STEVE WILSON

TRINITY ICON

A Michael Neill Adventure

Published by White Feather Press. (www.whitefeatherpress.com)

ISBN 978-1-61808-108-7

Printed in the United States of America

Cover design created by Steve Wilson

White Feather Press

Reaffirming Faith in God, Family, and Country!

For Adam and Luke,
who inspired the Michael Neill series

TRINITY ICON

Beginnings * The Warrior Priest

Christmas Eve, 1655
Poland

THE STALLION SPED NORTH, URGED ON BY his master's heels. Clumps of mud formed a wake in the air as the animal dashed ahead. With the onset of winter the soil lay fallow, dormant for now, and aside from horse and rider, there was no other living thing within sight.

Seeing anything at all on this moonless night would have been an accomplishment; the stars above offered little illumination, and Krystophor Nilscovic didn't bother looking back. His pursuers were miles behind him, and he knew that peril would most likely come from the western frontier, where a horde of Swedish infantry had swept across Poland's borders. But they were not the only hazard. On nights like this, marauders and highwaymen waylaid the unsuspecting, so Nilscovic had wisely avoided the most heavily traveled routes. He gripped the hilt of his *karabela*—the traditional sword of a nobleman—and managed a wry grin. In these troubled times, it was hard to make a distinction between armed invaders and common outlaws.

DOTTED by orchards of willow trees, the low country

of the Mazovian province was a fertile land of endless fields and meadows. Her plains stretched to the banks of the River Vistula, encompassing the tributaries that radiated into the heart of the nation. Narrow roads criss-crossed the countryside, but as wayfarers ventured further, these paths became few and far between.

A heavy rain had fallen and the ground was now covered in melting snow. Beneath the slush, the hearty grasses of the steppe waited for spring and the promise of renewed life. And surprisingly, by winter's standards, humid air began to push south, providing a respite to the season's chill.

On his left and right were marshes and lakes. Krystophor navigated his way around these and came upon a vast expanse of pastureland. During the day, but less so in winter, these fields would teem with herds of grazing horses, sheep and cattle. Watching over their flocks, anxious shepherds had taken to carrying arms for protection against hungry brigands—and the occasional bands of Cossack horsemen. At night the danger was not lessened, and Nilscovic would keep up his guard.

Cossacks! The thought left a bitter taste in Krystophor's mouth. He shifted in his saddle and spat on the ground. Stirred by the promise of revolution, those Godless ruffians had pushed west from Ruthenia and turned this landscape into a battlefield. The blood of many Poles now enriched the earth, and in spring not a day passed that a farmer's plow didn't turn up a weapon—or some fallen warrior's bones.

AFTER an hour of determined riding the horse cantered onto a broad path. Nilscovic stopped to get his bearings and to give the animal some rest. His eyes turned to the northeast. On a ridge that ran parallel to the road, the timbers of an abandoned outpost thrust up from the ground, a line of breastworks where men once stood watch. An ancient guardhouse buttressed the structure, but this too was now empty.

He whispered a prayer to the Blessed Virgin and loosened his hold on the reins. The horse pointed its nose forward, steam rising from its flanks. Had the air been cooler, the Pole would have been able to see his own breath.

He had made it this far. He set his eyes on the horizon and forced himself to relax. This was familiar territory, and Nilscovic knew the village of Olm was less than an hour away.

* * * *

KRYSTOPHOR'S STEED WAS FROM TURKISH stock, an Anatolian with eastern blood coursing through its veins. The animal's predecessors were bred for the famed *Husaria*, Poland's heavy cavalry. These mounted knights wore winged armor, and their tactics struck terror in the hearts of their enemies. More nimble than mere lancers, the Hussars had won a long string of victories from Byczyna to Trzciana—often against overwhelming odds. Nilscovic was proud to take his place among them, and in that respect he was different.

The Nilscovic family estate was humble but expansive. Generations had lived in the farmhouse modeled in the style of a mansion. Entitlement and favor had always been a Nilscovic birthright, and because of this, there was little about Krystophor's upbringing to explain the adventurous wanderlust in his soul.

The landed gentry—Poland's traditional nobility—enjoyed great privilege. The elder Nilscovic counted himself as one of these, and so did his offspring. Krystophor lived a life rich in family tradition, yet he embraced romanticism and the old order of chivalry. And above all, Nilscovic the younger was a patriotic Catholic.

In 1648, with his countrymen at his side, he had resisted the Ukrainian uprising, fighting fiercely against the Zaporozhian Cossacks and the Crimean Tartars from the east. The war of liberation from the Commonwealth wrested control from the aristocracy, decimating much of the nation's lands and costing great property loss to the Nilscovic family. Sacrifice had come in other ways, as well. In the course of one battle, Krystophor had nearly lost a leg—and the conflict had just begun.

THE horse's pace was faster now. Nilscovic recognized the homes of the families who lived just outside of Olm. At this hour, their shuttered windows were dark, and the road leading into the village was deserted. Slowing to a trot, the horse entered Olm's market square. The animal's shoes clopped loudly on the cobbled surface. Nestled in the heart of the township, Nilscovic's destination lay just ahead.

The Church of St. Mary the Virgin was the center of life for the poor village. Built in the Romanesque style, the abbey was like a miniature cathedral, with granite ashlars and a Baroque façade. Rising twice as high as the vaulting was the church tower, and at the top of this parapet, the *hejnal*—a five note anthem, recognized by faithful Poles—was sounded daily by trumpet call.

Stained glass windows were set between the arches framing the building. Through these, Krystophor could see that the inside of the church glowed with light. That was unusual, given the time. The exterior portal was also lit. And it was there that Nilscovic dismounted.

THE Pole took a moment to stretch. His joints were stiff from the journey, and the pain in his leg had grown. He adjusted his long tunic coat—called a *kontusz*—and then retrieved his karabela from its place on the saddle. This he thrust into the outer tasseled sash that acted as a waistband. The coat itself was a deep green, with a mustard colored lining and open sleeves that Krystophor had thrown over his shoulders. Covering the short-cropped hair on the top of his head was a piece of headgear called a *kolpak*.

Nilscovic moved away from his horse and looked overhead. Looming above, the blackened silhouette of the tower was darker than the night sky. The rain clouds had receded, and only a few stars were visible. A grin spread across his face. He had heard the hejnal since his youth, but as he entered the church, he had other plans for the spire.

THE narthex was brightened by candles and lanterns on both sides of the entrance. Nilscovic removed his kolpak and dipped his fingers in the font of holy water, quickly touching his forehead, chest and shoulders. He asked the Virgin to dispel the power of evil before pushing open the door and stepping into the sanctorum.

The church appeared empty. More candles lined the high altar, giving the far end of the chancel a comforting radiance. Flanking the entrance were two seraphim, chiseled from granite and emerging from the rear wall. Facing inward, their wings formed an arch over the doorway.

A sandstone center aisle split the room in half. The flooring here had been worn by a constant parade of the penitent. Krystophor approached the front and then slowed his pace out of reverence. He stopped at the rail, bending his knee to the ground. Again his hand repeated the gesture of faith, and before he could rise, Nilscovic realized he was not alone.

A familiar figure stood before the holy place. Clad in black, the priest wore a silver crucifix around his neck. He was broad-shouldered and tall, his face framed in a long, black beard. His arms were folded beneath his robes—but in his right hand he held an old Roman sword, candlelight glinting from the steel.

"Is this how a nobleman enters God's house?" The priest's eyes flashed. "Gone for months—and now you greet me with a weapon, leaving a trail of mud with every step."

Nilscovic instinctively went for his own blade, holding back a laugh. Standing now, he glanced downward. The hem of his coat was caked with dried soil.

"Forgive me, Father. The dirt is a gift from Malopolska. But what of you?" Krystophor stepped back. Seeing the holy man like this was a reminder of their days fighting Cossacks. *"Behold Jakob Sobieski!* You favor King Zygumunt—*God rest his soul*—with a sword in one hand, and a cross in the other."

The priest would have preferred a comparison to another king, Kazimierz the Great. A charismatic monarch, as well as a soldier and diplomat, it was said that Kazimierz had found

Poland of wood, but left it in stone. Jakob had made similar strides in Olm, adding to the church from his own family's fortune, and like the fourteenth century ruler, he had a talent for stonemasonry and woodwork.

Sobieski brandished the weapon before resting it on the rail. Both men felt great relief at the sight of the other. Father Jakob blessed Krystophor as he knelt again, and then he pulled the younger man to his feet.

"I see you have been busy. Gabriel arrived safely?" A trusted soldier, Krystophor had dispatched Gabriel the day before.

"At the noon meal," the priest confirmed. "He helped me empty the sacristy and load the wagon."

Nilscovic's smile returned. "Not before filling his stomach, I'm sure."

The nobleman's gaze settled on the high altar. The cere and linen cloths were missing from the stone, as was the coverlet. Also gone was the bell, rung at the Sanctus and during Mass. The chalice and ciborium were nowhere in sight. Every sacred vessel—including the tapestries and votive offerings—had been removed, giving the chancel table an austere feel.

Nilscovic focused on the wall behind the pedestal. Two paintings hung there; the first depicted the birth of Christ. The second illustrated His death on the cross. But between the two was a barren space, marked by the faint outline of soot on stone.

The vacancy in the middle marked the centerpiece of the triptych panels. This decorative frieze—now unseen—was an elaborate representation of the Holy Trinity, rendered in the Dutch Mannerist style. It was painted on a tabletop from the home of St. Luke—or so the legends said. There was no way to confirm that, but local tradition supported the story, and the villagers of Olm had seized on it.

Through the years other embellishments were added. The value of the icon went far beyond artistic merit or its links to holy tradition. Enclosing the piece was a fortune in gold filigree; precious gems were laid within the frame, and more gold was fashioned to surround the figures of the Father, the Son, and the

Holy Spirit. The latter was depicted as a dove, with spokes of light—also of gold—radiating out to the panel's edge.

"I can think of better ways to celebrate the Savior's birth," Krystophor announced.

"As can I, but God is gracious."

Nilscovic repeated the blessing. "Where is Gabriel now?"

"Sent house to house, to spread the warning." The priest glanced upward. "Your instructions have been heeded—gentry and commoner alike have taken refuge in the forest."

"An answered prayer," Nilscovic remarked, his grin widening. "Then we'll have no need of the tower."

"Heavens no. The bell would only draw the heathens."

"And the wagon?"

"Henryk holds the reins as we speak," Father Jakob replied. He waved a large hand behind him and started toward the rear of the church. "Do you bring news from Czestochowa?"

The Pole paused long enough for one last look at the empty wall. The center panel's absence reassured him.

"My regiment reconnoitered near Oblegorek. But word has filtered through." Leaving the sanctuary, Nilscovic tugged at the ends of his long moustache. His smile went unnoticed. "Your Pauline brothers fight like wolves."

The priest chuckled. "So they resist the Swedes?"

"Pah!" Krystophor would have spat again were they not on holy ground. "German mercenaries are at the heart of this—and a few traitorous Poles. Swedish troops are few, but they make their stench known."

"And how goes the battle?"

The two followed a narrow corridor and descended a small staircase. This passage led to a heavy oaken door, and beyond that an arched portal to the outside.

"They bring their twenty-four pounders to bear against the north wall," Nilscovic answered. The wet cobblestone patio behind the church reflected more lantern light. A tall maple stood nearby, with drops of rainwater falling as the wind rustled its leafless branches.

"But one cannon is already lost—possibly more. The hand of Providence is with the defenders."

"The siege continues?"

"Aye. But Jasna Gora still stands."

"Yet some are not content with attacking the monastery," Jakob snorted. "Tell me about those who travel to Olm."

Krystophor's fatigue gnawed at him. "A company of soldiers," he said. "Fifty strong. They know our efforts were meant to hinder their journey north. We harassed them near Kielce, but our numbers were much less."

The priest nodded. He knew the place. Trevano the architect had built a palace there. "Who leads them?"

"A Swedish captain," Nilscovic continued. "We believe his name to be Angstrom—a brutal man, Father." He knew what Jakob's next question would be. "I rode hard much of the way, hours ahead of their horses. We still have time, *towarzysz.*"

Krystophor saw the wagon now. An old nag was bridled before it. Huddled against the breeze was Henryk, crouching atop the carriage, the leather straps of the reins held loosely in his hands. Seeing the nobleman, the boy straightened in his seat and gave a respectful nod.

Nilscovic returned the gesture and inspected the lorry's cargo. Candlesticks and other vessels from the altar had been carefully placed inside. Several pieces were wrapped in hemp cloth; the largest of these matched the size and shape of the icon. Clearly, Father Jakob had no intention of allowing church treasures to fall into the hands of the Swedes.

Sobieski saw the exhaustion on Nilscovic's face. "Have you eaten anything? And when was the last time you slept?"

Krystophor brushed aside the priest's concerns. "I have bread and cheese in my pack, and I can sleep when I'm dead." He flashed a grin. "There are more pressing concerns, Father. Where would you have Henryk and me hide all of this?"

Jakob came forward, his dark eyes holding those of his friend. "Young Henryk has his orders. For you, I have another mission."

The Pole started to protest, but Jakob stopped him.

"One final ride, Krystophor. God will bless your service to His church. Now you must honor the wishes of your priest."

Nilscovic was too weary to argue. Only crumbs remained in the saddle bag, and his mouth was parched. He took hold of the cart and leaned against it. Standing on his own was an effort. Sheer determination—and the grace of God—had got him this far, but without rest, and some food and drink, the man would soon be undone.

"What would you have me do, Father?"

"Ride to my family's holdings. See to my sister's safety." Jakob's voice was both a balm and an irresistible force. "Troubled times have drained servants from the manor—few men remain, and none can handle a blade like you."

"Do you think she would accept my offer of protection?" Krystophor's voice caught in his throat. He lowered his eyes to the pavement. "I am a boorish man, Jakob. A fighting oaf." The bluster he displayed just moments before had melted away. A sincere humility replaced it as words began to fail. "Helena—"

"Helena is a woman, my warrior friend. Strong-willed and impetuous, but now is the season of the sword." Sobieski grinned broadly as he eyed the weapon at Nilscovic's side. "Your karabela was made for more than just ceremony." As an afterthought he added, "And Helena knows of your feelings for her."

The wind howled as if to punctuate Jakob's words. Krystophor was dumbstruck at this, and his tired eyes filled with moisture. "But she entertains no suitors," he stammered. "Why should—"

"You see so little, Krystophor." The priest's smile remained. "Helena suffers no man because she waits for you. Surely your heart is not so blind."

"I dared not hope."

The gale strengthened around them, wet leaves blowing through the patio and lifting into the air. It was growing colder. Startled by the sudden rush of wind, the nag grew restless, anxious to be on her way.

"Take the northeast road," Jakob pressed. "There are seven

leagues between us and the estate, and Helena knows nothing of the Swedes."

Nilscovic started to speak again, but the priest reached out and gripped his arm. "My place is here, Krystophor. God wills it. Now swear to me that Helena will be safe."

"On my life, Jakob."

"Then *go*." Sobieski's command was stern.

There was nothing else to be said. Tears filled Krystophor's eyes, and Jakob silently blessed him. Turning, Nilscovic followed the alley, favoring his stronger leg and giving the warrior priest one last look before reclaiming his horse.

* * * *

THE CART WAS DISPATCHED TO THE EAST. THE river road was narrow and little used—and chosen for just that reason. Pursuing horsemen would have no room to ride abreast, forced to follow single file.

Once Henryk was out of sight the priest extinguished the lanterns and returned to the chancel hall. The church was bare; cold now, save for the glow of candlelight. A faithless man would have felt alone, but Father Sobieski was comforted by God's presence.

He would need it.

Jakob knelt before the high altar one last time. He made the sign of the cross, his eyes fixed on the verse of Scripture carved above the railing. He recited the words and then bowed in prayer, smiling at his own cleverness.

The thought had barely crossed his mind before he confessed his pride. Beneath his knees, the sandstone floor was hard, and the priest accepted that as penance for his vanity.

* * * *

HE WAS STILL KNEELING WHEN THE COMPANY of soldiers rode into town. The clattering of horses filled the square, and raised voices echoed off the walls of the empty village.

Father Jakob could hear the Swedes as they advanced on the church. With their captain leading them, the raucous mob burst into the sanctuary. A few hid their contempt, chastened by conscience, but Johannes Angstrom had no such reverence for God's house.

The Swede marched toward the high altar. He lifted his eyes above, and then stopped halfway down the aisle. His blood ran cold. Candlelight illuminated the far wall, but the object of Angstrom's desire was lost to him.

The captain had heard stories of the icon, wild tales of fortune that excited his greed. He intended to use the relic to enrich himself—and, to a nominal degree, his men—but someone in this small hamlet had frustrated those plans. The penitent man at the far end of the room was the most likely suspect.

With an edge in his voice, the Swede advanced on the altar and demanded to know the icon's whereabouts. His grasp of Polish was poor. The monk appeared deaf, earning more of Angstrom's ire as he drew his sword. Even at the point of a blade the priest refused to reveal the treasure's location.

No amount of coaxing or threats changed that. This enraged the officer. Father Jakob persisted with his meditation, engulfed in the peace of God. He simply ignored the Swede and continued in prayer, repeating in Latin the words of Scripture that would define his legacy.

"Et exaltabitur sicut unicornis cornu meum et senectus mea in misericordia uberi…"

Johannes Angstrom would have none of the priest's incoherent babbling. He was a short-tempered man, and given to blind anger. Spittle flew from his mouth as he profaned the holy place, cursing God and Sobieski in the same breath.

The Swede raised an arm. His sword was crafted for cavalry use and designed with a sharp double edge. Angstrom had hefted its weight in battle many times. Driven by rage, he cared little for the fact that taking the priest's life might keep him from his prize.

Angstrom brought the blade down, striking between the nape of the priest's neck and his cowled shoulders. His men were shocked by his brutality. None suspected that his fury would come to this.

* * * *

FATHER JAKOB NEVER SAW THE BLOW THAT SENT him into eternity. His body was found the next day. The Swedes had left it where it had fallen, in a pool of blood at the high altar. The priest's very essence seemed to soak into the stones, and the grisly scene in the sanctuary shocked the villagers.

One of Angstrom's scouts had discovered tracks in the road—deep ruts left by the heavy wagon. The Swedes pursued Henryk as far as Deblin. There, the youth had followed Father Jakob's instructions to the letter. With the soldiers on his heels, Henryk abandoned the cart and hid in the tree line. When he emerged hours later, the invaders had stripped it bare and fled back into the west.

THE martyred priest was buried in a place of honor on the eastern side of the church. Each day the rising sun would cast its rays on the ground covering his grave; and from that year forward, the mass celebrating Christ's birth would reference the death of Jakob Sobieski.

For a short time Olm held out a naïve hope that the ornate relic might turn up. The villagers searched the countryside for months, and inquiries were made in the neighboring provinces. Appeals were sent to the church fathers in Warsaw. These requests fell on sympathetic ears, yet the diocese could do nothing. A petition got as far as the Swedish government but no one really expected results.

Olm had lost much in blood and treasure. A servant's life had been taken on one of Christendom's holiest days, and the icon had simply vanished. A reminder of the priest's stewardship could still be seen just above the church altar. Two of the triptych's panels hung on the wall, but the space between was conspicuously empty.

For the generations that followed, stories of the center-piece would bridge the gulf between reality, legend and myth, and the relic's disappearance would haunt the village for more than three hundred years . . .

TRINITY ICON

Chapter One * Evil Empire

International Operations and Intelligence,
Headquarters Marine Corps,
Arlington, Virginia

THE CONFERENCE ROOM WAS ADJACENT TO the C.O.'s office, connected by a door that gave the colonel direct access. It was long and narrow, with a proportionally-sized table that sat in the middle of the floor. An oak bookshelf and matching credenza crowded the rear of the space, and these appointments were seemingly at odds with their simple surroundings. The solitary figure who entered smiled at that. He supposed that these furnishings were just an overflow of the commanding officer's oversized cubicle.

Marine Captain Michael Neill leaned over the laptop positioned near the front and plugged in a set of coaxials. These cables were synched to a compact disc player and the big screen display that dominated one end of the room. In an earlier generation, a carousel slide projector would have been employed for this type of presentation, but in a more digital age, a laptop—or even a smart phone with the appropriate app—was the technology of choice.

Still tanned from a recent deployment, Neill stood six feet tall, with short, sandy-colored hair that was freshly cut. Like many Marines, he was broad-shouldered and athletically built. Staying in shape was second nature for the captain.

The young officer adjusted the blinds, noting the darkening skies outside the sprawling complex. Compared to the gloomy exterior, the overheads were a bit harsh, reflecting light from the twin silver bars fastened on each side of his collar and tie. The rank was a recent addition. Michael had distinguished himself eight months earlier in the South China Sea, and the Corps— along with one notable cabinet official—saw fit to reward his actions.

"Knock, knock." From the door came a young woman's voice, friendly and upbeat. Her words captured Neill's attention. "You got that?"

Staff Sergeant Christina Arrens—also newly promoted— stepped into the room, gesturing toward the audio/visual array. She wore her service uniform, and an additional stripe—called a rocker—just below the chevrons on her sleeves. Her blouse was crisp, with military creases and every ribbon and badge in place. The young sergeant also had an understated grace about her, with a professionalism that set her apart from her peers. She was one of those NCOs that made working in the office a real pleasure, and her beauty was not lost on anyone.

"Really?" she chided. "These are color-coded for a reason, Captain."

Arrens eased toward the laptop and removed two of the cables. Neill leaned in to watch as she reattached the leads— properly placed this time. Christina's expression was something like a smirk. The captain had seen that look before.

Hazel eyes fastened on hers. "I'm not *quite* the knuckle-dragger you think I am, Sergeant," he offered, just a hint of a smile on his face.

Neill's little quirks had an endearing quality. "This from a man who still uses a rolodex. And it's *Staff* Sergeant," Christina said, correcting the omission.

Teasing aside, she was right; Neill was a curious mix of old and new. As a missionary kid, he had grown up in Eastern

Europe, and access to electronic devices had been limited. During the past several years he played catch-up, but like most of his generation, he adapted quickly.

The two were side by side now. Arrens' perfume had a fresh, clean scent. Neill inhaled softly. He couldn't remember the name of it, which was altogether proper. Still, he might have complimented her choice of fragrance—but for that, he'd have to admit that he'd even noticed.

"Do you need audio for this?"

A shake of the head. "Nope."

"Okay—we can unplug this one, then." She stood and gave him a smile. Her auburn hair was arranged in a French twist, and she brushed aside the bangs in her dark eyes—the ones looking directly into his. "What would you do without me?"

For all her captivating charms, Arrens wasn't really a flirt. Rules were rules; especially in the Corps, and regulations governing fraternization were strictly applied. There was a line neither of them could cross, and regardless of how she felt—

Neill didn't respond immediately. It was an innocent question, and probably rhetorical. He couldn't tell if she was being coy or just offering a friendly jibe. She leaned in, ever so slightly, and he caught her scent once more as he found his voice.

"Let's hope I never have to find out."

His reply wasn't at all clever. Nor was it what she wanted to hear, but for now, it was the best she could hope for.

* * * *

THE BRIEFING BEGAN PROMPTLY AT NINE. Colonel Nicholas Terryton was present, along with Master Gunnery Sergeant Owen Ethridge, currently filling the role of company first sergeant—while riding a desk as a senior career planner.

It was Etheridge's job to channel those with leadership potential toward the top. In a roundabout way, he and career advisors like him grew the Corps by reducing its ranks; funneling qualified applicants upward to fill needed positions. High standards were maintained, and that kept the race for coveted slots very competitive. There was room on the tiller for only a few hands. And that was exactly where men like Etheridge applied their experience.

Terryton was marginally in charge of this morning's gathering, but Neill had the floor, directing everyone's attention to images being displayed on the screen. Staff Sergeant Arrens sat nearby, queuing up frames from the laptop.

"The Hemmat Industrial Complex," the captain began, standing just off to one side. He spoke slowly at first, a practice he'd learned from his father. "Outside of Tehran. This facility is responsible for the development of Iran's cruise and ballistic missile programs."

"Long-range or short?" Etheridge frowned. The dark-skinned, barrel chested man looked up from an open folder— the cover of which was stamped *top secret*. Not quite a quarter of an inch thick, the pages within contained a more detailed listing of the talking points. Terryton had an identical copy, while Neill referred to a smaller sheaf of notes.

"Both, Master Guns." The junior officer welcomed the question. He gave Christina a nod. "But our discussion today focuses on the former."

Arrens' fingertips danced lightly across the keypad, and the second frame appeared. Neill preferred using a mouse, and silently envied the young woman's adept touch with electronics. Her chin came up and she gave him a grin, along with a soft flip of her hair, tapping away and never missing a beat.

Showoff, Michael thought.

"The Iranians have spent fifteen years perfecting single-stage, medium-range weapons. At present, those have the capability to reach out and touch other Middle-Eastern countries."

"Like Israel," the colonel grunted.

"Roger that, sir," Neill allowed. "But they haven't demonstrated the technology needed to lob a warhead further—until two days ago."

A new image filled the screen. This one was grainy and depicted the launch of a multi-stage rocket system. The angle of the frame suggested the photo had been taken from ground level.

"A little blurry, but there's enough detail to identify this as a *three*-stage North Korean variant."

"The Taepo Dong?" Terryton asked.

"Yes, sir," Neill answered. "Intelligence in place says it's the Shahab-5. This one was code-named MIDAS by the Iranians. A single stage prototype of this vehicle was launched three weeks ago."

"I thought that project was shelved," Etheridge said.

"That was the general consensus, yes." For a retention advisor, the master gunny was well-informed. Michael silently gave him points for that. "But if our data is correct, we're going to have to reconsider that line of thought."

Terryton gave the captain a curious look. "How solid is this?"

Neill knew what he was asking. Intel from the field was broken down by category. Credible information provided actionable options. Anything else was flagged as marginal. The colonel's question went beyond the material's reliability, zeroing in on where it had come from.

"We have every confidence in its accuracy, sir," Neill replied.

"We?" So, he thought, *our friends in Kiev have a spy on Iranian soil.* The senior officer smiled. Good for them. "One of your proprietary sources, Captain?"

More than twenty months earlier, Neill—a lieutenant at the time—had worked closely with the government of Ukraine to ensure nuclear disarmament. His efforts there deepened the level of trust between the U.S. and the former Soviet republic. As a result, informal ties had been established with that country's State Security Directorate.

"You asked for my analysis, sir. If I questioned the credibility of this intelligence, it would be summarily dismissed." Michael stepped forward, adopting a persuasive tone. "It's not my intention to give credence to any material that doesn't pass muster."

Arrens caught a quick glimpse of the captain. On certain occasions, he dropped his calm demeanor and could be a real bulldog.

"And I have every confidence in your judgment, Captain," Terryton returned, raising a hand. It was clear that Neill trusted the intel. And he wasn't hesitant about standing behind it. The colonel didn't mind sources from the outside; they had to be vetted a little more carefully, but— "Please continue. What else do we know?"

The captain glanced back at his notes. "This version of the Shahab uses a Russian engine and burns liquid fuel, like their SS-4s. Earlier models were reportedly purposed to launch satellites." A wry smile formed. "Except Iran has never sent any into orbit."

"How were they able to get this one off the pad?" Etheridge was taking notes now.

"Outside assistance," Michael supplied. "North Korea—and definitely the Russians. Additional photographic evidence— next image, please—would indicate that they've borrowed technology from their earlier Ghadr rocket. That one used solid fuel."

"More advantageous for military applications," Terryton observed. "Why didn't they use that fuel to boost this launch?"

Neill shook his head. "We're not sure. Maybe the solid propellant wasn't readily available. It's possible they've developed a more combustible liquid, but for practicality's sake, that's not likely."

"Why not?" Etheridge asked.

"Liquid is old school, Master Guns. As the colonel said, solids are the preferred method. They're more easily loaded, for one thing. Faster, too. And they're much less volatile."

"I never knew the Iranians were such sticklers for safety," the master gunny grinned.

"They're not," Neill agreed. "But they are focused on results."

The colonel leaned back in his chair. "Speaking of which—how did this launch go?"

"The third stage managed to attain a low-Earth orbit. This payload was fairly light; several hundred pounds, comparable to a warhead with a three thousand kilometer range. It splashed down in the Indian Ocean four hours after lift-off." Another thought came to mind. "By way of contrast, the Koreans attempted a test last year, using a similar delivery system. That launch failed."

"No surprise there," Etheridge added sarcastically. "How did we track this flight?"

Neill made eye contact with Arrens. "Scroll to the map, please."

The staff sergeant clicked through to the end of the presentation. An image showing the boundaries of the eastern hemisphere appeared on the screen. Iran's borders were prominently marked.

"Ground-based radar followed the initial launch; satellites in geo-synchronous orbit—above these points—" the captain gestured toward the western reaches of the Islamic republic—"caught thermal images as it left the pad. Aerial assets also contributed. We usually have an aircraft or two aloft, keeping their eyes open."

"What about the ground-based stuff? Who provided that telemetry?"

"Various stations downrange."

"Ours?" Terryton pressed.

"Yes, sir. Lask was helpful," Neill said. He was referring to the American air base on Polish soil. "Our allies in Eastern Europe, as well."

"Ukraine?"

"Yes, sir."

Etheridge's mind wandered back to the facility near Tehran. "Does the Shemmat—" he paused, referring to his folder. "My mistake—the *Hemmat* facility—have additional rockets they've prepared for testing?"

"One other gantry has been cleared. Long-range photography suggests that pad is being readied, but no vehicles are currently visible."

"That could change in a heartbeat," the colonel quipped. "Nothing like success to jump-start a bad idea."

"But do they have the resources to go to the next level?" Etheridge was thinking ahead.

Neill was ready for that one. "In the past, they've been hampered on two fronts. For one thing, the international community has withheld the required hardware." He turned to Christina. "Staff Sergeant Arrens, could you bring up the third frame, please?"

Almost instantly the grainy image of the missile launch reappeared. "This photo clearly shows a three-stage rocket. As with any technology, the more moving parts there are—"

"—the more that can go wrong," Etheridge interrupted.

The captain gave another nod. "The evidence before you tells us that the Iranians are working to overcome certain technical obstacles. At some point in flight, re-entry vehicles need to break away from their boosters. This test is proof that Tehran now has stage-detachment technology."

"Courtesy of Moscow," Terryton remarked.

"And then there's propulsion," Neill continued. "Apparently they've solved that problem, too. We don't know how reliable their current guidance systems are, so I can't speak to that."

"What else has held them back?" This from the master gunny.

"Finances," Neill replied simply. "We can't forget that sanctions have hurt Iran far more than most people realize. With a restrained economy, they've had very little capital for military purposes. Of course, now that many of those have been lifted—"

"What changed? More outside assistance?"

"That's a fair bet," Neill said. "The CIA believes Russia's behind this as well, bankrolling much of their missile production."

The master gunny narrowed his eyes. "To what end?"

"To divine the Russian psyche is a difficult thing, sir. I was born over there and I still haven't figured them out." Michael began to grin. "All I can offer are theories."

"Those will have to keep." Terryton looked at his watch. "I'm presenting this to the joint chiefs at eleven hundred; after that, a closed door meeting with the chairman of the Armed Services Committee and the national security advisor."

Neill imagined that he saw the colonel wince. The chiefs were above the political fray—publicly, at least—and the chairman was a fair man. But the *rest* of the committee—

A presidential election was only weeks away, and the incumbents were losing ground. Tensions were running high in D.C.

Terryton eyed Neill thoughtfully. "Clear your schedule, Captain; given the breadth of this material, I could use your help up on the Hill."

"Aye, sir." It had been quite some time since Neill had seen Mr. Avery.

The C.O. remained in his seat. A wistful look spread across his face. Arrens and Etheridge stirred in their chairs, but remained in place out of respect for the colonel.

"Orlando, Florida. 1983."

Neill blinked. "Sir?"

"The 'evil empire'—that's what Reagan called the Soviet Union—back in the day." He regarded the younger Marines with a smile, but there was no humor behind the expression. "You're both too young to remember that."

Michael and Christina traded glances.

"Before my time, sir. But I am familiar with the reference."

"The USSR collapsed in 1991. The evil empire is dead." Terryton closed his folder and got to his feet. The others followed his example. He glanced forward, where the image of the Iranian missile was still displayed on the screen. "And then we discover that their influence is still being felt. Sometimes I wonder if they ever really left."

Captain Neill recalled the years he'd spent in Ukraine. He understood the colonel's sentiment. Growing up in the shadow of communism, he'd often wondered the same thing.

* * * *

THE EVIL EMPIRE HAD ENDED WITH A WHIMPER, and not a bang. Its demise was complicated. Woven into its death throes were equal parts tragedy and farce, with the historic melodrama playing out across eleven different time zones.

Behind the scenes, there had been a struggle between several factions. Hardliners tried to maintain totalitarian control. Their goal was to keep power out of the hands of the democratically-minded moderates—a fool's errand, but seventy years of iron-fisted rule died hard.

Western observers of the USSR saw little change in the sprawling nation—although subtle clues popped up occasionally. Residents of Moscow were the first to notice. Their day to day existence went on just as it had for decades; the only difference was that things had actually gotten worse.

It was difficult to ignore the truth, and the reality of life for Soviet citizens was framed by hardship and deprivation. The capitol itself was a dismal shell of misery. The Soviet infrastructure was at its lowest there. The streets were filthy, and public conveyances were best avoided—for safety's sake. Lines formed everywhere, but demand always exceeded supply, no matter what commodity was being sold.

In the winter of 1991, the crisis had reached a new level. Food became scarce. There were shortages of everything—flour, meat, salt; even bread was next to impossible to find. Hoarding followed, and the black market flourished.

The State had set up warehouses, but these were poorly managed. Countless lives were lost through inefficient distribution and the malignant corruption of the Russian mafia. Taking bribes and giving them no longer seemed scandalous in the hearts of most. In order to simply survive, Muscovites had resorted to desperate measures.

Parliament intervened, but prices for the most basic necessities—milk, medicine and fuel—had exploded beyond their normal costs—and that was when they could be found at all.

The very definition of *perestroika* meant re-structuring, but there was little about this program of reform that touched the common man—except poverty.

Yet, a revolution of another kind had sprung up—in the most unlikely of places. In the early years of *glasnost*—translated as 'openness'—the cries of a suddenly free press began to rise above the propaganda. Unlike their western counterparts, rife with bias, newspapers in the rapidly changing Soviet empire refused to accept anything as truth. The Russian populace embraced the novelty of investigative reporting, and the voice of the *Rodina*—the Motherland—now had a different tone.

Through the years, the fourth estate had been fed a steady diet of disinformation, and in many cases media scribes were complicit with the government in spreading more. That was the best way to stay alive, or to prevent being banished to some backwater republic. But in the waning days of the Soviet state, an expressive minority of the daily broadsheets began to publish the truth. Suspicious of the status quo, crusading reporters dug deeper.

It was an unprecedented time in Soviet history, and a new frontier for Russian journalism. But it was not to last. *Perestroika* had a brief shelf life, and after a few years, the media once more began to feel the jackboot of oppression.

After communism's fall, the Russian Federation imposed old restrictions. Censorship returned. The breath of fresh air was not much more than a breeze, and a liberated press would have to wait for the next generation before it could openly flourish again.

* * * *

THE LOBBY WAS ENCLOSED BY EXPANSIVE GLASS panels that ran from floor to ceiling. The visual effect was intentional. A local architect had designed the building, paying heed to the entrance, and giving the structure a certain symbolism. It was a nod to the newspaper's mission—providing transparency to life—but the metaphor was lost on most city-dwellers.

Viktoriya Gavrilenko checked her image in the glass, heels clattering as she exited the offices of the *Odesa Sivodnya*. Her outerwear did little to deflect attention, but that was never her goal. The coat she wore was a double-breasted trench, made of white leather, with wide lapels on either side of the cowl-neck sweater crowning her shoulders. An ivory belt was cinched around her narrow waist, with black denim jeans and matching shoes for contrast.

The young journalist took to the sidewalk and began moving east on Balkovskaya Street. Her appearance earned a few admiring glances, but Viktoriya paid no mind. Navigating through pedestrians, her head was tilted down as she checked her phone.

"SHE just came out." The man in the car had a wireless earpiece.

His accomplice was across the street, leaning against a kiosk and pretending to read the morning edition. He wore a similar device in his ear.

"Right on time."

SHE checked her email first. Viktoriya's in-box contained only a few messages—which was both a relief and a disappointment. A trending story on a news site caught her eye next. Archaeologists in neighboring Poland were poking around a riverbed near Warsaw. The report looked interesting; she scanned the highlights and then filed it away for later.

There was a chill in the air, not uncommon for Odessa on an October afternoon. Viktoriya clutched her collar just a bit closer and kept walking. A tram stop was one street over on Rozumovskaya. The aging conveyance was always on time, and if she caught the 5:05, she could be home in less than twenty minutes.

FROM half a block away, Sergei Holcek matched the

woman's pace and kept his distance. He allowed himself a smug grin. She was making his job easy. With the way she was dressed, it would be hard to lose her now.

A head taller than those around him, he was a stocky man, in his mid-forties with graying temples. He had been watching Viktoriya's movements for the past two days. She didn't own a car, and the towering Russian knew she'd hop on the trolley approaching from the far side of town.

"Get into position," Sergei ordered.

"On my way."

The driver revved the engine. The Mercedes crept past Viktoriya slowly, allowing him one last eyeful. The woman had more curves than—

"Focus on your driving, *tavarisch*," the Russian snapped.

The man in the car turned away.

"Such a waste."

He left Viktoriya and Sergei behind, and then turned on the next street, headed north.

HOLCEK stared ahead, scouting the terrain. The intersection was crowded with Ladas and other Eastern European models. The congestion didn't concern him; in fact, he was silently thankful for it. A glance to the north gave him a fix on his escape route, an alley between the main thoroughfare and Kolinsky Street. The Russian breathed deeply, measuring his steps and gauging the arrival of the tram.

Sergei resumed his surveillance. His mark was right where she should be, so the Russian began assessing obstacles. There were no militia cars in sight, and no officers walking a beat.

All the better, he thought.

Small groups began milling toward the corner, waiting for the trolley. Holcek glanced at those closest to Viktoriya and moved a little faster. She arrived at the stop just as he crossed Rozumovskaya.

It was time for one last check.

"Ready?"

The receiver crackled in Holcek's ear. "Waiting for you."

"Keep the motor running."

The driver could hear the anxiety in Sergei's voice. "I'll do my job. You do yours."

SHE was still alone. A loose-knit throng of commuters stood nearby. Sergei gave them a studied look. Most were simple office workers who wanted to go home. A few tourists had wandered up from the port, and students from the Institute huddled together, portfolios clutched under their arms. Close to the corner, an old sweater-clad *babushka* sold flowers, a display of nested *matryoshka* dolls on her cart.

The tourists and students weren't a concern. Holcek was more interested in picking out individuals. Beneath the stop's canopy, a transient weaved from side to side, his posture stooped. He wore a dirty, hooded sweatshirt; Holcek gave him a passing glance and then dismissed his presence. Another man was now standing to Viktoriya's left, stealing glances as she waited. A third—very tall—ignored everything else except his hand-held mobile device.

Truly a shame, Holcek reflected. Throughout his life he had been a connoisseur of beautiful women. Under different circumstances, he would have liked to enjoy this one; but business was business, and his handlers were paying him well. It was just too bad that Viktoriya Gavrilenko had to die.

The Russian stood patiently as the tram slowed. The students moved toward the street and would be the first to board. Holcek got into position next to the man with the roaming eyes while Viktoriya fell in behind the tourists.

"*Astarozheneh*," *Attention*; a metallic voice squeaked from a speaker. "*Dveri atkraviyetseh*,"—*doors opening*. No one disembarked at this stop, and the small group began crowding forward.

Holcek reached into his jacket. A 9 millimeter Beretta rested in a holster on his left side. The weapon was heavier than usual, equipped with a noise suppressor. The Russian had also chosen subsonic ammunition, not terribly effective over great distances—but certainly lethal at close range.

The plan was simple enough, and bold. Sergei would wait until Viktoriya took her first step into the tram. He would press in from the rear, raise the weapon to the base of her skull and fire two rounds.

Things would happen quickly from that point.

As the young woman fell forward, Holcek intended to make a hasty retreat, capitalizing on confusion and shock. Street traffic would slow anyone who might try to follow him. The Russian would then race into the alley, and the driver would take over, carrying the assassin on a pre-determined path out of town.

Holcek filled his lungs again. The tourists had taken their time—*had he imagined their sloth, or was he just nervous?*—but had finally entered the idling streetcar. Viktoriya paused as the last one ascended the steps, and then edged to the open door.

Time to move.

He tried to stay calm. The man to his right started toward the curb, but Holcek pushed past him. Sergei had always thought himself to be a smooth operator, yet anxiety caused his movements to be abrupt.

With a hand in his coat, the Russian began to retrieve the Beretta, but the pistol never cleared its holster. To Holcek's left, the disheveled transient stopped his side to side motion and surged toward him. His actions were surprisingly fluid, fast—and professional. He shoulder-blocked Sergei with the skill of a linebacker, pinning him against—of all people—the man with the wandering eyes.

Both wore tactical gloves, a clue to their real vocations, but Holcek saw this too late. Their combined efforts caught him off guard. He managed a surprised look, and then his arm—sans the weapon—was twisted behind his back. Sergei was now completely immobilized, and felt his body forced awkwardly to the rear.

The two aggressors had their tradecraft down perfectly. Each step put him off balance, and to remain upright, Holcek was compelled to yield to his captors' demands. From the rear, the commuter with the mobile device had put away his tablet and held a syringe.

The Russian felt a pinch as the needle was pushed into the side of his neck. He struggled, but was no match for the solution flowing through his veins. The drug acted quickly, and Sergei was limp within seconds.

* * * *

HOLCEK HADN'T BEEN PAYING ATTENTION. IF he had, he might have noticed a few characteristics of the men waiting for him.

Their superior strength barely registered before he slipped into darkness. As the world receded, the Russian looked into the face of the 'transient.' Beneath his hood, the square-jawed man smiled, his close-cropped hair neatly trimmed, military style. Had he remained conscious, Sergei would have seen identical cuts worn by the other two.

They were Special Purpose Police—a Berkut unit, tasked to fight against organized crime. Institutional descendants of federalized Soviet troops, they were responsible for public security, and were a fixture in most provinces of the republic.

Aleksander Voskov—Xander, for short—led this team. Under the dirty, hooded sweatshirt, Holcek had mistaken him for a homeless derelict. Voskov's bobbing stance and vacant stare gave him all the cover he needed. A natural-born showman, it wasn't the first time someone had underestimated Xander's abilities.

The commuter with the tablet used the device to monitor the Mercedes, and then signaled a separate team to apprehend the driver. And the shifty-eyed man—his name was Yegor—hadn't been ogling Viktoriya; instead, he was fixing the Russian in his peripheral vision. All of that was just a snapshot of their surveillance; the quick reaction force worked closely with the Ukrainian SSD—the State Security Directorate. Holcek's presence in Ukraine was known from the moment he entered the country.

The Berkut unit's tactics were well-rehearsed. Acting in concert, the two groups accomplished their mission in under a minute. Sergei Holcek never suspected a thing—until it was too late.

"Load up," Voskov snapped. His comrades, including the fourth team member, Iosef, dragged the motionless Russian away from the curb.

"He's heavy, Captain," grunted the tallest of the three. His name was Yuri Tereshenko. The tablet was stuffed in his coat.

"Then I'm thankful for your muscles," Xander grinned.

* * * *

Few on the streets of Odessa saw what had happened, and those who did ignored it. It was best that way. Getting involved with a militia matter, if that's what it was, just wasn't worth the effort. And if it was something else—

Viktoriya greeted the conductor with a smile—the highlight of his day—and then eased into the streetcar's interior. Preferring to stand, the young woman found a space close to the rear exit. She gripped the overhead rail for support as the tram surged to life again, taking in the cityscape through streaked windows. Hearty sycamores spread their branches on either side of Balkovskaya. Some of the broadleaf foliage had already fallen. The rest would succumb to winter's touch during the first hard freeze.

Up and down the street, the tenements reflected an old world charm as they absorbed the hues of the setting sun. While the Berkut unit trundled a pliant Holcek into a waiting van, Xander Voskov caught a glimpse of the tram lurching across Rozumovskaya. The irony of the situation brought a smile.

Ukraine's most famous journalist was completely unaware

that someone had tried to kill her. For all of her intuitive skills, Viktoriya was ignorant of the attempt on her life. And what was it; the second—or *third*—failed effort? Voskov's gaze fell on the Russian's body as the door slammed shut. Thinking more soberly now, he decided that someone should probably warn the woman.

The captain shook off that thought; he could make a recommendation, but ultimately decisions like that were above his pay-grade. In the front of the van, Yuri took the wheel. Xander climbed into the passenger seat and gave him a nod, feeling satisfaction for another successful operation. They had done their jobs. Now it was time to clean up the mess.

Sergei was little more than an amateur, but that wasn't the only reason he'd failed. He was simply in over his head. Against a trained Berkut squad with superior tactics, the outcome was never in doubt.

His employers had erred in sending a novice, but they had other men on retainer—experienced professionals who could get the job done. One of those assassins was particularly skilled. Holcek's handlers wouldn't make the same mistake twice.

Chapter Two * Incognito

Two Days Later
Hemmat Industrial Complex,
Outside of Tehran

THE PLAIN WAS ARID AND FEATURELESS, SAVE for the pillboxes hugging the rocky dunes. Identical in size and construction, and dusted weekly by sandstorms, these squat structures were crowned above with electronics, ranging from communications gear to radar dishes. All had been covered with the dry silt of the Iranian desert.

One kilometer distant, near the eastern edge of the compound, two missile gantries reached into the sky. Both towers were scarred at their base by multiple tests, the metal frames blackened by rocket exhaust. They sat on the hardened concrete that served as launch pads—also scored by fire—and were separated by two thousand meters of windswept terrain.

Between the two spires was an ancient utility truck, handed down from a government that no longer existed. Summers had taken their toll. The truck was sandblasted to a khaki finish, still bearing the Cyrillic letters of the USSR. The markings hung on, but these had faded and were barely legible.

Ruslan Petrov had the window rolled down, his arm perched on the door. Like the truck, the weathered technician had spent too many days in the elements. Even in late fall, his skin was leathery and deeply tanned—which was odd for a native of Moscow.

Petrov gunned the motor and steered toward Gantry One. In contrast to the second tower, this one hosted a multi-stage rocket. Several figures scurried beneath it, attaching cables and priming pumps within an open cowling. Ruslan recognized several of them; the ground-based support teams were largely Korean—*North* Korean. The mechanics and technicians—tasked with doing the heavy lifting—were Russian and fewer in number. All wore heavy polyester coveralls that were suitable for the colder days.

A smattering of Iranians stood nearby and simply watched. They were easy to pick out, their haircuts and beards emulating the style of the engineer-turned-president now running the country. Two even wore suit coats and dress shirts—without ties, of course. From a distance, Petrov recognized them as supervisors. He smiled. Aspiring to success here meant dressing in lockstep with the Republic's leadership.

Cretins, the Russian decided.

A mechanic by trade, it was Ruslan's job to keep the truck running. When it did, he ferried small components and parts to the launch sites. A forklift moved the heavier equipment, and Petrov occasionally drove that as well. Little more than a laborer, his role as a driver gave him a certain anonymity, allowing the discretion needed to perform other duties.

The small group of Russian technicians and mechanics had been sent by the Kremlin, but Petrov had other masters. Before his posting in Iran, the Ukrainian SSD had quietly recruited him to gather and report intelligence. Petrov did this on a weekly basis, or anytime some milestone was achieved at the missile complex, and his method of relaying the information was a thing of beauty.

Ruslan was the outgoing and garrulous type. Socially forward—another oddity for a Muscovite—he spent much of his free time with friends back in the workers' quarters. An inexpensive digital camera was his constant companion. He used it to capture photos and videos of his comrades—drinking parties mostly—in the dorm common room. Petrov was also an avid gardener. He grew a variety of brightly colored perennials in flowerbeds outside his apartment. Every few days he recorded their progress, uploading the images and movies to a popular video sharing site—and with no one ever being the wiser.

Ruslan's comrades thought these antics were peculiar—the man *was* eccentric—but they understood his need to share a part of his life with family back home. They resisted his constant urgings to view the online offerings. Those who did found the videos extremely boring. But that didn't stop Petrov from encouraging them to watch *just one more . . .*

The prodding had the desired effect. Ruslan knew that if he made a nuisance of himself, his actions would never rise above suspicion. His contact in the SSD had told him so—and the man had been right. Superiors no longer asked him about social media, and in time, they accepted the Russian's shutterbug tendencies as part of his personality.

But the camera had a dual purpose, with capabilities few could have guessed at. Petrov had been taught to toggle through to a feature not found on other photographic equipment. In this mode, images captured by the lens were compressed to a micro-dot and stored separately. Uploaded to a simple laptop—equipped with the right software—they could be retrieved later from the innocuous files Petrov posted online.

Everything was under the hood from that point. The micro-dot utilized a bracketed encryption that made detection nearly impossible. Downrange, a member of the Ukrainian clandestine services reviewed Ruslan's footage on a regular basis. From his desk in Kiev, the SSD operative would use an algorithm that searched for a specific digital signature. Once that was found, the embedded intel could be transferred and expanded for analysis.

Petrov had seen it in use on a few occasions. The application itself had been built from scratch—with a distinctly Western flavor. It certainly had none of the earmarks of Ukrainian technology. The cash-strapped republic just wasn't that advanced. Ruslan shrugged it off. The politics of the operation weren't his concern. The former Soviet satellite had partnered with NATO on other projects; agriculture, economics, manufacturing and energy.

Why not espionage?

Ruslan had made use of his spy craft when the first rocket blasted into orbit. He watched from the cab of his truck—while discreetly snapping photos of the launch. The next test was less than a week away. Such occurrences were 'all-hands' events, and Petrov could count on being there for that as well. He would be sure to bring his camera.

THE truck edged closer to the gantry. Ruslan slowed to a stop, shifting into reverse while applying the parking brake. He craned his neck, eyes following the sleek, white fuselage of the missile, its nose pointed skyward. The sun blinded his view of the third stage, but he could easily read the moniker used to christen the arrow-like projectile.

Of late, the Iranians had taken to plucking titles from Greek mythology, yet something about this name bothered Petrov. He couldn't quite place what it was, and for that, he could be excused. Most of his education was focused on hard science and engineering, and he was unable to fit the epithet in context. Schools in Moscow were not as tightly controlled since the end of the Soviet era, but the patterns of instruction had been laid down, and Ruslan's tutelage proved adequate—even without the benefit of the liberal arts.

Petrov's eyes scanned east, to the second spire where the first missile had been flung into space. The rocket motor had ignited and shook the Earth, sending a wave of heat across the dunes. The blast was more intense than previous launches, but that was as it should be. A three-stage vehicle demanded greater thrust.

MIDAS—*that* name Petrov knew. He was a king. And there was something about gold, or a golden touch, anyway. He dredged his memory. It galled him to think that he couldn't remember more, but that didn't matter. MIDAS had successfully lifted off its pad five days earlier. ICARUS would follow in just a few more.

* * * *

EVEN ON WEEKENDS, NEILL FOUND IT DIFFI-cult to sleep in.

Resisting the alarm clock just wasn't in his nature. His Academy days had forged that habit, and the Corps' zero-dark-thirty mentality reinforced the behavior. Michael had also grown accustomed to a certain level of white noise to help him doze; the rush of traffic on the freeway helped, but on Saturday mornings, the sound of cars motoring along the Beltway was greatly diminished.

Neill had slept well. He stirred before sunrise and was up by six, pulling on his favorite jeans before moving to the kitchen. The coffee maker was his first stop. The Marine had prepped it the night before, and with the flip of a switch, the aroma of dark roast began to fill the air. Next he retrieved a carton of half and half, along with a flavored creamer that he considered a guilty pleasure. He smiled at the thought. Probably too much sugar, he decided, but it was a vice he was willing to indulge.

The daily routine started with devotions as he nursed the contents of his mug. This morning's schedule would be some-what abbreviated. Michael was meeting the master gunny—his uncle Daniel—at a Denny's in Anacostia. The two Marines had staked out the restaurant as their favorite, and the younger Neill was looking forward to a full breakfast and a second cup of cof-fee before they drove into the countryside for a day at the range.

Thoughts of his uncle etched a frown on Michael's face. Since his return eight months earlier, he had noticed a change in Daniel Neill's behavior. The master gunny was characteristi-cally cranky, but lately his personality had shifted from irascible to subdued. The captain disliked this turnabout, and spent much of his time trying to draw the man out of his funk.

He considered where the career NCO had been. On his third

tour in Iraq, the elder Neill had lost his right leg to an IED—traumatic for anyone, and no less for the hardened master gunnery sergeant. Many veterans of that war were still coming to terms with the effects of combat and post-traumatic stress. On top of that, Daniel had never married, and by his own admission, he spent too much time alone. Taking everything into account, Michael mused that Daniel's experiences were simply catching up with him.

Michael put his concerns aside and checked his cell. Still plenty of time to shower. Breakfast wouldn't take long, and the range didn't open till nine-thirty. He'd skip shaving this morning; it was Saturday, after all, and the Marine wanted to give his face a break.

The phone lit up just as he laid it on the nightstand. Neill focused on the display. The small screen ID erased his frown and brought a smile.

"*Dobro'd nyah.*" *Good afternoon.* The air base at Nikolayev was six hours ahead. Michael launched into his best Ukrainian accent. He did so effortlessly, having learned English and the Slavic tongue at the same time. "*Zheneral* Ulyanov, I presume?"

There was a pause from halfway around the world. Andrei Ulyanov chuckled softly before answering.

"Your presumption is correct, Captain," he boomed. Reception was crystal clear, and it was good to hear Michael's voice. As he aged, the young man sounded more like his father. "I trust I didn't wake you?"

"No, sir. Just finished my first cup of coffee."

Neill heard a sigh on the other end. "Have you forgotten your upbringing, *Mischa*? True Ukrainians drink tea."

"I can't argue with that," Michael conceded. "But no one here can make it like you—and certainly not Irina."

An amused laugh. "You should consider the diplomatic service when you leave the United States Marines."

Neill turned on a lamp and stepped toward the gun safe in the corner. He dialed the combination and opened the door—before tacking in a different direction. "I hear you're up for a second star." It sounded like a question.

"Two for two, Michael," Ulyanov allowed. "The president is padding my resumé, it would seem. A meritorious promotion—" he hesitated, "—at the request of your State Department."

"I won't ask." *Interesting*, Michael thought silently. He lifted first one, then another shooter's bag from the safe's interior. One held a .12 gauge shotgun; the other a .22 rifle. "General-*Lieutenant* Ulyanov. Has a nice ring to it—but over here the rank would be lieutenant-*general*."

"That sounds like a demotion." The complexities of the English language always befuddled Andrei, with the confusion sometimes going both ways. "However, that's not why I called."

"Glad to hear it," Neill answered. "Bragging doesn't suit you. Is Irina okay?"

"She's fine, Michael; although she does lament the end of fall. November is here and winter is just around the corner." His tone became hushed. "The woman has been canning all season. We have more cabbage and sugar beets than ever—and you know how I feel about cabbage."

Michael winced. "Any apples? I'm all about apples."

"Two whole shelves." Ulyanov grew enthusiastic. "You'll have to come for a visit."

"I'd like that. My mouth is watering at the prospect of one of Irina's pies. So—you were saying . . .?"

The general took the hint. "Yes, of course. Is this a secure line?"

A reflexive nod. "My apartment came with mil-spec encryption." That was an exaggeration, but the required equipment had been installed. "You can speak freely. What's up?"

"It's your journalist friend." Ulyanov's deep voice grew somber. "There's been another attempt on her life."

"Viktoriya? Is she all right?"

"Don't worry, Michael. Miss Gavrilenko is as vibrant as ever. Thankfully her assailant was incompetent; apparently Moscow is handing out firearms to imbeciles." He now wore a rueful smile. "He will no longer be a threat to anyone."

"What happened?"

Andrei spent the next minute relaying what he knew about the incident. A bare-bones assessment landed on the general's desk the day before. The report included no names, and personal details were omitted to protect the operatives involved.

"You've heard of our Berkut units?" Ulyanov growled.

"Golden Eagles. The guys with the burgundy berets," Neill replied. "Subordinate units of the Ministry of Internal Affairs, if I'm not mistaken—not somebody I'd want to tangle with." He removed a box of .12 gauge slugs from the safe; the range didn't allow buckshot. "I didn't know you had a team in Odessa."

"We don't. This one was dispatched—" Ulyanov hesitated, another smile forming, "—from a separate location." The general shifted gears. "You realize this has everything to do with President Murovanka?"

The captain reflected on that. Since his last visit to Ukraine, Viktoriya had done quite a bit of digging. Using evidence provided by Ivan Malyev, she had uncovered ties linking the Russian president to acts of terrorism. The information had been posted online and in print—under a pseudonym, of course—but efforts to safeguard the journalist's identity had begun to erode.

"That thought did cross my mind. What are we going to do about it?"

Both men felt responsible for Viktoriya. The idea to enlist her services had come from Ulyanov, but Neill had talked her into cooperating—while dangling the prospect of an exclusive. They had assumed—naively, perhaps—that the Ukrainian security services could protect her; but with *two* attempts against her life—

"Her luck won't last forever, Michael. Even a blind squirrel finds a nut now and again." The general's words carried a fatherly concern. "I've spoken to the SSD about this. Her editors in Kiev have been informed as well. They agree that a posting *outside* the country—for reasons of health, if you will—might be an attractive short-term solution."

"Where?" Neill asked.

The Marine knew that Arkadi Murovanka had a long reach, as did his right hand man, Leonid Karpenko. Viktoriya had exerted tremendous pressure on the Russians, but now they were pushing back—and their agents only had to be successful once.

"That's entirely up to her. Personally, I think it best if neither of us knows. Hiding in plain sight might be the best option—but not in Ukraine."

Time to go incognito. "Close enough to keep an eye on, but out of immediate danger." Michael thought back to the time he'd spent with Viktoriya in Odessa. "Either way, she's pretty stubborn—probably best if she thought the whole thing was her idea."

THE two spoke for another ten minutes. Michael ended the call and laid the phone next to his weapons. A trip into the kitchen followed; he split a bagel in two and popped it into the toaster. The conversation with Ulyanov had delayed breakfast, and he hoped a taste of cinnamon and raisins would suffice for the moment.

He showered and dressed, choosing tactical khakis and a hooded sweatshirt bearing the Henderson Hall imprint over the pocket. The design was simple enough; anything bolder would be deemed too *moto* by Daniel Neill. The choice was practical, too; November's arrival had brought cold weather, and Michael was thankful they'd be spending the day at an indoor range.

The young captain had other reasons for carving out time with his uncle. The presidential election was just days away. Media coverage had saturated the airwaves. Daniel Neill was a news junkie, and while the president's party appeared to be on the ropes, fixating on the political back and forth only agitated the retired veteran. The gunny had a professional's touch when it came to firearms, and Michael hoped that a little target practice might distract him, giving him a chance to vent his frustrations at the same time.

Family was never far from his thoughts, but the general's words spurred new concerns. Viktoriya Gavrilenko had done her country a great service. It could be argued that the citizens of Russia were equally in her debt, but the journalist's devotion to ferreting out corruption had put her in Murovanka's crosshairs.

Neill picked up his cell and tabbed through the photo archive. Viktoriya's face smiled back. The images had been taken at the opera house nearly two years before. He hadn't seen her since, although the two exchanged emails a few times each month. He kept things friendly but professional. Viktoriya had done the same. On occasion she tested the waters with a coy remark; and there were times when her subtle advances reminded him of—

The captain hefted the shooter's bags from the bed. Locking the door behind him, he bounded down the stairs to his car. The sun was up and he was a little behind schedule, but traffic would be light for the drive north. He pushed his cares aside, filling his mind with thoughts of eggs and bacon. Michael had always been big-hearted, but there were times when his stomach simply took over.

He had started the day preoccupied with his uncle. Ulyanov's call had changed all that. Now the Marine had someone else to be worried about.

The Washington Hilton
One hour later

THE CADILLAC LOOKED HEAVIER THAN MOST, and given its occupant, probably armored. Approaching the D.C. landmark from Leroy Place, the limo eased up the ramp and circled the turnabout, chugging exhaust as the car slowed to a stop.

Emerging from the hotel's T Street exit, Charles 'Chuck' Cassidy appeared positively ebullient; he'd been waiting for this guest to arrive and wanted to be the first to greet him. Warm and engaging, he played host naturally. That was part of his appeal, and it came across as genuine—unlike many politicians.

The tall black man was clad in slacks and a powder-blue Oxford shirt, without coat and tie at present, his sleeves folded neatly below the elbows. Striding toward the limousine, the physician-turned-presidential candidate had a relaxed air about him, in contrast to the stern Secret Service agents flanking his left and right. Their anxiety was understandable. This was the very spot where Reagan had been attacked by a gunman more than thirty years before.

"Glad you could make it," Cassidy grinned. He crossed the sidewalk and extended a hand.

At street level, another agent shadowed his charge. Closing the limo's door behind him, the dignitary stepped away from the curb in Cassidy's direction. He wore a double-breasted raincoat that was slightly oversized; the expensive outerwear was rumpled, giving the big man a somewhat disheveled look. A crisp breeze caught hold of his wavy hair, tossing it at an unflattering angle.

"Thanks for the invitation," Willis Avery returned. He smiled warmly and accepted the proffered hand. He had expected a crush of reporters, but they were curiously absent.

"My pleasure. Now what do you say we go someplace warmer?" The candidate shivered. "The coffee's waiting, and it's a little chilly out here."

INSIDE, one whole floor had been reserved for the campaign staff. An adjoining dining room had also been retained, along with a kitchen, and as they entered, the aroma of breakfast foods filled the air. A small cadre of assistants scurried about. One of these—Avery recognized the campaign director—led the men to a table at the center of the room. The national security advisor shed his coat and handed it off to one of the candidate's energetic assistants.

They exchanged pleasantries as Cassidy lifted a steaming carafe. He filled two cups and then wheeled a serving cart closer, providing his guest a choice of cream and sugar. Avery noted his actions with admiration; the man certainly wasn't one to simply sit back and be waited on.

Chuck Cassidy gestured to the buffet cart, and the two men began dishing food onto their plates. Avery filled his with scrambled eggs and hash browns, and then noticed a menu item that ranked on his list of weaknesses.

"You set a fine table, Mr. Cassidy." He added a biscuit to his plate, "—although I doubt there are many heart docs who would recommend the sausage gravy."

The physician chuckled softly. "Everything in moderation, Mr. Avery. I think everyone can enjoy the *occasional* indulgence. I prefer to think in terms of balance."

"Balance it is." Avery helped himself. "And why don't you call me Willis?"

The two attacked their food in silence. The hall could accommodate more than three hundred people, but was largely empty, save for the candidate and his guest. It was some time before Avery noticed that the staff had receded, leaving the men completely alone.

Finishing the meal, they pushed back from the table as Cassidy refilled their cups. With breakfast out of the way, it was time to focus on the reason behind their meeting.

"Looks like the press hasn't caught wind of our little get-together," Avery observed. He scanned the room. The pre-requisite campaign signs and placards dotted the walls. Most prevalent were the ones declaring that *The Doctor Is In!*

Cassidy's face spread into a broad grin. "The press thinks I'm back home in Sioux City. I hear there's a contingent camped out in my driveway." The thought was clearly amusing. "Besides that, your boss insisted on discretion. I have to admit, I was a little surprised he agreed to this meeting at all."

"Mark Breese is a pragmatist, Mr. Cassidy. He's foreseen the inevitable."

"Call me Charles. Everyone else does."

Avery nodded. "All right—Charles. Of course, we all know that will change after Tuesday; by then I'll be addressing you as *Mr. President-elect.*"

Cassidy raised a hand. "Let's not count our chickens yet."

Avery gave him a shrewd look. "You've seen the polls. So has the president. Every major pundit has you winning by a landslide." He shrugged. "The vice president would love the job, but he's incompetent and trailing by double digits. You've achieved the unthinkable; capturing most of the opposition's base while uniting your own. No one could have seen this coming."

The candidate said nothing, a blank expression on his face.

"And then there's the press," Avery continued. "They don't know what to do with you. Back when you and I were growing up, they held a sacred trust. 'Comforting the afflicted, and afflicting the comfortable.' "

Cassidy wore a smile once more. "Not so much over the past eight years, but I do remember that phrase."

"The fourth estate has taken to shaping the news instead of reporting it; if it fits their agenda, then it leads. The dailies are the worst. Small wonder no one reads the papers anymore." Avery grinned, catching himself. He sipped from his mug, becoming more relaxed. "But that's not why we're here. You requested a national security brief, so let's get started."

Cassidy became focused. "You didn't bring any notes."

Avery shook his head. "Don't need any. This stuff crosses my desk every day, and I get plenty of updates. We'll begin with the highlight reel." He drew in a breath. "First on my list is Russia. Yours too, come January."

"I'm listening."

"The wheels started coming off that wagon nearly two years ago. You might recall that incident. They crippled an unarmed Navy plane flying reconnaissance. Killed one of our aviators."

"I remember that. Sea of Japan, right?"

A grunt. "Things got a little dicey, but we managed to gain some valuable intel out of the whole affair."

"Fast forward to the present."

Avery pressed on. "President Arkadi Murovanka has suffered politically ever since, and a mounting body of evidence links him to corruption and acts of terror. He's not just a nationalist; the man's an *ultra*-nationalist. His actions have put the hardliners under the microscope—and they don't like that." He drummed his fingers on the table, reflecting on the irony. "The Russian prime minister is in the awkward position of chastising the man who put *him* in office."

"That mess in Crimea didn't help, either," Cassidy offered.

"Not to mention the rest of Ukraine. These are troubled times for Pavlovsk's administration." A new thought came to mind. "And then there's the State Duma. They've had a falling out with Murovanka, too. We've heard from a back-channel source that some members are calling for a vote of no-confidence."

"Did we have a hand in that, Mr. Avery?" Cassidy waded slowly into that one. "I've heard a rumor or two."

The national security advisor deflected. "I can promise a more in-depth discussion *after* the election."

"Understood. What's next on our list?"

"Iran. Probably not a surprise; but for all their bluster, they've recently made strides with regard to their ballistic missile program. They were able to successfully launch a multi-stage vehicle last week—with assistance from the Russians and North Koreans—so they've managed to upgrade their airframes considerably."

"And China?"

Avery's countenance shifted. His face now bore a curious cast. "Something odd has manifested itself in Beijing. I hesitate to comment. We're getting a hodgepodge of analysis from the field—some conflicting, I'm afraid. I'd prefer not to weigh in until I know more."

"Fair enough," Cassidy stated. The man was intrigued, but he deferred to Avery's judgment. Rather than press the issue he took a different approach. "What about you, Willis? If you're right—and the landscape here in D.C. changes in the coming days—what plans do you have?"

Avery sensed a deeper motive to the question. "I might go back to Kentucky; do a little teaching at the university level. Or there's a think tank out west that's offered a lucrative salary. I could retire comfortably—"

Chuck Cassidy was shaking his head. "Retirement's not in

your foreseeable future, Willis. You've been in government service your entire career. A cushy private sector job doesn't suit
you." He was firm in his assessment—one that seemed to be
leading to something else. "I understand you and Allan Hayes
are friends. Have the two of you talked lately?"

"The Secretary of Defense." Avery winced. "Prostate cancer.
Advanced, from what I hear. He submitted his resignation to the
president in mid-October."

From across the table Cassidy nodded slowly. "You might be
surprised to learn that I've taken a look at his labs," he smiled.
"He wanted a second opinion. I'm a thoracic guy, mind you, but
I can read a blood panel—"

Avery wasn't surprised at all; the physician had a reputation for helping where he could, even in areas outside of his
expertise. "Allan told me. Sounds like he might have a fighting
chance." His eyes fixed on one of the placards hanging just a
few feet away. "And the Doctor *is* in."

"I'm optimistic." Cassidy was guarded. "Still, his absence
will create a void in Defense. I'm not ready to settle for that.
What can you tell me about MacGinnis—the under-secretary?"

"Patrick's a good man." For someone charged with giving
advice, Avery sounded noncommittal.

"But not strong on the big decisions," Cassidy suggested.

"True; but adequate for the interim, until you can find a more
suitable replacement." There was an awkward silence. Avery
knew where this was going, but hadn't entertained the possibility of a job offer. Besides—

"I'm speaking out of turn, Mr. Cassidy. Allan will have to
make that call. He's the Secretary of Defense, not me."

"At least not yet." There. It was out in the open now.

Avery resisted. "My plate's a little full these days. You've
heard about Poland?"

The candidate frowned. "Doesn't ring a bell. What can you
tell me?"

"Missile emplacements. A shield in Central Europe. A few
years back we approached the Poles with a phased adoptive

policy; sea-based defenses at first, leading to ground installations—on their soil."

"And?"

"The plan was to take baby steps. A system of defense in
incremental stages. Sea-going weapons would have come first,
followed by missiles being placed in Romania and Poland. The
goal was to counter the threat of an ICBM launch from Tehran."

"The so-called Theater High Altitude . . . something or other.
Breese killed that initiative." Cassidy was close; the name had
changed of late. Currently the system was branded as *Terminal*
High Altitude Area Defense. It was called THAAD for short.

"He was part of it, that's true," Avery hedged. "But politics
on the ground didn't help either; the Polish president—Karl
Dobrogost—got heat from Moscow. The Kremlin decided such
actions were provocative and would lead to another arms race."
He sampled his coffee but it had grown cold. "I can understand
that sentiment—up to a point. In our defense, the Russians are
propping up radicals in Iran, so I think we have a legitimate
grievance."

The candidate lifted the carafe and warmed the contents of
each mug. "Where does this all rest now?"

"We're working on a few angles. State is twisting some arms
in one of the republics." The U.S. had leveraged the Ukrainian
president, but Avery wasn't quite ready to reveal that fact.
"Negotiations have been on-going, but for the moment, we're
stuck with our initial contingency; making the most of our
Aegis-based system."

"Is that anywhere near as effective as the Iron Dome program?" Cassidy was referring to the stellar achievements of
Israel's anti-missile batteries.

"No, sir, it's not," Avery breathed. "Needless to say, this
has been a coup for Moscow; they view Dobrogost's rejection
of our aid as a chance to undermine U.S. goals abroad—and
they've jumped on it."

This news didn't surprise Cassidy. "What happens in the
meantime?"

Avery responded with a shrug. He considered offering something pithy; about hoping for the best, but then scrapped the idea. Factoring in Iran just complicated things, and where Russia was involved, resorting to wishful thinking just wasn't good policy.

Chapter Three * The Assignment

Central Moscow,
Russian Federation

GENERAL LEONID KARPENKO SAT IN THE back of the Zil as his driver took the exit. Far from the straight, broad *prospekts* of the city's main arteries—away from the Rublyovo-Uspenskoye highway—the road here was curved, following the bends in the ice-choked river. A fresh snow blanketed the ground, and frozen crystals glistened in the afternoon sun as the bulky sedan motored south.

One of the general's subordinates had joined him today, an officer from the southern military district, a region that ran along the border with Ukraine. Like Karpenko, the major wore an Army uniform. At length, the car passed an urban construction site. Neither man spoke as the car slowed, allowing Leonid a chance to survey the property.

The brick and mortar shell at its center was nothing like the garden houses of the past. This was truly a *gosdacha*, or state house, an elaborate display of power sitting on twenty-five fir-covered acres of land. Much of the surrounding forest had been uprooted to give contractors and engineers greater access, but this was only temporary. Saplings would be planted later to obscure the view.

This was to be the general's retirement villa, but for all its once and future grandeur, the structure was now impotent. Its growth had been stunted by scandal—a reproach of Karpenko's own making. For much of his career, he had allied himself with Arkadi Murovanka, and their mutual rise to power was often built on corruption. The two men had taken steps to hide their involvement, but for the past year, their efforts had come to naught.

The trouble had begun in Ukraine. It spread to the outlying republics. A media barrage had been unleashed; published reports cited a conspiracy to reinstate Soviet control over the Commonwealth. The journalistic attack went far beyond innuendo. Murovanka's name figured prominently in the stories. So did the general's. A series of allegations came to light daily; and in each case, the evidence was irrefutable. The news outlets not only repeated the accusations, they sent copies of documents to the federal agencies charged with investigating government activities.

Someone had declared war on the Russian president—and that someone was a member of the press. It had taken some time, but a name finally surfaced. Karpenko nursed that thought bitterly. His plans had begun to unravel not long after—

The officer on Leonid's right stirred in the leather seat.

"Holcek has failed." Major Pirogov's words came abruptly, but did little to bring Karpenko out of his reverie.

The general stared through the glass at the mansion and sighed. The *dacha* would never be completed now. He was sure of it. Eighteen months had passed since construction began, and along the western banks of the Moscow River, the two story edifice was still only half finished.

"Do you see that patio in front?" Karpenko gestured to his left. "That would have been a fountain." He gave a disaffected smile. "I had the garden completed first. A denouement to entice Anna; but these days she prefers not to visit." His expression faded. "You assured me that Sergei was perfect for the job."

Pirogov swallowed. "We agreed that simple jobs require

simple tools. If we had recruited a professional—"

"—then we might have staunched the flow," Karpenko grunted. He waved a hand toward his property. "And all of this might still become a reality."

"Yes, General. Sergei was a poor choice."

There was little the major could say to defend the assassin, and Karpenko didn't intend to give him the chance. He produced a sheet of newsprint from the leather satchel at his side.

"Have you seen this?"

"Today's *Pravda*?" Pirogov took the creased paper and scanned the headlines. Above the fold was a story of particular interest. Eight columns of type dominated the page, crowding out everything that was less newsworthy. The major's face began to pale. "They can prove this?"

"Our assets are sheltered in numbered accounts," Karpenko replied. "That should have been enough."

Pirogov was already aware of that. A vast pool of funds had been siphoned into the Army's coffers—financial resources under the general's control. The bookkeeping had been carefully arranged, and the accounts were only accessible to senior bank officers—men on Karpenko's payroll. These electronic ledgers were all password protected. The money was moved from time to time, filtered through legitimate businesses, but always at the president's disposal. Murovanka had insisted on it—and it had become his Achilles' heel.

Pirogov continued to read. "Yet someone has gained access."

Karpenko nodded. "Tracing payouts to the Lithuanian underground."

The major almost cringed. Staring back at him from the page were two names he instantly recognized—agents he had enlisted himself. Both were on the run now, suspected of planting radioactive canisters in the parks and railway stations of Vilnius—a ploy to encourage the former republic to seek Moscow's protection.

He had often wondered why Lithuania had been chosen as a target. The country's membership in the Soviet Union was never ironclad. The southern Baltic state was fiercely independent as well. Pirogov had always thought it best to let it go, but those decisions were above him.

"How could they get this information?"

The general drew in a deep breath and fixed his gaze on the unfinished mansion. The past had seemingly returned. On Karpenko's orders, some of it had been buried in Bryansk. The major had seen to it personally; but Karpenko had begun to question some assumptions.

Sasha Kobrin and Ivan Malyev had paid a high price for their allegiances. But too many details were coming to light. It was foolhardy to dismiss the possibility of an informant, and the senior officer wondered if their forest graves might be empty.

"They had help, Alexei. Access like this is beyond the grasp of a mere journalist." He retrieved the newsprint from Pirogov's hands. "We live in a digital age. Anonymity is an illusion now. Ukraine's Security Directorate is quite good, but they would require Western assistance."

"The Americans?"

Karpenko heaved a shoulder. "Possibly the British." He pulled a folder from his attaché, eyeing it warily before handing it over to the major. "They have a few scores to settle as well."

The dossier's cover was blank, as was the index tab. Pirogov opened the file to the first page. What he read there excited his interest. He quickly leafed through several more sheets before turning to face the senior officer.

"The REMORA file?" He lifted the docket reverently, eyes wide. "I saw a copy of this report years ago; that one was heavily redacted."

"This one is not."

"So I see," Pirogov marveled, studying the folder again. "Why are you showing me this?"

Karpenko didn't answer. He gave the major additional time to absorb the data. A full two minutes passed as he scrutinized the portfolio's content, a mixture of surprise and awe on his face.

"He was FSB?" Pirogov asked. He was referring to the Federal Security Service of the Russian Federation.

"Yes."

"And FSK?" Before being reorganized, the intelligence agency went by another acronym.

Another nod from Karpenko. "Briefly KGB, then FSK. After that, he was seconded to the FSB."

The major blinked. "And the Hungarian Secret Police, as well." He closed the file. The general's intentions were clear. "You want him to finish the job Holcek started."

Pirogov's semantics were incorrect. "I want him to *do* the job Sergei was hired for." Karpenko tapped the folder with his index finger. "This man will see it done."

"But surely he's retired by now—if he isn't dead," the major protested. "His age alone—"

"Our affiliation with him is deniable," Karpenko muttered. "Reinstate his credentials. He's living in Sverdlovsk. Move him south, closer to the border."

"To Bryansk?" Pirogov had spoken without even thinking, but it seemed logical.

"We closed that camp," the general remarked with a smile. At the time the facility had been used to train terrorists. President Murovanka ordered it shuttered, to conceal his own liaisons. "We could reopen it, given these . . . special circumstances."

"What then?"

Karpenko looked thoughtful. "Once he's settled, we'll send him into northern Ukraine. The military prison at Chernihiv."

"A visit to Major Mayakovsky?"

The general nodded. "A simple test of his skills."

"Bryansk first," Pirogov said. He wanted to be sure. "The dacha—quite a large facility for one man."

"He enjoys his privacy. But you're right. Assign a four man team for perimeter security."

"Will they double as his protectorate?"

A soft laugh. "That won't be necessary. Advise them to stay clear," Karpenko replied. "REMORA can take care of himself."

Odessa, Ukraine
1,300 kilometers from Moscow

"YOU CALL THIS A CHOICE OF ASSIGNMENTS?"

Viktoriya Gavrilenko was livid. In her hand she held a single sheet of paper, a page filled with double-spaced copy in three paragraphs. She began ticking off the list of bulleted items.

"Kyrgyzstan wants to 'restructure its crumbling pension plan for state workers.'" Her eyes focused on the next line. "A port strike in Greece 'threatens vegetable exports.' And here's the best one—a German oil firm has been accused of 'age discrimination.'" She dropped the sheet as if it were a filthy rag. "What does that even mean?"

The managing editor might have smiled at her theatrics—had he not been on the receiving end of her harangue. Instead, he shrugged and offered a less than satisfactory explanation.

"Not every story cuts to the root of some perceived corruption, Viktoriya."

Valery Bukin regarded the young woman with care. She operated on two different levels; overly-dramatic—or alluringly coy. The latter was most effective on the opposite sex. Bukin noted she wasn't using that method now.

"You need a change of pace," he said quietly. "Something less pedantic."

"Pedantic?" She feigned comprehension, but would have to look that one up. "These aren't even human interest stories." She leaned forward and tapped a red fingernail on the page as it lay on Bukin's desk. "I can't gin up readership over this drivel—am I being punished for something?"

"Not at all." It was time for a little damage control. "But it's healthy to adjust our views from time to time. Get a different perspective on life." Valery had practiced this, and tried a conciliatory tone. It didn't sound authentic. And he immediately regretted using the word—

"*Healthy?*" Viktoriya was suspicious. "Whose idea was this? Not—"

Bukin didn't let her finish. "This comes straight from Kiev, Viktoriya. The publisher himself. He wants you out of the country—the sooner the better," he blurted.

Her hands were firmly on her hips. "Why?" she demanded.

"Because your life is in danger," the editor relented. Normally he spoke in measured tones, but his words slipped out faster than intended. "*Bozhe moi*, Viktoriya! Can't you simply accept an assignment without badgering me?"

She blinked. "Danger?"

"And stop repeating everything I say," Bukin spat out. On occasion, she raised his blood pressure—and not always out of exasperation. He ran a hand through his graying hair. "You'll be the death of me, *zhinka*."

"What about my work here?" Valery's warning hadn't quite registered. "You know what I've been doing."

Bukin was fully aware of what Viktoriya had been up to. More than a year had passed since the SSD descended on his office. The agents in dark suits cajoled Valery, alternately extending a carrot—and a stick—to enlist his cooperation. The managing editor knew better than to resist.

"Your features are already written. I'll see to it they get in the pipeline—that's what an editor's for, in case you hadn't noticed."

Viktoriya's demeanor settled. Her posture relaxed, and the color in her face returned to normal. In an instant, she seemed vulnerable—and much less ready to pounce. "Valery," she exhaled softly. "Please—tell me what you know." Viktoriya wasn't employing her coquettish wiles, but it had the same effect.

"Four days ago," Bukin started, "on your way home. We'd be planning your funeral now, had it not been for your guardian angels."

"Who?" Another question—but at least she wasn't parroting his words.

Valery told her everything he knew. It was less than what General Ulyanov had been told—but it was enough. The report had been written by a government drone and lacked the spark of imagination a journalist might have included. Nonetheless, the *apparatchik's* words chilled the young woman. Bukin relayed them as gently as possible, but his tender elocution did little to blunt the effect.

"Now I understand." There were tears in her eyes. "This is why you picked Greece and Germany." After a pause she seemed to compose herself. "But you can forget about Kyrgyzstan. It's too cold there this time of year—I have nothing to wear, and I look terrible in a parka."

Bukin raised an eyebrow. "Those are your criteria for assignments abroad?" He'd been ready to step around the desk, to give the fragile woman standing before him the embrace he felt she needed. But with her focus back on wardrobe, it was clear she was beyond that.

She gave Valery a smile. "I know just the place."

Viktoriya glowed as she marched through Bukin's door. Her workspace was just two desks away. She plucked a page pinned to the cubicle divider and turned on her heel.

Almost giddy, the journalist re-entered the office. "Send me here." She thrust the sheet under Bukin's nose.

Valery pulled a pair of glasses from his shirt pocket. "Warsaw?" He appeared to be relieved—which Viktoriya took as encouragement. The page included a photograph taken near a riverbed. "What's in Poland that would arouse your interests?"

"A dry rainy season." She stepped closer and now stood at Bukin's side. He caught the scent of lavender. "They've had two. The Vistula is receding from its banks."

"Hardly newsworthy," Bukin scoffed.

"In and of itself, no." Her eyes brightened, and she laid a hand on Valery's arm. "But read on."

The woman's touch cast a spell on him. He looked at the page and read aloud—mumbling at first, but then his voice rose.

"Droughts and extreme conditions have lowered the river's waterline, exposing long-lost treasures from the past."

She pressed in, picking up the narrative. "Of particular interest are ancient barges used by the Swedes during the 1600s.

With the lower sea level—"

"It's a river, Viktoriya," Bukin corrected.

"I know—but whatever." She squeezed his arm. Effusive and bubbly, the charm offensive was on. Bukin found it entertaining and completely irresistible. "After sacking Poland's cathedrals and palaces, the invading troops loaded their spoils on barges, intending to send them back home. It was the war between the Polish-Lithuanian Commonwealth—"

"The Deluge—that's what the Poles call it," Bukin interrupted.

"—and Sweden." An excited nod. "Right. But some of them sank—a result of improper loading, storms—or just poor seamanship. Now a French team is trying to recover them."

Valery removed his glasses. "And this is where you want me to send you?"

"Think of it, Valery." She was almost pleading. "This has everything."

The wheels were already turning. As much as he hated to admit it, Viktoriya was right. The story had all the elements of a good feature: history, conflict, and drama—maybe even romance, with the proper spin. Fundamental ingredients to heighten interest—and expand the paper's readership. Additionally, there would be no language barrier; the French were involved, and Viktoriya was quite fluent.

Bukin was sold.

"It does get you out of Ukraine," he pointed out with a sigh.

"So everybody's happy—me, you. The publisher."

"All right," Bukin agreed. "Warsaw it is."

Viktoriya squealed. For a woman with a price on her head, she was awfully pleased. "When can you be ready to leave?"

"I'll have to pack—day after tomorrow, I should think."

"That won't give you much time to update your apparel." The comment was intended as sarcasm.

"Warsaw's *very* Eastern European. My winter attire will be fine." She caught the gentle taunt without missing a beat, but then her expression deepened, "—but I might need to do a little research."

"Regarding?"

"The 1600s," she purred. Her eyes met his. "Valery—what was it like back then?"

"Get out of my office—before I have payroll restrict your expense account." He raised an index finger for added emphasis, pointing to the door. Viktoriya gave him a quick embrace and a peck on the cheek. Before he could react, she was bounding into the hall, laughter rippling behind her as she went.

Chapter Four * Morning Assessment

Arlington, Virginia
Election Day

NEILL IGNORED THE ELEVATOR, TAKING THE stairwell instead and bounding up the steps two at a time. He was casually dressed, but still in uniform, wearing PT gear and running shoes. His rucksack was slung over one shoulder. He carried a fresh set of service alphas, still wrapped in plastic, as he reached the landing on the second floor.

The Headquarters and Service battalion held their company run every Friday, but there were rare exceptions to that rule. The Marine Corps birthday, for one—less than two weeks hence—or some other special occasion or patriotic event. A presidential election certainly fit the bill, particularly this one. And today's run would send a subtle message. After eight years of budget cuts and a waning focus on defense, the Corps was putting its stamp of approval on the man expected to change all that.

The battalion would form up at 0700. Shortly afterward, the Commandant, General Bradley Cole, would lead the group of Marines, and a smattering of sailors, on a five mile circuit of the campus. As acting first sergeant, Owen Etheridge would be at his side, running with the guidon and trying to keep pace with the Corps' senior officer. That thought brought a grin. The old man was in tip-top shape, while the master gunny, after twenty-eight years of service, had seen better days.

Neill pushed through the hatch and entered the hall. Light spilled across the floor at the far end; the door to the International Operations and Intelligence Office—Russian/Eastern European branch—was already open.

"You're here bright and early."

The captain eased through the entryway, dropping the ruck at his work station. Normally the first one in, he was surprised to find Christina at her cubicle. The overheads were still out, but the lamps at her desk—and Neill's—were glowing.

"Early, yes; bright, not so much."

Christina's voice was low—sultry to Michael's ears. The staff sergeant was similarly dressed, her hair in a pony-tail. She was tapping away at her keyboard, light from the monitor reflecting in her eyes. Neill gave her a quick glance and a smile, then did a double-take. He was tempted to stare, but she would have noticed.

Lord, You made her beautiful, he decided; *extremely so*. He kept that thought to himself.

"CIA assessment on your desk," she announced. "Duty officer logged it in at 0400."

"I guess they never sleep." Neill found a hook for his dry cleaning. He picked up the envelope, looking down as he broke the seal. Placed carefully in the center of the desk were his ribbons and rank insignia, in addition to his shooting badges. Christina must have laid them out when she came in. Michael amended his earlier appraisal; the staff sergeant was not just beautiful—she was efficient, as well. The PC police would probably deem that sexist, but Neill meant no harm.

He smiled, noting something different in the air.

"New perfume?"

The remark caught her off-guard. She hit the wrong key, but corrected the typo.

"Amber—by Colleen," she said. Pausing for a micro-second, she elected to do some fishing. "Why? Do you like it?"

"It has a pleasant fragrance." Neill had already started reading, and his answer was detached.

Christina sighed. *Just what a woman wants to hear. Can't you just say that I smell good?* Occasionally, he came close to paying her a compliment—before pulling back. The man could be infuriating, and she wondered if he would *ever* notice her.

"What's in the assessment?"

"Nothing good."

She looked up. A frown darkened Neill's face, and the dimple in his left cheek became more pronounced—one of several appealing characteristics she had catalogued in the young officer.

"How so?"

"A finding by the British Defense Ministry." His expression softened a bit. "That's *Defense* with a *'c'*, by the way. The Royal Navy's been shadowing Russia's Northern Fleet—surface ships and subs."

"And?"

He read further. "Vessels bearing the tri-color standard of the Northern Fleet have engaged in unorthodox maneuvers, within close proximity to glacial masses or shorelines with high cliffs—a last resort tactic intended to defeat the tracking systems of cruise missiles and other low-altitude, sea-based weapons."

He noted James Wainwright's name attached to the data. The commodore had supplied intel for the report. That was no surprise; the man certainly knew the Russian Navy. Seeing the British officer's contribution reminded Neill of his time aboard the *Industrious*.

Christina's words brought him back around. "Not very effective, given current NATO technology," she answered.

"Hence the term *last resort*," Michael asserted. "Additionally, they've sortied their subs—in two separate tests—at high speeds, sending them to supposed safe havens beneath arctic pack ice."

"Defensive measures," Christina judged. "So why are they suddenly so interested in protecting their fleet?"

"Contingency plans, that's my guess. The Russians are always thinking two or three steps ahead."

"What about their ground forces? Any movement there?"

Michael flipped to a second page. "Plenty—but I'll cut straight to the Ministry's conclusions: 'through economic ineptitude, the current administration has signaled to the world that America's strength has faded. Russia sees this weakness and has made plans that include the possibility of probing attacks on U.S. military installations in Europe.' "

He let his words sink in. That was pretty tall talk for an ally. His gut told him the Brits had misread their Cold War adversary—and his instincts were usually spot on when it came to the disbanded Soviet empire.

The captain's analytic instincts kicked in. He read the report once more, digesting the missive's finer points. At long last, he set the memo aside and relaxed his focus.

"No," Neill began. "As good as our English brothers are, I'm not buying it. This is a reaction to something." The first rays of dawn seeped through the blinds, dispelling the darkness. "The Russians will bide their time—right now they're just testing the waters." Another phrase had come to mind, but *saber-rattling* was so overused. "Adopting a defensive posture requires the assumption of worst-case scenarios. The Kremlin's doing what they do best. In my estimation we're about to see a major shift in Moscow's thinking—Arkadi Murovanka won't want to cross a hawk like Charles Cassidy." His grin returned. "Now I'm starting to sound like my uncle."

"And how is the master gunny?" Christina had met Daniel Neill several times and liked the man.

"He's doing better. I saw him this weekend. We did some shooting over at the range."

"Tell him I said hi."

"I'll do that," Michael promised. *That will definitely make his day.*

There was movement in the hall as the rest of the staff began filtering in. Neill placed the report in a separate folder—Colonel Terryton would want to be briefed—and then leaned back, checking the time.

"Polls open at seven. The Skipper plans to secure us after PT—provided everybody heads to their respective precincts. By the way, you didn't hear that from me."

Arrens turned and met his eyes. The early morning light gave her face a warm look.

"I dropped off my ballot two weeks ago."

"An early voter," Michael observed. His tone became playful. "I wouldn't broadcast that; the boss might make you put in a full day." It was one of his rare forays into humor.

Christina's demeanor shifted. "What makes you think I don't have the boss wrapped around my little finger?"

Back to sultry. The dulcet resonance in her voice was practically hypnotic. Now it was the captain's turn to glow.

Chapter Five * Icarus Rising

Hemmat Industrial Complex,
Outside of Tehran

ONLY A DOZEN TECHNICIANS WORKED THE day shift. Known as Flight Command, they were a select group charged with launching rockets and tracking their ascent. Seated at their consoles, each man's eyes were now glued to various instruments; digital, for the most part, but there were still a few old-fashioned gauges left. These were the preferred choice for the range officers with little faith in automation. For them, low-tech was simply better.

The project manager was another story. Young and often brilliant, Ashok Attil scoffed at the technology of previous generations. He knew that sophisticated weaponry required advanced avionics, and computers had always been crucial to successful rocketry. A stand-out at the University of Tehran, the mechanical engineer had overseen the launch of MIDAS, and was poised for even greater responsibility as the Islamic Republic expanded their missile program.

Attil prepared to lead his team through their pre-flight checks. Mechanics and support personnel crowded the bunker, squeezing into corners and grabbing available chairs. The rest stood in the back, craning their necks for a look at the monitor trained on Gantry One.

Today's event was low-key; there would be none of the usual formalities. ICARUS was the third vehicle in the Shahab series, and the success of its predecessors ensured that fewer eyes would be following this launch. That wasn't to say that Iran's leaders weren't interested; members of the Ministry of Science—and the military—would be watching from the comfort of their offices and conference rooms, viewing the lift-off via closed-circuit video feeds.

The absence of bureaucrats didn't bother anyone in the room. Having them underfoot was an unnecessary distraction. The engineer preferred the simplicity of tests that required a small team—sending missiles into orbit was serious business, and he had little patience for putting on a show.

Attil checked the digital clock above the monitor. The countdown was proceeding on schedule. His eyes swept the command center, and then the engineer cleared his throat and activated the comm system shared by the flight personnel.

"Systems check; all stations report."

The man to Attil's left didn't hesitate. "Gantry Control, all ready."

"Propellant mixture, set." This came from Fuels.

Guidance was next. His words crackled in Attil's ear. "Go for launch."

"Flight path?" Attil asked.

"Air traffic has been re-routed away from our position." It wouldn't do for ICARUS to collide with a jetliner, as unlikely as that might be.

One by one, the rest of the team checked in. Satisfied with the reports from each station, Attil turned to the launch director. "Clear for launch. Flight?"

"Flight concurs; all protocols are matched for lift-off."

Attil nodded his acceptance. Everything was ready; it was almost time to go. When the countdown clock reached zero, he stretched out a hand and flipped a key embedded in the console.

* * * *

ELECTRICAL SIGNALS RACED FROM THE BUNKER to the gantry half a mile away. The rocket motor ignited first, showering the pad with sparks and flame. There was a deafening roar, and the ground shook as an inverted cloud of dust and smoke rolled upward.

Systems within the missile came to life. Pulses relayed to the gyro determined that the vehicle was stable, aside from a two degree vertical shift. At a command from the onboard computer, support armature running the length of the tower began to disengage and swing clear. Sensing that the airframe was now free, the main engine increased thrust, and ICARUS began clawing its way into the sky.

But one of the arms resisted. When it finally detached, a flange connected to the tower failed; structural fatigue and repeated use split the metal collar in half. With nothing to govern its movements, the cradling beam whipped away from the missile, struck the tower framework and snapped free.

RUSLAN Petrov saw everything. The technician was outside, safe within a concrete dugout. The narrow bunker was in a pocket between dunes and covered by a metal awning.

Petrov felt a subtle change in air pressure as the blast wave rippled across the desert. The Russian peered over the berm, his eyes protected from the elements by a pair of polarized sunglasses. He was just about to take a few photos when he caught a glint of sunlight from the tower.

THE steel arm tumbled as it fell. With the mass of a small car, it struck the missile hard, its weight smashing a section of the tail fin. The flat surface of the stabilizer was joined by a series of rivets. Impact with the beam caused several to break free, but the fin managed to hang on.

The damage had been done, but it was only the beginning.

ICARUS had barely cleared the gantry when its slender fuselage began a slow, clockwise spiral.

* * * *

ATTIL LOOKED AWAY FROM THE SCREEN AND down at his instruments. Something was wrong.

"Check for yaw, Flight," he ordered. A frown marked his brow.

The flight director noted the rapidly changing numbers. "Pitch is off, as well." He gripped a joystick and attempted a course correction, but the long axis of the vehicle continued on its path. Gaining altitude and speed, the deviation became more pronounced.

"Controls are sluggish. I can't restore attitude."

Attil took over. "Propulsion, give me a five percent increase in thrust. We'll jockey her back into position."

* * * *

THE MISSILE WAS DESIGNED TO TRAVEL VERTI-cally before arcing into an orbital trajectory. With a damaged stabilizer, it strayed from its original course, the nose cone dipping much too early.

ICARUS was going the wrong way.

Flight Command had their hands full. The control surfaces of the external fins could be easily finessed under optimum conditions, trimmed to maneuver the vehicle as it ascended. That option no longer existed. The busted wing interrupted the smooth flow of air around the missile, introducing a variable that was difficult to compensate for.

Attil had almost regained a measure of control when another rivet came loose. Only two now held the fin in place, but those wouldn't last. Increased drag stressed the frame, tugging at the wildly flapping tail section and snapping the last of the connectors.

In an instant, the broken stabilizer sheared away from its

mounts, tumbling end over end as it fell back to earth.

NORAD,
Cheyenne Mountain Complex,
Colorado

"HEAT BLOOM—LAUNCH SIGNATURE IN THE IN-frared range!"

The lieutenant's voice rose. It was six in the morning, and his shift would have ended soon. Buried deep in the underground facility, the gangly Air Force officer hadn't expected this.

"Walk me through it, Reston." The major kept his cool. *And fall back on your training, son.*

Reston's eyes locked on his instrumentation. "Confirmed launch; Iranian desert." It was enough to get his blood flowing.

Major Montez didn't like the sound of that, but he wasn't too worried. Tehran didn't have the technology needed to strike the U.S.

"Second one in as many weeks. Trajectory?"

"A little sketchy right now, sir, but FELIX is working on it."

That was more of a nickname than a military acronym; it referred to the Combined Aerial Telemetry system, or CAT. Somewhere along the way the application was branded FELIX—and the label stuck.

The system worked fast. "Altitude has surpassed five thousand feet. Projected path is due north."

"North?" Montez was now at Reston's side. "Their last test ended in the Indian Ocean."

The lieutenant studied the screen plotting the missile's progress. "Unless they're taking the scenic route, I'd say they're a little off course."

The major picked up the phone. There were calls to make; first, to the National Reconnaissance Office—the NRO—to flag the threat and acquire signals intelligence. The next would go to the J-3 Directorate at the Pentagon. The National Military Command Center was linked directly to COM/TAC, and the two defense agencies worked in tandem to piece together information from the field.

Montez pressed the receiver against his ear. He glanced at the monitor dominating the far wall. "What's his current position?"

* * * *

"CROSSING INTO RUSSIAN AIRSPACE." FLIGHT bit his lip. He had started sweating.

"Over the Caspian Sea," Attil noted. "Thrust?"

"Nominal, but falling off. Speed is eight thousand KPH," Flight answered. He began considering alternatives. "Increased altitude *could* enhance control."

The project manager shook his head. "ICARUS will never reach the thinner atmosphere. It's too far from the threshold."

There was no controlling it now. Attil had only one option left.

National Reconnaissance Office
Chantilly, Virginia

THE ANALYST'S THREAT BOARD WAS ACTIVE, AND it didn't take long to find a screen monitoring southwest Asia. Within seconds, he was following the course of the Iranian missile. In rapid succession, a multitude of agencies had confirmed the launch. AFTAC—the *Air Force Technical Applications Center,* down in Florida—was the latest to sound the alarm.

"I didn't think ICBMs had a self-destruct feature," the NRO operative announced into the phone.

"That's all Hollywood," Major Montez replied. "This is a prototype. The Iranians don't want one of their rockets landing in downtown Tabriz. Our intel suggests they've got charges on each of their test platforms."

The analyst considered that as he watched the screen. He hoped Montez was right; currently the rocket was angling north by northwest.

"They better do it quick, then," he muttered. "If they blow it once it's over land—"

* * * *

"—WE'LL HAVE THIRTY TONS OF STEEL RAINING down on a civilian populace," Flight grated out. "Over southern Russia, no less; not an attractive outcome."

"Then we have to act now." Attil looked at the downrange telemetry. Flight Command had trained for this contingency, but no one expected it would ever crop up. And there wasn't time—

One of the phones began ringing, followed by another. *Inquiries from the Ministry of Science,* Attil reasoned—*or the military.* He ignored the calls; his most pressing responsibility at the moment was to kill ICARUS.

The engineer gripped a key. With a glance at the data, he turned his wrist to the right, sending one final command to the renegade traveler.

* * * *

The White House

"CAN'T WE SHOOT IT DOWN?"

Richard Aultman was breathless as he and Willis Avery entered the situation room. Election Day had barely started and they were already facing a crisis.

"With *what?*" The national security advisor snorted. "THAAD's been put on hold. And our Aegis-based weapons can't touch this." He gestured toward the large, cartographic display now depicting the country of Iran. An image representing the Iranian rocket was shifting across the screen. "Besides, the best chance of knocking down an ICBM is during boost phase; we're a little late for that."

Other members of the president's staff began filing into the room, including Admiral Eric Davies, chairman of the joint chiefs.

"So what are we looking at—is this a first strike?"

"Against Russia? Not likely," Avery frowned. "Think it through, Richard; the Russians have advisors on Iranian soil. Their people are *helping* Tehran. I can't picture Iran lobbing a missile over the border. Still—" he turned to face Davies, "Might be prudent to know what Ivan's up to right now—" he stepped forward, tracing a finger around the western edge of the Caspian Sea, "—in this general vicinity."

The admiral gave a nod and then leaned over the control console. Using a mouse, he clicked on the map, expanding the image.

"FIRESTEPPE," Davies intoned. He tapped a few keys. The display shifted to satellite mode, and a string of glowing boxes appeared on the screen. "Also known as the REDWOLF Perimeter Command Directorate. Most likely they've been bird-dogging that rocket since it popped up over the horizon." He singled out the line of rectangles. "These keyframes represent Russia's southern border defenses—near Lagan in Kalmykia. The ones in red have just gone on alert."

"They're *all* red," Aultman observed.

Davies nodded. "Tell me about it," he added dryly.

Command Bunker,
FIRESTEPPE/REDWOLF

GENERAL-LIEUTENANT VASILY LAVROV HAD A front row seat. Like his Western counterparts, the commander of Russia's southern perimeter relied on a series of visuals to follow ICARUS' movements. Cameras were now tracking the missile, and a high-def retina-display monitor offered a split-screen view of the inbound rocket.

"Course and speed," Lavrov barked.

The radar officer was ready with an answer. "North by north-west. Speed is twelve thousand KPH."

"Altitude?"

"Twenty-one thousand meters, sir."

The general pursed his lips. Lavrov had more than a few arrows in his quiver—and the command authority to use them.

FIRESTEPPE had a small inventory of interceptor missiles, chiefly the Fifty-Three Tango-Six. That weapon had been developed to knock incoming vehicles out of the sky. Unfortunately, the Fifty-Threes came with certain limitations.

The defensive weapon had a range of one hundred kilometers, and it was only effective against warheads on a re-entry path. The inbound was still ascending and moving fast. Additionally, the Fifty-Three was armed with a nuclear tip, and the general was hesitant about employing—

Lavrov discarded that thought. He was charged with defending Russia's southern frontier, and he would use all means necessary—however slim the chances of success might be.

The Russian officer moved from one station to the next, checking the status of the interceptors' launch containers. He was prepared to blow the silo covers when the radar officer called his attention back to the screen.

Above the Caspian Sea

THERE WERE FOUR EXPLOSIVE CHARGES ABOARD ICARUS. One was mounted next to the inertial guidance system. The rest were placed near the propellant tanks at the base of the missile.

Attil's directive was relayed to the wayward rocket via radio waves, but the fail-safe was only partially successful. The device in the nose cone obliterated the vehicle's communications suite. Contact with the ground was lost immediately. Two charges in the tail section inexplicably failed, and only one of the three managed to detonate.

The blast had some unintended side-effects. Several side panels were thrown clear of the airframe, just above the point where the stabilizer fin had been ripped away. There was now extensive damage to the rocket's lower half—further degrading maneuverability.

Within the fuselage, the booster continued to burn, but not for long. The engine was fed by turbo-pumps that channeled the fuel through a set of thrust chambers. Both were shut down at detonation, and for an instant, ICARUS became silent.

That, too, was not to last. Engine cut-off triggered an automatic response. The first stage was jettisoned, and as it fell, the missile's sustainer rocket ignited.

* * * *

"I SEE IT, CAPTAIN," LAVROV BREATHED.

One hundred and twenty kilometers to the east, the rocket bucked wildly in flight. For an instant, its erratic course was anyone's guess. The images provided by the video feed were remarkably clear, and all eyes were on the screen as the view abruptly changed.

The projectile arcing across the sky altered its appearance. What had once been a single object became two. One of the pieces tumbled seaward, while the other half continued along its original path. As the first stage plunged out of visual range, there was an intense burst of light from the portion of the vehicle still aloft.

Freed from a quarter of its weight, ICARUS blazed ahead. Stage separation jarred the fuselage, sending the missile in a slightly different direction. It found new life as the sustainer engine began its burn.

Near the nose cone, four vernier rockets ignited, providing adjustments to speed and trim. ICARUS was now traveling due west, following the curvature of the Earth. In six minutes the remaining fuel would be consumed, and the missile would reach apogee, the highest point of its flight.

General-Lieutenant Lavrov was relieved at this sudden turn of events. His Fifty-Threes were untested in a crisis scenario, and for today, they would remain so. The troops of FIRESTEPPE/ REDWOLF became spectators. They could watch, but nothing more. At the moment, that was all anyone could do.

Chapter Six * The Fall of Icarus

Lask Air Base,
Poland

THE SENIOR MASTER SERGEANT WATCHED flight ops from the edge of the tarmac. A cargo plane was parked just ahead, and all four engines were turning. Even at this distance, the prop wash was strong, and the air was filled with the smell of fuel as it was blown across the taxiway.

"We call them *gray-tails*." The sergeant squinted as the fumes burned his eyes. His voice rose above the din, and an interpreter translated his words. "Not an official designation, mind you, but accurate."

A group of Polish non-commissioned officers had gathered at Geoffrey Welles' side. He didn't speak their language, but his friendly personality helped to bridge the gap between cultures.

Welles reached into a pocket to retrieve his goggles, but gloved hands made that effort cumbersome. He also wore hearing protection; mouse ears, as they were called, and a pair of steel-tipped boots. The reinforced footwear had come in handy on more than one occasion, and he smiled at the thought. After all this time—twenty-five years in the Air Force—it was the simple things that helped to protect life and limb.

A transporter rumbled past, edging onto the flight line as the group observed the afternoon exercise. The plane before them had lowered its ramp, and an American loadmaster was schooling his Polish counterpart. Both focused on the lumbering vehicle to the rear. Officially called a Tunner, the loader was remarkable for its tiny control cabin, massive chassis, and the twenty wheels tucked underneath. It could carry up to six pallets of cargo, using its conveyor system and elevated deck to service any aircraft in the world.

"And that's a K-loader," Welles continued. His audience nodded appreciatively. The Tunner was the talk of the base, and had been since a C-17 delivered it days earlier. "60K, for short."

"You have more of these?" A lieutenant in the Polish Army, the interpreter's name was Pyotr Stanislaw.

"Lots more," Welles said. "And they come in different sizes. We have a smaller version called the Halvorsen—carries up to twenty-five thousand pounds." He wasn't sure what that meant in kilograms.

"And these vehicles; they are expensive?" The young officer had just a trace of an accent.

"More than I make in a year," Welles grinned. "Hey, where did you learn to speak English?"

Stanislaw returned the smile. "An American missionary—in Ukraine. But that's a long story."

THE group turned back to the flight line. The C-130 looked like any other, but on closer inspection, something was different. A J-model, the plane's tail carried the roundel of the Polish Air Force; red and white squares in a checkerboard pattern. Two other planes were likewise marked and positioned at the yawning mouth of a nearby hangar. These were recent additions to Poland's military—no doubt purchased with U.S. foreign aid, Welles mused.

The senior sergeant didn't begrudge the Poles for that. The two nations now shared common goals, and the former Soviet satellite was a member of NATO. The relationship gave the U.S.

a foothold near Russian soil—and for the old hardliners in the Kremlin, that was the rub.

Welles was halfway through a six month tour, acting as superintendent for the operations group. His posting to Lask was a progressive step, and checking off the box in Poland would ensure his promotion to Chief, the last rung on the Air Force enlisted ladder.

He was unique among his fellow airmen in several ways. Standing over six foot four, he had a shock of white hair and a boyishly round face. A smile seemed forever etched there. His deep baritone voice commanded respect, and his unusual height made him hard to miss in any crowd. He was also a reservist, which meant he had to balance his civilian occupation along with a military career.

Being in Europe was a refreshing change. His previous assignment had been in eastern Afghanistan. While at Bagram Airfield, Welles was forced to carry a weapon—even in the chow hall. At the time it was an annoyance, but in hindsight, having armed troops covering the base proved a deterrent.

A deployment to Lask was nothing like a stint in the war zone. In Poland, there were no such requirements. Battle rattle was unheard of, and the risk of a mortar or rocket dropping out of the sky was practically nonexistent.

THE pilot throttled back, giving Welles a chance to be heard. With Stanislaw's help, the tall American continued to explain airfield procedures. He was emphasizing the importance of safety when the loadmaster's actions caught his eye.

The load was looking aft, standing on the ramp's edge. The broad tail section of the plane obscured the skyline, so he bent at the waist for a better view. In an instant, he crossed his arms at the wrists, signaling a stop to ground operations.

To the southeast, something streaked across the sky, bright flashes of sunlight reflecting from its surface. The object began to descend, falling at a tremendous rate of speed. Seeing the puzzled expression on Welles' face, the airman dropped to one knee and pointed to the horizon.

* * * *

LIKE ITS NAMESAKE, ICARUS HAD SHED ITS WINGS. Alarms were going off all over Eastern Europe. Early warning systems from Kaliningrad to Minsk announced the presence of ICARUS as it traveled across the sky. These were silenced as the threat moved west, and ground personnel had little time to respond before the unwanted visitor disappeared from their screens.

There was no contrail; that would have required exhaust. During ascent, the missile cruised under tremendous thrust, but now that the last of the fuel was gone, the blue and gold skies above were unscarred by the vehicle's passage. The rocket had failed to achieve orbit, and began its ballistic arc back to Earth.

At this stage of flight, ICARUS had become nothing more than a projectile. It passed over Russia, soaring far to the north of Kiev before entering Belarusian airspace. Here the inert fuselage began a sharp descent. Gravity had taken over, and combined with the vehicle's terminal velocity, the second and third stages were falling toward the Polish heartland.

White House Situation Room

"WE'RE IN LUCK," ADMIRAL DAVIES ANNOUNCED. "NORAD's projecting an impact point here—" he clicked the mouse, enlarging the display, "—roughly one hundred kilometers southeast of Warsaw. Combined aerial telemetry confirms. Looks like some farmland, out in the sticks."

Willis Avery narrowed his eyes, scrutinizing the map. "ETA?"

"Under three minutes," Davies answered.

"What about real-time orbital views?"

The naval officer shook his head. "Nothing available at the moment."

"Population density?"

"I do have a template for that."

Davies tapped at the keyboard, selecting a dropdown from the menu. In seconds, a grid overlaid the satellite view, digital icons forming a pattern of shapes clumped near inhabited areas.

"Those squares depict the estimated populace per thousand," the admiral explained. He used the mouse once more, choosing a region in the center of the screen. A red square appeared. "This is ground zero."

Avery eyed the monitor. "Eric, can you get in touch with the allied commander in Europe? We need to jump on this."

Admiral Davies turned away from the screen to face the national security advisor. "NATO or SACEUR?"

"You can inform the Secretary General, but call Sid Ecklund first—I want a full court press from an American officer. Have him get a damage assessment and then report back to us."

Richard Aultman smiled. "Playing an angle?"

Avery gave a slight shrug. Political motivations aside, he still had legitimate concerns about casualties.

"If this happened on U.S. soil, our allies would offer *their* assistance. Lending a hand is what makes us the good guys. I'll contact Dobrogost personally; let him know the president will be in touch."

East Central Poland

ICARUS BEGAN TUMBLING. THE SPENT FUSELAGE was traveling at a fraction of its initial velocity; drag increased as it encountered thicker air, and the missile's speed slowed. It burst through a thin layer of clouds, hurtling forward at nearly sixteen hundred kilometers per hour. The terrain in its path was a carpet of pastures, potato fields, and the occasional marsh.

Landfall came at the edge of a narrow heath. Eighteen tons of steel thundered against the earth, ripping a hundred meter gash in the soil. There was no fire, and no detonation; just the instantaneous dissolution of the rocket's metallic shell.

Pieces of the shattered hulk tore through the air in a lethal wave, concentrated in a narrow cone but expanding after impact. What was left of the upper stages fragmented, with chunks of the airframe's ribs and superstructure cartwheeling over the open plain.

THE steppes were draped in the colors of fall, and vast acres of woodland were still green. Train tracks bordered the meadow, winding between forests on either side. Earlier that morning, construction crews had begun laying a spur near the tree line. This double-ended artery was intended as a storage point for the state-owned railroad. An exuberant group of vocational students from Czersk had gathered to help, and it was just another class assignment—until the pastureland exploded.

* * * *

THE HEAVIEST DEBRIS SKIPPED ACROSS THE landscape like stones on a pond. A two ton instrument package remained intact, bouncing ahead of the other wreckage, and the dummy warhead in the nose cone followed closely behind.

Inertia propelled the remnants toward the workers' camp. There was no time to react. Shards of steel and copper slammed into the group, severing limbs and snuffing out lives before a single head could turn. Smaller pieces of the rocket came to rest along the spur, while the larger chunks were catapulted far beyond the track, landing on the banks of a tributary feeding the Vistula.

The admiral's hopes had been premature. Eleven students from the technical school—teenaged boys and girls—were killed instantly, along with seven railway workers. A total of nine others were seriously injured. In a tragic twist, the workday was almost over. Had ICARUS fallen an hour later, the construction zone would have been deserted.

* * * *

"WE HAVE IMPACT."

The Situation Room fell silent. Admiral Davies studied feeds from several sources. "SBIRS GEO-6 is registering an abrupt deceleration; we have a KH-11 over Sweden that concurs." These satellites used infrared and optical imaging to scope out areas of interest.

On the display, a new image appeared. A small yellow rectangle now bracketed a point close to the projected crash site, and the square red icon winked out. The admiral used the mouse, and a few keystrokes later, a dialog box popped up on the screen.

"FELIX was off by only two kilometers—not bad for a three thousand mile journey." The comment sounded tactless, and Davies instantly regretted it.

Richard Aultman stepped toward the monitor. He was focused on the symbol that rested near the impact point.

"What can you tell us about the target area?"

Davies consulted the display. "It's a region called the Mazovian province—an agricultural center. There's a small village nearby, about five kilometers distant."

Avery frowned. "Does that village have a name?"

"Yes, sir, it does." Davies toggled to a map view of the area. Additional details were now available. "A quaint little township not far from the Vistula.

"It's called Olm."

Chapter Seven * Smooth Stone

Southern Russia

THE DACHA WAS EXPANSIVE, PRACTICALLY an estate by Western standards; but in spite of its size, it offered little in the way of comfort. The barn-like structure was cold and drafty, and parts of it were in disrepair. It had been recalled to service just weeks before, and for nearly two years the lodge sat empty and forgotten.

Nestled in a grove of maple and oak, the chalet could pass for a frontier hideaway, but crossing its threshold, the interior suggested a more utilitarian purpose. The inner rooms had the look and feel of a barracks, harsh and austere. Stacks of bunks filled a squad bay in the east wing, next to an adjoining dining hall. Shower facilities were outside, and a small armory—empty of weapons—was tucked in between.

Originally purposed as a training camp, this site had been chosen for its remoteness. The retreat had few modern amenities. An electrician had shored up the wiring—it was a temporary fix—and a natural spring provided running water. Industrial-grade appliances could be found in the kitchen, but these were older models, fashioned nearly two decades earlier in some nameless state factory. That they were still functional was something of a miracle, although at times, even the Russian Federation could produce a reliable product—so long as it wasn't *too* complicated.

* * * *

THE OLD MAN ROSE EARLY. HE HAD THE APPEARance of a commoner—his features were unremarkable—with a dappled, neatly-trimmed beard. Long-limbed, he carried himself well for someone of his years. He was lean but powerfully built, with a thick matte of gray hair and terse eyes that always matched the hue of his garb. He favored slate.

His morning ritual was the first order of business, and that meant tea and breakfast. A search of the cupboards revealed plenty of food—packaged goods, mostly—from a German supplier to the west. None of it was appealing, so he moved to the icebox. This was well-stocked, with eggs, cheese, and even some milk. There was also black bread—a Russian staple—and a sausage roll the length of his forearm.

He seasoned the eggs with dill, and carved the bread and cheese into open faced sandwiches. Thick slices of cooked sausage were layered on top. He sipped the first cup of *chai* and took his meal in silence, then poured a refill and pushed himself away from the table.

The kitchen's back door held a thick window, and the first traces of dawn spilled through the trees. In the stillness of the morning, he considered his reasons for traveling to Bryansk. As much as anything else, Karpenko's promise had brought him here. The general had offered him one last assignment, and pledged a very generous fee in return. The old man could retire in style—and not on a paltry state pension—to live out the rest of his days in comfort.

But first, he had to prove himself.

There was movement outside as the day shift came on duty. A Land Rover eased onto the access road, slowing to a stop near the tree line. The vehicle's lights dimmed and the passenger door opened. He recognized a member of the security team— the swarthy guard's first name was Anton, but he couldn't recall anything more.

The detail was charged with safeguarding the property. A four man contingent, they checked in at the beginning of each rotation. Anton would expect that now, and the dacha's new occupant decided to accommodate the sentinels and get on with his day. He stepped out the back door, drawing in his breath as the frigid air pricked his skin. Anton saw him emerge and was the first to speak.

"Another day has dawned, *tavarisch*." A thin covering of snow crunched underfoot. The first rays of sunlight would remove that.

"Indeed," the old man grunted. He could see the caution Anton exercised in the presence of his host.

"And you slept well, Ilya Nikolayevich?"

More small talk. Ilya hated it, but these low-level *apparatchiks* needed something to begin a conversation. He sighed and accepted the idle chatter.

"Ah, *sleep*," he observed. " *'those little slices of death . . . '* Do you know who said that, comrade?"

Anton's brow furrowed. "Dostoyevsky?"

Ilya shook his head. "Edgar Allan Poe."

The watchman wore a perplexed look. It was far too early for philosophy—or whatever it was the old man was attempting.

Ilya Nikolayevich Maersk didn't press the issue. It was time to get to work.

"A package should arrive in a few days. When it does, you are to bring it to me." He gave an icy stare. "See to it that it remains unopened."

Anton nodded. "I will instruct the others."

"Make sure that you do." The Russian turned and climbed the steps, tossing a warning over his shoulder. "Your very lives will depend on it."

Anton didn't argue. It was best to pay heed to Ilya's words.

REMORA was not a man to be trifled with.

Marine Corps Birthday Ball,
Westin Hotel, Washington, D.C.

"CHICKEN OR BEEF?" MICHAEL ASKED.

Master Gunnery Sergeant Daniel Gavin Neill, retired, gave the menu a cursory glance.

"Definitely the prime rib." He leaned to his right, where his nephew was seated. "They served chicken last year; a little bland. Don't you remember?"

"You're thinking of two years ago." The captain surveyed their surroundings. The ballroom was filling up fast. "I was deployed during last year's shindig."

"That's right," Daniel reflected. "With the Thirty-Second."

Blues were encouraged for the evening's festivities. Both men wore their mess dress, complete with scarlet cummerbunds. The elder Neill sported a black bowtie, while Michael's uniform was slightly different, enclosed at the top by an embroidered collar.

More service members began filtering in—Marines and their guests, for the most part—along with a smaller group of sailors. Representatives from the Army and the Air Force were also in attendance, but these were few and far between. This night truly belonged to the Corps.

A week had passed since the election—and the tragedy in Poland. Charles Cassidy proved the pundits right; he was swept into office by a wide margin, maintaining a double-digit lead over the vice-president. His victory wasn't *quite* the landslide that had been predicted, but it did offer the legitimacy to call for wholesale change.

After the polls closed, the VP offered his congratulations and conceded the choice of the people. The new president-elect accepted his well wishes with a humble spirit, and used the opportunity to extend an olive branch to the opposition. Media outlets were in full swing, offering coverage of the one-sided political drama—while also keeping a weather eye on the unfolding events in Central Europe.

A young sergeant and his date took their seats across the table. Daniel growled a friendly greeting, with Michael giving a cordial nod and a smile. He continued his inspection of the hall, while at the same time pulling out the chair on his right, laying a printed program on the cushioned seat.

The captain's actions didn't go unnoticed by the master gunny. "Saving a spot for someone?"

"Staff Sergeant Arrens might appreciate the courtesy." He made every effort to sound non-chalant while avoiding his uncle's stare.

"So you're holding a seat at the table for *one*," Daniel observed. "What if she's not alone?"

The younger Neill was caught off guard. "That thought hadn't crossed my mind."

Daniel fished out his cell, checking the time. "Relax, poster boy. This *soiree* doesn't kick off for another twenty minutes. She'll be here."

"Yeah, but she's usually early." Michael's troubled expression gave way to a smile. "I thought you got a *new* phone."

The senior NCO looked offended. "I did," he carped.

"Let me see that." The captain took the cell and turned it over in his hands. He stopped long enough to examine one end, giving the device an extra measure of scrutiny. "Where's the string?"

"What string?"

"You know—the one that connects to the other can."

"Very funny, Captain. I'll have you know it came free with my contract. It gets the job done. You can call me, I can call you." He gave a sardonic grin and retrieved the phone. "I didn't know they taught humor at the Academy. Maybe you could do a little stand-up after the cake-cutting."

Michael waved him off with a laugh. "I think I'll pass. If you want humor, you'll just have to watch me dance."

Daniel relaxed, settling into his chair. It was good to see his nephew break a smile. The sound of conversation filled the hall, and the gunny's eyes were drawn to the entrance.

"Wow—is that her?"

Michael looked toward the back of the room. "That would be her," he breathed slowly.

Staff Sergeant Christina Arrens stepped across the threshold, accepting a bulletin as she entered. She was turned out in her evening dress bravo uniform, with a long sleeved jacket and a cummerbund of her own. This version of formalwear included a short skirt that stopped at the knee—and was much less matronly than the dress alphas, which featured a floor-length garment. She greeted the usher with a smile—he was a lance corporal with a nervous cast—and then turned instinctively to face the Neill men. Her grin widened, and she offered the two a friendly wave.

Michael got up from his seat—a little too quickly to project a casual air. He returned her gesture and then pointed to the empty place at his side.

"What was that all about?" Daniel grinned.

"What was what all about?" The captain took his seat. From across the room, Christina began moving in their direction, stopping at a few tables along the way. Both men followed her progress.

"Looks like she's alone."

"That's what it looks like," Michael answered. He sounded relieved.

"If I were twenty years younger . . ." Daniel's voice trailed off. "You want my advice, Mike?"

"Not especially." He'd heard this speech before. "You know the rules, Master Guns."

"I also know what they *say* about the rules," Daniel entreated.

MICHAEL didn't get the chance to respond. Christina's arrival silenced the conversation and brought the men to their feet.

"*Bon jour, mademoiselle.*" Daniel's eyes sparkled in greeting, and he extended a hand.

She beamed in response. "*Ravie de te voir.*" *Good to see*

you. Christina's French was excellent. "Sorry I'm late; new rank, new uniform." There was no need to apologize. Her delayed arrival was worth the wait, and neither Marine had ever seen her more lovely.

She smoothed the front of the skirt, her white ceremonial gloves vivid against the dark fabric. "And put that away." She brushed aside Daniel's hand, drawing closer and surprising the senior NCO with a hug. Her smile never faded.

Thoroughly pleased with the attention, the elder Neill gave his nephew a wink. "Bet you never got one of those, Mike."

The young woman turned to the captain. In a more chivalrous age, she might have curtsied. Her stance conveyed a friendly but demure openness. Dark eyes locked with his, and by raising a single brow, her countenance changed to something more artful.

"We wouldn't want to get the captain into trouble now, would we, Master Guns?" Christina said playfully.

And besides—the night's still young, she couldn't add.

THE ball was replete with pageantry. Following the social hour, Master Gunnery Sergeant Ethridge took charge, serving in the role of adjutant. It was his job to moderate the ceremonial aspects of the event. The senior NCO took his post near the entrance as the drum and bugle corps sounded Officer's Call.

Servers lit candles in the center of each table. The lights dimmed. Guests found their seats, and several junior Marines appeared with roped stanchions to mark the processional aisle. With the floor now cleared, Etheridge directed the musicians to continue with Adjutant's Call. The color and honor guards stepped off with precision, advancing toward the front of the room as the orchestral group played *Semper Fidelis*.

"SO who's the guest speaker?" Daniel whispered. By now, everyone in the venue stood tall.

"You'll see." Michael recalled the program, and the elegant

calligraphy spelling out the dignitary's name.

"I smell a conspiracy," Daniel grunted.

"*Hush*," Christina urged.

The master gunny needn't have asked. Just as the music ended, the official party entered the hall, led by Colonel Terryton, General Cole, and another familiar face. Daniel took a moment to recognize the man in the crumpled suit, but Michael would have known the national security advisor anywhere.

"Willis Avery," Daniel breathed. Having a table in the rear of the hall had its advantages. The retired Marine was free to comment without being heard. "Impressive."

Arriving at the front of the room, the officers and the president's advisor faced about to receive honors. A chill ran up Michael's spine as the orchestra launched into the *Stars and Stripes Forever*. From the rear, Etheridge bellowed the traditional *"Long live the United States, and success to the Marines."*

DINNER came next, and what followed afterwards was a flurry of pomp and circumstance. There was fanfare and reverence as the colors were carried to the dais. Assembled guests stood straighter, and hand salutes were rendered by those under cover. Pride surged as the musicians played *The Marines' Hymn*—another indispensable element of the Corps' history.

No birthday celebration was complete without dessert. A large sheet cake—trimmed in shades of scarlet and gold—was wheeled in by a four man escort, and positioned beside the official party. After a few more procedural details, Willis Avery was invited to stand front and center.

His speech was short. He paid tribute to the Corps' long and illustrious history, gaining points for his brevity. His listeners were relieved; the ceremonial trappings were nearly at an end, and only one thing remained.

A sergeant in blues marched smartly to the dais and produced a sword. This was presented to General Cole, who deferred to the national security advisor, giving him the honor of cutting the cake. After Avery finished, a piece was given to the oldest and youngest Marines present.

The colonel directed everyone to take their seats. The captain settled into his chair, and the other guests did the same. It was time for the Commandant to mark the end of the ceremonies, and as the general moved to the podium, Michael leaned to his right. He was rewarded with the captivating scent of Christina's perfume.

Fortune favors the bold, he decided. There was probably a Scripture verse to match that sentiment, but at the moment he couldn't place it.

"Would you be offended if I paid you a compliment?"

Christina blinked. "I'd be offended if you didn't."

"You look absolutely and positively stunning this evening," Neill whispered.

Two adverbs in one sentence. Christina's heart skipped a beat, and with the lights turned down, she was thankful that no one could see her blush.

"Thank you—Michael." Her voice was low. She cupped a hand to her lips and turned in his direction. "And I don't believe I've ever seen a more handsome officer."

The two were shoulder to shoulder. Michael felt the breath of her voice in his ear—she made sure of that—and each could sense the warmth of the other. He could have stayed there longer, but Christina slowly pulled back, and both of them pretended to listen as the Commandant concluded his remarks.

* * * *

"You want a beer, Mike?" Daniel got up— haltingly at first, maneuvering his prosthetic leg beneath him. His tone became less brusque. "And what will you have, Staff Sergeant? It's on me."

Christina brightened. "A glass of Cabernet, please."

"I've got this, Guns." Michael stood and straightened his jacket. "Your money's no good here."

Stringed instruments began to play. Neill crossed the hall— angling around couples on their way to the dance floor—before reaching the bar. Near the front of the room, the official party had left their seats and waded into the crowd, a cluster of attendees parting before them. Willis Avery was busy pressing the flesh, but seeing Neill, he started moving in his direction.

"Go easy on that stuff, Captain." The voice from behind was unexpected. Neill turned and braced slightly, but Colonel Terryton raised a hand.

"At ease." Less formally attired, Willis Avery stood at the senior officer's side, wearing a wide grin; in fact, both men were smiling. "You'll need to keep your wits about you."

"Always, sir."

"Good to see you again, Neill." Avery extended a hand. "Can you spare a minute?"

"For you, sir—I can spare *two*," Michael answered. "I heard a rumor you might show up. Glad you could make it."

"I managed to finagle an invite. You leathernecks throw a fine party." Avery craned his neck, inspecting Neill's table, and Staff Sergeant Arrens in particular. "This won't take too long—there's a small conference room down the hall. I'll have you back in no time."

* * * *

"Uh-oh." Daniel eyed the convergence. "Now what's that all about?"

Christina's chin came up. "Looks like some very important people have ambushed our captain," she sighed. Her face sported an exaggerated pout. "I guess that drink will have to wait."

From across the room, Neill met their gaze and offered a shrug. The two watched as the small group moved toward the exit.

"His loss," Daniel grinned.

The orchestra struck up a waltz, thinning the couples who had taken to the floor. The elder Neill stood and reached out a hand.

"Miss Arrens—would you care to dance?"

The terse Marine sounded very polite. Laying her fingertips in his palm, Christina gave Daniel a winsome smile.

"I would be honored."

AVERY guided the Marines through the door. On the other side, a man in a dark suit became alert, giving way to the national security advisor. An agent, Neill surmised. One more waited down the hall. As they approached, the captain recognized someone else.

"Mr. Aultman."

"Captain Neill," Avery's assistant reciprocated in kind. "Shall we?"

Richard Aultman directed the three principals into an anteroom. He closed the door behind them, leaving the protective detail outside.

"WE'LL keep this somewhat informal, gentlemen," Avery began. "Specifics will follow sometime next week." He gestured to the chairs ringing the conference table. "But I'm forgetting my manners. Is anybody thirsty?"

Another grin from Terryton. "This is the birthday ball, Willis. Every Marine's thirsty on this occasion."

"Quite right," Avery chuckled. A micro-fridge took up space in the corner. "What'll you have?"

Aultman grabbed a couple of dark ales, handing one off to his boss. The colonel asked for a light beer. Richard began twisting lids, while Avery regarded Neill with a smile.

"The hard stuff's next door, Captain. But I don't imagine you're interested in that."

"Ginger ale's fine."

Avery passed a bottle across the table as everyone sat down. "We've just been handed an unexpected opportunity. Tragedy's like that sometimes." He stretched out in his chair. "A door just opened—and we're going to step through it."

Terryton sipped from his beer. "Poland would be my guess."

Avery dipped his head. "In terms of recent events, eighteen of their citizens died when that Iranian missile struck the country's interior." He winced. "We've sent teams to assist the Poles—hazmat crews and the like. It wasn't pretty."

"How's that shaped our foreign policy?"

"It's reversed the course of some options," Avery began. "One in particular."

"THAAD?" Terryton asked.

"Bingo," Avery replied. "We offered it to the Poles a while back; they turned it down."

"And of course the Russians had nothing to do with that." The colonel's tone was clearly sarcastic.

Avery countered with a grin. "Dropped because of funding; at least that's what the administration claims."

"More likely political pressure from Moscow," Neill tossed in. He'd heard all the chatter. "Murovanka threatened an arms race. Dobrogost got nervous and backed out."

The man in the creased suit continued to smile. "You don't mince words, do you, Captain?"

"We don't pay him to sugar-coat things, Willis." Colonel Terryton looked pleased.

Avery couldn't disagree. "THAAD is a practical alternative to the old Strategic Defense Initiative—Star Wars. A land-based missile shield—using off-the-shelf technology. David meets Goliath. To be fair, the press releases issued by the White House might have *some* merit."

"In what respects?"

"The Kremlin's still not happy—even after we scaled back. Plan B was to rely on our Aegis-based systems at sea. Now the Russians want assurances. And our friends in the House and Senate could have gotten it right, too."

The national security advisor startled his audience. It wasn't often he played devil's advocate for Congress *and* the Kremlin.

"That might explain the intel we got from the British Defence Ministry," Michael said.

"Oh?" Avery raised an eyebrow. "How's that?"

"The Russian Navy's ramped up operations. Some of their ground forces, too." The captain nodded slowly. Things were starting to make sense. "I'll bet they caught wind of your efforts in Poland."

"Can't argue with that." Avery pressed on. "But Tehran's wayward missile has changed everything. If you'll forgive my timing, I'd like to read both of you in."

* * * *

DANIEL WAS QUITE PROUD OF HIMSELF. TWO slow dances had come and gone—and he hadn't stepped on Christina's toes once.

"I think you had Mike worried." He held her gently as they moved.

She pulled back, tilting her head. "What about?"

He dodged a little. "You. Here—all alone."

Christina smiled. The expression was disarming.

"But I'm not alone," she countered. "I'm with my friends."

Daniel followed with something more direct. "And how many invites did you get for this clambake?"

She paused before answering. "Three."

"And you turned them all down?"

A soft laugh. She squeezed his arm. "I wasn't willing to settle."

"Good answer." The orchestra continued to play. "You wouldn't be sending some kind of message, would you?"

"I'm not sure what you mean."

Tactically evasive. This one was sly. Daniel could appreciate that.

"Mike probably wouldn't want me to say this—"

"Then don't." Christina's eyes flashed. She laid an index finger across his lips. "*Please*, Guns."

Her look became imploring. Daniel couldn't resist. Christina rested her head on his shoulder, and not another word was spoken.

A petty officer third class appeared, interrupting the moment.

"Mind if I cut in?"

The master gunny glared, feeling very paternal.

"Take a hike, junior."

* * * *

"SO THAAD'S BACK ON THE TABLE?" TERRYTON INquired.

Avery went on with his talking points. "I'm envisioning an even broader network, providing security to nations bordering Russia. Karl Dobrogost agrees."

"What's the big picture?" Neill asked.

"The system will use a blend of Polish and American technology," Avery went on. "We'll provide most of the hardware—SM3 missiles—fine-tuned by U.S. technicians and contractors."

Michael was impressed. "On their soil?"

"We've gotten a little more ambitious than that, Captain," Avery said wryly. "THAAD doesn't have the necessary range. We're working to extend its capabilities, but to make the shield truly effective, we need the cooperation of other European nations. Radar installations, listening posts—additional weapons batteries, if we can arrange it."

"Then you can expect the Russians to counter," Neill advised. "Probably someplace like Kaliningrad—using their Triumf air defense system. Murovanka's allocated billions as a hedge against our missiles; that goes back several years. You can bet he and Leonid Karpenko will make the most of this opportunity—they'll probably throw in some kind of exercise, give Dobrogost something to think about."

"Recommendation?"

The captain had an answer ready. "We roll out an exercise of our own. NATO has contingencies for this, don't they?"

"RESILIENT EAGLE," Avery replied. "Elements from various partners could be fielded with just a few days' notice. Mechanized infantry; NBC battalions, aircraft, some surface ships. We could build on that, beef up the troop levels if the need arises."

"Location?" Neill asked.

"Central Europe," Avery said. He considered something else. "And it might be a good test of NATO's Response Force. Of course, I'd have to coordinate with SECDEF."

"That would signal our resolve," Michael agreed, and then dangled a suspicion. "I hear the State Department's enlisted Ukraine's help."

It was Avery's turn to be surprised. "I take it you've spoken to General Ulyanov?"

"It might have come up," Neill hedged.

"Operational designation?" This question came from the colonel.

"The expanded program has been hastily resurrected. We've dubbed it SHORT SPEAR, a concession to THAAD's limited capabilities."

"You should have a little more faith, sir," Michael chuckled.

"In what way?"

The captain downed a little of his ginger ale. "Earlier you mentioned an Old Testament match-up. David brought down a giant in the book of 1st Samuel." A mischievous light danced in his eyes. "Do you remember what he used as a weapon?"

"My grand-pappy was a preacher, Captain," Avery sighed. "He'll roll over in his grave if I get this wrong—it was a sling."

"That was just the delivery system. The weapon itself—"

"—was a smooth stone." Avery recalled the reference with a smile. "David chose five, but only needed one." He turned to Aultman. "Make a note; SHORT SPEAR is getting a new handle."

"Got it." Richard grinned. "Probably best if we defer to the Marines on this."

Avery moved on. "You grew up in that neighborhood, Neill. What can you tell me about Poland?"

Michael deliberated before picking a starting point. "As a

nation, the country straddles East and West. That's put them in the crosshairs more than once. They were wiped off the map in the eighteenth century. Since then, they've been savaged by the Nazis and subjugated by communists." A smile appeared. "But like any anvil, they've proven their mettle."

"Providence?" Avery asked.

"No doubt."

"And what about the present day?"

"Booming market economy; good record of human rights," Neill said. "The Poles have a democratic government, and they're a new member of NATO—relatively speaking."

"With your background, I'm guessing you have some other insight." Avery had come to expect that.

Michael was thoughtful. "There's a facet of their culture that's often missed. That would be the spiritual element. Poland's a land of castles, cathedrals and churches—you can see it in their history. Faith's a very big part of everyday life."

Avery absorbed Neill's words. There was a pause, and then he leaned forward.

"And how's your Polish, Captain?"

The Marine blinked. "I don't mean to disappoint, sir, but—"

"You haven't let me down yet, son. Do you have a grasp of the language or not?"

Neill was hesitant. "I understand more than I speak. I'm not even conversational."

"We'll change that." Avery was undisturbed. "I need someone to help me twist a few arms. Somebody I can trust."

"A liaison?" Terryton piped up.

"We're on something of a tight schedule. Dobrogost's the key. He's championed the missile shield from the beginning—but he runs hot and cold."

"—and bends like a reed in the wind," Aultman interjected.

Avery shrugged. "That's just politics. He's thoroughly on board now."

"What's next on the calendar?" Michael asked.

"The Poles want an American delegation on their soil by

mid-December. Warsaw, specifically. Dobrogost has invited deputies from Central and Eastern Europe to hash things out. Between our respective countries—and NATO—we're hoping for a signed agreement by Christmas."

"Doesn't the diplomatic corps have their own interpreters?"

"Plenty." Avery took a long draw from his bottle. "We've already lined up a few. Neill will provide background; gauge the mood, if you will. Advise our side. He has a track record I've come to admire."

"With all due respect, Mr. Avery, you're asking me to re-assign key personnel at a critical juncture." Neill could see his boss bristle. "If you're expecting fluency—"

"The man already speaks Russian, Ukrainian and English. How hard can it be?"

"Your schedule doesn't leave much time," the colonel observed tersely.

"I won't deny that," Avery agreed. "But I need Neill spun up. Four weeks at the Defense Language Institute should do it."

"Monterey?"

Avery shook his head. "We'd lose time sending you out west. DLI has a campus at Arlington Hall. We've arranged for five days of one-on-one instruction; after that, you'll join a class already in progress."

"Sounds challenging," Neill said. He was warming to the idea.

"It's just down the street from Henderson Hall, Captain. You can visit your office every few days—" the national security advisor grinned, "—provided your homework's done."

* * * *

AVERY KEPT HIS WORD. MINUTES LATER, THE Marines rejoined the ball, while Aultman and his boss exited through the building's garage.

Neill returned just as the orchestra finished. A faster beat filled the air—a DJ had taken charge—and younger couples took to the floor. Christina found Michael soon enough. She hooked her arm in his and pulled him toward the center of the room.

"Dance with me, Captain."

Michael protested at first, but Christina would have none of it. She led him into the crowd, with Daniel watching as his nephew tried to keep up.

That girl's a spitfire, he grinned. *God help you, Michael Neill.*

* * * *

"THAT WENT WELL," AULTMAN REMARKED. HE gave Avery a look as the limo advanced west on M Street. "Although I think you left something out."

"It's a ball, Richard." The national security advisor loosened his tie. "Not the appropriate time."

Aultman silently conceded the point. The car turned left onto Fifteenth for the trip back to the White House.

"But you are going to tell him—the man deserves to know."

"The possibility exists that he already does," Avery replied evenly.

Richard shook his head. "His father wanted to protect him. Besides—"

"—Neill was too young," Avery finished. Aultman was right. "He couldn't fully appreciate the circumstances—not at that age." Something else occurred to him. "Might even be best to get SECDEF involved; he has all the operational details."

Aultman weighed that thought. "Do you think the Secretary feels responsible?"

"Allan was just the case officer," Avery answered after a moment. "If you want to assign blame, maybe you should start with the president himself."

* * * *

"NOW THAT'S ODD."

Lieutenant Reston looked up. "How do you mean, sir?"

Deep in the heart of Cheyenne Mountain, Major Montez was doing some homework of his own. A ream of paperwork had been generated to document ICARUS' flight, and it was his job to mine the data for relevance.

Montez began flipping pages. "Just reviewing the Iranian's trajectory." A frown darkened his face. "This must be wrong."

The lieutenant grimaced. Hard copies were *so* last generation.

"Second opinion?"

The major nodded. "Pull up WIREFRAME."

Reston turned to his computer. "Last four?"

"Seven-seven-six-three."

He plowed through the database and found the incident code. "You want the animation, too?"

Montez grunted. It sounded like a yes.

The junior officer was already on it. "Might take a minute. Lots of compressed information."

Another grunt. The major looked at the clock. There were still six hours left on this shift.

Montez waited for the software while poring over the documents. Portions of the datum raised a flag; the major's eye was drawn to the report's technical appendices. These required a different level of interpretation, and while Montez knew his stuff, something puzzled him about the final leg of the missile's flight.

A flat depiction of the path didn't offer much. This was illustrated in a short series of diagrams and charts. One unimaginative table simply traced the launch to the point of impact. More elaborate details were available in a three-dimensional view—and that's where WIREFRAME offered a unique perspective.

"She's up, sir. What are we looking for?"

The major wheeled over in his chair. "Terminal inclination. Angle of attack—from apogee to the crash site."

Reston went to work. After a few keystrokes, the application rendered the trajectory in a simple, fast display mode. This enabled the user to navigate the battle space without waiting for the software to constantly refresh. The bells and whistles would come later.

Using a mouse, the lieutenant clicked on the rocket's track—a digital arc on the darkened monitor. Reston isolated the highest point of flight and then clicked on the vehicle's terminus. He thumbed a track ball at his fingertips, allowing the officers to see the selection from any angle.

"Simple overview?"

"Put some meat on the bone," Montez directed.

Reston tapped away. "Automating layers. Full channel view—here we go."

WIREFRAME began communicating with FELIX. Combining telemetry from a host of sources—including Google maps—the program began assimilating and interpreting data, translating features like buildings, forests, and bodies of water into an easily viewed format—complete with 3-D modeling.

The lieutenant was ready to launch the animation. "Low resolution, Major?"

Montez eyed the default setting. "Double the frame count. We'll need smooth transitions."

Reston changed the digits and tabbed a radio button. The results were quite impressive. The screen resolved, and once more, ICARUS arced toward Earth—a digital representation this time. Montez followed its progress by cross-referencing the print-outs with the screen's timeline.

Seconds passed. "Slow it down—same frame rate, but half the speed." The major leaned in. "Right—*there*. Did you see it?"

The lieutenant's eyes widened. "That's a marked deviation." He checked the software, selecting a drop-down menu. "At twenty-one thousand feet. Nine-tenths of a degree—maybe less."

"Enough to constitute a statistical anomaly—and change the glide path," Montez agreed. "So the figures were right."

Reston ran it again. And then a third time. "What could have caused it?"

The senior officer leaned back in his seat, drawing a hand

across his chin. "Weather, maybe? An inversion layer?"

"Kind of a stretch, sir."

"And how would *you* explain it, Lieutenant?"

He was on the spot. "Maybe one of the verniers kicked in—air pressure forced some remaining fuel into the line."

"A thruster re-ignited—*after* the propellant was exhausted?" Montez smiled broadly, but Reston was focused on the monitor.

"As long as we're speculating—" he accessed the menu. "Let's remove the deviation—see what FORECASTER can tell us."

Reston scrubbed the variable while preserving the rest of the data. The extension now displayed a very different trajectory.

"Alter the view," the major suggested. "Does the impact point change?"

The lieutenant switched modes. He whistled softly as the software recalibrated the new end point.

"Five clicks due east. Smack dab in the middle of that village." Reston shook his head. "Could've been a whole lot worse." He pointed to the screen. "And look where the deviation occurred."

Montez' eyes narrowed. "Is that—*yeah*," he muttered. "The very boundary of Polish airspace."

"There's your answer," Reston blurted.

A double take. "Come again?"

"The deviation." The lieutenant was about to go out on a very big limb. He wasn't sure how the major would take it. Reston wasn't convinced himself, and he could already feel the hairs stand up on the back of his neck.

"It was an act of God."

Chapter Eight * Captains Three

Near Gora Kalwaria,
South of Warsaw

J EAN-PAUL TOUSSAINT WAS ECSTATIC. HE HAD the warm glow of a man in love. Given his audience, that was understandable, but the presence of his guest wasn't the only reason for his enthusiasm.

"This is a spectacular find, *ma bell juene femme*. We are on the cusp of history."

Viktoriya Gavrilenko stood at his side on the western bank of the River Vistula. Passing overhead, a Russian Mi8 helicopter moved into position. A cable hung beneath its long underbelly, and a metal hook dangled from the end. The aircraft was on loan from the military, a collaboration between Warsaw and Toussaint's research firm, the prestigious *Archaeologique François*.

The young journalist watched as the chopper slowed its pace. Descending sharply, it hovered above the eastern side of the river. A team of workmen busied themselves on a barge anchored in the shallows. As the aircraft approached, the group gathered in the midst of the platform, all eyes focused skyward.

"These items are priceless national treasures," Toussaint continued. He was in the habit of offering expressive gestures, and extended his arms, palms up, toward the river. The suave

Frenchman had the look of a symphony conductor, inviting applause. Viktoriya smiled behind her sunglasses. Recognizing his arrogance, she was certain that any homage he received would not be shared with anyone else.

She had to admit that he was refined and quite attractive. Since they met, she had employed her own allure to gain his attention, and the tactic had proven very effective.

"What have you recovered so far?"

"Alabaster ornaments; marble statues," Toussaint paused, mentally cataloguing the trove of riches. "Sculpted busts, jewelry, archways—most plundered from castles and palaces." His eyes widened. "And all are remarkably well-preserved."

The din from the chopper's massive blades made conversation difficult, and the gale produced by the rotors had reached them. Both were chilled by the gusting December air.

"Allow me, *mademoiselle*." Jean-Paul gestured toward a portable office squatting on the bank nearby. He offered her his arm. "Your boots are very fashionable, but not made for practicality, I'm afraid."

Viktoriya was getting the full tour. It had taken two weeks to gain an audience with Toussaint. After their initial meeting he had practically begged her to return, and the visit today was her second trip to the site.

"You certainly have passion for your work," she observed. The soil beneath her feet was soft and wet, and she gripped Toussaint's wrist for support.

He wore a rueful smile, and made no effort to mask his appreciation for her beauty. "I become intimately involved in *all* of my projects, *ma cherie*. I find success in my endeavors because they fascinate me."

Viktoriya lost count of the personal pronouns. The entrepreneur's characteristic charm was on full display.

Arrogance, indeed.

Toussaint's gaze lingered. She broke his concentration with a question, raising her voice to be heard.

"And what made you search here, *monsieur*?"

"Call me Jean-Paul, *s'il vous plaît?*" He appeared puzzled but pleased. "Your French is very good. But your accent—you are Russian, *oui?*"

"Oui—*Jean-Paul*." She smiled. In truth, she was Ukrainian by birth, and the State Security Directorate had persuaded her to adopt an alias. "You were saying?"

"We are in possession of several letters," the Frenchman answered. They made their way along the water's edge, steadily climbing the gravel embankment. The footing here was more stable, and on either side of the river, the landscape was marked by gentle hills. "Most were written by Swedish officers—after the Deluge. Their correspondence enabled us to locate these spoils." He turned as they reached the site's command post. Toussaint's men had secured the cable to a stone artifact, and the chopper slowly lifted it from the deck of the barge.

"I should add that this is not a new find. The Poles discovered several canal boats more than a hundred years ago."

"Why didn't they retrieve them?"

Jean-Paul shrugged. "The water levels were much higher then, and the technology did not exist to make recovery possible."

He reluctantly freed his hand and pulled open the trailer's door. "Come inside, Viktoriya. I have something you might like to see."

* * * *

ABOVE THE GORGE, TWO WORKERS CLEARED brush from a relay station. One of the men ambled closer to the ravine's edge, watching the chopper ferry its cargo. As the aircraft soared above, Xander Voskov cast a glance down the bank and then rejoined his comrade. The rest of his team was back in Warsaw, prepping for the night shift.

Yuri Tereshenko cursed under his breath and dropped an armload of brambles. Frowning, he shook his hand in pain.

"I told you to wear gloves, *tavarisch*," Voskov scolded.

"And you were right, boss." Tereshenko sucked blood

from his wound. "Where are they now?"

The Berkut captain made a pretense of gathering brush-wood. "They've gone inside."

Yuri shook his head and frowned. "We can't protect her if we can't see her." It was an axiom of their trade, and Voskov didn't need the reminder. Still, Ukraine's security services had been quite clear—be discreet, they directed.

"We have our orders." A scowl hung on Xander's face. "But *Monsieur* Toussaint doesn't believe in subtleties—he's fawning over her like a schoolboy."

"Does that surprise you?" Yuri smiled. His discomfort had lessened. "He is French, after all." Tereshenko decided to goad his friend a little, and asked, "Are you jealous?"

Pain flashed in Voskov's eyes. Tereshenko regretted the comment at once, and muttered a hasty apology. For his part, Xander simply ignored the remark and attacked the thicket with renewed vigor.

"She's just an assignment, Yuri," he grunted.

* * * *

THE PORTABLE'S INTERIOR WAS A HIVE OF AC-tivity. Workers pored over a chart in one corner. The men's heads came up as the door opened, giving Viktoriya a second look as she entered the confined space. Seeing Toussaint, they offered respectful nods before returning to the diagram on the table.

"Henri Minouche—my excavation chief." Jean-Paul re-moved his coat; Viktoriya did likewise, earning more apprecia-tive glances. "I fancy myself an archaeologist, but Henri is the true craftsman."

The team's senior member stepped forward and mumbled a greeting. He was dressed in layers of worn denim and flannel-wear, and despite the cold, his sleeves were rolled to the elbows. Viktoriya smiled and shook his hand.

Toussaint peered over the man's shoulder. "Hand me the let-ter, *monsieur*."

Minouche pulled open a drawer. He wordlessly retrieved a weathered parchment—protected in a Mylar sleeve—and presented it to Jean-Paul.

"One such memoir is particularly enlightening." Toussaint held the document gingerly for Viktoriya to inspect. A handwritten script flowed across the page. "This was couriered to Sweden three hundred and fifty years ago."

"The penmanship is beautiful," she remarked.

"Ah, *oui!* And valuable for other reasons, as well—I paid fifty thousand francs to possess it." That was meant to impress her. "It's an inventory, of such. An account of military campaigns—with a listing of stolen treasures."

Viktoriya casually produced a small notepad. "Who wrote it?"

Jean-Paul smiled. "Probably a junior officer. Or a scribe, perhaps. It was dictated by a man we know to be somewhat brutish, if you will—with a vicious tendency for swordplay." He gazed through a window. A bridge spanned the river upstream, and the countryside had the stark look of winter. "He drowned when his barge sank—just days after sending this letter home. Perhaps the wrath of Jehovah God Himself."

A chill ran up Viktoriya's spine. "What makes you say that?"

"This soldier was a plunderer," he explained. "Before his death he looted a church to the south—murdering the parish priest." Toussaint laid the parchment aside. "This final testament mentions what he calls 'the wealth of the sacristy'."

"The sacred vessels?"

"*Oui*—and I suspect something of more intrinsic value." He let that statement hang in the air for a moment, but then his exuberance overwhelmed him again. "As I said, we are on the brink of a fantastic find."

Viktoriya offered her most beguiling smile. "And what else can you tell me?"

In spite of her probing Jean-Paul was noncommittal. "We will make an announcement very soon, *ma cherie.*"

Her instincts told her to steer in a different direction. She studied the letter before them. While the longhand was exquisitely rendered, the signature itself was quite crude.

"And whose name appears at the bottom?"

"He was a Swedish officer," Jean-Paul announced. "A cavalryman. His name was Johannes Angstrom."

There were limits to what he was willing to reveal, she realized. The man was clearly stringing her along, but she didn't mind that. He had already given her a great deal, and in time, he would provide more. It might even prove to be an exclusive.

Henderson Hall,
Arlington, Virginia

Terryton's eyes drifted from the report on his desk. He looked up as a presence filled the doorway.

"You wanted to see me, sir?"

Neill wore his service alphas—the green and khaki business suit of the Corps. Even at five p.m. his uniform was crisp. The captain, on the other hand, appeared a bit frazzled.

Neill presented himself in true Marine fashion before the colonel directed him to a chair. "Two weeks in, two more to go," Terryton mused. "How are you holding up?"

"Ready for the swing shift, sir." Michael gave a tired grin. "I got your text—I take it you have something for me?"

The colonel stretched in his seat. He was comfortably dressed in PT gear, his day uniform hanging from the conference room door. "Tell me about classes first."

Neill drew in a breath and seemed to relax. "The one-on-one sessions were a big help—good prep for the first week. The basics are similar to what I grew up with; a little choppy in some respects, but much the same. Subject, verb, and object are pretty standard. And no definite articles—just like Russian."

"How's the curriculum structured?" Terryton's skills extended to German—fluency in more than one tongue was a job requirement for those in the International Operations and Intelligence Office.

"As you know, language is spoken, first and foremost. The

focus is on verbal skills," Neill replied. "It's a contextual approach, with hours of immersion thrown in. The class roster is made up of diplomats headed off to embassies and consulates; the instructors recognize that, and don't spend much time on the written word."

"What about your current skill sets—do those give you an edge?"

The junior officer nodded thoughtfully. "I find myself reverting to Ukrainian at times. There's some give and take—borrowed words and phrases. Also a surprising mix of German idioms."

Terryton wore an amused expression. "A little tougher than you thought, Captain?"

"It's not like I can just phone it in, sir." Neill's face matched that of his C.O. "The trick is distinguishing between regional variations."

"Dialects," the colonel grunted.

"Roger that," Michael agreed. "Fortunately, the class is small and geared toward Mazovian—that should make things easier when I get to Warsaw."

"And the grammar?"

"Never my best subject," Neill deflected. "But I'm catching on."

Terryton pressed a little. "So you'll be fluent, then?"

Neill laughed, and didn't hesitate in the slightest. "Not a chance."

"At least you're honest," the colonel chuckled. He opened a folder and produced a single sheet of paper, sliding it across the desk. It was time to shift the conversation. "I need your assessment on some raw data." A pause. "I should warn you—"

Neill scanned the first line, suppressing his shock. "When did this happen?"

"About six hours ago. The Russians tend to move slowly—but sometimes they can really ramp things up."

"Both houses, too." The captain continued to read, a look of exhaustion evident. "I never saw this coming—not this soon, anyway."

The colonel noted Neill's weariness. "Somewhat under-standable, Captain. You've been burning the candle at both ends. Full class schedule; and then you show up here—for hours on end—to analyze the intel dumps." He shook his head, and a measure of irritation crept into his voice. "My patience for this arrangement is wearing a little thin."

Michael inhaled deeply. "Two more weeks, sir. After that—"

"—after that you'll be in Poland, and things will only get worse." Terryton managed to temper his emotions, regretting the outburst. "I'm not upset with you, Neill. The national security advisor thinks you work for him. Given the chain of command, there's not much I can do about that." Both men could tell when fatigue was doing the talking.

Neill didn't press the point. "I wish I had the answer, sir."

Terryton considered that. Langley had tried filling in the gaps, and the shop had endured fourteen days of their analysis. The colonel wasn't impressed; CIA's interpretations seldom matched Neill's insight.

"Don't worry about it, Captain." Terryton's tone softened. "The first sergeant and I have been comparing notes. Between the two of us, I think we've come up with a workable solution.

"You'll just have to remember to behave yourself."

* * * *

SEVERAL OFFICES WERE ALREADY SHUTTERED. Michael fished for his keys, but then noticed that the shop was still open.

He stepped through the door and took in the view. Christmas lights decorated the workspace; a twinkling strand hung from Neill's desk, with more brightening Arrens' cubicle as well. Christina looked up from her desk and offered him a smile.

"The tree's a nice touch," Michael grinned back.

A spot next to the copier had been cleared, and a small Douglas fir, complete with ornaments, now stood in the space. The overheads were off, and the room had a festive, almost romantic, glow.

"Looks like we've even had a visit from the North Pole." He knelt and retrieved a wrapped gift tagged with his name.

"Don't shake that," Christina warned. "Santa knows when you've been naughty."

"I'm pretty sure I'm on his good list." Neill glanced at his desk. Two stacks of documents sat on top. "Did Kris Kringle leave those as well?"

"I've separated that stuff; raw data on the left, completed assessments on the right." In Neill's absence, Christina's role had become largely administrative—and unquestionably mundane. "We've missed you, Captain."

"I appreciate the sentiment." Neill handed over the memo Colonel Terryton had given him. "Have you seen this?"

Arrens read the page. Her frown was enough of an answer. The communique was time-stamped at 1600—four p.m., local time.

"They finally did it."

Michael nodded. "The Federal Assembly has issued a vote of no-confidence—Arkadi Murovanka has been removed from office."

"—and charged with abuse of power," Christina noted. Her frown deepened. "What about Karpenko? He and Murovanka are practically joined at the hip."

Neill appeared to shrug. "Oddly enough, he's not even mentioned."

The staff sergeant was incredulous. She looked up from the report, eyeing the officer evenly. It was obvious the man was tired. Christina wished there was something she could do to help. "Any word on Murovanka's replacement?"

"The situation's still fluid, but the colonel thinks they'll go with Rurik."

"Anatoly Rurik?"

A nod. "One and the same. Both chambers have vested him with full plentil—plenit—"

"Plenipotentiary powers?"

"That's it—thank you."

She smiled. "English really is your second language, isn't it?"

Michael ignored that, and Christina pressed on.

"So the Russians *pass* on the general—and choose Rurik. Makes sense—Karpenko's too toxic. He's been linked to the same criminal activities. Which begs the question; why didn't they give *him* the axe?" The wheels were turning now. "Are we sure the military's not behind this?"

Neill's brow furrowed. "I'm not following you."

She paced herself. "We know the hard-liners weren't happy with the president. So they make him take the fall." Christina turned to her computer. News alerts were popping up, with several sites reporting the story to varying degrees. She took a moment to check her sources as Michael looked over her shoulder. "But there's nothing online about the general being sacked. I find that a little suspicious. Who's to say the military—or one of their proxies—didn't put pressure on the Assembly?"

Neill was impressed. Arrens' theory had merit; he'd have to pass it along to Willis Avery. "You make a good point. Their legislature seldom agrees on anything—but what's the end game?" He wanted her to tease this out a bit.

"Control," she stated flatly. "Everybody's been calling for Murovanka's head on a pike, and this gives the international community what they want. With Karpenko still in the mix the *de facto* government retains power."

"So the general's calling the shots?"

Christina shrugged. "The CIA thinks we can work with Rurik. I'm not so sure. You've read his file. His background suggests he's just another communist." She turned away, facing the screen. "I suppose your journalist friend will be happy about this."

"Viktoriya?" Neill hadn't considered that. "I haven't heard from her in over a month." It had been five and a half weeks, but saying so wouldn't earn the captain any points. He thought it best to move on.

Michael sighed heavily. "Guess I'll just have to figure all this out while I'm in Poland." He studied the calendar pinned to the wall. "On top of that, Colonel Terryton wants fresh analysis while I'm there."

"Sounds like you'll be busy."

The shift was abrupt. There was silence. Christina lowered her eyes, a melancholy look on her face. The two Marines worked well together, and she relished these brain-storming sessions. But with Neill soon to be out of the country—

It was always something. The birthday ball was just one more example. She had hoped for a few quiet moments with the captain—just one slow dance—until Willis Avery showed up. Obstacles seemed to appear at the most inopportune times, and in the coming days Neill's tasking to Central Europe would separate them again.

Michael read her mood, and while tired, he wasn't beyond a little mischief.

"That reminds me. The colonel's had a few thoughts." He paused. "He wants to send another analyst along for the ride. Think you can initiate a second set of orders?"

"Sure," she managed. Her response was emotionless, and was followed by a frown. "Wait—what? Which analyst?"

"Arrens. Christina F., staff sergeant." Neill collapsed in his chair and stretched. "Should you write that down?"

Something like a gasp escaped her lips, and he found her surprised look enchanting.

"I'm going to Poland?"

"You are an oh-two-eleven —counterintelligence," Michael pointed out. He was referring to her MOS, or military occupa-tional specialty. "This should give you a better grasp of the region—and besides, I might need someone to help carry my luggage."

She crumpled the memo into a tight ball. Neill half expected that. Practically useless as a weapon, the wad of paper arced across the room with surprising velocity. He managed to catch it before she beaned him.

Military Stockade,
Chernihiv, Ukraine

HE FEIGNED SLEEP, BUT LIKE EVERY OTHER PRIS-
oner, Vadim Mayakovsky could hear the shouts. The guards
were at it again, berating a fresh batch of convicts on their
first day in the quadrangle. It was completely routine, and the
former military officer turned on his side and tried to ignore
the bedlam.

These were weekly occurrences. Invariably, it happened in
the early hours of the morning. The old bus would roll in, stopping at the receiving barracks with a new crop of detainees. The
jailers would then appear, truncheons in hand, while the canine
squad kept their animals at bay. The latest collection of misfits
would be blind-folded, increasing their disorientation; and once
inside, most would never leave the stockade again.

The custodians at this facility were hardly *corrections officers;* that would imply an attempt at rehabilitation—and far too
many inmates were lost causes. Life behind bars was enough of
a deterrent, and while civil rights for criminals was a popular
concept in the West, the former Soviet republics had a different philosophy. Incarceration was the main goal here, with strict
adherence to the rules placing a close second.

The guard dogs were the best means of enforcing that discipline. Caucasian Ovcharkas had a reputation for ferocity, with
a mouthful of teeth to match, and long, coarse hair that only
magnified their presence. The animals weighed twice as much
as a man. Standing on their hind legs, they were well over six
feet tall. The beasts were prehistoric to some—but that was exactly the point.

ALMOST two years had passed since Mayakovsky's ar-
rest. He had been convicted of a number of crimes, and each
carried a life sentence. Treason and reckless endangerment
were his most egregious sins. Enticed by a pledge of cash,
his collaboration with Leonid Karpenko had ended in Odessa,

and now—

"On your feet, comrade."

A boot crashed against the bunk, forcing him to abandon sleep. Mayakovsky struggled to become upright. Standard procedure was to toss each cell every half hour, beginning at sunrise, but it was far too early for that. Vadim was shocked by the watchman's appearance. He collected his wits, nursing a bitter resentment for this impertinent guard.

The major reeked of alcohol and cigarettes. The jailers traded on the black market, and even here nearly anything could be had for a price. They brought liquor several times a week, and the fee for Vadim's drink also included the time needed to sleep it off.

But not today.

Mayakovsky pulled himself to the edge of the bed and surveyed his unwelcome guest. He was a stranger. A single bulb illuminated the hall. Silhouetted against the light, Vadim could make out a tall, broad-shouldered figure, with a short beard framing his features. He was not a young man, and now stood immobile, gripping a night stick in both hands.

There was a surveillance camera above the intruder's head. It was the only piece of modern equipment in the cell. Oddly enough, the red glow of the activation light had dimmed, and in his stupor, Mayakovsky didn't find that relevant.

Abruptly, the guard stepped forward, extending his arm toward the major. The baton was shoved rudely into his gut, and Mayakovsky felt something sharp pierce his skin. He cried out in pain as he was forced back onto the bunk.

Vadim instinctively lifted his shirt. The wound was red, a pinprick of blood forming on the surface. He raised his arm to protect against another blow, but his attacker had withdrawn. When he looked up again, the cell door clanged shut, and the room was empty.

LATER that morning, Vadim developed a fever. By nightfall he suffered from an extreme case of diarrhea and went into shock. His body temperature continued to rise. The following day, he became convulsive before slipping into a coma, and within thirty-six hours, Mayakovsky was dead.

The prison doctor who performed the autopsy found a small, metal pellet embedded in the major's abdomen. It would take some time, but a forensic examination determined that the bolus contained a lethal dose of ricin. All of the guards were interviewed, but none could shed any light on who the mysterious assailant had been.

The camera in Mayakovsky's cell inexplicably failed, and the monitors in the hall had also winked out. There were no still photos, and fingerprints at the crime scene were non-existent.

Not a soul could remember seeing the imposter. He appeared like a ghost, and vanished like a vapor. The major never heard the man enter his cell. Somehow, the killer had silently infiltrated a maximum security prison and murdered an inmate. The assassin shadowed his victim, and no one knew he was there. He got close and managed to stay close.

That was how REMORA earned his name.

Chapter Nine * En Route

Passenger terminal,
Andrews Air Force Base, Maryland
Twelve days later

NEILL HELD A RUCKSACK IN ONE HAND AND a cell phone in the other. Classes had been cut short, and he was glad to be going somewhere again. He stared beyond the windows as a C-17 cargo plane taxied to the ramp a hundred yards away. Rolling ahead of the aircraft, a 'follow me' truck played escort, comically small compared to the massive flying machine that trailed behind.

The Globemaster was a workhorse of the airlift community. Its appearance could be deceiving. From head-on, the bird had a bulbous look, but its lateral profile was sleek and aerodynamic. Four jet engines hung from its wings, and the plane's interior could hold troops and materiel—or a combination of both.

"We're in the sterile area now," Neill was saying. He eyed the room, sparsely filled with other passengers. Staff Sergeant Arrens stood nearby, and both Marines were dressed in woodland utilities. "I saw Mr. Aultman at the AMC counter—he has quite the entourage."

"The advance team is leaving today, same as you." Willis Avery was at his desk in the White House. "They'll arrive in Warsaw tonight. Richard's traveling with a token group from

State—along with a modest number of agents. I'll fly out in three days."

Modest? Michael grinned. The security complement stuck out in the crowd, completely overshadowing the Foreign Service corps.

"If you don't mind my asking—why aren't the diplomats taking point on this?" Neill was pushing things a little. Christina was surprised by the question.

"Is that rhetorical, Captain?" It was Avery's turn to smile. "SECSTATE hasn't exactly distinguished himself over the past few years. The Poles don't trust him."

Outside, the Globemaster exited the runway and taxied closer to a parking spot, its ramp lowered. Sunlight flashed on the wings as the plane made the turn. "And Poland's president prefers dealing with your office."

The national security advisor shrugged. "We've been working with Karl for some time, establishing our *bona fides*. It's been worthwhile." Another thought came to mind. "You get the list of emplacement sites?"

"Yes, sir."

"Excellent. Check out a couple before I get there; I'd like an update on construction. Then meet us at the Hotel Bristol." Avery paused. "One more thing—you did pack your blues, right? If we're successful, you'll need 'em for the signing—" he chuckled, "—not to mention the state dinner."

"The state dinner?" Michael repeated.

"Karl's big on ceremony. He's already making plans for a celebration. Should be first class."

"Roger that." A soft tone chirped in Neill's ear. "Sir, can I get back with you? I've got another call coming in."

"I'm done talking," Avery grunted. "You have a safe flight, Captain."

✳ ✳ ✳ ✳

"THE AIRCRAFT JUST PARKED. I HOPE THEY'VE turned up the heat."

Michael got a laugh in reply. On the other end, Daniel Neill listened attentively. "A little chilly there, Mike?"

"Not especially—but you know how cold gray-tails get at altitude. I might have to borrow a pair of Arrens' socks."

He smiled at Christina and gave her a wink—something he rarely did. She returned the look by sticking out her tongue. The friendly expression faded as she knelt to retrieve her pack.

The elder Neill shivered in empathy. A medical team had flown him to Germany after he'd lost his leg. The master gunny's memories of that time were spotty, and he decided to move on to a more pleasant topic.

"I imagine Christina's pretty happy about this trip," he opined.

Neill's gaze held fast on the young woman. "Like a kid in a candy store. I guess the thought of spending Christmas in Europe can do that."

Arrens stepped forward. "Is that your uncle?"

"Yep."

She smiled openly now—and Michael found the look appealing. She leaned in to grip the phone, her fingers curling around the captain's hand. He couldn't help but notice the warmth of her touch.

"I'll send you a postcard, Master Guns. Stay sweet."

A gate agent entered the room, clutching a manifest. He started counting heads while referring to the sheet.

"Time to go, Gunny," Neill announced. "The Air Force is ready to crank up the bus. I'll call you when we get to Lask."

"You do that, junior—and take good care of my girl," he growled, and then added, "You could open up a little. She cares about you. We had a nice heart to heart at the ball."

"Oh?" Michael blinked. "That's a terrifying thought."

"It doesn't hurt to have friends, Mike."

"Look who's talking."

Daniel brushed that aside. "Exactly my point; don't make the same mistakes I have."

Neill wondered at that. When it came to matters of the heart, his uncle was usually right.

"Okay, I'll keep that in mind." The captain decided to shift gears. "Thanks for the mothering, by the way—you would have made a fine officer."

At his home in Anacostia, Daniel Gavin Neill winced.

"Mike, you really know how to hurt a guy."

CIA Headquarters,
Langley, Virginia

THE EDUCATIONAL ANNEX SAT ON THE SOUTH-ern edge of the property. Students here filled a narrow niche—under the Agency's watchful eye—and in each case, the curriculum was tailored for their specific needs. It was geared toward issues of national security. Throughout the building, classes were small, and the courses and enrollees were kept out of the public's view.

Natasha Lenkov taught English, and had been employed by the CIA for nearly two years. She instructed only one pupil, yet each morning her routine was the same; at the beginning of class, she stood at the front of the narrow room—her diminutive form easy to miss behind the podium—and took roll.

The reasons were very practical. The Americans had given Ivan Malyev another identity. He was Mr. Orlov now, and through rote repetition, his new surname was burned into his memory. Natasha's solitary student found the practice eccentric, but Ivan never questioned her behavior. It was just part of the dance, and once the roster had been dutifully checked, the real work began.

Ivan had done well. He applied himself from the very beginning. Learning the English alphabet came first. Simple words and phrases followed, and under Natasha's instruction, he mastered pronunciation and shed much of his accent. With the basics out of the way, the two Russians waded cautiously into the world of syntax and grammar, and Ivan Orlov challenged the language of the country that adopted him.

Things were to be different on this crisp December morning. Mrs. Lenkov had asked her driver to stop on their way in. While her work at Langley paid well—Willis Avery had seen to that—she had no car of her own. The thought of navigating the Beltway made her shudder; it was arduous enough for a younger generation, and Natasha had no interest in developing her defensive driving skills.

Ivan was delivered to the CIA's doorstep in much the same way, but for different reasons. High value assets required constant protection. His chauffeur was an Agency operative, one of three who saw to his safety. Well-armed, Orlov's detail provided transportation—and a separate layer of security.

THE car arrived at the usual time. Ivan entered the annex and found Mrs. Lenkov, poised at a table in the rear of the classroom. The aroma of dark roast was in the air—an acquired taste for Russians, but one that Orlov now preferred.

Natasha held a china cup; black tea was her beverage of choice. As she sipped she gave Ivan a nod and a smile. Both gestures were out of place for the stern widow. Even more surprising were the pastries, baguette and box of coffee that now graced the narrow credenza.

"I felt a little celebration might be appropriate today, Mr. Orlov," the elderly woman announced. Her expression said more than her words.

Ivan's gaze went to the calendar above the table. "But Christmas break doesn't start for another week, *moi uchitel.* What are we to celebrate?"

A contraction. *Excellent*, she thought. They had been working on those.

"Haven't you been following the news, Ivan?" She retrieved the morning edition from a desk behind her. "There's yet another story about Russia's former president."

Ivan scanned the headline above the fold. Articles about Murovanka had appeared frequently for the past few weeks, ever since his abrupt dismissal from office. Most outlined his rise to power, and the allegations that led to his downfall, but today's front page told a different story.

Mr. Orlov absorbed the first paragraph and began reading aloud. "Officials have denied assertions that Murovanka was toppled by a turned Russian dissident." He placed the newspaper on the table, selecting a cruller from the box. "Where does such nonsense come from?" he deflected.

Ivan's diction was commendable, and Mrs. Lenkov took his response as a confirmation of sorts. She chose a fruit-filled turnover and poured herself a second cup. "Your elocution is exemplary, Mr. Orlov. Today's lesson will be short—finish the reading and we'll call it a day."

His eyes brightened. *"Razveh?" Really?* The prospect of ending classes early had great appeal. "Surely you jest."

Natasha maintained a flinty cast. "Everyone deserves a break now and again, Ivan." She took a long sip of her tea.

"Even turned Russian dissidents."

Moscow

AT FIRST GLANCE, THE CHANGES WERE SLIGHT. Only someone with the advantage of years and experience would have noticed—save for the tourists—and casual observers always missed them.

The dour remnants of communism were hard to erase, and vestiges still hung on in unlikely places. While statues of Lenin had been largely removed, a few could still be found in the far-flung corners of the Russian capitol. There was little to explain their continued presence. For Western visitors, and there were many of those these days, they were a photo op. For the common citizen, they served as a reminder of the past—an era never to be repeated. But to the disciples of dormant Marxism, they fueled hope for a restored Soviet empire.

Nearly all of Moscow's major landmarks had been sanitized. These were merely cosmetic alterations, and none re-shaped the skyline in a significant way. The city's spires remained, and Stalin's indelible mark was clearly evident. One edifice seemed permanently embedded among the Seven Hills. The Kremlin would always be the Kremlin—its storied history made it a symbol of Russia—yet it, too, had undergone a subtle facelift.

The massive fortification was framed in antiquity. Its walls enclosed four churches and five palaces, while the entire complex was ringed with more than a dozen watchtowers. The Moskva River marked its southern boundary. Red Square—*Krasnaya Ploschad*—lay on its eastern side, and included St. Basil's Cathedral. The colorful church was a ubiquitous reminder of the nation's Christian roots—and the fact that it survived the Soviet State was something of a wonder in itself.

Squatting just above the banks of the Moskva was the Grand Kremlin Palace. The most telling changes were here. Its façade had once borne the stamp of socialism, but that stain had been scrubbed clean. Five coat-of-arms—double-headed Russian eagles—now graced the building's pinnacle, replacing the Cyrillic CCCP that had once dominated the view from the river.

* * * *

ALEXEI PIROGOV CARED LITTLE FOR THE SWEEP of history. He was in his early twenties when the Soviet Union dissolved. For him, the change in government went unnoticed. There were more pressing concerns; food was still scarce, and hope was non-existent. Career choices were limited, and for many disaffected citizens, there were few options available. Alexei was fortunate in two respects; he had his youth, as well as a university degree. Both were requirements for the Russian Army's officer corps, and the young Muscovite seized his opportunity.

That was the past. Pirogov now moved from checkpoint to checkpoint, displaying his credentials as he made his way deeper within the citadel. At length, he arrived at a corner office on the second floor, where he presented his photo ID once again. The watch officer nodded curtly and allowed Pirogov to pass.

Alexei had been here many times before. Stepping inside, he closed the door behind him. The office was large, but not egregiously so, and a single lamp glowed at the far end of the room.

"Alexei Ivanovich." Karpenko looked up from his desk.

"*Dobre veecher*, General," Pirogov said in greeting. *Good evening.*

In contrast, Leonid Karpenko's career straddled two eras—the Party years, as well as this current exercise in democracy. He was old enough to remember the changes inflicted on the *Rodina,* and had witnessed the crimson flag of the USSR lowered for the last time. The passage from one bureaucracy to another was unremarkable; there was no ceremonial retreat, and the very next day, the red, white and blue standard of the Russian Federation snapped in the breeze.

"I would welcome some good news." The general stretched in his seat, reaching for a bottle of *mineralnaya vada.* "Is that what you bring me?"

"*Da,*" Pirogov answered. He permitted himself a smile. In truth, it was a mixed bag, but with the right spin— "I received a call from Bryansk earlier this week. Our problem in Chernihiv has recently been solved."

Karpenko understood and nodded thoughtfully. He took another sip before speaking. "And Ilya Nikolayevich?"

A satisfied smug. "He acquitted himself well."

"Then he can move on to his next objective," the general announced. "Direct him to continue; provide whatever operational support he requires—within reason." He leaned forward. "And the journalist?"

Pirogov avoided the general's eyes. "For the moment, she eludes us," he admitted.

Karpenko was unperturbed, much to Alexei's surprise. "Ilya will find her." The implication of his words was chilling. "And what news from Belarus?"

The major happily moved to a different topic. "Our *rezident* in Minsk has heard whispers," Alexei continued. "Satellite imagery would seem to confirm specific rumors."

"To the southwest?" the general ventured.

"The Poles have been stirred," Pirogov said. "Dobrogost has renewed his collaboration with the West. Five ground locations have been cleared, and they all share the same characteristics; isolated, equidistantly spaced, and each can be found in an arc running from the north—in Warmia—to the southeast, in the Malopolska region. All are a kilometer's distance from a rail line."

Karpenko grunted. "Hardware?"

A slight shrug. "None, as of yet. We suspect they will employ the American SM3 airframes."

"Aegis?" Karpenko frowned. "Those are sea-based weapons. Anti-aircraft, yes?"

"A modified variant *could* be effective against incoming missiles—provided the delivery vehicle is robust enough." He shook his head. "I must confess, we have only speculation at this point. The rocket launched from Iran has complicated things. For the Poles, international opinion is in their favor. No one can deny them the means to protect themselves—"

"—if they are truly defensive in nature," the general snorted. "But the modifications you speak of could create an offensive weapon."

Karpenko's scowl deepened. He thought this issue settled, but the Poles continued to be a troublesome lot. In the past, Dobrogost had been cowed by Russia's looming shadow. Now Tehran's blundering had set them on edge again.

"That remains to be seen," Alexei cautioned. "As I said, they have no munitions in place." An idea sparked in his mind. "There are steps we can take—countering their move."

Karpenko closed his eyes, stretching once more. "And what do you suggest, Major?"

"We have an opportunity to influence their negotiations. At the moment, two of our regiments are stationed near Georgia—rocket batteries, with a dozen Triumf missiles in each. Two more companies are scheduled for the same region."

"When do they deploy?" The general began to see potential in this line of reasoning.

"Tomorrow—unless their tasking changes."

A half-smile formed on Karpenko's face. He considered Pirogov's words and then weighed his options. Taking the next step could create further tension between East and West—but the American president was weak, and Leonid could afford to push him a little.

"Re-route the Rocket Forces," the general directed. He scanned a map on the wall. "Send them in the opposite direction—to Kaliningrad." He turned and stared at his subordinate evenly. "A simple exercise in mobility, Alexei."

The major's eyes held a question. "And a message?"

"*Da*," Karpenko returned. "A message indeed."

Chapter Ten * Along the Royal Route

Warsaw

MAJESTIC WAS AS GOOD A WORD AS ANY TO describe the Hotel Bristol—but in some ways, even that wasn't nearly enough. Situated in the heart of the Royal Route—the famous enclave of Polish nobility—the landmark of Old Town embodied history and prestige. Its location next to the Presidential Palace gave it further distinction. With its new-Renaissance façade and art deco interiors, the jewel of Warsaw was known for its romantic elegance, and had become the herald of a proud nation.

A few steps off the lobby, the Slowacki Salon was just one extension of the Bristol's grandeur. Like every other part of the hotel, this room was richly appointed in every detail. Hues of blue and white dominated the space from floor to ceiling. Distinctive wall coverings complemented the patterned carpet. Its decorative touches gave it a contented feel, and the Salon could be purposed for small dinner parties, meetings, or press conferences.

Jean-Paul Toussaint was intent on using it for the latter. The employees of Archaeologique François had rearranged the floor space—under the watchful eye of the staff—crowding fifty chairs into a room that comfortably held twenty-four. A lectern with microphones stood at the far end, between the windows and bookcases on either side. Beyond the panes of glass, night had fallen, and at the podium, one of Toussaint's associates fussed with the company's insignia. The Salon came alive as the media crowded in.

YURI Tereshenko found the room's beryl cast oddly soothing. Dressed in a suit—his shirt collar chafing against his neck—the Ukrainian sat in the back, wedged between journalists from as far as Sweden and France. His attire helped mask his chiseled physique, but there was no disguising his uncommon height.

The Berkut member's eyes swept the room. He noted the presence of a dozen photographers, but finding Viktoriya in this gaggle was easy enough. His principal was seated in the front row—Toussaint had seen to that—her coiffure shifting this way and that as she spoke with her peers.

Yuri smiled. Such fashionable tresses required a great deal of attention, and he wondered how she found the time. Her wardrobe was equally flattering. Tereshenko's mind began to stray. While hair and clothing added to Viktoriya's beauty, the young man pondered her other attributes. What was it about her that drew everyone's eye? Something other than her physical appearance? The way she carried herself, perhaps?

No, he ultimately decided. *It must be the make-up.*

That thought brought a smile. His father called it 'painting the barn', but the old man had always been one for homespun analogies. Yuri shrugged. There was no doubt that Viktoriya was pleasing to the eye—not even the stoic Captain Voskov would dispute that fact. He had caught Xander eyeing the woman on more than one occasion, and Yuri wondered—

"Are you in place?"

The voice crackled in Tereshenko's ear. He reached into his jacket, adjusting the gain on his wireless. His hand brushed lightly against the holster shielding his Walther sidearm.

"Speak of the devil and he'll steal your last chance," Yuri muttered. A young man to his left gave him a puzzled look. "Yes, boss. I'm here."

"Do you have her in sight?"

Again, the Ukrainian answered in the affirmative. "I do."

Yuri turned slightly as a separate entourage filed into the room. Jean-Paul Toussaint led the troupe. A few academic types followed, one wearing a ridiculously checkered bow tie. Henri Minouche brought up the rear, appropriately dressed in a business suit, but clearly uncomfortable without his trademark fleece and flannel.

"It looks like the first course has arrived," Tereshenko smiled. "I believe the hotel is serving us a large order of peacock. Can you tell?"

From across the street, Xander Voskov leaned against a lamp, the cold evening air swirling around him. His eyes were fixed on the big windows framing the Salon. The bright interior and parted curtains offered a clear view.

"I can see him now," the captain chuckled. "Even without my field scope—his ego is impossible to miss."

EVERY head turned as two beautiful women—eye candy for Toussaint's audience—entered the room. Their sequined gowns and broad smiles flashed. Each pushed a cart bearing finds from the excavation site, and the photographers began snapping pictures.

Henri Minouche now stood at the podium wearing a wide grin. The room quieted, and he gave an opening statement. A handful of interpreters parsed his words into Polish, Ukrainian, German—and even English.

With the obligatory courtesies at an end, he launched into a lavish introduction of Jean-Paul, and then a vigorous summary of the team's efforts along the Vistula. Minouche took a few questions along the way. Many were shallow and uninformed, and the Frenchman skirted those in favor of broadening the journalists' awareness.

"We have long known that such treasures existed," Henri continued. He waved a hand toward the artifacts on display. Yuri found the team chief's voice both deep and tranquil. "But until recent times, we were uncertain as to their whereabouts."

"What changed that?" It was the young man at Tereshenko's side that spoke up.

Minouche acknowledged the question with a nod. "A combination of factors; new technology, advanced underwater techniques. And with the Vistula's reduced water levels, our job has been further simplified." He bowed slightly, the gesture directed toward a uniformed officer in the front row. "Of course, with the gracious assistance of the Polish military, we can expedite the retrieval of many of the larger objects."

Yuri saw Viktoriya lean forward.

"But surely, *monsieur*, you're seeking spoils far more valuable than marble busts."

A light now danced in Henri's eyes. "We have saved the best for last, *mademoiselle*. And with that, I give you Jean-Paul Toussaint—our society's founder, and a man with great passion and respect for Poland's lost treasures."

There were more flashes—and a smattering of applause—as the entrepreneur strode to the lectern. Drawing himself up to his full height, he projected a regal bearing. Toussaint eyed the room and waited for silence.

Much like Moses—come down from the mountain, Yuri smiled.

"Our goals on Polish soil are summed up in one word," Jean-Paul intoned, "—and that word is *restoration*. We seek to mend the offenses of the past—to heal the wounds of long ago—and return this nation's treasures to their rightful owners."

As if on cue—and it certainly was—one of the models produced a large print and walked to Toussaint's side. Lifting it to eye level, the two held it between them, and the image it bore caught everyone's attention.

"Archival documents have given us additional clues. This is an artist's representation, of course—" Jean-Paul drew a finger across the full color image, "—based on historical accounts and letters from antiquity. If those are correct, then we are only days away from a great discovery."

Even Yuri was impressed. The elaborate illustration depicted a portrait of the Trinity, framed in gold filigree and encrusted with jewels. Spokes radiated out toward the edges—more gold, Tereshenko judged—and the figures themselves were also enclosed by the precious metal.

"To the south lies a humble village. More than three hundred years ago, this priceless relic was seized from that township by Swedish troops. A priest gave his life to stop them, but his efforts were in vain." Toussaint carefully retrieved a weathered document from the podium—the same parchment Viktoriya had seen at the river's edge. He held it up for all to see.

"We have located a barge, and from this vessel we have retrieved many of the items listed by Swedish troops from the seventeenth century. Correspondence like this gives us the final pieces of the puzzle. This letter details the last military campaign of the man who took the priest's life—and also the valuables stolen by this . . . *murderous ruffian*."

The Frenchman fairly spat out the words, and Tereshenko grinned at Jean-Paul's theatrics.

"But at the bottom of a river—for three centuries—what would be left?" Viktoriya wasn't quite as taken by Toussaint's narrative.

An arrogant smile creased the entrepreneur's face. "We shall soon see, *mademoiselle*. I must admit, much of the painting's exterior features are probably gone—but this icon has a price far beyond its artistic worth. We know the exact size of this relic—" *How could he be so sure?* Tereshenko wondered, "—down to the inch—and have calculated its worth in the millions."

Yuri raised an eyebrow, but the Frenchman said nothing more, allowing his words to register. The tactic was effective; the reporters had a new-found respect for the image in Jean-Paul's hands. If the artist's rendering was correct, the gold embellishments alone would be worth a fortune.

* * * *

AN HOUR LATER, VIKTORIYA LEFT THE BRISTOL and took a cab southwest to her flat. Toussaint had invited her to a late supper, but she had a deadline to meet, and begged off—much to Jean-Paul's disappointment. Voskov and Tereshenko followed from a distance.

For the ride across town—past the Saxon Gardens, the Palace of Culture and Science looming in the distance—Viktoriya read a series of press releases. She began absorbing names, dates and locations from Poland's past, and smiled at the abundance of material. Archaeologique François had a fully engaged public relations department. They had done a masterful job of laying the groundwork; all Viktoriya needed to do was to verify details, wedge in some names—and craft the story with an eye toward human interest.

Given the story's tragic elements, that wouldn't be hard. She already knew the cavalry officer's name; now, based on the handouts, Viktoriya had the identity of the long-dead priest. There was pathos here, a dramatic tale of blood and treasure. The young woman had promised her editor as much, and with Toussaint's assistance, she could soon deliver on that pledge.

She needed to put the story into context. For that, a trip to the south was required. The name of the little village was mentioned several times in the media releases. It tugged at her memory. Recent events explained that, and she realized the small hamlet had a peripheral connection to Iran's catastrophic missile test.

Viktoriya hadn't given that story much focus. Valery Bukin had pressed her for coverage, but at the time, she was fully immersed in Toussaint's excavations. Now the past had seemingly intersected the present, giving her a reason to explore both.

The journalist had a small car at her disposal. Poland's roads were notoriously bad, but in the coming days, Viktoriya would use the vehicle to pay a visit to Olm—gathering background on the lost icon—and at the same time, satisfying her boss's demands.

Chapter Eleven * Night Flight

THE GLOBEMASTER CARRYING NEILL AND Arrens was designated REACH-961. Twenty-one reservists were also aboard—from Homestead, Florida, according to the loadmaster—bound for Ramstein Air Base and two weeks of training. The airmen from the south regarded the Marines curiously, yet didn't begrudge them a ride on their plane.

In truth, it was the other way around. Michael and Christina's mission gave *them* an elevated priority—but the Air Force wouldn't send the bird aloft without other passengers. Fuel was expensive. So was maintaining the aircraft, and if the DoD could maximize resources—

Cargo had also been manifested for the flight. An F-16 engine dominated the center aisle, carefully secured to a pallet train with a series of chains and devices. The big Pratt and Whitney turbofan was bound for Aviano, Italy. Behind that was a separate pallet with the reservists' baggage.

The Marines' gear was floor-loaded near the front, their garment bags stuffed. Assignments dealing with protocol required an extra uniform or two—in this case, the mess dress each had worn to the birthday ball, less than a month earlier.

Inboard-facing seats ran on both sides of the aircraft, from the crew door in front to the ramp at the rear. The two picked spots along the starboard bulkhead just across from the jet engine. Stowing their rucks beneath them, they settled in for the trip across the Atlantic.

Neill had been right. Once they reached cruising altitude, the temperature dropped within the pressurized aircraft. Two hours later, he and Christina donned their fleece liners. They passed the time with tablets and readers. The captain reviewed Polish phrases; Staff Sergeant Arrens entertained herself with a novel. It was an historical romance of unrequited love. She showed him the cover, and made a point of describing the plot—in great detail—before delving into the book's final chapters.

The plane stopped at Bangor, Maine to take on more pax. Half a dozen Army officers came aboard—doctors bound for the military hospital in Landstuhl—and then the ramp came up as they taxied to the runway.

Airborne once more, Neill caught a nap.

REACH-961 stopped in Lakenheath for concurrent servicing. It was late in the evening when they arrived. Michael looked at his watch. He wasn't surprised to hear that their departure would be delayed. Ramstein operated under 'quiet hours' during the night, and air operations were restricted as a concession to the surrounding community.

Disembarking the aircraft, the Marines had several hours before their next leg. They took advantage of the time by freshening up and grabbing some food. That helped, and getting off the plane restored some of their vigor, but the interruptions in their journey were taking a toll. They were ready for some real sleep.

"Never been to England before," Neill said. After their meal he and Arrens found their way back to the gate.

"And you still haven't," the staff sergeant answered tiredly. "Four hours in the pax terminal doesn't count."

"Guess you've got a point," he grinned.

"I'll bet Avery's assistant isn't sleeping in an airport right now." Christina's eyes were half-closed.

"Probably not," Neill agreed. "I'm sure he's enjoying all the amenities of a Warsaw hotel."

"And a nice soft bed," she yawned.

* * * *

THE FLIGHT TO GERMANY WAS UNEVENTFUL. Transiting the Channel, REACH-961 arrived just before dawn. Morning glowed over the snow-draped hills, and air traffic was light as the plane's wheels brushed against the runway.

With the aircraft parked on the ramp, the loadmaster released their gear. Christina got to her feet and started to move forward, but then stopped.

"Would you be a dear, Captain?" She batted her eyes, and her voice was melodic. "My sea bag's a little heavy."

"Yes, ma'am." Neill gave her a knowing look. A smile crossed his weary face, and she returned the expression. His comment about luggage had come back to haunt him, yet he didn't mind at all.

They exited through the crew door, where a Dodge six-pack awaited. They could see their breaths in the chill of the air. Michael helped load their belongings in the back of the truck, and Ramstein's port dawgs took over. Their connecting flight was waiting, and the vehicle sped across the tarmac.

A bus delivered the passengers to the terminal. Neill took in the sprawling structure as the morning frost covered its surfaces. It had been less than two years since his most recent visit, and for that trip, Ramstein had been his last stop before heading to Odessa, Ukraine.

* * * *

SMALLER THAN A C-17, CHROME-356 WAS A PROP-driven C-130 aircraft, a J-model. There was less space to stretch out, and given the number of passengers, the flight promised to be a cozy one.

The two gravitated once more to the starboard side of the plane. Accommodations were more austere than the Globemaster. Air Force personnel—also bound for Lask—crowded the interior.

The zoomies segregated themselves, and sitting together, Neill and Arrens were surprised to find empty seats on either side. Christina pulled out her reader and burrowed into the canvas seating while Michael listened to music.

Their time on the ground dragged. It wasn't terribly cold, but with the ramp down, cool air filled the compartment, and the young woman edged nearer. They were shoulder to shoulder now, and Neill enjoyed the closeness. As the cargo plane taxied, Arrens abruptly powered down her device and pushed it back into her ruck.

"Stupid book," she grumped. Her voice was barely audible over the sound of the turboprops.

Michael pulled out his ear buds. "Did you finish?"

"Yes." She sounded disappointed.

"Did the hero get the girl?"

She sighed. "Not this time."

"Maybe in the sequel," he offered.

"I guess." She tapped Neill's MP3 player. "What are you listening to?" Without waiting for an answer, a warm hand enclosed his, and she lifted it to her ear.

"I know that song." A grin now. "Disco. From the eighties?"

"Late seventies. One of my dad's favorite groups."

Christina tilted her head, still holding his hand next to her cheek. "That's so sweet." Her voice had an almost adoring tone.

Michael blinked. "How's that?"

"You like your father's music. It's *sweet*."

She released Neill's hand, much to his disappointment. Her gaze lingered, and he could almost predict the next question. He deflected it with one of his own.

"You really like those stories, don't you?"

"Stories?" The comment caught her off guard. "Oh—*stories*. Yes, I do." Christina shivered, pressing in just a little. Her eyes bored into his. "I can't help it. I'm just a hopeless romantic."

* * * *

Neill was spent. The drone of the engines produced a hypnotic effect, and with the J-model climbing into the sky, most passengers drifted off, the captain included. Light turbulence created a rocking motion, and with his chin in his chest, the Marine slumbered deeply.

He stirred some time later, waking to the soft scent of Christina's perfume. Turning slightly, he found her head resting on his shoulder. On the ground, she had resisted closing her eyes, but the young woman lost the battle shortly after take-off. Her body was relaxed, snuggled in the seat as the aircraft approached the Polish border.

It was a little awkward, but Neill stayed where he was, reluctant to wake her. The fragrance she wore conjured memories. At the ball, the two had shared a tender moment, and the magic of the evening tempered the distance between them. Neither would admit it, but they were drawn to each other. Michael reflected on that, but instead of banishing the thought, he re-lived that point in time. The chemistry between them that night might have been encouraged by the occasion—but was something else now at work?

The two had meshed from the start, despite their varied experiences and separate career tracks. It was a relationship based on respect. Neill was quick to acknowledge the staff sergeant's professional skills, and Arrens had always esteemed the captain's aptitude for language. Over the past few years, their friendship had grown, and now he sensed a deeper connection. That truth came slowly. Embracing intangible concepts had made him good at his job, yet understanding his own feelings could often be a struggle. In those instances, he would push them aside—especially when it came to the young woman sleeping next to him.

There was good reason for that. The rules regarding fraternization were never far from his mind. Michael could understand the reasons for those. Allegations of improper relationships had recently tarnished the military. Most had been tawdry, immoral and completely unprofessional. The regulations were in place to protect members—regardless of rank—and to ensure discipline.

They were well-intended, to be sure, but the coaxing of youth was a powerful inducement, and human nature was a strong force to contend with at any age.

Neill had dated in the past, but those interactions were brief and unfulfilling. From what he knew of Arrens, her experiences had been much the same. Edging closer to their late twenties, neither felt compelled to make commitments beyond their own careers.

The captain smiled to himself. These were weighty matters to consider, and probably better suited for another time. He felt a curious mix of emotions; an odd satisfaction, combined with a longing from within. Falling back on old habits, he tried to suppress them. When that failed, he simply ignored the sentiments.

In that respect, Neill was typically male.

The plane hit a patch of rough air. Asleep in the canvas netting, Christina shifted against him, and before dozing off again, Michael felt strangely at peace.

Chapter Twelve * On Foreign Soil

Lask, Poland

LONG BEFORE CHROME-356 PARKED, THE LOAD-master dropped the ramp, allowing everyone a glimpse of this new location. Neill and Arrens looked aft, past the 'honey pot'—a receptacle in the bulkhead—to the Polish countryside beyond. A somber gray sky stretched in every direction, and Christina's stare held as she gathered first impressions.

It was mid-morning and bitterly cold. The sun's face was masked by a thick layer of clouds, and snow was in the forecast. This part of Central Europe was mostly flatland, with beech trees, hornbeam and oaks lining the edges of the airfield. Half a dozen F-16s, part of Poland's Tenth Tactical Squadron, sat neatly in a row on the tarmac. Some distance away, a couple of F-22 Raptors were parked, augmenting the Tenth for RESILIENT EAGLE.

The cargo plane made the turn from the taxiway to its parking spot. As it slowed to a halt, a white six-pack rolled up from behind. Driving was the air field representative—the RAMPCO—along with someone riding shotgun in the passenger seat. A bus arrived to collect the Air Force personnel and waited nearby.

"GEOFFREY Welles." The tall, senior NCO was waiting on

the ground. He grinned boyishly and stuck out his hand. "Been expecting you, Captain. Pulled the manifest out of the system and found your names."

The Marines had disembarked last. Neill hefted his ruck and stepped off the plane. On the J-Model's ramp he was as tall as Welles, but standing on the flight line, the Air Force sergeant towered over him.

"Nice to meet you." Neill raised his voice above the sound of the turbo-props. The aircraft was doing an ERO—an engine running offload. Noting the stripes on his sleeve, Neill asked, "Senior Master Sergeant, correct?"

The zoomie's head bobbed, and his chin came up as Arrens descended the ramp. He all but ignored the captain now, turning to the staff sergeant.

"Ma'am," the senior chirped, his smile widening. Further introductions were made. "You folks bring any gear?"

"Baggage pallet," Michael said, nodding toward the back of the plane.

"No worries. Forklift's on the way," he announced.

A Caterpillar 10K was positioned well behind the aircraft, the driver staring ahead. Welles was prepared to marshal him in when Arrens climbed back up the ramp. The plane's loadmaster met her as she reached the main deck, a small black case in his hands.

"Can't forget this," she grinned. "Need to see my custodian's letter?"

The load—a senior airman—smiled back at the young woman. "No, ma'am." He gave Christina the case. "I'm sure you know how to handle these."

THEY hopped in the truck for the ride back. The cab was warm, and the seats much more comfortable than what they'd experienced on the plane. The two newcomers began to relax as they covered the half mile distance to the terminal.

"From what I've been told, you'll be our guests for a couple of nights," Welles announced. Beyond that, he knew very little.

"What happens after that?"

Neill took in the view from his window. "We'll be headed to Warsaw. The State Department's made arrangements for us there." A few thin shafts of sunlight had begun to pierce the clouds. "What do you have in the way of lodging?"

Welles turned to the rear. "Most of our buildings are situated around the pax terminal; two Cadillac's out back—one male, the other female—and a sprung on the west side. We get a lot of DVs through the port, so billeting won't be a problem."

"Sprung?" Michael knew that a Cadillac referred to the head, or bathroom. The other term was unfamiliar.

"Portable tensioned structure ," Christina explained. "Like a tent, but with steel ribs and a stronger skin. We had some in Afghanistan."

The senior flashed his perpetual smile. "Ours are divided into separate quarters. Plenty of room." Welles gave her a sideways look. "Where were you deployed, Staff Sergeant?"

"Camp Leatherneck. What about you, Senior?"

"Bagram," he answered, a measure of pride in his voice. "Four months in a B-hut. Ever seen one?"

Christina nodded and reflected his grin. "Just once. I wasn't impressed."

"Neither was I," the senior agreed. "Nothin' but plywood firetraps."

Welles didn't want to slight the captain. He faced Neill once more. "We'll stop by air ops first, and after that I'll have a few airmen grab your bags and we'll get you to your rooms."

THE air operations center was a busy place, and a mix of Polish and American personnel worked side by side. Squadron insignia for the respective air groups were proudly displayed, with ready rooms and a conference space separated by a long hall. A few heads came up as they entered, and Welles directed the weary Marines to a row of couches in the reception area.

The travelers dropped their packs and Neill checked the

room. A map of Central Europe dominated the rear wall. To the east was Ukraine, and Michael's gaze went from Kiev to Odessa, skimming over a dozen smaller townships in between. The names on the chart brought back a few memories, and he found himself feeling just a little nostalgic.

Welles took notice. "Ever been to this part of the world before, Captain?" the senior asked.

Arrens glanced at her boss with a ready smile. Neill had begun to peel off his Gore-Tex when a laugh came from behind.

"Captain Neill grew up here, Sergeant Welles." A pause, "—well, perhaps not *here*. You would say 'next door', yes, *Mischa?*"

Michael turned and stared. For a moment he was stunned. Fatigue had dulled his senses, but recognition came quickly.

"Pyotr?" His puzzled look became a smile, and he shook his head. "Can't be. The Pyotr Stanislaw I knew was a skinny little kid. Just a horsefly."

"But that was more than ten years ago," the Polish officer said, raising a hand in protest. "A lot has happened since then, *moi przyjaciel.*"

He wore camouflage, not unlike his American counterparts. Standing just feet apart, Stanislaw and Neill were evenly matched in height and build. Pyotr stepped forward; Neill did the same, and the two men embraced like brothers. Welles and Arrens watched the reunion in silence. Both regarded the exchange with mild amusement, and it was clear that the two men were old friends.

The captain studied Stanislaw's uniform. "It's good to see you, horsefly. How have you been?" Neill had shifted languages, gauging the lieutenant's reaction.

"Will wonders never cease?" A surprised look hung on Pyotr's face. "You speak Polish now, Mischa?"

"Only a little," Michael warned. He switched back to English. "Quite a coincidence, finding you here."

The Pole chuckled. "You know what your father would say about that, Michael."

His grin faded, and the Marine became more guarded. "I remember, *towarzysz*."

To Christina, Neill appeared to pull back. She chalked that up to fatigue, and the surprise he must have felt at seeing a familiar face. They now stood on foreign soil, in a country he had never visited—but one that must have seemed very much like Ukraine. Given his lack of sleep, the man was bound to experience a few odd moments, yet none of that fully explained the melancholy Arrens saw in his eyes.

His reaction now called to mind their discussion at Ramstein—and the artful way he dodged questions about family. She knew his parents had been missionaries, and were gone, but little more. In the past she'd just considered him a very private person. Something about his behavior now made her wonder. The young woman was about to bookmark the impression when the old Neill returned.

"I'm forgetting myself," he announced. Names were passed around, with the captain leading the introductions. "Pyotr and I go way back. We both grew up just outside of Kiev. Spent a lot of seasons playing rugby—" a broad grin "—although horsefly's soccer skills are a little questionable. How's the family?"

"They are well, Michael. My parents speak of you often—" A gleam came into Pyotr's eye, "—and Tula will be pleased to know that you're here."

* * * *

SOMEONE'S STOMACH GROWLED. CHRISTINA hoped it wasn't hers. Welles must have heard it too, and steered the group toward thoughts of an early lunch.

The Marines stowed their gear first. Arrens' black case was locked away in the armory, while their bags were taken to the sprung. From there it was off to the dining facility.

The offerings didn't disappoint—especially for the two hungry Marines. Pyotr acted as host, recommending items in the hot food line. Pierogies and soup were on the menu, along with sausage, black bread, and butter. Welles and Stanislaw went for the steak tartar, but Neill and Arrens passed on the raw food.

The meal had lifted everyone's spirits. The group jumped back into the six-pack, and with Senior Master Sergeant Welles at the wheel, a tour of the base followed. Ambling along perimeter road, the field was not unlike any other expansive military installation—which meant there wasn't much to see. The sun had chased away the low, somber clouds, and a light layer of snow clung to the ground, receding as the day wore on.

The trek around the base was intended to stave off sleep and the effects of jet lag, but the truck's cab warmed quickly. Within minutes the heavy lunch began to take its toll. Neill's head bobbed, and Arrens was also ready to doze off.

* * * *

"NEW UNIFORM, STAFF SERGEANT ARRENS?"

"Don't laugh," she advised. Her voice was appropriately stern.

"Wouldn't think of it." Neill wore his PT gear, a shaving kit under one arm. "Feeling better?"

"Much," Christina answered. A hot shower had restored her senses. Clad in sweats and flip-flops, she was also wrapped in a heavy robe, and carried a toiletry bag through the sprung's hall. Her hair was held in a thick towel, bringing a smile to Neill's face.

She felt the need to shift his focus. "Must have been quite a shock, seeing the lieutenant."

"Didn't recognize him at first," he admitted. "It's been awhile."

"Uh-huh." She cocked her head to one side, viewing him with an exaggerated squint. "And who's Tula? An old girlfriend?"

A little color came to Michael's ears. "Pyotr's sister."

Christina smiled. This was unexplored territory, and she decided to tease him. "Were you a heartbreaker, Captain?"

"His *little* sister," he was quick to explain. "I was seventeen when his family came back to Poland. Tula was eleven."

"Why did they leave?"

He drew in a breath. "Pyotr's father was—*is*, I should say—an engineer. Poland's economy improved after the Soviet Union fell. His dad took a job with the state railway. He moved the family back—"

Neill's head came up, his expression bearing a trace of surprise. Arrens raised an eyebrow.

"Back where?"

"Olm." The captain chided himself. The connection had eluded him. "That's where the Stanislaws are from."

"Olm?" Christina repeated. "That's close to—"

"The crash site; I know." He had a faraway look in his eye. "I guess it really is a small world."

"Another coincidence?" She recalled his earlier words, and wanted to press him further. "What was Pyotr talking about—when he mentioned your father?"

"Remind me to tell you sometime," Michael deflected. He abruptly changed the subject. "Did you get all your bags?"

Christina nodded. "You?"

The moment slipped away, and Neill didn't answer; he was too taken by Arrens' appearance. Without make-up, her eyes were dewy, with a natural look, and her face had a fresh-scrubbed glow all its own. Even under layers of terry-cloth and cotton, he found her absolutely beautiful, and both of them realized that the captain was staring.

"I'm sorry—what?" His response was almost comical.

"Someone's sleepy," she laughed softly. That melodious tone had crept into her voice again. She took a step forward, studying Michael's chin. "And I think he needs a shave, too."

Arrens felt a bit self-conscious, dressed as she was in a bathrobe. Neill seemed to enjoy the view, and she savored the moment of innocent attention, but there was little point in encouraging it.

Christina moved toward her quarters. Giving him a mischievous smile, she disappeared inside, closing the door slowly behind her.

That feeling surfaced again—the intangible *something* Neill couldn't put his finger on. The longing he'd felt on the plane tugged at him once more. Another man might have explored his options, but that wasn't Michael's style. He watched her go, offering no reply, and then turned and headed for the showers.

Chapter Thirteen * Relics

Her Majesty's Naval Base,
Portsmouth, British Isles

ARRY WAINWRIGHT SCOWLED, HIS EYES fixed on the collection of reports covering his desk. Spread out before him was little more than conjecture, hashed together by the spooks at MI6 and the intelligence branch of the British Royal Navy. It was a mixed bag, competing interpretations that touched on the truth—and then veered off in tangents, reminiscent of a wild goose chase.

Little of it coalesced into anything meaningful. The commodore shook his head. For that he'd have to cut through the commentary and study the raw data. His face broke out in a wan smile. Wainwright had a discerning mind, and over the past few years, his analytical expertise had been called for quite often.

He sometimes wondered why the analysts got involved at all. Too often they relied on opinion rather than substantive evidence. That seemed to be their default setting—the younger ones, at least. Wainwright considered that wryly. There was a phrase used by the Americans—*when your only tool is a hammer, every problem looks like a nail.*

That assessment wasn't meant to be demeaning; there was some value to what the youngsters had to offer. Most were academic types, gifted pundits, sitting cloistered in their cubicles at the Admiralty. Many had simply checked off the right boxes and gone to the requisite schools, but a diminishing list of those operatives had ever put to sea.

And that was why the commodore's skills were in such demand.

It wasn't just the paperwork that had put the frown on Wainwright's face. Lean and driven, the Royal Navy man preferred a deck below his feet and didn't like being sidelined in an office. His current command, HMS *Industrious*, was tied up at the dock; the return to port was unexpected, and while the ship was still brand new, upgrades to OVERTURE meant an extensive refit of her comm gear.

A schedule for the undertaking was tacked to the wall. The work was slated to last through December and into the next year. The Christmas holiday was fast approaching, which further extended the delay. Wainwright mulled that over with a glance through the window. He was effectively marooned ashore, the home waters of Portsmouth glimmering in the distance.

Sir Harry broke from his reverie and concentrated on the task at hand. He began sifting through the more cogent analyses. One consensus had emerged, something he could agree with. Over the past few years, the antics of the Russian Federation had become steadily more erratic.

First, the Kremlin had provoked the Chinese, massing troops far too close to their shared border—for what was termed as an 'exercise'. Then came the attack on the American reconnaissance plane. A Navy pilot had been killed in that incident. And there were whispers that Moscow had resorted to acts of nuclear terrorism . . .

Those rumors had proven true, and as a result, Arkadi Murovanka's goose was cooked. MI6 speculated on the CIA's involvement, but Wainwright wasn't convinced. He'd seen nothing to validate those suspicions. If the colonials were behind sacking the Russian president, they'd managed to keep the lid on extremely well. In and of itself, that might have been confirmation enough.

He brushed aside the analyst's contributions. So much of that was simply a distraction, so Harry turned elsewhere. Field intel was the best source. Observations by line officers gave men like Wainwright something to chew on, and if he wanted to sort through the clutter, that's where he needed to go.

The communique in his hand was less than three hours old. It had been sent from a position near the mouth of the Skagerrak Strait, between Denmark and Norway . Wainwright eyed a chart on the wall. That patch of ocean would be very cold this time of year. A yeoman had marked the spot with a red push-pin, and considering the relative geography, the location was practically in the British Isles back yard.

Wainwright contemplated the report. During the night, a Royal Navy frigate had crossed paths with a warship—a Russian missile cruiser steaming south. Sighting a former adversary on the high seas wasn't rare, and certainly not in international waters. That was a common enough occurrence, but the vessel's class—part of the 1164 series—raised a few flags.

She wasn't always known as the *Moskva*. Launched in the late seventies, she was christened the *Slava*. Names aside, the commodore remembered her from his Cold War days, and he hadn't forgotten her purpose. The old Soviet-era ship was packed with armament; her decks were laden with tube launchers, dual purpose guns and close-in weapons systems. She was designed to inflict damage, and NATO had dubbed her a carrier-killer . To men of Wainwright's caliber—masters of ships like the *Industrious*—that was the most chilling title of all.

The message went on to list two other vessels; the *Smetlivy*, even older than *Moskva*, and the anti-submarine destroyer *Admiral Panteleyev*. These ships were relics of communism, but that didn't make them any less lethal. All three had rounded Norway's coastline, transiting the Norwegian Sea on a southerly course as they left the Barents. That much was clear, and the memo before him didn't trade in speculation. What worried Wainwright was the convoy's timing and the stand-off capabilities of each ship.

Earlier intelligence had linked the *Moskva* to a weapons facility near Archangelsk, in Russia. Details were spotty, but the munitions factory there was thought to produce long-range missiles. Then came a more tenuous connection; an Ilyushin-76 had flown from Talagi Air Field to Murmansk. The four-engine cargo jet was similar in size to the American C-17, and two days later, the missile cruiser had slipped out of the icy port with her escorts.

The commodore sat back in his chair and turned that over in his mind. Only recently the *Moskva* and her support ships had been part of Russia's naval operations in the Barents. Now they were loitering in the frigid waters of the North Sea.

There was other activity that concerned him. In the slightly warmer climes of the eastern Mediterranean, the *Aleksander Shabalin* and the *Novocherkassk* were passing through the Bosporus on a course that would take them to the Black Sea. The Russian Defense Ministry had claimed that the maneuvers were simply fleet rotations, designed to keep their crews fresh. Wainwright had to concede that as a possibility; none of the ships had demonstrated provocation, and no single vessel—or group—posed an imminent threat. Yet it stood as too much of a coincidence to be believable.

On the face of it, the Russian Navy was projecting power. In doing so they sent a message. Wainwright had been privy to all the Admiralty briefings. Poland had once again embraced the West's offer of protection. The general public was oblivious to this collaboration, but the Kremlin was not; and with the subtlety of two armed flotillas, the Russians were making their displeasure known.

* * * *

"YOU SHOULD BE IN BED." AULTMAN'S VOICE drifted from the phone in Avery's hand. "What time does your flight leave Andrews?"

The national security advisor glanced at his watch—an archaic piece of jewelry in this age of cell phones and mobile devices.

"Seven a.m.," Avery grumped. He was puttering around the kitchen, working on his second cup of coffee. His wife Madeline—Maddie, as Willis called her—was in the bedroom, laying out his shirt and tie. "The driver's picking me up at six. What time is it there?"

"A little after ten o'clock." Aultman was enjoying the view of Warsaw from the Hotel Bristol. "I was about to get something to eat."

"Try the Marconi." Avery placed his mug in the microwave. It was after four a.m., and his coffee needed a warm-up—and a lot more caramel creamer. "Better hurry. They stop serving breakfast at ten-thirty."

Aultman already knew that. This was his second full day in Warsaw. "I'm on my way," he answered. Richard grabbed his jacket, and then checked the pocket for the room key card. "Anything happening on your end?" The boss rarely called just to chat.

"More like your neck of the woods," Avery chuckled, but there was little humor in his voice. "I got a call from the signals office, about an hour ago. Suvorov's upped the ante again."

"Suvorov? General of the Army?"

"Chief of the General Staff," Avery corrected. "At the risk of understating things, the Russians are a little unhappy."

Aultman considered that Moscow probably knew all about the renewed plans for the missile shield. "What's he bleating about now?"

"Apparently the threat of an arms race wasn't enough." Avery stirred his coffee. "Now he's blustering about a strike against NATO."

Richard stopped in his tracks. The Russians were big on hyperbole, but this was over the top. "Did you get confirmation from General Ecklund?"

"It was Sid who called the White House," Avery informed him. "SECSTATE's on it—or will be, as soon as the sun's up."

Aultman didn't comment. Breese's appointee to the office

had little in the way of diplomatic skills. "What about Karpenko? I'm guessing he's staying out of this."

"The general has wisely decided to let Suvorov play the bad guy." Avery was impressed, but his subordinate always did catch on quickly. "In any case, this doesn't rise to the top of my list of concerns. We've heard this kind of swagger before. Suvorov's trying to rattle Turkey. And Romania. He doesn't want to see radar sites in those countries."

"Much less missiles in Poland."

"Agreed—but there's more to it than just that."

"I'm listening."

"Their forces are on the move. A division of motorized infantry just deployed to the south—close to Ukraine. Four tank companies are now evenly spaced on the border, and two missile regiments just took up housekeeping in Kaliningrad."

Richard blinked. "Rocket batteries?"

Avery grunted and leaned against the counter-top. "Packing Triumfs . Twenty-four total, if the intel's correct."

"Neill was right," Aultman breathed. He shook his head. "*Son of a gun*—we need to put him on our payroll."

"Not a bad idea," the national security advisor barked. "I'd love to get his take on what they'll do next."

"Then this is all about Poland?" Aultman asked.

"Suvorov said as much. He's no diplomat, of course. Their military tends to blunder through affairs of state. This is just an excuse to build up their weapons stockpile. The shifting power base in Moscow hasn't helped. And then there's RESILIENT EAGLE." NATO's contingency operation had rolled out a week earlier and was building steam.

A new thought sprang to mind. "The Russians are like our friends on Wall Street, Richard—they hate uncertainty; and next month we'll swear in a new president—a rather hawkish one, from their perspective."

Aultman gauged the potential threats. "Do you think they'll pull the trigger on either option?"

"That's hard to say. Personally, I think Suvorov's just feeling his oats. But given the current climate, they might go for both. Ecklund says that two of their ships are passing through the Dardanelles, on their way to join the Black Sea Fleet."

Recent history jogged the younger man's memory. "Didn't Suvorov once propose a joint missile shield? A cooperative effort between Russia and NATO?"

Avery grinned. For a man on his way to breakfast, Aultman asked a lot of questions.

"He did," Willis replied. "A stalling tactic. Their military voted it down. The alliance nixed it too."

"More paranoia?" Richard suggested.

"Possibly on both sides," Avery carped. He looked at his watch again. It was time to get out of his pajamas and into the shower. "I need to get dressed. I'll call you when the plane lands."

"Hang on." Aultman wasn't so easily dismissed. "What about SECDEF?"

Avery grumbled under his breath. He knew exactly what the man was asking. "Hayes authorized the release. I have the file in my briefcase." He also suspected what the next question would be. "I'll sit down with the good captain after I get there."

"He deserves to know."

"So you keep telling me," Avery said. But he knew Aultman was right. "In the meantime, let's hope the Russians can exercise their better natures until this agreement is signed."

Aultman ended the call, his mind swirling. He wasn't sure which prospect raised more concern. The possibility of military action was hard to imagine, but a new build-up of weapons carried other implications.

With the Kremlin involved, either circumstance could prove deadly.

* * * *

BREAKFAST WAS EXCELLENT, WITH A LOCAL FLAvor. The dining facility's cooks were Polish nationals hired from Lask. There was plenty of black bread and sausage, and the chef even indulged Michael's appetite for eggs over easy.

Neill had managed to sleep in and missed the breakfast crowd. He'd brought his tablet, and was reading the *Gazeta Warszawa*—or trying to. The captain stumbled over a host of words before giving up and switching to the English version.

One story piqued his interest. The feature was prominently placed 'above the fold', crammed into the top half of the page, along with other content. Two photos competed for attention. One was taken beside a river; the other depicted some type of historical artifact. Michael scrolled down and read the captions, then absorbed the article over coffee. Most compelling of all was the narrative's byline.

"Good morning, Mischa." Pyotr Stanislaw slid into the seat across from Neill. His words were Ukrainian. "You slept well?"

The Marine nodded. "I was whipped."

The Pole smiled and sipped from his mug. "No tea?"

"No one makes it the way *mati* does."

"Mine or yours?"

"Either," Neill grinned. "You've eaten?"

"Hours ago. I'm an early riser." Pyotr's eyes swept the hall. "And where did you leave your *starshy serzhant*?"

"Asleep, I guess," he answered. Michael considered knocking on Christina's door, then thought better of it. He'd left a note instead. The Marines had spent too much time aboard aircraft, and he felt she could use the rest.

Neill regarded Pyotr's uniform. "I didn't know you'd joined the army."

"I followed your example. The military seemed like a good fit." He drank his tea, giving Michael a roguish look. "After seeing your friend, I can understand why you became a United States Marine."

"It's not like that. Staff Sergeant Arrens is—" Neill paused, drawing a breath, "—just a colleague."

"Just? *Pah!* For such a colleague, I would be most thankful," Stanislaw teased, choosing his words carefully.

"You don't think men and women can just be friends?" Neill was prodding him now.

"I believe it's a good place to begin," Pyotr came back. He thought to say more—but then his chin came up. "She rises from slumber."

Christina carried a tray and was moving in their direction. Arriving at their table, she parked it next to Michael.

"Good morning, *Serzhant*." Both men stood—Pyotr bowing dramatically.

"Good morning, Lieutenant; Captain." She inspected Neill's face. "Looks like someone shaved."

"An improvement?" Michael asked.

"It's a start," she beamed. Fishing for compliments was unexpected; *the boss must have slept well,* she thought. "Did you call your uncle?"

"Last night," Neill said. "Just before I conked out."

She thought as much. Christina heard his muffled voice through the vinyl walls of the sprung. Their rooms were next to each other.

"Mind if I join you?" Arrens asked.

Stanislaw bent at the waist again. "I would be hurt if you didn't."

* * * *

CONVERSATION WAS LIGHT AS CHRISTINA ATE her food. Over more coffee and tea, the two men traded questions, most dealing with life in their respective militaries. For his part, Pyotr never strayed into serious matters. Michael did ask about the Stanislaws, but nothing he said revealed much about his own parents—and Christina sensed that was intentional.

Out of respect, the officers spoke in English. Neither man lapsed into a dialect that would exclude her from the discussion. Arrens finished her meal and made a little small talk of her own, biding her time before wading in.

"The captain tells me you have a younger sister." She

sipped from her mug. "Does she live nearby?"

Pyotr brightened. "Tula?" He shook his head. "No; she is still at home. But only for a short time—in the spring, she will go to the abbey in Krakow to become a novice."

Neill appeared visibly surprised. "A nun?"

A nod, and another smile. "Don't look so shocked, Mischa."

"Then your family is Catholic?" Christina asked.

"Most Poles are, *Serzhant* Arrens."

"Please—call me Christina."

Pyotr's grin remained. "That would be my pleasure— Christina." His tone became more serious. "Do you know the meaning of your name?"

"Follower of Christ?" she replied.

The lieutenant agreed, but added, "It also means 'beautiful'—and in your case, I can't disagree." He looked to Neill. "And then we have Mischa—'one favored by God.' "

She laughed softly, glancing Michael's way. "I don't think I've heard that one before. Why don't you tell me about your home, Lieutenant."

"To the south. A village called Olm." He finished his tea. "You've heard of it?"

"Olm's been in the news a lot lately," Neill injected.

"Tragically, yes," Pyotr said. "The Iranians. Their missile took many lives."

"I wasn't referring to that, *moi przyjaciel.*" Michael touched the tablet, refreshing the screen. "You've seen this?"

Stanislaw took the device and scrolled through the story. "I have," he answered slowly. A photo of Jean-Paul Toussaint appeared at the bottom. "The Frenchman. He's been digging around Gora Kalwaria, looking for treasure." He handed it back across the table.

"Treasure stolen from Olm, it would seem," Neill observed. *Another surprise.* Pyotr didn't appear to be impressed.

Christina skimmed more of the story. "What kind of treasure?"

"A religious artifact. An icon," the lieutenant responded.

"Taken by the Swedes in the seventeenth century. Our village calls it the Treasure of the Heart."

"According to this, it was lost in the Vistula," Michael added.

Stanislaw was indifferent. He waved a hand at the screen. "And this foreigner thinks he's found it."

"But you don't?"

Pyotr gave Christina a shrug. "He's found many things. I just don't believe the icon is one of them."

Neill sat back in his chair. "I thought you'd be excited about this."

"It doesn't work that way, Mischa." The lieutenant stared at his friend, slightly irritated. "You think you've arrived here to witness some great discovery. But this isn't the first time. Years ago, an art collector claimed to have found the icon in a cathedral. The university tried to verify his story, but it was a hoax." Pyotr had an unsettled look about him. "During the war, the Nazis had it; and then it was spirited away to the Kremlin Museum. Neither story was true. Not long ago, a Vatican priest came across the centerpiece in a storeroom—or so he thought."

"The centerpiece?" Christina asked.

"The icon is part of a triptych," he explained. "Three paintings in all. Only two remain." Pyotr continued; "For each so-called 'revelation', Tula's hopes were dashed. You know how much she loves the church, Michael."

"She was always very devout."

Christina sat quietly. "You're trying to protect her."

The lieutenant became more relaxed. "I don't want to see my sister hurt. If the icon was lost in the Vistula, then the river has taken it back to God, and it will never be recovered."

"What do you think happened to it?"

"There is a local tradition." Stanislaw was pacing his words again. "A prophecy, of sorts. As a child, my grandmother had a dream, or a vision. In it, she was told that the Virgin Mary would one day choose a maiden, and a nobleman's son, to restore the icon."

Arrens leaned forward. "Do you think it still exists?"

Pyotr shrugged. "There is always hope. At the Mass on Christmas Eve, the priest prays over the village youth, asking God to bring the icon home. But with the passage of years—I fear it may just be an old wives' tale."

"And Tula?" Michael asked.

"Like you said, Mischa; my sister is very devout. I think she secretly hopes that the Virgin will one day choose her."

"And you, of course, would be the nobleman's son," Neill teased.

Pyotr was quick to reply. "There's no royal blood in my veins."

Christina was drawn in by Pyotr's story. She studied the tablet, gleaning other details. "Who wrote this? It doesn't read like a newspaper article." She scrolled to the top of the page. "Special to the Gazette, by Viktoriya Turandot." Her gaze fell on Neill. "What was the name of your journalist friend—that Ukrainian woman?"

Subtle, Michael decided. "I thought I'd told you."

"Refresh my memory."

"Viktoriya." The captain almost smiled. "Viktoriya Gavrilenko."

A polished nail tapped the screen. "*Turandot* is also an opera."

"I've seen it," he confessed.

"So you've said." Christina's voice was flat. "I wonder what the odds are—"

"The thought did cross my mind," Neill relented. "There have been a few attempts on Ms. Gavrilenko's life. *Turandot* could be an alias; something she's using while plying her ... doing her job." He cleared his throat. "Writing."

"Uh-huh."

Pyotr was intrigued. "You know this woman?"

"It's possible." Michael avoided Christina's stare. "We met once in Odessa. Her pose is—" he caught himself, "her *prose* is very similar."

"Yes." The staff sergeant narrowed her eyes. "Her prose is very similar."

There was an awkward pause, and Pyotr felt the need to step in. "These stories *have* excited Poland's interest," he admitted. "Who can say?" He thought it best to change the subject. "But enough of that; these treasures can wait. The day is still young, Mischa. What are your plans?"

Neill drank the last of his coffee. "I'd like to inspect a few of the emplacement sites." He was all business now. "Our national security advisor arrives in a day or so. He'll want an update on construction."

A nod from Stanislaw. "That can be arranged. One of the locations is thirty kilometers east of Olm. Another is near Lublin."

"I'd love to see the countryside." Arrens' mood lightened. She seldom got the chance to needle the Captain, but now it was time to get to work. "Can we rent a car?"

The Pole frowned. "You can—but I don't recommend it. Our roads are not very good. Especially at night; you can't see the potholes."

Michael wore an amused expression. "Just like Ukraine?"

"*Tak*," the lieutenant grinned back. "Just like Ukraine."

"Then what options do we have?"

"Trains," Neill replied. "We can probably be in Deblin in three hours."

"From Lodz, two and a half," Pyotr countered. "The express lines connect bigger cities. Tickets cost more, but are worth the price."

"And from there?"

"Tula can pick us up at the station." The lieutenant was genuinely enthused. He slapped his knee for good measure. "It's settled, then. We detour east to make your inspection—then cross the river to Olm."

"It would be nice to see your family," Neill allowed. "But I'd prefer to keep a low profile." He fingered the rank on his collar. "We should probably change out of these uniforms first."

"As you wish, Mischa." Pyotr faced the woman across the table. His tone was soft. "Did you bring anything warm to wear, Christina?"

It was Neill's turn for a little ribbing. "Clearly you've never carried her luggage," the captain grinned. Arrens' head came around.

"I'm sure she can find something."

Chapter Fourteen * Whispers in the East

PLA-Naval Division headquarters,
Beijing, China

EAST OR WEST, NO CHAIN OF COMMAND could escape the often impractical demands of its leadership. All hierarchies were subject to such taskings, and in some cases, these requirements were based on the whims of an uninformed brass. It was the job of those in the middle to sort through the petitions, to distinguish need from want; and invariably, making those determinations could displace the essentials.

Beijing was six hours ahead of Warsaw, and twelve hours ahead of Washington, D.C. The staff at the People's Liberation Army-Naval headquarters was nearing the end of another long shift. Busy days passed quickly; that was one advantage of a crowded schedule. On the downside—and every yin had its yang—it also brought home the fact that a considerable chunk of one's life had just been swept away and could never be replaced.

The key was to use that time wisely. Hours filled with the inane or superficial were a waste, and focus was crucial. Anything less bred indifference. It was important to find meaning in individual effort, and so it fell to the Chinese officer to follow a Biblical admonition.

"Redeeming the time, because the days are evil . . ."

That a uniformed member of Beijing's armed forces would embrace such a worldview was unusual. China was one of the last bastions of communism, and faith of any kind was anathema to its system of government. Adherents to Christianity kept their convictions without fanfare, pledging their loyalty on a very private level—especially those whose Party affiliations left them open to scrutiny.

The senior officer was not a man to squander opportunity. He was efficient and direct, and had risen to the top through diligence and the sheer force of will. Having a work ethic borne of his faith helped, but there were few who recognized the origins of his character traits. He was simply regarded as a rigidly moral officer, and many—even the Premier— mistakenly assumed that his love of the Party shaped his actions.

Captain Zhu Ling had quietly cultivated that persona. In consideration of his last posting, and the man to whom he once reported to, certainly no one would have pegged him as a follower of Christ. Since spring, a very different picture of the officer had been framed in the minds of his colleagues. During that time, a cadre of the senior staff had attempted a blockade of Taiwan, and there were whispers that Ling put a stop to their treason.

Toppling Xian Lee was no mean feat, and if the rumors were correct—and they were—then there was no doubt that the captain had been involved. Only someone with knowledge of Lee's intentions and the evidence to back it up could have exacted such an outcome. Ling was in a position to have both. It was an enterprise few would have attempted, but the senior captain had prevailed.

And now he had the Party Secretary's ear.

Not at this particular moment, however. Today Ling's docket was consumed by other matters. The secretary had retained him as adjutant, to the commander of China's Naval Forces in the Pacific. Zhu Ling's role was no different than before, but the man he now served was a far cry from Xian Lee.

"THE *Shandong* is delayed," Ling announced soberly. "The *Luzhou* and her escorts proceed apace. Her captain expects to arrive in Australian waters within twenty-four hours."

Admiral Wu Chang was unmoved by the ship's status. He checked his list. "Replace *Shandong* with the *Linyi*. I would prefer not to hinder the progress of this exercise." From across his desk, Chang directed a smile at his subordinate and added, "*Or* disappoint our hosts. Has there been further reaction from Formosa?"

"Taiwan has been assured that this collaboration is limited." Whether they believed that or not was something else, Ling didn't say.

"They are understandably concerned," Chang conceded. "Taiwan looks to the United States for assurances."

That was a bit understated. China's dalliance with the American Navy—even for something as innocuous as a humanitarian drill—had set the island nation on edge. Nine months had passed since Beijing's ships had encircled Taiwan; Party Secretary Chengdu had little regard for the American president, but even he saw the value in tamping down Western tensions after Lee's coup.

"Operating jointly is necessary for diplomatic relations," the Admiral continued. "The United States will not stop her march across the Pacific—this 'pivoting', as they are fond of calling it. Insulating ourselves from that encroachment would not be wise."

Naval interaction between the U.S. and China was rare, but not unheard of. Similar operations had been conducted each year. Chang had quietly advised that Chengdu accept the invitation to participate in RIMPAC—the Rim of the Pacific exercise—as a way of restoring faith in the PRC's intentions. It was a politically expedient move, and also quite practical in helping to assure peace in the region. For Chang, that was just a subterfuge; its underlying appeal focused on achieving harmony between superpowers, and masked the spiritual goals behind the admiral's suggestion.

Chang put that aside. His list beckoned. "And what of the *Yue Fei?*"

"She will launch on schedule," Ling replied. The sister ship to the ill-fated *Gansu Province* was being readied in the port of Qingdao. "Sea trials will commence with the new year." He paused, his gaze steady. "Admiral, if I may . . ."

Chang raised a brow. "Please, Captain."

The younger man passed a memo across the desk. Chang studied it for some time before speaking again.

"Is this a naval matter, Ling?" The former submarine master was making a point.

"It is not, Admiral."

Chang responded with a narrow smile. "I thought as much. I would be very surprised to learn that the Russians have ships between Bryansk—" he looked down at the report, "—and northern Ukraine. Why are you bringing this to my attention?"

"I felt compelled," Ling said simply. He offered no other explanation.

He didn't need to. Chang understood the meaning behind the captain's words. A believer within the ranks of the admiralty was one thing. But finding *two*—

"Assassination," the senior officer intoned. The word jumped from the page. Even more obvious was the report's origin. "This came by way of Third Department. A former colleague?"

"More than one," Ling allowed.

Third Department had achieved a nearly mythical status in the realm of intelligence gathering. The section monitored comm traffic from a list of nations, and their SIGINT network was the most elaborate of all in the Asian-Pacific region. Manning for the Directorate was rumored to be in the thousands. Zhu Ling had begun his career there after graduating from the linguistic school in Luoyang.

"So the Kremlin is running a new op." Chang reflected on the missive's content. The finished assessment was detailed but concise. "Has Third confirmed the principals?"

Ling nodded. "Based on intercepts tied to the western district. Since 2010, that region has included Moscow. Third sees a connection between the incident at Chernihiv and the Ukrainian reporter."

The admiral could almost imagine the linguist, huddled in some listening post, his ear pressed to a headset. "What makes this journalist such a threat?"

State-sanctioned killings were distasteful affairs—Chang knew that from personal experience. Presenting this news to the admiral meant that Ling hoped to find a receptive audience.

"For the past year, media reports have linked Russia with nuclear terrorism. Just weeks ago their president received a vote of no-confidence—and was removed from office."

Corruption bred some very imaginative tactics, and Chang knew it was best not to underestimate the Russians. "So I hear." He studied the communique again. "And this reporter—from Eastern Europe, no less—was behind that?"

"We suspect that she was."

"She?" Chang was visibly surprised.

"We also believe that she had assistance."

"Western assistance?"

Again, a nod. "Yes, Admiral."

"And what action should we take?" Chang was asking for a recommendation.

"We should monitor this. Third has the operative's alias, but I find that name difficult to accept. Do I have your permission to pursue this further?"

"Proceed." The admiral often deferred to the captain's good judgment. "It might be time for our accord to flex its muscles. And if this woman has accomplished what you say, then she has done her country a great service."

And then came the questions. They always did.

"Do you miss that life, Zhu? Do you miss Moscow?"

Ling smiled broadly. "There is enough intrigue in Beijing to satisfy my interests, Admiral."

"But what of espionage? Where does the future lie?"

Zhu couldn't say. The dissolution of the Soviet Union—so

long ago—had shifted the landscape of the spy game, altering the strategies of East and West alike. Changing fortunes made forecasting the future untenable; the present was enough of a mystery, and would occupy White Dragon's thinking for some time to come.

*   *   *   *

EUROPE'S RAIL LINES WERE HARD TO BEAT, Neill thought. After a short drive from the base, Senior Welles dropped the travelers off in Lodz. Michael bought three tickets at the station—his Polish was better than expected—and thirty minutes later, the trio found themselves headed east on an express.

Trains in the former Soviet Union were efficient, but certainly not plush. Poland's transportation system was a step up from most. The PKP, the national railway, operated a commuter line that was very comfortable. Neill and Arrens picked window seats, facing each other, while Lieutenant Stanislaw chose a spot across the center aisle.

The Marines made small talk as they took in the scenery. Winter had cast the woodlands in shades of gray and white. Outside, it was bitterly cold, and by the time they reached Warsaw, the motion of the car and the heated interior had lulled Pyotr to sleep. Christina gave Michael a grin as the Pole began to snore, but as the train turned south, she succumbed to the ride and nodded off as well.

It was only the second time Neill had seen her sleeping, and he took the opportunity to appreciate the view. The captain smiled to himself. He'd been right; Arrens had indeed found something for the trip, and he silently, but heartily approved of her apparel.

She was clad in a cashmere turtleneck and wrapped in a lamb's wool jacket, tailored for a decidedly feminine fit. The hood was trimmed in fox fur, and below, Christina's blue jeans looked brand new. The tan boots she wore went to her knees, and were worlds away from her combat footwear.

Michael's clothing was more simple. He wore a sweatshirt, leather bomber jacket, and a faded but comfortable pair of trousers. Pyotr was dressed the same way; both men's attire marked them as Central European, but Arrens' look was markedly different.

The most appealing aspect of Christina's appearance was her hair. Neill was used to seeing it pulled up; in a French braid, or some other style that kept it out of her face. At other times, she wore it in a pony-tail, but only for PT. Now it fell around her shoulders, and Neill found himself staring.

Snap out of it, he told himself. The Marine was enjoying the view far too much. He turned to the window, but could have admired her for much longer. His father's words came back to him; '*When God created woman, he did a great job.*' That was always followed with a smile—'*… and I got the best one.*'

* * * *

AT LEAST THE GPS WAS WORKING. VIKTORIYA checked it constantly and steered slightly east, away from Gora Kalwaria, on a course that would take her between Czersk and Garwolin . She was familiar with the region near the excavation site, but had never traveled further south.

The highways were as bad as those in Ukraine, but she never gave them a second thought. It was noon, and the sun had burned through the cloud cover. Her rental—a Dacia Duster—was getting warmer. She switched off the heater and adjusted her sunglasses. To the west, the sun's rays glinted off an express as it raced deeper into the countryside. Viktoriya had no way of knowing it, but the train's passage to Deblin—and her own journey—were about to intersect.

She looked at the dash clock, and then the GPS display. Plenty of time to make the appointment. The priest had agreed to meet her at three, offering a tour of St. Mary's. Viktoriya had worried there might be a language barrier, but the Father spoke Ukrainian quite fluently.

A look to either side told her that Poland was much like her own country. There was little to see on this particular stretch of road, but that wasn't really a consideration. She wasn't here on holiday. The journalist had a job to do, and she was headed to Olm to make sure that no one else got the story first.

To do so, Viktoriya Gavrilenko would have to travel back in time.

* * * *

NEILL WAS READY TO DOZE WHEN CHRISTINA began to stir. The train's passage south mesmerized him, and the songs he listened to had taken him to another place.

"Must've been more tired than I thought," she stretched, sleepy eyes meeting his. "I didn't do anything goofy, did I?"

"You want the truth?" Michael smiled.

She pretended to be concerned. "Was it bad?"

Neill hesitated. *Time to play nice,* he told himself.

"Not at all. In fact, you've never been lovelier." He meant it.

Her eyes widened, but she quickly adjusted. "Dear Diary; Michael Neill just paid me a compliment." She had an impish gleam and then changed the subject. "More of your dad's music?"

He removed his ear buds, showing her the player's small screen. "Made a big splash in the eighties and nineties. Ever hear of him?"

Christina shook her head. "Can't say that I have. Good stuff?"

"Great stuff," Neill smiled again.

"Is that a mullet?"

"Hey. It *was* the nineties," he countered.

"I think I'm seeing a pattern here." She decided to probe a little deeper. "Your dad was really special, wasn't he?"

The question was delicately framed. It stung, nonetheless.

"He was the best."

Michael drew in a breath and recalled his uncle's words. Maybe he *should* open up some. Squaring his shoulders, he sat back in the seat and lifted his chin.

"There was something else you wanted to ask."

Christina blinked. There were several ways she could have responded, but she wasn't going blindly down that road.

"I'm sorry?"

"In Ramstein. After you asked about my dad's music."

"I remember," she replied. So he *had* noticed. "I just wondered—about your father—"

"How he died?"

She flinched slightly. "If you don't want to talk about it—"

Neill quietly stopped her. "You're counter-intelligence. I'm surprised you don't know already."

"I've never been one to pry." That much was true.

The captain relented. "Maybe it's time I did talk about it." His gaze followed the scenery outside.

"Do you mind if I ask you something first?"

He turned back, and their eyes met again. "Go ahead."

Here goes. She started slowly. "I know the rules. You do, too, and you're always careful to avoid anything inappropriate. I get that. But when we're together, you've always got your guard up."

"Is there a question in there someplace?" He immediately regretted the comment.

"Look," Christina leaned forward. "I'm not asking you to go against your own code of conduct. But couldn't you let me in—just a little?"

Neill looked down, somewhat embarrassed. Arrens thought she might be losing him.

"Captain—Michael, look at me." She paused for effect, and then continued. "You're not alone. You have friends who care about you. The truth is, I care about you, too." *More than you realize*, she didn't add.

Neill felt like a dolt. He hadn't meant to be flippant.

"So—where was I?"

"Your dad."

"Right," Michael breathed. He glanced across the aisle.

Pyotr was still sleeping. "It was one of those wrong place, wrong time situations, when I was seventeen. There was a Chechen separatist, with a gun and an attitude." The words caught in Neill's throat. "He shot my dad during a political rally in Kiev."

Christina's hand went to her mouth. "I'm so sorry."

Neill nodded, his lips becoming a tight line. He looked up at the ceiling, and Arrens thought she saw a tear in the captain's eyes. She was hesitant to ask for more details, not wanting to inflict pain on the man she—

"Did they catch him?" The question spilled out, in spite of her best efforts to contain it.

Again, a nod. "Two days later, the Ukrainian Militia found a cell holed up downtown. They killed all five members in a firefight; one of them matched the description of the man who shot my dad."

"What about your mom?"

"She was already sick," Michael swallowed hard. It was difficult to tell, but Christina thought she saw his chin quiver. "Losing my dad—she never got over that." There was no mistaking the tears in his eyes now. "They're buried just outside of Kiev."

"Not in the States?"

He shook his head. "That was my choice. At the time it just felt right—Ukraine was their life's work."

"Pretty heavy decision—especially for someone seventeen years old."

"I didn't make it alone," Neill admitted. "The Ulyanovs were right there with me." He blinked away the tears, and a smile pulled at the corners of his mouth. "They were ready to adopt me on the spot."

Christina had never seen him so vulnerable. She leaned forward again, her own eyes misting. At that point the rules didn't matter. She slipped her hand into his and held it tight. It felt perfectly natural, and brought a measure of peace to her heart.

There was movement across the aisle. Christina released her grip. Pyotr cleared his throat, and the Marines turned to see the lieutenant rising sleepily from his spot. He pretended not to see Christina's gesture, but then grinned and gave Neill a nod.

"I'm going to the dining car," Stanislaw announced. "Mischa, would you, or your—*colleague*—like me to bring something back?"

"I'm holding out for mati's cooking." Neill had recovered his poise, and caught his friend's subtle jibe.

"Me, too," the young woman answered. Her tone held less composure than she would have liked.

Pyotr gripped Michael's shoulder as he passed, and Christina pulled a tissue from her purse.

"That was a little awkward," she drew in a deep breath and dabbed her eyes. "I hope I didn't—"

"No, it's okay," Neill replied. His tone was compassionate. "Don't worry about it."

"You've been holding that in for a long time," Christina noted. "What happened after that?"

The captain thought the conversation was at an end, and as painful as it was, he indulged the question. "The only family I had left was my uncle," he replied. "He came over and brought me back to the States. I stayed with him, finished high school and got an appointment to the Academy."

"And the rest is history."

"Something like that."

"And the day we arrived," Christina reminded him. "What did Pyotr mean—about your dad, and coincidences?"

The memory flashed through Neill's mind. "My dad always said that coincidences were simply times when God intervened—but chose to remain anonymous."

He stared into her eyes, and she didn't look away.

"Christina—" His voice was barely audible.

"Yes?"

"Thank you."

His words were sincere, and she could tell. The tears welled up again. "You're welcome."

Michael's thoughts went to Scripture. *"Bear ye one another's burdens, and so fulfill the law of Christ."*

"Sunday school—right?"

His head bobbed. "My mother's favorite verse." He looked at her in a way she'd never seen before. "You two would have gotten along very well." He was grinning now. The weight had lifted. "Do you mind if I ask you something?"

She was puzzled. "What would you like to know?" Her reply was cautious.

"Where did you learn to dance like that?"

The young woman blinked. "What?"

"At the ball. You were cutting a move. Where did you learn that?"

"*Busting* a move," she corrected. A quirky smile appeared on her face. "Did you like it?"

Neill's short laugh surprised her. "Honestly?" He was reluctant, but then spoke up. "I couldn't take my eyes off you."

Christina gave him a shrewd stare. "Are you flirting with me, Captain?"

He was anxious, until he saw her smile. "I just wondered, that's all," he said. "You were a natural—and I had two left feet."

That mischievous gleam returned, and she reached out and took hold of his music. "Well," she began, regarding the player, "while *you* were listening to disco—I was practicing for the school dance." She tossed the device back into his lap, and her face lit up. "I could teach you—if you'd like."

Christina waited for his response, and Michael grinned back.

"I'd like that very much," he said, astonishing the staff sergeant for the umpteenth time that day.

Chapter Fifteen * Reunions

Nikolayev, Ukraine

AS A FIGHTER, THE SUKHOI-27—DUBBED
FLANKER by NATO—had impeccable lines, and
looked much more elegant than any of its Western
counterparts—at least in the opinion of Russian experts. Its
aerodynamic features embraced fluidity, giving it an almost
serpentine appearance. At first glance the design was artful, and in the eye of the beholder, the aircraft had a graceful
quality that was hard to dismiss.

That was how General Andrei Ulyanov viewed the plane.
The one he was watching now was camouflaged in hues of gray,
white, and sky blue, matching the palette of colors supplied by
winter. A two-seater, this jet seemed to float in the air as the pilot
adjusted the flaps, descending on the runway that stretched from
one end of the base to the other.

Ulyanov turned from the window and back to his guest,
feeling a touch of melancholy. "We were friends, once," he
shrugged, and then a frown. *No, that wasn't quite right.* He
amended his statement. "Associates, at least."

There was something about Vadim that made it hard to call
him a friend. Andrei reflected on that. Greed was a particularly
ugly trait, and Mayakovsky's weakness for it had surfaced early.
Like most character flaws, that one had led to more serious de-

ficiencies—some criminal—and for the past two years, the former Army officer had been imprisoned for treason.

"And the Security Directorate has nothing to go on?"

"Just the cause of death."

From across the general's desk, Major Dmitri Yaroslav shifted in his chair. The red markings on his shoulder boards identified him as a member of the Strategic Rocket Forces, but of late, the younger officer had been partnered with Ukraine's clandestine services.

"No photos? No surveillance footage?"

"None, *Zheneral*," Yaroslav shook his head. "But perhaps that is telling."

Ulyanov's eyes narrowed. "How so?"

"It speaks to the professionalism of the assassin. This was an action with impressive tradecraft. He slipped in and out without anyone seeing him. And he used ricin to murder Mayakovsky—not the common killer's weapon of choice."

The general considered the attempt on Viktoriya Gavrilenko. The memory brought a smile. Sergei Holcek planned to use a pistol, until the Berkut unit stopped him. That Russian had been a clumsy oaf, but not so with the assailant who took Vadim's life.

"Then this was state-sanctioned." It wasn't a question. For Ulyanov, that was the only conclusion left. Which, by extension, meant— "Leonid Karpenko is behind this."

The major raised a brow. "A Russian undertaking?"

"That concept should not surprise you, Dmitri." Ulyanov's broad chest filled with air. "Do you know how many contract killings there are in Moscow each year?"

Yaroslav offered a humorless smile. "You seem well informed on the subject."

"I've come to expect such things from Murovanka's henchmen," he growled. The general planted his forearms on the desk; it was time to discuss something else. "And how do you like your new job?"

"I find it intriguing."

"More so than artillery?"

"Much more," Dmitri answered. "And not as loud. Perhaps we can discuss it over dinner. Are you free tomorrow?"

Ulyanov shook his head. "I leave for Warsaw in the morning."

"President Dobrogost's summit?"

The general grunted a yes, with a glance through the window. The very jet he'd been watching earlier would transport him to Central Europe. Andrei eyed his former adjutant evenly.

"I understand the SSD will be sending someone?"

A real smile now broke out on Yaroslav's face. "The Directorate will be well-represented," he announced. There was a self-important tone in his voice. "I leave the day after you."

* * * *

THE TRAIN TOOK THREE HOURS, PULLING INTO Deblin station at one thirty-five local time. The trio claimed their packs from the overheads and walked off the express; Pyotr led the way, and Michael had barely stepped onto the platform when the three were welcomed with a squeal of delight.

Tula Stanislaw fairly bounced into the Marine's arms, squeezing him tight and planting a kiss on his cheek. Tall and a little on the thin side, she wore a long, black coat that further emphasized her slender frame. Her sand-colored hair was tucked under a knit cap.

"I thought you'd be in uniform." She pouted, and before Neill could blush, she surprised Arrens with an enthusiastic hug. "*Dzien dobry; jestem Tula.* And you must be—I'm sorry—"

"It's Christina." The staff sergeant couldn't help but like the bubbly young woman. "Your English is excellent."

Tula seemed to bounce on the heels of her feet. "Not so good as Pyotr. But God is gracious, and I learn." She took Christina's hand, squeezing it, then leaned in to give her brother a peck. With a warm and friendly smile, she looked into each face and then asked, "Are we ready?"

* * * *

"NICE CAR," CHRISTINA SAID ALOUD.

Tula turned to the right. She was an aggressive driver, and they were jetting east now.

"You call them mini-vans, yes?"

Arrens nodded. The vehicle was an Opel, butterscotch in color, and characteristically smaller than an American model.

"It belongs to my brother," Tula explained. "He lets me drive it during the week." With one hand on the wheel, she reached behind and squeezed Pyotr's knee—getting a yelp from the lieutenant. "I *love* my brother!"

"Watch the road," Pyotr barked.

The Polish woman's personality was in sharp contrast to her sibling. There was a child-like innocence about her. Tula's affectionate nature was contagious, and brought a smile to Christina's face. She turned in her seat and gave the captain a knowing look. It was easy to imagine the crush Tula must have had on Michael as they grew up in Ukraine.

* * * *

VIKTORIYA WAS HEADED WEST. HER GPS HAD failed, and then came back online again. Unable to get a signal, a series of turns followed, and the navigational system directed her the wrong way.

But the journalist was not deterred; she pulled over and retrieved a map from the glove box. Within minutes, the little Duster had passed the train depot in Deblin and was back on the road.

* * * *

THE EMPLACEMENT SITE WAS TEN KILOMETERS distant. Crews had resurfaced the highway; the Polish government wanted to ease access for contractors. The terrain surrounding the construction zone was flat, bordering a marsh on one side and a forest on the other. Tula circled the encampment slowly, giving Neill a chance to inspect the workers' progress.

Christina snapped a few photos with her phone. Stacks of rebar sat behind a chain link fence; footings had been poured, and rows of electrical conduits were positioned nearby. Neill took note of the buildup, but it was hard to judge when the facility might be ready. A group of laborers watched the van curiously, and then continued using a backhoe to claw at the frozen ground.

"I've seen enough," Michael declared.

Tula glanced at the Marine in her rearview. "Where to now?"

"Olm," Pyotr answered for him. He turned to face his friend. "There's something I want to show you, Mischa."

TRAFFIC was light on the way to the township. A cold front had pushed south, bringing back a canopy of scudding clouds that blocked the sun. Twenty minutes after crossing the Vistula, Tula slowed the van and edged onto the shoulder.

"We have to stop here," she announced.

"Is something wrong?" Christina asked.

Both Stanislaws released their seat belts. "It's time to pay our respects," Tula answered, "—before we reach the village."

To the right, on the crest of a mound, was a patch of soil enclosed by a small iron fence. In the center of the space there appeared to be a memorial of some kind. Plastic bouquets and a few votive offerings lined the railing, and the entire scene was framed in shades of white.

A light snow had fallen, and it crunched underfoot as Tula exited the vehicle. She bounded around to the passenger side, opening Arren's door and reaching out for the Marine's hand.

"Hurry, Christina—I want to plead the Virgin's favor on you and Mischa!"

She didn't wait for Michael or Pyotr. Neill found it entertaining, watching as the wispy young girl tugged on Christina's elbow. Linked arm in arm, the two women dashed up the embankment.

"A roadside shrine," Michael observed. He'd seen several in Ukraine, but those generally marked the site of a tragedy.

"In Polish, they're called *kapliczki*. This one honors the priest."

"The priest?" The two spoke Ukrainian now. "The one mentioned in the newspaper story?"

The lieutenant nodded. "An ancient family wanted to re-member his sacrifice." He scratched his head. "I'm sad to say I don't recall their name—Nemscovik, Nilscovic—something like that."

Michael regarded the memorial once more. It did look old. Kneeling at the small shrine, Tula made the sign of the cross. Head bowed, she was fervent in prayer. Christina did likewise and knelt beside her. In less than two hours, the women had become fast friends.

Neill looked past the bend in the road ahead. Through the barren limbs of the trees he could faintly see a few buildings.

"Olm, I presume."

Another nod from Pyotr. He chuckled softly as he regarded his sister. "Tula will ask a special blessing on your visit. She's a very loving woman, Mischa."

"That's the Spirit of God within her," Michael affirmed.

Pyotr gauged his friend's response. "Please," he gave Neill a stern look. "Try not to confuse her feelings."

"That's not my intention," Neill answered. A glance over Pyotr's shoulder gave him a reason to change the subject. "Car coming. Maybe we should get out of the road."

The Marine stepped away, and Stanislaw did the same. Michael watched as the vehicle approached. He wanted to make sure that the driver saw them.

And she certainly did.

As the little Duster crept past, Neill could hear the engine downshifting. The vehicle slowed, giving the van a wide berth, and while it rolled forward, a dazed sense of recognition came over the captain.

"No way," he muttered, loud enough for Pyotr to hear.

"What is it?"

The car coasted just past the shrine and parked. Both men could hear the distinctive sound of the parking brake being applied, and then the driver's side door swung open.

* * * *

"MICHAEL?" VIKTORIYA COULD SEE HER BREATH in the air. She broke into a trot, nearly slipping on the icy surface of the road. Stopping mid-stride, she wasn't quite convinced by what she saw with her own eyes.

Neill was having a hard time believing it himself, but he stepped off in the young woman's direction. There was no room for doubt now. A broad grin stretched across his face, and the two met at the foot of the rise, below the memorial site.

"It *is* you!" Viktoriya couldn't contain her joy. She threw herself into Neill's arms with a laugh, hugging him tightly. *"Bozhe moi!* Michael, what are you doing in Poland?"

"I might ask you the same thing—Miss Turandot."

She braced, her eyes wide.

"Don't look so surprised," Neill continued. "Did you think I wouldn't notice?"

"My editor's idea," Viktoriya explained. Her arms were still wrapped around him. "And the Security Directorate— Michael, someone tried to—"

"I know. We'll talk about that later."

The Marine was pleased to see her, but tried to extricate himself nonetheless. He'd nearly succeeded, but the familiar scent of lavender surrounded the young woman. Viktoriya's perfume was a strong inducement to memory, and called to mind the time they'd spent together in Odessa.

* * * *

"Now who do you suppose that is?"

Viktoriya didn't wander far without an escort. The Ukrainian SSD made sure of that. A Mercedes followed the Duster and now idled at a distance.

"Someone known to her; clearly an intimate acquaintance." Xander Voskov released his grip on the wheel. "Two men and two women."

Yuri Tereshenko lifted a digital SLR from the console between them. He pointed the camera's telephoto lens and squinted through the viewfinder.

"The one with the leather jacket looks military. So does the other male."

"And the women?"

"A blonde. She looks like someone's kid sister—definitely not my type, boss." He gave Xander a grin and then continued his observations. "The brunette, on the other hand—"

"Get close-ups," Voskov barked. He wasn't smiling. "I want tight shots."

"Facial recognition?"

The captain nodded. "We'll run the images once we get back."

* * * *

The commotion by the road captured Tula's eye. Christina turned just in time to see the journalist press her lips to Michael's cheek. The two got to their feet, but not before Arrens felt an intense flash of—*something*.

"Your hair. It's red," Neill said, his voice flat.

Viktoriya raised an eyebrow. "How do women resist such charm?" Her tone was sarcastic.

The Marine tried to recover. "I just meant—"

"Oh, never mind." Viktoriya waved her hand and then squeezed him again. She was now aware of the other members of the party. She stepped back, subduing her enthusiasm until she could sort out the ties binding the little group. Her instincts told her that might be wise, especially when it came to the dark haired woman descending the hill.

"Who's she?" Viktoriya asked.

Michael was evasive. "Who's who?"

"The one with the daggers in her eyes," she answered.

"ANOTHER friend of Mischa's." Tula outpaced Christina, and her trademark embrace disarmed the moment. Hearing the journalist's greeting, she spoke first in Ukrainian, then switched to English for Arrens' benefit. She took charge of the introductions, putting everyone at ease with her simple ways, and the openness she displayed warmed even Viktoriya's heart.

Michael found himself at Christina's side. Her eyes narrowed, and she stared ahead—away from the parked Mercedes.

"We've got company."

"So I've noticed." The captain's voice was low. "A chance occurrence?"

"I doubt it," Christina whispered. She was now wearing a quirky grin. Michael had seen that look before.

"You okay?" he asked.

"Looks like this country's just chock full of coincidences," she muttered. With a gloved hand she pulled a tissue from her pocket. "And what's that on your cheek, Captain?" Christina stepped forward—toe to toe with Michael—and eyed the spot where Tula had pledged her affection. She dabbed at the smudge, feigning shock. "Is that a new shade of camo—or just lipstick?"

The humor helped to break the ice. There was a bit of a language barrier, but Viktoriya's English was improving. She caught on quickly. "On this side, too," she purred. With her index finger, she gently stroked Neill's other cheek.

Christina shook her head. "You might want to pace yourself, loverboy; who knows how many other towns—"

She couldn't finish. Tula started giggling, which spread to the rest of the bunch. Watching the women shower Michael with their favor, Pyotr nodded his approval. Neill's embarrassment was real, and it occurred to him that the remainder of the afternoon would be far more interesting than he could have imagined.

Chapter Sixteen * Blood of the Martyr

TWO RAPTORS LIFTED OFF THE RUNWAY IN Ramstein, banking east for the relatively short flight to the exercise area marked for RESILIENT EAGLE. The fighters climbed to twenty-six thousand feet and then cruised north to patrol the airspace above Poland's Warmia region. The province was directly south of the border with Kaliningrad, a politically annoying enclave of the former Soviet Union, and with no direct land ties to Russia itself.

After one hour on station, the F-22s were topped off by a lone KC-135, forward deployed from MacDill Air Force Base in Tampa. Four F-16s from Lask—Polish birds—joined the Raptors not long after that. The mixed group began crisscrossing their area of responsibility in an east-west pattern, their eyes, and radars, sweeping the northern territory for any activity fielded by the Russian Air Force.

The respective squadrons didn't have to wait very long. Their presence aloft was noted by ground-based radar installations near Chernyakhovsk . Thirty minutes later, the skies on either side of the border started to fill with the angular shapes of fighter aircraft.

Getting a little crowded up here. Christian Prentice, the American colonel flying lead, could easily distinguish the silhouettes of support planes on the horizon. The biggest of those was an Ilyushin-78, a flying gas station, currently providing fuel to a couple of Sukhoi-designed interceptors. *I guess both sides have decided to send a message . . .*

"They look like frogs," came a voice crackling in Christian's headset.

"Say again, JOLLY ROGER." The colonel's first thoughts went to the nickname given to the French.

"Like the ones you see in those shows about rain forests," his wingman replied. "All multi-colored and bright. Check out that dash thirty-four."

JOLLY ROGER's vision was unerring. The colonel's eyes gazed to the left. NATO had designated the Russian fighter FULLBACK. It was a sleek, twin-seat fighter-bomber that was designed, oddly enough, around crew comfort. And the pilot was right; squinting into the distance, Prentice could see that the plane was marked with distinctively bright hues.

Yet the color scheme was deceptive. Each Russian fighter carried air-to-air missiles on their wingtips. A fur ball in the skies over Central Europe was always a possibility, but that outcome was predictable. The superior weaponry of Alliance aircraft would no doubt carry the day, and the flying skills of his squadron were unrivaled. Compared to the West, Russian flyers got very little air time. Training was everything, and without it, going up against coalition forces was a recipe for disaster.

His comm went silent again, which was just as well. The colonel didn't want to caution his wingman about radio discipline. As it was, the senior officer had a lot on his mind. He'd been fully briefed days earlier, and the warnings about playing nice still rung in his ears.

That Russian general—Suvorov, was it?—had made no bones about threatening a new arms race, not to mention his allusion to a strike against Polish missile batteries. The flight lead shook his head.

If anyone needed encouragement to behave themselves, the Russians should be the first ones in line.

✳ ✳ ✳ ✳

FOR THE SHORT RIDE INTO THE VILLAGE—AND at Tula's urging—the three women had chosen Viktoriya's car. The arrangement created its share of tension. There was an awkwardness between the journalist and the Marine; the situation called for a buffer, and Tula's presence did help. Her excitement at having guests had grown, and she found it difficult to keep still in the seat behind Christina.

Few words were spoken as the Duster navigated Olm's narrow streets, but the disparity of language was only partially responsible. In Michael's absence, the subtle discord had only deepened.

"Park there, Viktoriya," Tula advised. She leaned forward, her arm extended between the seats. Her finger waved in the air, eventually pointing in the general direction of St. Mary's.

The car rolled into market square and came to a halt next to the church. Tula gave her new friends a chance, but neither seemed ready to ease the breach. As they silently reached for the door handles, she decided the two might need an intermediary.

She used English, then switched to Ukrainian. "Things might go easier if we found a common language." Russian was her first choice, but while Viktoriya was fluent, Christina recognized only a few words.

"German?" The women shook their heads. Tula was thankful for that; her grasp of the tongue was very poor.

Polish was definitely out, and Spanish simply wouldn't do. Her young mind raced. The list of options was growing short, and she was prepared to give up, and then blurted out—

"French?"

"Oui."

The same startled look from each face. Their responses came together, and the two were now smiling.

✳ ✳ ✳ ✳

Pyotr and Michael followed, finding a spot for the Opel a few spaces away. They sat patiently, but the trio in Viktoriya's car appeared deep in a discussion of some kind.

"What are they waiting for?" Stanislaw asked.

Neill shrugged. "Tula looks happy." He turned to his friend. "That's a good thing, right?"

"Good for whom, Mischa?" Pyotr grinned. "I don't envy your predicament."

Michael frowned. "I'm sure I don't know what you're talking about."

* * * *

There was an abrupt shift in the divide. "This could be interesting. Where did you learn the language?" Christina asked.

"Boarding school, in Donetsk. And the university in Kiev," Viktoriya answered. "And you?"

"With a name like Arrens?" Christina laughed. "Third generation French immigrant. I grew up speaking it." In the back seat, Tula was clearly pleased with the turn of events.

An unexpected option had just presented itself. "You realize this gives us something of an advantage," Viktoriya suggested. "As far as I know, Michael doesn't speak—"

"No, he doesn't." Christina turned in her seat, glancing at the parked van. "I think I see your point."

The two locked eyes. Viktoriya offered the Marine a friendly look—and then stuck out her hand.

"Truce?" She asked with a laugh.

Arrens regarded the journalist cautiously, but gave in.

"Truce," she agreed. Christina smiled openly and was practically giddy. "Now let's go have some fun."

"They're getting out," Pyotr observed. His eyes crinkled. "I wonder what's made them so happy."

Neill eased his door open. "I can only imagine."

Tucked beneath the shadow of the Romanesque abbey, the travelers exited the vehicles and moved toward the cobblestone sidewalk. Michael surveyed the streets, but the dark sedan from the road was nowhere to be seen.

The women laughed as Tula skipped ahead. "Mischa— you'll never guess!"

Neill's hands went into the pockets of his jacket. "What am I guessing about?"

Tula was at his side now, her arm locked in his. "Someone here speaks *French.*" Her palm was turned up, extended toward Viktoriya and Christina. "Isn't it wonderful?"

Michael forced a smile. "Fantastic."

"We can communicate, Michael. You should be excited," Viktoriya gushed, switching easily to Ukrainian. She reached out and pinched the side of his face. "Just think of the things we can tell each other now."

The captain's head bobbed slowly. "I was just thinking that."

PYOTR let the girls have their fun and then raised his hands and gestured broadly. "The Church of St. Mary the Virgin," he announced, "—and the heart of Olm. This is what I wanted you to see, Mischa."

There was magnificence to the small cathedral. The arched vaulting spoke of another age, a time when craftsmanship governed architectural considerations. Pointing skyward, the tower loomed above. The lunettes encasing the stained glass gave the chancel a breathtaking appearance, and even in daylight, the decorative windows dazzled the eye. The entire scene possessed a charm that evoked the past.

"It's beautiful," Christina allowed. She stepped back to take in the view, then gave Michael a warm look. No one else was aware of it, but the captain saw her whisper a silent *thank you*. He wondered what she meant.

Surrounding the little basilica—at a respectable distance— were the shops and businesses that made up the market district. These were clustered near the center of town, and were a hive of activity for the locals.

"Can we go inside?" Neill asked.

"The priest should be here," Viktoriya said. She looked at her cell phone. "I have an appointment with him at three."

"It is a bit cold," Pyotr granted. He turned to his sister. "Tula can lead the way."

Cheeks pink in the bitter weather, the youngest Stanislaw clasped the other women's hands and began pulling them toward the rear of the sanctuary. Neill started to protest.

"But the front—"

The lieutenant waved him off. "That entrance is never used, Mischa—well, *almost* never. I'll explain once we're inside."

Olm's priest met them at the back of the church. He ushered them in through an ancient portal, introduced himself, and graciously supplied the troupe with refreshments. It was a meager offering, however; the Father was a congenial host, but he had been expecting only Viktoriya, and not a party of four.

* * * *

NEILL STOOD IN THE CENTER AISLE AND STARED toward the front of the church. His eyes were fixed on the images flanking the arch. Carved from granite, the two seraphim appeared to guard the heavy door leading to the narthex.

"They used to terrify me, even as a teenager." The words were whispered. Pyotr was at Michael's side, quietly regarding the chiseled messengers.

"I can see why," Neill replied. Each of the angels held a sword, and resembled mythic warriors.

The captain turned, looking at the wall above the altar. Venerated in the center were two of the triptych's panels, undisturbed after three hundred years. And despite the passage of centuries, the faint outline of the icon's presence still remained.

Hanging along the rear wall were hundreds of rosaries.

These were clustered in groups, and crowded the space close to the remaining panels. Pyotr took a moment to explain.

"Those represent the prayers of the church, asking God to return the Treasure of the Heart." He shook his head. "There is always a chance, I suppose."

Near the altar, Viktoriya took notes while the priest relayed parish history. Tula was having a conversation with Christina, speaking in hushed tones. Neill smiled. The young woman was having a difficult time containing herself, and her voice would rise and fall in deference to the setting.

The sanctuary had a worn but thoroughly peaceful air. A diffused light spilled in from the windows facing west. Neill took a step forward, noting the splash of colors on the floor. One spot stood out. Just before the railing was an irregularly shaped stain; it was dark-hued, and blotted the corners of several stones centered before the sacred table.

Moving closer, the Marine knelt. He reached out a hand and drew his fingers across the floor's coarse surface. It was cold to the touch, and there was something about its texture that brought a chill.

Tula's animated chatter came to a halt. Pyotr was frozen in place, and both watched to see what Neill would do next. Even the priest was intrigued.

"This is blood," Michael breathed. The statement surprised him; his voice seemed to belong to someone else. He got to his feet, his brows knit together. "Old, yes. But it's blood."

The lieutenant gave Neill an approving and respectful nod. Tula was more expressive. Silently clapping her hands, the young woman beamed while bouncing in place.

Pyotr advanced. "This is where Father Jakob was slain, Mischa. The Swedes beheaded him on this very spot."

"Only the pure in heart even notice the stones," Tula gushed. "The eyes of the righteous are drawn to the martyr's blood."

The captain had stumbled into the province of legend. He wasn't quite ready to attach spiritual significance to what he saw, but it was hard to deny first impressions.

"No disrespect intended, but after three hundred years, how can you explain—"

"Who can say?" Pyotr shrugged. "The porous nature of sandstone; the viscosity of hemoglobin." It was a list he was very familiar with. "Or the presence of a natural spring, far beneath the foundation. I have heard all the theories. In any case, something has preserved it."

Neill turned slowly. "And what about the front door? You said it's never used."

"Almost never. And only on Christmas Eve." The Pole was intentionally drawing this out, adding a bit of flair to his presentation.

"Okay; I'll bite," Michael smiled. "Is that somehow related to Father Jakob, too?"

The lieutenant gave another nod of his head. "Nearing midnight, before the Mass, the priest slides the key into the door and turns the lock. And every year, it swings open on its own—"

"—allowing the spirit of Jakob Sobieski to enter," Tula finished. "It remains sealed for the next twelve months."

"Christmas Eve," Arrens whispered. "That's ten days from now."

Viktoriya had joined them, and Christina switched gears, explaining everything to her in French. She was barely done when Pyotr's expression brightened.

"There is one last commemorative you must see."

* * * *

THE GROUP FOLLOWED STANISLAW TO THE REAR of the church, descending a small staircase. This passage led through another wooden door, and beyond that, an arched portal to the outside. Standing on a stone patio, Pyotr waved a hand toward a snow-covered knoll, shrouded by maples.

At the base of the hillock was a hewn slab, standing upright and springing from the white drifts. Austere in appearance, it was hemmed in by rails and nestled in a quiet corner of the church property.

"A headstone," Neill announced. "Very old, at that." He heard a chuckle from his friend.

"By American standards, everything is old here, Mischa."

Michael gave his friend a look. "Don't forget that I'm a son of Ukraine."

"Point taken," Pyotr conceded.

No one else spoke. The air was clean and still, and the newcomers had a sense of reverence as they approached the grave. After a moment, Neill asked, "Father Jakob's?"

The elder Stanislaw nodded soberly. "Father Jakob's." He made the sign of the cross and Tula did the same. Standing beside Pyotr, Viktoriya used her tablet to capture a few images.

Michael edged closer. The image of a bearded man had been fashioned on the marker's face; a simple carving, worn by the years, but still quite distinct. In one hand, the figure held a carpenter's saw; in the other, he balanced something that looked like a church. His eyes were cast to the right, and seemed to behold a smaller, fortress-like structure that was chiseled at the base of the slab.

Neill began to interpret the symbolism. "The meaning of the tool is obvious," the captain said, conversing in English now. "The priest was skilled with his hands—am I right?"

"Woodworking," Pyotr acknowledged. "And also masonry." He pointed to the lower corner. "At the bottom—"

"Czestochowa?"

The lieutenant dropped his arm. "How did you know that?"

Neill shrugged. "He's looking down and to his right—to the southwest," he said. "The carving is primitive, but matches the shape of the monastery. Hang on—" A persistent whirring came from his jacket and he moved off toward the church. "Phone hasn't blown up all day—"

Christina looked at Tula. "What's Czestochowa?"

"The stronghold of the Pauline order," the younger woman answered. "The monastery was under seige on the night of

Father Jakob's death. The monks there were his brothers."

"What happened?"

Tula smiled proudly. "The priests fought off the Swedes." Her face became sullen, and she added, "Jakob never knew of their victory."

Neill slipped the phone back into his pocket, rejoining the group. "Text from Richard Aultman. BLUEGRASS is arriving tonight."

"Who?" Pyotr asked.

Michael smiled wryly. "Willis Avery—our national security advisor," he replied. "We should get going. Anybody hungry?"

Pyotr's sister pulled Viktoriya close. "Can you come?" She was speaking Ukrainian again.

"Not this time, Tula." The journalist was disappointed. "I promised my editor—photos from the crash site." The skies above were becoming gloomy again. "It will be dark in a few hours. I don't want to lose the light." She turned to Neill. "Will I see you again?—all of you, I mean. You still haven't told me why you're here."

"We'll get around to that," Michael dodged.

"Just like Odessa," Viktoriya chuckled, giving him a knowing smile. "Where will you go next?"

"Dinner's first. Then to Deblin." Michael saw Tula's face fall. "We'll take the train back to Lask. Tomorrow it's on to Warsaw. The State Department's booked rooms for us at the Bristol."

"Impressive." Viktoriya said. "I have an apartment in Warsaw. We've had so little time today—perhaps we can get together." For Christina's benefit, she repeated her suggestion in French.

Arrens joined the conversation. Her words were also in French, and she smiled. "I'm sure we can all find time for that."

Bryansk,
Southern Russia

POLAND'S MEDIA REFORMATION BEGAN IN THE

late eighties, following the dissolution of the communist regime. From an ideological perspective, it was easy to distinguish the roots of any number of news outlets, based simply on their editorial stands, and how they separated hard fact from opinion—or if they made any kind of distinction at all.

Print was the predominant news source, and the country enjoyed a rich tradition of newspaper publishing. Dailies and tabloids established during the Soviet era still existed, but many of those had been bought up by foreign investors. The recent crop of periodicals favored an independent tone, and reflected the heart of a more liberated Poland. And with the specter of the Soviet Union dispelled, profit had replaced propaganda.

At the dacha, Ilya Maersk was staring at the mastheads of several broadsheets, his palms planted firmly on the kitchen table. His eyes scanned the papers spread out before him. Each one represented a major metropolitan region. A few were opened to stories that continued inside. Maersk had pored over them for some time and the newsprint stained the Russian's fingertips; while the West embraced cleaner inks, the practice had not quite caught on in Central Europe.

REMORA muttered under his breath and offered an editorial opinion of his own. His interest in these pages was simply a means to an end. He was scouring their contents for clues, but was now mired in commentary. Ilya shook his head. These rags did nothing to disguise their political agenda, and it was clear that their editors had little journalistic integrity. Their essays were meant to sway readers, and in his view, their goals weren't much different from the institutionalized hype of the previous era.

Maersk swept that aside, and a smug satisfaction began to take root. His quarry had initially eluded him. She had vanished from Odessa more than a month before, but Ilya knew the journalist wouldn't stray far from her chosen path. This Gavrilenko woman was an unusually focused individual, honing her craft to perfection. It was inevitable that she surface eventually; Maersk had only to search for patterns of thought and stylistic interpretation. In some ways, her professional acumen matched his.

She was far too polished to rely on cliché, and her writing skills rarely employed echoing—the tendency on the part of amateurs to repeat common words and phrases. Viktoriya's prose displayed an evolving process, and simply scrutinizing small details wouldn't reveal her location. It was only when Ilya stepped back, taking in the bigger picture—

That was when he found her.

* * * *

IT WAS VIKTORIYA'S PRACTICED HAND AT STO-rytelling that gave her away. She could mask everything else, but not her style, or her consistent reach toward excellence with the written word.

Maersk moved through the empty rooms of the training camp, mentally cataloguing the items he would need for his next assignment. There was no need to rush the process. Most were already packed, but his new destination would require a few adjustments. Entering his personal quarters, his eyes were drawn to the Dragunov rifle on the wall. Exacting and lethal, it was the instrument of choice for many sniper operations, but far too much weapon for the mission at hand.

He turned instead to the corner, where a shooter's bag con-cealed a Mosin-Nagant carbine—an M59 variant—along with a cache of fifty rounds. That number would be more than suf-ficient. The bolt-action rifle was an older model, but still clean and capable, and Ilya was comfortable with its reliability.

Maersk had other resources at his disposal. Locked away in the armory was a package, much like the one he'd received be-fore traveling to Chernihiv. That, too, would become part of his kit, and put to good use should the rifle prove to be an unsuitable option.

There was another contingency to plan for. Sending the jour-nalist away from Odessa was only one step in protecting her life. The Russian had to consider that a security detail would be close by; a faction of the SSD, a military team, or possibly even one of Ukraine's elite Berkut units. Sergei Holcek had paid the price for his carelessness, but Maersk was well-prepared for any and all possibilities.

In his previous life, hidden under the mantle of a false alias, Ilya had come to admire the smooth performance of a Walther semi-automatic pistol. He had several to choose from, and selected a P99 sidearm, a 9 millimeter with a fifteen round capacity. He would supplement the weapon's firepower with two fully loaded, high-capacity magazines.

Transportation was also a concern, but Maersk didn't worry. The logistical side of the house belonged to his handlers, and they would supply everything. The following morning the dacha would be shuttered once more; REMORA's carbine would disappear from the corner, the armory would be emptied, and General Karpenko's assassin would begin his journey southwest to the city of Warsaw.

Chapter Seventeen * Warsaw

"EVERYBODY HAVE A GOOD TIME DOWN south?"

Senior Master Sergeant Welles was driving again, behind the wheel of 'Big Blue'. The eight passenger van was used for a variety of transportation needs by the Americans at Lask. Neill was to his right, with Arrens and Stanislaw in the seats to the rear.

"Very enjoyable," the captain yawned. "Good company; good food. And we got to see quite a bit of the countryside."

The senior sported his boyish grin. "You got in late, I take it."

Michael nodded. "The lieutenant's family wouldn't let us leave." He managed a glance over his shoulder. "We had to make a break for it."

"Pah!" Neill's comment had roused Pyotr from his fatigue. "The *serzhant* and I had to drag you away."

"The man does have a weakness for herring," Christina quipped. Her eyes were sleepy. "Not to mention Polish pickles."

"Which you just mentioned," Neill pointed out. The vents on the dash were pumping hot air. He leaned forward, warming his hands. "I'm also a sucker for black bread and sausage. Mati sets a fine table."

Mati had, indeed, gone all out. As in Ukraine, the kitchens of Polish families made good use of soups, breads, dumplings and vegetables—potatoes and cabbage foremost among them.

Michael and Pyotr had grown up on such fare, and enjoying a meal around the Stanislaw table brought back pleasant memories for both young men.

The toughest part of their visit was leaving Olm behind. Tula had shed a few tears as the trio departed. The women traded numbers, and Christina promised they would visit again before Christmas.

"We appreciate the ride, Senior," Neill said. He sat back in the seat, adjusting his coat. The Marines wore their service alphas, and the Polish lieutenant was also in uniform. Given the cold weather, Christina could have opted for serge green pants but chose to tough it out in her skirt instead.

"I wasn't about to let you take the train again," Welles boomed. "Station's not far from your hotel, but then you'd have to find a taxi." He shrugged. "They're not expensive, but hey, I rarely get to Warsaw. This is no trouble at all."

More than an hour later, Big Blue was navigating the outskirts of the capital. Welles steered east, rolling through the City Center—and relying almost exclusively on a GPS device fixed to the windshield.

Several shops had decorations gracing their storefronts. Approaching the Royal Route, the Christmas spirit was on full display. Christina was sitting behind Neill and took in the view.

"Is that it?"

Pyotr dipped his head and peered through her window. "No, that's the Victoria. You'll know the Bristol when you see her."

"Her?" Arrens turned, flashing a winsome smile.

The lieutenant tried to mirror her expression. "She is the jewel of the city."

As the van cruised *Ulica Krolewska*, Pyotr decided to be helpful. "Make a left at this intersection, *Serzhant* Welles."

The senior NCO squinted ahead. "*Krakov—Krakowsk—*"

"*Krakowskie Przedmiescie*." Pyotr was quick with the assist, and the voice of the navigation system chimed in for good measure.

* * * *

"OH, MY."

Christina was breathless. Stepping from the van, the Bristol's façade enchanted her. A light snow had begun to fall, and the Polish flag and hotel standard lifted in the breeze. "I see what you mean."

"She is even lovelier at dusk. Softly lit, with the colors of sunset gracing her face." Pyotr was in a good mood. "Just like a beautiful woman."

"Flatterer."

The Bristol's service was well known, and two porters instantly appeared to help with the luggage. Welles said his good-byes and eased the van back into traffic. The trio entered the lobby, enveloped in more luxury as they moved past the reception area to the front desk.

"Can you do this, Mischa?" Stanislaw viewed his friend with a critical eye.

Christina grinned. "Yes, *Mischa*. Can you do this?"

Neill smirked. "Buying train tickets; checking into hotels. Right up my alley," he answered. "Wait here."

The desk clerk became attentive at Neill's presence. He presented their IDs. The concierge wore the *les clefs d'or*—the keys of gold—on her coat, and her name tag read Lidia.

"Capitan Neill; Serzhant Arrens." She studied the photo on Pyotr's credentials. "Is the lieutenant a member of your party?"

"A last minute addition," Neill answered. He'd channeled that request before leaving for Olm. "Our State Department—"

Lidia switched to English, which was quite good. She looked at her computer. "Yes—I have a room for him on the second floor." The young woman lifted her chin, glancing at Christina. "Yours are on the fourth. And my compliments."

"Come again?"

"Your language skills. Most guests don't even try." She gave him a friendly smile. "Your Polish is—"

"—not nearly as good as your English," Neill granted.

Lidia circled their reservations on a floor diagram, and then activated three room keys. There was a pause. "Capitan?"

"Yes?"

"If you wish—" she hesitated, "—alternate accommodations *are* available." Her voice was softer now. "Adjoining rooms."

Neill didn't understand. "I'm sorry?"

"For you and the *serzhant*. With a connecting door." Her face reddened slightly. "For discretion."

"I see." Michael was catching on. He turned, and from across the room received an innocent smile from Christina. "But that won't be necessary. After all, the sergeant is a lady; we wouldn't want to stain her reputation now, would we?"

"Not at all, *Capitan* Neill." The concierge was embarrassed. "Please accept my apologies."

Michael became more serious. "There is one thing you might do."

"Yes?" Lidia seemed willing to redeem her missed step.

Neill held up the diagram. "I have a corner room?"

"Yes, sir; it's larger, a concession to your rank."

He rested his forearm on the counter and leaned in. "Could you make an exchange—switch our accommodations, give my room to the sergeant?"

"We don't normally—"

"Consider it a favor. To me," Michael smiled. "If you'd prefer, we could discuss it with your supervisor. I wouldn't want you to get into any trouble."

Lidia caught the implied threat. "I think I can comply with your request," she answered slowly. Using the computer, she made a few adjustments, and then slid their credentials and key cards his way.

The concierge watched as the captain rejoined his friends. The cut of his uniform and the way he carried himself was striking. It occurred to her that an honorable man had just checked into the hotel, and she was encouraged and disappointed, all at the same time.

✶ ✶ ✶ ✶

"YOU'RE IN THE BUILDING?"

Richard Aultman's voice was nearly a whisper, but his words came through loud and clear.

"Just checked in," Neill replied. "Where are you?"

"The presidential residence." The battery display on Aultman's cell was blinking, the consequence of multiple calls. It had been a busy day. "It's a palace; starts with an 'N'. I'm not even gonna try to pronounce it, but we're right next door. This place overlooks the Bristol, and vice versa."

"Mr. Avery's with you?"

"He's got me on a very short leash," Richard chuckled. "A lot's been happening. Some of the delegates are already here, and the rest are due tomorrow."

"I saw a few downstairs," Neill replied. He stood in the center of the room, his sea bag and luggage heaped by the bed. The clock on the nightstand read three p.m. "What's on the docket for the rest of the day?"

Aultman sighed heavily. "Briefings. Dinner with Dobrogost's cabinet at six. Be glad you're not here. Tonight's shot. Can you do breakfast—tomorrow morning at eight?"

"Absolutely. But my posse will be hungry, too."

"Bring the whole bunch," Aultman invited. "The Marconi's a good choice, and it's in the hotel. In the meantime, take the rest of the day off. Get something to eat, or go for a stroll downtown. And try to rest—we hit the ground running tomorrow."

The captain loosened his tie. That thought had already occurred to him.

* * * *

MICHAEL ENDED THE CALL JUST AS A KNOCK came. He opened the door to find a beaming Christina on the other side.

"Come see my room!" She took hold of his arm and pulled him into the hall. "I've never stayed in a place this nice."

Arrens wasn't exaggerating. The suite was quite elegant,

finished off in a blend of contemporary and art-deco styles. Corner windows faced two streets and offered a spectacular view of the city.

"I believe it's called the Grand." Neill had a pleased look on his face. He left the door open, his eyes sweeping the room's interior. Another man might have kicked himself for giving it up, but Michael relished in Christina's joy.

"Grand is how I'd describe it," she gushed. Her coat was laid neatly across the back of a chair. She kicked off her shoes, allowing her stocking feet to sink into the plush carpet. Her exuberance reminded Neill of the day before, and he eased toward the center of the living room.

"I was wondering—"

Christina took a step forward, loosening her neck tab and top button. "What about?"

"Yesterday; at the church." His eyes followed the contour of her face. "You thanked me for something—at least that's what it looked like."

"I remember. I was in the moment, I guess." She lowered her chin. "You didn't have to bring me here—I know that. But I'm glad you did." She found her smile again. "I just wanted to say thanks, that's all."

"You're not gonna kiss me on the cheek, are you?" He feigned alarm. "There's been a lot of that lately—maybe you should make an appointment. I think I'm free tomorrow—"

She stood inches away now, snarling good-naturedly. "You're impossible, Captain." Christina tried ushering him from the room. "Now get out—*sir*."

Arrens' bangs had come loose and were hanging in her eyes. Michael was amused by her actions, and the sight of the barefoot young woman was almost comical—and quite endearing. She pushed him to the door, and the two were reduced to laughter.

Neill escaped into the hall. Looking over his shoulder, he feared she might throw a pillow—or something more substantial.

Teasing aside, neither of them really wanted him to go.

Chapter Eighteen * The Eyes of Mother Russia

TELLING THE TRUTH WAS A BASIC TENET OF journalism. That cornerstone was linked to credibility, and credibility was the handmaiden of reporters. Without it, a fair and comprehensive accounting of the facts was suspect—and casting doubt on the truth was the quickest way to destroy trust.

Such standards were the least of Viktoriya Gavrilenko's concerns. Her bona fides were well established, and her peers and readers regarded the young woman as one of Ukraine's foremost journalists. Gaining recognition for those skills had come easy; but keeping it required a lot of digging, and that was what separated her from the rest of her colleagues.

And separate she was. The distinctions that marked her renown had also placed her in an isolated niche. By the age of twenty-seven, Viktoriya had outdistanced both associates and rivals. She had stoked her credentials by delving into the seedier side of human nature; specifically, the black market economy that fed the existence of so many across the former Soviet Union. Her accounts of corruption in high places brought a loyal following, earning every award Ukraine's fourth estate had to offer. They were also a boon to the ambitions of the editors she worked for. And while exposing illicit trade had secured Viktoriya's professional standing, it had also made her a target of those who profited from it.

She was pragmatic enough to take one problem at a time, and with her reputation solidly in place, Viktoriya focused on surviving her chosen career. Persevering under those conditions had become a distraction. She was frustrated by the inconvenience of it all, oddly detached from the potential for harm that came with it. Viktoriya's bosses knew that rationale defied logic, but crusaders seemed to possess a sense of invincibility. Valery Bukin had recognized that early on, and not even he could explain it.

Media watchdogs had noted 'negative trends' toward Ukrainian correspondents. That was something of an understatement. Violence against journalists—and editors—was rising. Threats persisted, and in some provinces the local authorities were slow to act.

Before the Ukrainian president came to power, opposition newspapers had been shut down by the government. Under Pavlovsk's rule those restrictions had eased. The real danger came from organized crime. Several reporters had died or gone missing, and many of those were from Odessa. An editor-in-chief had been shot dead on his way to a board meeting. More were found hanging in their apartments. These brutal attacks sent a clear message, and in hindsight, Viktoriya should have been more circumspect about choosing her assignments.

There was an irony to it all. In countries where the press enjoyed greater freedoms, journalists were less likely to stir the pot. Reporters like Viktoriya resisted the status quo, and were more willing to probe deeper—another paradox that defied explanation.

It was hard to hit a moving target. Not even Viktoriya could argue that point. She had uprooted her life on two occasions; first, to Odessa, the port city on the Black Sea. That was where she and Michael had met. Now she found herself in Warsaw, and the dashing American was back in her life.

Neill's presence had been a precursor to exclusives in the past. Viktoriya's life was always more interesting when the humble young officer was around. Still, she had her hands full covering the river excavations, and the background she'd gathered in Olm would give that story a fresh angle. Sacrifice, blood and treasure sold newspapers and increased readership. Viktoriya was more concerned for the latter, and if she could somehow find a romantic connection—

She ignored that for the moment. The media was abuzz with the news of President Dobrogost's summit. Like her associates, Viktoriya subscribed to alerts sent to Poland's press pool. An email had arrived just that morning, listing a timeline for events connected with the conference. Of particular note was a question and answer session slated for that afternoon at the Hotel Bristol.

Mention of that opulent landmark jogged Viktoriya's memory. She knew that Michael had accommodations there—Christina, too, for that matter, as well as the rest of the U.S. delegation—and his arrival in Central Europe hinted at something big.

A vague recollection surfaced; references to a land-based missile shield, a proposal that somehow irked the Russian Federation. Viktoriya chided herself for not knowing more, but she would rectify that.

Breakfast came first, and then a trip to her wardrobe followed. She would be very selective about today's apparel; the press gaggle was slated for one p.m., and Viktoriya planned on standing out among her peers.

To do so, she intended to arrive very early.

* * * *

XANDER VOSKOV STARED AT THE SCREEN. "HE'S Ukrainian."

"No, boss. He's American," Tereshenko countered. He enjoyed disagreeing with the captain from time to time. It kept Voskov on his toes, although the senior officer was rarely off his game.

"He's both," Xander grumped.

One block from Viktoriya's flat, a kilometer west of the City Center, the two men were accessing the SSD's facial recognition database. The link was tenuous, at best, and the retrieval system was a recent addition to the Directorate's resources, making it limited in scope.

Yuri read further. "A United States Marine. So what's he doing in Poland?"

"The summit," Xander ventured. "It starts tomorrow."

"In that case, we may see him again," Tereshenko clucked. He leaned in, scrutinizing the display. "What about the woman?"

"The dark-haired one? No hits," Voskov replied. "She's not in our system." He regarded his colleague with a scowl. "Put your tongue back in your head, *tavarisch*."

The taller man pouted. "I'm disappointed."

"You're a pig," the captain answered, the beginnings of a smile forming on his face.

"What man isn't, boss?" Yuri grinned back. "At least I have good taste."

* * * *

WILLIS AVERY ENTERED THE MARCONI IN CLASsic style.

As always, the tussled mass of hair on top of his head was a stranger to combs and brushes. His suit coat was wrinkled, and he wore a button-downed Oxford, with a four-in-hand necktie—slightly askew—cinched under his collar. Very little about his appearance suggested permanent press, but beneath his unruly cowlick was an intellect that often surprised both friends and enemies alike.

"I know, I know," he growled. "I'm late. Sorry to keep you waiting."

The big man's approach got the expected reaction. Seated around the breakfast table, Neill, Stanislaw, and Arrens got to their feet. Richard Aultman did likewise.

A few introductions were in order. "Lieutenant Stanislaw," Avery drawled. He needed coffee. "Neill says good things about you. Nice to have you on board." He turned to Christina, and his expression came alive. "Staff Sergeant; truly a pleasure. Your expertise will be needed, and you bring an elegance to our gathering that's most welcome."

A server arrived and filled their cups. "Everybody relax," Avery directed. "Food first, and then I'll give you the lay of the land."

A buffet had been set up on the opposite side of the room. The group scooped food onto their plates, and the intimate setting began to fill with hungry guests. Neill recognized cabinet officials from several Eastern European nations and a few from scattered points to the west. The presence of some surprised him.

Lithuania lingered over the bread cart. "The defense minister is fond of pastry," Neill observed quietly. He took his seat next to Christina.

"Look who's talking. And I'd go easy on those hash browns, Captain," she teased. "No PT for days, and your waistline—"

"As you were, Staff Sergeant," Michael advised. He sucked in his gut, and added, "I'm very pleased with my girlish figure." A grin. "You just keep all that elegance in check."

Christina gave him a sour look. "Behave yourself," she whispered.

THEY ate quietly, making polite conversation between bites. Avery finished first. He was ready to sail into his presentation.

"Let's not forget the importance of what we're trying to do here," he began. "In this part of the world, there's a shadow that lurks in the dark. It's been here for some time, casting its influence. The Cold War may be over—or maybe not—but you don't have to go far to look into the eyes of Mother Russia."

Avery's gaze swept the table. "You'll have to forgive me if I get a bit poetic," he grinned. "Talking about shadows sounds a tad dramatic, I know."

"But we live by the light," Neill stirred. "*Watch the flame,* my dad always said." His comment got a chuckle from the national security advisor.

"A spiritual application. Just what I'd expect from you, Captain Neill." Avery settled back in his chair. "Keep the big picture in mind, people. This was a good idea even before that Iranian missile business." He sipped his coffee, giving Pyotr a nod. "The Polish government is in our corner—but we have yet to convince the other players.

"The esteemed ambassador from Estonia, for example." His focus shifted. "That republic's roots go way back, all the way to 1918. They lived under Soviet rule. I was hoping for a more senior official; Mr. Rutan speaks for his government, but he's not a decision-maker."

Christina caught a glimpse of the ambassador and then turned away. "The Russians haven't helped. They signed a treaty with them but never formally recognized their border."

Avery was impressed. "And now they're part of NATO."

"And the European Union," Arrens pointed out.

"A trend that's given Moscow pause," Avery noted. "They don't like it when their former satellites align with the West." A glance across the room found the defense minister from Vilnius. The boss decided to test the young woman's knowledge. "What can you tell me about Lithuania?"

Christina drew in a breath. "A signatory to several international agreements. Also a member of NATO and the EU. They've butted heads with Poland—notably during the Moscow coup, back in '91—but everybody's made nice since then." Her mind raced. "And on the plus side, they've been pushing Belarus to strengthen their reforms—a positive step for Eastern Europe."

"A fair summation," Avery granted. He suppressed a smile. The staff sergeant sounded like Neill. "Where do they stand with Russia?"

She pursed her lips. It was an expression the captain had come to appreciate. "Tensions exist; some disputes over trade and customs practices. And there's a call to condemn the crimes of the Soviet era; occupation and annexation, namely."

"Which brings us to the subject of Ukraine," Willis intoned. A scowl hung on his face, and Neill seemed to wince.

Christina frowned. "More bad news, sir?"

"Story broke this morning. The cable news is all over it," Michael announced.

"Their neighbor to the north is exerting some pressure." Avery fingered his collar. He disliked ties. "Pavlovsk was inching closer to a formal alliance with NATO. Now he's leaning the other way."

Aultman joined in. "And Moscow keeps gobbling up chunks of their eastern provinces."

"On top of that, Russia supplies a great deal of their energy needs," Michael volunteered. "And it's winter—they could make things very difficult."

Avery continued. "Free trade with Europe has already strengthened Ukraine economically. Up till now they've maintained a non-aligned status. The Russians see this as one more move toward the West."

"But what about Poland? They're already allied with NATO," Christina protested. "And I thought President Pavlovsk was one of our biggest cheerleaders."

"Correct on both counts. But Moscow wants to keep them under their thumb," Avery replied. "They'd like to see Ukraine withdraw their support for the shield. If they do, the talks could collapse—and everybody would pack up their marbles and go home." He focused on Neill. "I need you to speak with General Ulyanov. Get his read on what Ukraine will do."

"I don't suppose we could go it alone," Aultman chanced. He was simply being hopeful.

It was Neill who shook his head. "For this to work, we need the cooperation of the other nations in the region. Ground stations, radar networks—a picket line of electronic surveillance. Without that, we couldn't hope to field an effective defensive system."

"So it's politics as usual," Pyotr spoke for the first time. He shrugged. "My country has endured such times before."

"I like your optimism, Lieutenant," Avery said.

"What's the venue for the summit?" Christina asked.

"The Palace of Culture and Science." The NSA weighed the looks on the faces of those around him. Neill returned his scrutiny with a question.

"Is that a political statement by Dobrogost?"

"One can only guess at the president's intentions. But I'd say that was a fair bet."

Only Richard was puzzled. "What's the significance of that?"

"The Palace was a gift to the Polish people—from Josef Stalin. He had it built in the fifties." Christina laughed softly. "Dobrogost is sending Moscow a message."

"How so?" Aultman pressed.

"The president has gathered the republics on our soil—to unify them, in a stand against Russian wishes," Pyotr explained. "The Palace was a symbol of Soviet domination, but the tables have turned now. My country is thumbing its nose at them."

"Poetic justice?" Richard quipped.

"Subtle, but pointed." Avery finished his coffee. "Let's get moving. We have a meeting at the presidential residence at nine-thirty."

"Karl Dobrogost?" Stanislaw's chin came up.

"Tomas Krol; the president's minister of defense." The group began pushing back from the table. "We'll meet in the lobby in thirty minutes."

"Want the car brought up?" Aultman asked.

Avery shook his head. "No, it's just around the corner—and we need to walk off this breakfast."

* * * *

VASILY BRESLOV'S FATHER WAS BORIS, WHICH meant that in formal settings, the younger man was called Vasily Borisovich. That was how the former munitions worker was addressed by his comrades in *Fraktsiya Krasny*—Faction Red—and it was also the name that appeared on Interpol's watch list of known terrorists.

It was only natural for Faction anarchists to blame a litany of woes on the West. Their current animus was sharpened by American 'atrocities' in Afghanistan. Breslov's own views were selective and completely myopic, and he was oblivious to Russia's involvement there more than thirty years before.

He had become more militant and disaffected of late. An ardent supporter of Russia's president, Vasily embraced the Faction's manifesto, an unimaginative and predictable document calling for war with Western nations. The cell was prepared to take things to the next level, and Breslov was more than willing to act as their point man.

For more than a week the media had reported the specifics of the Polish/NATO summit. Faction Red was far too isolated to take their fight to the West, but now they might not have to; according to the press, their target of choice was in Warsaw.

Fraktsiya Krasny's roots lay in Islamic extremism. They had identified Willis Avery as the most visible symbol of American aggression, and no one was surprised when the group convened a court to hear evidence against him. Juiced on their own rhetoric, the Faction's high council convicted Avery of war crimes and pronounced judgment. The verdict they rendered condemned the national security advisor to death, and they dispatched Breslov to carry out their sentence.

* * * *

Viktoriya's car moved north, edging past Warsaw University and the Church of the Visitation. She regretted not taking a taxi. Tourists would soon begin to fill the Royal Route, and finding a place to park might not be easy.

The skies clouded, giving her a chill. Viktoriya ignored the row of vehicles in front of the Bristol; there wasn't an open space in sight. She made a right-hand turn before reaching the hotel. Just days before—during Toussaint's press conference—she'd found a spot across from the Sociology Institute. Oddly enough, the same space was now vacant. She wheeled the Duster between the lanes and killed the engine.

* * * *

HALF A BLOCK AWAY, VASILY BORISOVICH WAS A passenger in a car parked along *Krakowskie Przedmiescie*. His driver was Yevgeniy Borla. Yevgeniy's father was unknown, so determining his formal name was out of the question.

The national security advisor's presence in the hotel had been noted in the morning paper. Putting eyes on that location was easy. A corner café offered an excellent view of *Ulica Karowa,* running east and west, and the main thoroughfare that tracked north and south. And then there were the Bristol's windows.

The first floor façade was marked by tall, glass portals that faced the avenue, offering an unobstructed look into the building. Seeing Avery and his entourage as they ambled through the front door would not be a problem.

* * * *

"I DON'T LIKE THIS," VOSKOV GRATED OUT. HIS eyes scoured the streets. "No place to park."

Tereshenko wasn't one to limit his options. He searched the length of Karowa, and then pointed the car toward a space reserved for faculty. Half a dozen vehicles separated the Berkut team from Viktoriya.

"We're too close," Xander warned.

"Stop whining—just act like a tenured professor and she'll never even notice."

* * * *

CHRISTINA TURNED TO FACE MICHAEL. THE two were the first ones back in the lobby.

"Dental hygiene?"

He offered a toothy grin. "Check," and then, "Uh-oh."

"What?"

"Pepper; or maybe sausage." He shook his head. "Between your front teeth."

"Is not," Christina fired back. "Now act your age."

"I'm an officer and a gentleman," he defended. "*Fseegdah.*" *Always*.

"Sometimes," she sighed, "—and I know what that means."

The elevator opened, revealing the rest of their party. "Everybody ready?" Willis boomed.

He didn't wait for an answer. The group moved forward. Two agents braced at the far side of the room. As the national security advisor came near, they peered through the windows, surveying the building's exterior.

Avery pushed ahead; Neill couldn't get in front now. He inserted himself directly behind and followed the big man to the exit.

* * * *

"THEY'RE COMING OUT."

Breslov's heart raced; he couldn't believe their good fortune. Gripping the handle, he threw his shoulder against the door frame. "Time to deliver justice."

Borla was both somber and resolved. *"Insha'Allah."*

Exiting the car at the same time was a tactical error. It attracted too much attention—and there was something awkward about Breslov's movements.

Borla's pace was too hurried to be casual. The lead agent should have seen it sooner, but he was momentarily distracted by the red-headed woman advancing from his left.

* * * *

"SHE'S IN THE OPEN."

An odd foreboding tugged at Voskov. The hair on the back of his neck went up, and he quickened his steps. And something just ahead—

"Yuri—!"

"I see it, boss," Tereshenko snapped.

Xander's caution was not misplaced. There were times when a coat was just a coat, but to the captain's practiced eye, the apparel worn by the bearded men was out of place. The lapels of each were open, and the arms of both strangers were briefly concealed in the heavy poplin.

BRESLOV pulled back his trench, revealing a weapon. The fabric caught on the rifle's front sight post. Vasily jerked it free and hefted the AKM to his shoulder. Yevgeniy was also armed, and did the same, but neither man wanted to risk missing their target.

That was their second mistake.

* * * *

"GUN." YURI'S WARNING WAS MATTER OF FACT. "Boss—get the girl!"

He pushed Xander in Viktoriya's direction and raced ahead, his long legs propelling him into harm's way. Voskov didn't argue, and each man dashed to the corner.

* * * *

THE SECOND AGENT BROUGHT UP HIS SIG, BUT acted too late. He raised the service pistol just as Borla squeezed off a burst. Impacting his mid-section, the rounds knocked the officer to the pavement before he could return fire.

The lead member of the detail had more time to react. He brought his weapon to bear on Yevgeniy first; one slug struck his chest, while the second entered his skull, killing Borla instantly. The exit wound was not a pretty sight

Screams came from the street. Some ran for cover; others were frozen in place. Breslov ignored the din and focused on the shooter before him. He pulled hard on the trigger. Three rounds struck the agent center mass, dropping him to the sidewalk. Two more went high, chipping granite from the Bristol's façade. He directed his aim toward the entryway, spraying another five round burst, but these went over Avery's head, shattering the windows above the entrance.

NEILL acted instantly. Reaching forward, he took hold of Avery's overcoat and pulled him violently to the rear. As the two fell backward, broken glass cascaded around them. Before landing in a heap, the Marine collided with Arrens and Stanislaw, sending them rudely to the deck.

* * * *

WITH AVERY'S PROTECTORATE SIDELINED, Vasily was free to complete his mission—or so he thought.

Marching forward, Breslov cradled his weapon at the waist, pointing the end of the barrel where his target had fallen. Neill could do little more than place his body over Avery's. He was prepared to charge the shooter, but then his vision clouded as a dark fluid filled his right eye.

Viktoriya tensed as the world exploded. Even with the chaos around her, she knew that moving forward was a bad idea. One gunman was down, and the other was unaware of her presence. The journalist started to retreat—but her efforts were thwarted as she was tackled from behind.

* * * *

BRESLOV'S HEAD SNAPPED TO THE RIGHT, AND he saw Xander Voskov diving toward Viktoriya. The sight was impressive; the rescuer wrapped his body around the woman, twisting in flight and landing on his back. The impact forced the air from his lungs.

The surviving member of the Faction hit squad returned his gaze to the front of the building. The image greeting his eyes startled him, and in the space of a heartbeat the gunman hesitated.

✴ ✴ ✴ ✴

"STAY DOWN!"

Neill could only see with his left eye. A sharp pain came from the top of his head, and the two conditions left him dazed. Avery stirred and glass crunched beneath him, but the captain managed to keep him from rising. As he tried clearing his vision, Neill heard the sound of a slide being released on an M45 semi-automatic.

Stanislaw started to get up, his hand clutching the holster on his belt. *"Mischa!"* There was no response.

Aultman did a swift low crawl toward Neill and Avery. Arrens was on her feet now, stepping across the figures lying prone in the sea of glass. Her arms were extended, and she held a Colt 1911 with the business end aimed squarely at the attacker's chest. Her finger moved from the dust cover to the trigger; she was preparing to squeeze when Yuri Tereshenko burst onto the scene.

It was indecision that robbed Breslov of success. The tall Ukrainian hit low and hard. He and the Russian tumbled across the flagstone, the rifle clattering out of reach. The two rolled to a stop. Yuri took a knee, pinning the shooter to the ground, and a stunned silence hung over the street.

The security detail began to move. Shocked but unhurt, they had been protected by their vests. The agents gripped their sidearms and got unsteadily to their feet.

Christina's eyes and hands swept the area. She led with the pistol's muzzle. Her priority was in judging the threat; one of the assailants was clearly dead, and the other lay subdued near the street. To her left was a woman who looked remarkably like Viktoriya Gavrilenko. On closer inspection—

"Christina!" It was Michael's voice. He reached out, his hand gripping her leg.

That's a first, she thought dryly.

"We're clear." Arrens relaxed, but didn't drop her guard.

The captain recovered, crouching over the national security advisor. He pulled Avery into a sitting position. Small chunks of glass fell from each man as they got up.

"You hurt?" One eye was screwed shut, but Neill gave his charge a quick once-over. He was pleased to see that the man in the ruffled suit was uninjured. The sound of sirens came from blocks away.

"I'm fine." Avery's face was a portrait of surprise. He looked at the Marine. "Good Lord, Neill, you've been hit."

Arrens dropped her gaze. "Oh, God—"

MICHAEL touched his scalp; it was wet with blood. More covered the right side of his face, and there was a dull ache at the top of his head.

"Doesn't feel like I've been hit. But I think I'm bleeding—"

"Really, Captain Obvious?" Christina was kneeling. She put her weapon down and ran her fingers through Michael's hair. She stopped, pulling a shard of glass from his broken skin.

Avery provided his handkerchief. "Here—take this." Arrens pressed the material against the wound.

"Hey," Michael resisted her probing touch. "Go easy up there."

"Shut up," she ordered. Pyotr was now at her side. "I need to see how bad this is. Lieutenant, go check on Viktoriya."

"She's here?" Stanislaw was up and took off past the columns on either side of the entrance. More agents had come out of the woodwork and followed closely behind.

Christina clasped Michael's head in her hands, feeling his neck and skull. She ran a thumb gently over his eyelid. "Now follow my finger."

Neill did as he was directed. His responses were good, and his pupil reacted briskly.

"What's your diagnosis, doc?"

"I think you'll pull through," Arrens replied. Her hands had started shaking.

Neill's hair was tussled. He held one eye closed, and his features were marred with blood as it dried. A few dark splotches could be seen on the front of his uniform.

"You're a mess," Christina observed.

Neill flashed a grin. "But a squared-away mess, right?"

Beijing, China

"THIS IS BAD, CAPTAIN." THE THIRD Department operative had a disturbed look. He held a scrap of paper before Ling. "This is *very* bad."

The senior officer inspected the name on the missive with a frown. Third's chief responsibility was gathering intelligence, but they had very capable analysts, and the captain wasn't about to second-guess their current assessment.

"Confirmation," Ling muttered. He'd been afraid of this, but not surprised. Now there was no doubt. The Directorate had an elaborate metadata and telecom network. While the United States could only see the tip of the iceberg—or so they claimed—Third's abilities went much deeper.

Ling glared at the memo. The evidence was irrefutable. Third Department wouldn't publish such a bold conclusion if it wasn't, and SIGINT—Signals Intelligence—had corroborated the intel. The first clue was the one-sided nature of the traffic. The primary used sophisticated equipment, with an encryption hierarchy that suggested nation-state involvement—undeniably Russian.

The secondary, on the other hand, was nothing if not primitive; the Directorate had identified that one easily enough, tracing it to Bryansk. The contact there relied on a pre-paid phone, but only as a storage system for messages. It was a pattern of behavior that fit the target's profile; sometimes hours would pass before the communiques were retrieved, a clear indication that the user rejected current technology and wasn't tied to his mobile.

"Walk me through your sources," Ling instructed. He was interested in the provenance of the information.

"Moscow was sloppy," the junior operative answered. "Their agent proceeded from Sverdlovsk; we ascertained that from their earliest communications. It took some time, but with a point of origin, we were able to work backward to establish an identity."

"REMORA," Ling observed woodenly. "I thought him dead."

A mournful expression. "The British tried that," Third replied. "They failed, but not for lack of effort."

"Where is he now?"

"There have been no exchanges for days."

"Then he's on the move," the captain decided. He could guess the destination. "Is the woman still in Warsaw?"

The operative nodded. "It might be helpful to warn her." The man looked pained. "Ilya Maersk has never failed, Captain."

Ling grunted. "MI6 must have a file. Can you get it?"

A shake of the head. "Only portions. Vauxhall Cross has security almost as good as the Americans. They're using OVERTURE now. We haven't been able to crack that."

"Phone records?"

Third produced a folder. "The REMORA intercepts comprise the bulk of this report. The Ukrainian's list has been collated on the top sheet. May I?" He opened the dossier and traced a finger down the page. "She's made a few calls to Russia. All of her other contacts are in Eastern or Central Europe. Except for this one—" he stopped toward the bottom, "—an American."

The captain's eyes widened and moved to the column on the right side. "And this is his number?"

Another nod. "We have also determined his location, Captain. He, too, is in Poland."

That was unexpected news, and sent Ling's thoughts elsewhere.

"Years ago, REMORA was involved in another operation." His pad came out, and he jotted something down. "Do you have someone who can confirm this?"

The operative read what Ling had written. He compared it to the transcripts in the dossier. The last names on both sheets were identical.

"Are these men related in some way?"

Ling didn't answer. His course of action became clear, but he would need time to put it in place. "Set up a secure line. To the American's phone. Can you arrange it?"

A rueful smile replaced Third's dour expression. "So you do intend to warn her."

Zhu Ling planned to do more than that. He gave his subordinate a purposed stare. "If at all possible, the People's Republic will interrupt REMORA's plans—and save this woman's life."

Chapter Nineteen * Close Call

ULICA KAROWA WAS STILL OPEN, BUT THAT wouldn't last. Voskov and Tereshenko had slipped away and returned to their vehicle. Yuri slid behind the wheel and gunned the motor, then backed the car into the street.

"Which way, boss?"

"Anywhere but here," Xander ordered. "Make for the river. Then we'll circle back and wait."

Yuri made a hard right. There was an incline ahead and the Mercedes climbed the Markiewicz Viaduct. The road corkscrewed before heading east toward the Vistula. Safely away from the Policja's focus, Tereshenko glanced at his superior.

"She reminds you of Anya, doesn't she, boss?"

Yuri was out on a limb. He almost regretted the question, half expecting Xander's wrath. But the captain was thoughtful. He sat quietly for a moment, and his sigh was all the answer Tereshenko needed.

* * * *

LAW ENFORCEMENT ARRIVED FIRST; SOME ON foot, but the majority in blue and silver Astras, standard livery of the *Policja Kryminalna*. These were followed by no fewer than three emergency vehicles. Red and white lights soon flashed everywhere, and within minutes the responders had cordoned off the block and halted all traffic in front of the hotel.

Falling glass had caused Neill's wound, not a stray round. He sat in an ambulance while an EMT tended to his injury. The captain's language skills served him briefly, but after a few puzzled looks, Neill waved Stanislaw over to translate. They traded words and then Pyotr turned to Michael.

"It's a deep laceration, Mischa, but not serious. Nine centimeters in length." He chuckled. "Fortunately, your wound affects the least vulnerable part of your body."

"Very funny," the Marine replied. Michael's coat had been removed, and his tie and collar loosened. Splotches of dried blood could be seen on his shirt and more covered the right side of his face. "Where's Christina?"

Stanislaw looked back toward the hotel entrance. "She's checking on Viktoriya." He turned, an appreciative look on his face. "She bought us some time, and your boss is alive because of her actions."

"She did good," Michael said proudly.

"And you helped," Pyotr admitted.

The color had returned to the captain's cheeks. "Maybe a little."

"A word of advice?"

"Go ahead," Neill answered.

The lieutenant now wore a crafty expression. "Don't make that one mad."

THERE was activity everywhere. The Policja worked the scene, clustered in groups, and investigators took statements from witnesses. The American contingent did the same. Borla's body lay covered with a sheet, and the surviving shooter had been carted away. A crowd in dark suits had joined the party; burly men for the most part, and all with serious casts. Undoubtedly a security team from the presidential residence, Neill judged.

The local constabulary had frowned on Christina's sidearm. They complained at length until Avery exerted some diplomatic influence. After that, they dropped the matter and turned their focus back to the perpetrators.

The Marine could see Avery and Aultman near a second ambulance. Both men appeared calm and were surrounded by agents of the Secret Service. Michael whispered a prayer of thanks as the EMT began cleaning the blood from his face.

"Anybody else get hurt?"

Pyotr eyed the body in the street. "No one of consequence."

Neill touched his scalp. His hair was matted. "Stitches?"

More dialogue from the tech. "Staples," Pyotr translated. "Four should close the wound." He could see the two women moving in their direction. "We can do it here or go to the hospital."

Michael shook his head. "No hospital. I don't have time for that."

Pyotr gave the paramedic a nod.

"Who were those guys, anyway?" A whole list of questions flooded Neill's mind.

"An ultra-nationalist group," Stanislaw answered. "Faction Red, most likely. Oh, and you're going to feel a slight pinch."

The paramedic gave Neill two injections of lidocaine.

"*Ouch*—that stuff stings."

"Stop complaining. You sound like an old woman. Okay, Mischa, we do this on three—"

"There were two others. The guy who jumped the shooter. And the one who grabbed Viktoriya." Michael scanned the crowd. "Where did they go?"

Pyotr frowned. "I haven't seen them since the police arrived."

"Neither have we," Christina told them.

"Are you two all right?" Neill asked.

Viktoriya looked the worse for wear. Despite two attempts on her life, the day's events marked the first time she had come face to face with an armed assailant.

"One—" Pyotr began.

"We're fine," Christina spoke for both women. "Viktoriya's a little shook up." Arrens put her arm around the journalist and gave her a squeeze. Michael found her compassion touching.

Viktoriya was trembling, a combination of nerves and the frigid temperature. She laid a hand on the captain's knee and managed to find a smile. "Never a dull moment with Michael around."

"Two—"

Neill suddenly felt pressure, but no pain.

"You didn't say three."

Pyotr shrugged. "I lost count."

"What a big baby," Arrens grinned.

*   *   *   *

THE POLICJANT BRACED. TWO MILITARY MEN stood before the barricade, each wearing Ukrainian uniforms. The officers presented their credentials and marched past before the patrolman could stop them.

"Why am I not surprised to find you involved in this fracas?" Andrei Ulyanov's voice boomed in Neill's ears. "What have you done now, little Michael?"

Neill grinned at the sight of his old friend. "Nothing you wouldn't have, *Zheneral*." The captain hopped down from his seat. He shook hands with Major Yaroslav, and then embraced Ulyanov warmly. "It's about time you got here."

IT took a few minutes to put faces with names. After introductions were made, Neill began to explain the morning's events. Ulyanov expressed concern, but seemed more interested in something else.

"Would you excuse us?" The general controlled the group with the poise of a master.

"The captain and I have an urgent matter to discuss."

* * * *

"WHAT'S UP?"

Neill, Ulyanov and the major had found a quiet patch of sidewalk for their discussion.

"Vadim Mayakovsky is dead, Michael." The general's statement was delivered flatly. "He was poisoned."

It took a moment for the name to register. "Mayakovsky. The major who helped steal the nuke. When did this happen?"

"More than a week ago. A professional job," the general emphasized.

"Assassinated." Michael touched the top of his scalp. The staples felt odd. "Any idea who did it?"

"None, but I can guess who's behind it," Ulyanov replied, "—as well as their motives."

"Murovanka. Or Karpenko," Neill wagered. "Maybe both."

Ulyanov nodded. His young friend was catching on.

Dmitri spoke up. "And Viktoriya's life has been threatened—on two occasions."

"You think it's all connected?" the Marine asked.

"Can there be any doubt?" Andrei snorted. "Michael, the Russians have been stung. Your plan has worked all too well. Now they want to clean things up and move on." His eyes drifted toward the young woman in the crowd. "Viktoriya is in their sights now. Simply moving her from one location to the next isn't going to work much longer. And given all this—" he gestured toward the street.

Neill shook his head. "They were gunning for Avery." He turned to Yaroslav. "Have you two checked in?"

Dmitri shook his head. "Our cab is down the street." He smiled. "Along with our luggage."

"What about Irina? Is she coming?"

"She promised she would," Ulyanov grinned. "But only if all parties agree to the treaty."

✻ ✻ ✻ ✻

AULTMAN PUSHED THE PRESS CONFERENCE back to four p.m. In light of the circumstances, no one objected. The hotel staff made swift work of cleaning up the damage. Broken shards were quickly removed, and a glass company had already arrived to measure for the replacement panes.

Breslov and Borla's brass casings were collected by the Policja as evidence. The scene was photographed extensively. It took time, but eventually the crowds dispersed, the barricades were removed, and life returned to normal along Krakowskie Przedmiescie.

It was turning colder, and the hotel's guests filtered back inside where it was warm. Most were shaken. Arrens took Viktoriya to her suite for a chance to freshen up. Pyotr escorted the women to Christina's door while Michael returned to his own room.

THE captain's hair was thick with betadine solution. He stripped out of his uniform and jumped into the shower. The wound was swollen, but the injections had done their work. He managed to wash out the remaining traces of blood and felt no pain in the process.

He emerged from the stall and toweled off. His shirt and coat were next. He rinsed both, and then used a brush on the stains, filling the sink with water. Neill was about to pull an ice tray from the freezer when he heard a knock.

"Just a minute."

Michael slipped off his robe and put on a white t-shirt and a pair of jeans. He opened the door to find Christina on the other side.

"Just wanted to check on things," she smiled. "Are you feeling okay?"

"I'm fine," Neill grinned back. "What about you?"

He'd posed that question several times; in the lobby, on the elevator—

"Not even a run in my hose," she answered.

He remembered his manners. "Come on in. I was just about to soak my blouse."

She stepped through, and Neill closed the door. He could smell her perfume as she passed. "I read somewhere that cold water's best," he said. "Probably the officer's manual."

"That's my captain. Always by the book." Christina found his shirt on the chair. "This isn't so bad. How's your coat?"

Michael's eyebrows went up. "It's a little worse. There's some club soda in the fridge; I was going to try that, or maybe some peroxide."

She was smiling again. "Who travels with peroxide?" She found the ice tray and dumped the cubes in the sink. "The soda's not a bad idea, but let's soak it in water first. Make sure the stains don't set. And I'll bet the hotel has dry cleaning— we can take it downstairs later." She immersed the shirt collar and moved away from the basin. "Can I see your boo-boo?"

"Excuse me?"

"Your cut. Does it hurt?"

"I've had worse." Michael stepped closer, and then sat on the arm of the couch. "Hey, I wanted to ask you something."

"Shoot." Arrens was standing over him now, delicate fingers probing his scalp. Her other hand rested on the back of his neck, and Neill found her touch to be the most pleasant sensation of the day. "What's your question?"

"I knew you brought a sidearm; but where did you get that cannon?"

"The Colt?" Christina laughed softly, lingering over the injury. The two had never shared this much physical contact, and they were both starting to enjoy it. "That was Ethridge's idea. I've been keeping it in my purse."

"Not exactly standard issue." Michael got to his feet, and Christina didn't step away. They were facing each other. "Don't get me wrong; you saved some lives today."

She was blushing fully now. "You didn't do so bad your-self." Christina's voice was a whisper. She dropped her head, and her bangs came loose, falling into her face. "I'm just glad you're all right. You gave me quite a scare. All that blood—"

Neill wanted to reassure her. He gently touched her chin and lifted her head. Somehow they had moved closer. Using his index finger, he brushed aside the strands of her hair. His actions now were completely spontaneous.

Michael felt warm. He said nothing, and Christina didn't utter a sound. Each was lost in the moment. She caught the scent of cologne on his palm and drank it in. Their faces were just inches apart.

"Christina," Neill swallowed hard.

Her cheeks felt hot. "Michael—" *Don't do this,* she told herself. "Captain; your door—"

Neill wasn't listening. His fingertips rested against her temple. She closed her eyes and didn't resist, bringing her hand up and laying it on his, then pulling back as if stung.

"I should go—"

Both Marines had regained their composure.

"I think you're right." Neill stepped aside. "You need to check on Viktoriya. See how she's doing."

Arrens headed for the hall. Reaching the door, she took hold of the handle and paused, searching for some way to preserve what had just happened. She needed to let him know she wasn't offended.

"Would you like to get something to eat?" Her heart was racing. "It's already past noon."

Michael didn't move. He wanted to encourage her feelings, but the words escaped him.

"I am pretty hungry."

"There's a surprise," she teased.

It was a hollow taunt, but he enjoyed it. "Let me get dressed and I'll call you."

Christina opened the door and turned away. "Promise?"

A smile. "I promise."

HER eyes crinkled as she slipped into the hall. Pulling the

door closed, Christina caught her breath. The pounding in her chest had lessened, and she hoped Viktoriya wouldn't notice the flushed look on her face.

Danger close was a tactical phrase, but suitable for matters of the heart. She weighed that thought and winced. What if she'd allowed his touch to remain? Deep down, that's what she really wanted. She couldn't push that aside any longer and sensed the same conflict in Neill.

Christina balanced her feelings with reality. If they had taken the next step—if he had kissed her—would it have violated their core values? The regulations said yes, but wasn't denying the truth a greater sin? She searched for clarity. *Snap out of it, Arrens*, she told herself. Nothing had changed, and it was painfully obvious that the rules were still the rules.

The Marines had experienced a traumatic event. It was only natural to seek comfort from a friend, she reasoned. Christina had come to his room hoping for something—and then pulled away when she almost got it.

He would call soon, she was sure of that. A promise from Michael Neill was as good as gold. She nursed a deep resolve in her heart, and moving toward her own suite, part of her wondered what other promises she might be able to extract from the young captain.

Chapter Twenty * Old Town

THE GUEST LIFTS WERE LIKE GILDED CAR-riages. Framed in white steel and brass, they were another nod to extravagance; and with elevators as opulent as these, it was just wrong to rely on the stairs.

Neill and the women rode to the first floor and stepped into the lobby. Staff members were busy near the entrance; thick plastic sheets draped the window frames, and the material seemed to breathe as the outside air pushed in.

"Viktoriya, would you excuse us?" Michael asked. He turned to face Christina. "I just need a moment."

There was a tenderness to his words. Viktoriya had seen that quality before; and in each instance, it was in Christina's presence. She recalled that trait from their time in Odessa—but the expression now was much deeper.

And it didn't take a journalist to understand why.

"Of course," she smiled; first at Neill, and then at Christina. She took a step toward the concierge desk. "Take your time."

* * * *

"I'D LIKE TO CLEAR THE AIR," NEILL BEGAN. "About—upstairs." He shook his head, and kept his eyes on Christina. "I just wasn't thinking. It won't happen again."

"It's all right." She tried to stop him. His explanation was starting to sound like regret, and she didn't want that. "You don't need to apologize."

"I wasn't going to," Michael countered. "If you felt uncomfortable, or were offended, I certainly would. Otherwise—"

Christina was taken by surprise. She'd expected something like this, but the captain had veered in a different direction.

"I wasn't offended. And I wasn't uncomfortable. To be honest," she paused, wondering if honesty was best right now, "—I didn't want that moment to end."

Michael smiled. "We can talk about it later." The elevator doors opened again, revealing Pyotr and Dmitri. "Right now we should get going."

* * * *

IT WAS A SHORT WALK FROM THE HOTEL TO MARket square. Pyotr suggested lunch at an outdoor café and Neill agreed. It seemed best to distance themselves from the Royal Route and leave the morning's events behind. The group strolled through neighborhoods dotted with tributes to the city's past, and at length, they came to a stately palace.

"Ladies and gentlemen—and Mischa—I give you the Royal Castle." Pyotr's flair for melodrama had returned, and he waved a hand to his right.

The symbol of Polish independence was imposing, dominating much of the skyline. A massive clock tower bisected the structure's western façade, and a statue of King Zygumunt stood nearby. This towering column was one of the oldest effigies in Warsaw.

"A fitting welcome to *Stare Miasto*—Old Town. We'll pass a few more landmarks on our way."

Pyotr led his companions down a narrow street. They moved briskly. The sun had broken through, but the high walls above them cast shadows that blocked its warmth.

Viktoriya filled her lungs with cool air. She was surrounded by friends, old and new, and felt much more secure in their presence. Her case of nerves had vanished. She stayed close to Christina—and the Marine's slightly oversized but completely regulation purse, and Dmitri Yaroslav was glad for the chance to mingle with the somewhat younger crowd.

ULICA Swietojanska ran north and emptied near the southwest corner of Old Town Square. This part of the city was geared for pedestrian traffic, with townhouses springing up on all sides and open air cafés hugging the perimeter. Several shops had seasonal displays in their windows.

Christina was radiant. "I'll bet this place is gorgeous at night."

"Especially this time of year," Pyotr put in. "And when the sun goes down, the square is filled with lovers walking hand in hand."

Arrens didn't respond to that. Neill gave her a quick glance, but the young woman's eyes were fixed on a small bistro close by. "Contact left," she announced. "Doner-kebabs." A knife hand pointed straight ahead. "Everybody follow me."

* * * *

THE TURKISH SANDWICHES WERE A HIT WITH everyone. Michael polished off his, and then consumed half of Christina's when she couldn't finish.

Arrens located an ice cream parlor and polled the group for their choices. Neill waved her off. "I've had enough for now."

She gave him a stern and insistent look. "I'll need help with the order, Captain."

Michael got to his feet. "I think I'll help you with the order, Staff Sergeant."

"If you'd like—" Yaroslav started to push back his chair.

"I'm on it, Dmitri," the captain replied. "Desserts are my specialty."

* * * *

"ALL RIGHT," NEILL BEGAN. "WHAT IS IT YOU'RE trying so hard to bring to my attention?"

They stood outside the dessert shop, staring into the plate glass window at a tub of mint chocolate chip.

"Did you get a good look at our rescuers this morning?"

Michael blinked. "I was focused on Avery. And I couldn't see much with that blood in my eye. Why do you ask?"

She turned to face him and pretended to straighten his collar. "Over my right shoulder. Those two having lattes."

Neill gazed ahead. A couple of military types were seated nearby. "On the corner?"

"Bingo." Christina adjusted his tie. "There—you're almost presentable. Now let's get some ice cream."

"Hang on." The captain pulled out his cell phone. "I don't have any pictures of you in Warsaw."

The device did its work, but Neill frowned. "Uh-oh. Your eyes were crossed."

"They were not."

He snapped another photo—but not before zooming in on the patrons several tables away.

* * * *

TERESHENKO AND VOSKOV WERE SIPPING espressos, not lattes. Sunlight bathed the plaza, and the two were quite comfortable as they kept an eye on their protectee. Both noticed the Americans' interest in the creamery.

"*Morozhevo?*" Yuri was surprised. "A bit cold for a frozen treat, don't you think?"

"Not my first choice," Xander returned. The captain was relaxed. He spied a pastry shop and his gaze lingered over slices of Polish cream cake. The square was a public place, and with Viktoriya in the company of friends, the Berkut team's job had just become a little easier.

* * * *

THE MARINES BROUGHT BACK SOMETHING FOR everyone. Dessert boosted the group's mood, and they all agreed that the afternoon outing was the perfect remedy for what had gone before.

Michael had changed his mind, returning with a chocolate shake. He'd nearly finished when his phone began to whir. He pulled it from his pocket and stared, thinking that the display couldn't be right.

The caller ID was his own number.

"HOW'S Warsaw, Captain Neill?" The voice on the other end spoke Russian.

"Enchanting; but I'm still settling in," Michael answered. Winking at Christina, he got up from his chair and strolled away from the table. "Who is this—and how did you hijack my phone?"

"To put it bluntly—I'm the first-fruits of your father's labor."

The reply was both abrupt and unsettling, and froze Neill in place. "Can you be a little more specific?"

There was a pause. "Let me jog your memory, Captain. Think back to an island chain in the South China Sea. You wore green; my uniform was gray. If I recall correctly, it was raining at the time."

"White Dragon."

A soft laugh. "You once told me to do the right thing. I think you'll be pleased to learn that I took your advice."

"That would explain a few things," Neill granted. He was moving again, approaching the Statue of the Mermaid. "Do you have a message—or did you just call to wish me a Merry Christmas?"

The Chinese officer smiled thinly. "I'm intimate with details you might not be aware of, Captain. Consider this call not only a professional courtesy—but something more."

"You've got my attention."

On a darkened street in Beijing, Zhu Ling came right to the point. "The Kremlin has launched a new undertaking. An assassination. Someone you know is in grave danger."

"A young woman?" Neill turned instinctively, locking his eyes on Viktoriya. She was chatting amiably with Major Yaroslav.

"I could identify her, but you would profit more by knowing the assassin."

"I'm listening."

"*Ilya Nikolayevich Maersk.* Have you heard of him?"

Michael frowned. "Can't say that I have."

There was a heavy sigh in China. This wouldn't be easy. "He goes by other names," Ling offered. "No one is sure which is real. London may know more. Maersk has—a history, shall we say?"

"With the Brits?"

"MI6," came the reply. "He killed five of their agents. But not *just* Her Majesty's operatives." Ling's pacing slowed, and his tone dropped an octave. "All told, we believe he's responsible for a score of other deaths.

"*Mikhail Davidovich Neill*—forgive me." Captain Ling drew in an agonized breath, and let it out slowly. "There's something else you need to know."

* * * *

VIKTORIYA FOUGHT TO SUPPRESS A LAUGH. "HE doesn't really walk—have you noticed?"

She eyed Michael from afar, sharing her confidences in French.

"I think the sugar's gone to your head," Christina observed. She shivered, and regretted wearing a skirt for their tour.

"You're deflecting," Viktoriya noted. Her journalistic tendencies surfaced, and she smiled. "Why are you so guarded?"

"We follow regulations," Arrens explained. "It's all about decorum." Her tone was stiff; more so than she intended. She walked it back a little, adding, "But you're right—it's more like a *march*." *Or a strut,* she thought. *And the man can certainly rock a pair of combat boots—*

"But you don't like these rules," Viktoriya probed. She continued to stare, a restrained but slightly wild look in her eye. "You have to admit, he's very handsome—coming or going."

"Now I'm sure of it. No more ice cream for you," the Marine responded. Her gaze drifted back toward the square. As she watched, Michael found a bench, lowering himself to sit on one end. He ended the call, but remained in place, peering into the distance.

"Wait here," Christina advised.

To Viktoriya, it sounded like an order.

* * * *

"ARE YOU ALL RIGHT?" THE STAFF SERGEANT edged closer. "Who was that?"

Neill's head came up slowly. "A Chinese officer. His name is Zhu Ling."

"He was on the island." Christina had read the after-action report, despite its highly classified nature.

"That's right," the captain nodded. "It's all a bit complicated, but apparently I've been sold a bill of goods—led down a path with false information." He shook his head. "Ilya Maersk is part of it."

Christina claimed a portion of the bench next to Michael. "And why is he important?"

His eyes met hers, and the vulnerability she'd witnessed days before had returned.

"That's the name of the man who murdered my father," he said, and he began to share what he knew.

The Vistula
North of Gora Kalwaria

OFFSHORE SALVAGE WAS DIFFERENT THAN work in protected waters. Operators had to contend with exposure to the elements. Waves and weather posed constant threats, and dictated schedules that were beyond man's control. The best results were achieved when skilled labor could be on station, and all too often, environmental conditions made that requirement difficult to meet.

Efforts in sheltered waters were different. In some ways, that meant it was easier—especially if the vessel being recovered wasn't a hazard to navigation. Riverine operations weren't as complicated, and the needed equipment was far more accessible. Maneuvering A-frames and rigging cranes into position was less arduous, and the practical risks could be better managed.

The barge itself had no intrinsic value. Apart from an historical context, only its cargo was important. Archaeologique François had shepherded this excavation with an eye toward future projects. This enterprise represented a sizable expenditure, to be sure, but their *pro bono* efforts had earned the media's focus, providing a platform not available through traditional marketing sources.

And there was nothing like charity to get the public's recognition.

* * * *

THE SUV WAS A HIGHER END MODEL, AND PART of the fleet of vehicles owned and operated by the French society. Toussaint's driver sped south, following a stretch of frontage road that paralleled the main highway. He doubled back after missing a turn; crews had bulldozed a new path, providing direct access to the riverfront.

The 4x4 lumbered to a halt near the top of the ridge. Jean-Paul exited the car and began a loping descent to the water's edge. The excavation site lay below; a derrick boat hugged the shore, and the ever-present project office sat nearby. Toussaint clambered up the steps to the shack and found Henri Minouche waiting for him, bundled against the cold in a fleece liner.

"What have you found?" The entrepreneur was breathless.

"Not here, *monsieur*." Minouche pointed toward the waterline. "Our latest discovery is still on the salvage flat."

Henri led the way and the two trudged the gravel beach to the equipment barge. Ascending the main deck, they navigated around heavy machinery, minding their steps to avoid the cables and hoses that littered their path. The scene reeked of oil; pumps sputtering in the background, while compressors fueled air to points beneath the Vistula's surface.

At one corner of the barge was a low, rectangular basin filled with water. Toussaint recognized a few students—volunteers from the university—gingerly examining its contents. They withdrew as the Frenchman came near, allowing Jean-Paul a closer examination. What he saw prompted a gasp.

"A ciborium," Minouche announced. "The divers retrieved this an hour ago." He knelt and hefted the chalice from the tank. Ice cold water and silt drained from the sacred vessel as he handed it to Toussaint.

"The cross surmounting the top is still intact. And also this—" the project leader turned and bent at the waist, his palm landing on a bell-shaped object. Its patina marked it as old, but there was no question as to what it was.

Jean-Paul's eyes widened. "The Sanctus bell?"

Henri nodded. "And both are from Olm," he grinned.

"How can you be sure?" This was too good to be true.

Minouche took the chalice, turning it carefully on its end. "Here—stamped at the base. The crest of St. Mary's." He gestured toward the bell. "The same can be found on the outer casing—along with the city seal."

"You found these below?"

"Directly under our feet," the man answered. "There were a few other items—a candelabra, an angelus from the altar. All four are specifically mentioned in the Angstrom parchment."

"Then we've found it." Toussaint's eyes gleamed.

"This is science, Jean-Paul," Minouche warned. "Not a treasure hunt. I am cautiously optimistic, but there is still work to be done."

"Of course." Toussaint checked his exhilaration. "What's

our next step?"

Henri found a rag and dried his chilled hands. "There are no short cuts, *monsieur*. We must proceed carefully. I will not risk my men by sending them into the boat's hold. The water is too deep here, and the interior could collapse around them."

Jean-Paul understood the implications of that. "Then we'll stick to the original plan." He looked up at the derrick. "Attach straps to the hull and lift it to the surface."

"That's not as straightforward as you might think. This boat is fragile, and the river will not release her grip easily." He could see the expression on Toussaint's face. Minouche was beginning to sound like a man making excuses. It was time for a concession. "Nevertheless, if we work diligently, and handle this maiden with a gentleman's touch—our efforts might be rewarded."

Henri had a wistful look. The vessel below had already sailed once, and her cargo had not enriched the previous owners.

"She may yield the icon, Jean-Paul; or she may not. The Swedes could still have the last laugh." Both men stared into the black, frigid depths. "Only time will tell."

Chapter Twenty-One * Iron Harvest

THE GROUP RETURNED TO THE BRISTOL AND went their separate ways. Dmitri Yaroslav headed upstairs to unpack. Pyotr and Michael took the elevator with him. Viktoriya wanted to stick around for the press conference, and offered to treat Christina to coffee.

The women watched as the officers headed for the lifts. "Definitely a march," Viktoriya decided. Her eyes were fastened on Neill.

Christina didn't respond; in fact, she'd been sullen for most the trip back. Michael was also different. Their stroll to the square had been casual, but returning to the hotel, the Marines had led with a more purposed intensity.

"What's gotten into him?" Viktoriya whispered.

Arrens followed the captain with a concerned look.

"This whole thing just became personal." She forced a smile. "Come on. As long as you're buying, we'll talk about it over cappuccino."

* * * *

NEILL TURNED TO FACE YAROSLAV. "SO YOU'RE with the Security Directorate now." He was speaking Ukrainian, and held up his mobile. "Do you recognize these men?"

The major studied the screen. "Not at first glance, no. Should I?"

"I think they might be Berkut troops," Michael answered. "Possibly attached to the SSD."

"What makes you think that?"

"They intervened this morning. One grabbed Viktoriya, while the tall man sacked the surviving shooter."

Dmitri looked closer at the photos. "This is the square. You took these today?"

Michael nodded. "Less than an hour ago."

"Why Berkut?"

"It's just a hunch," Neill shrugged. "They protected her in Odessa."

"I know all about your hunches, Michael," Dmitri grinned.

The captain pressed on. "They've shown up twice now. Both times, Viktoriya's been part of the picture. Since they're obviously not here to *kill* her—"

"Send the images to my phone. I'll make a few inquiries," Yaroslav promised.

* * * *

RICHARD AULTMAN HAD A FROWN.

"Captain Neill would like a word."

Avery looked up from his desk—and over his glasses. He had a master suite on the fifth floor, complete with office. Willis didn't mind the interruption, but something about Richard's expression raised a flag.

"It would be a little awkward to put off the man who saved my life," Avery replied. He waited for a response, but his executive assistant wasn't humored.

"Something tells me this isn't a social call," Aultman warned.

The national security advisor considered that and heaved a sigh.

"All right. Show him in."

* * * *

"What's on your mind, Captain?"

Neill didn't pace in Avery's presence. He showed deference, but there was nothing hat-in-hand about his entrance. The young officer displayed no emotion.

Avery had seen that calm demeanor before, when the Marine debriefed him after returning from Ukraine. During that meeting, Neill had been in full command of the facts, yet the current situation was different. He possessed some details, but the bigger picture was incomplete.

"I was hoping you could provide a few answers," Neill returned. "I'm just not sure where to start."

"Oh?" Avery was on his feet now. His guest's composure was disarming. "The beginning's usually a good place."

"Not a bad idea," the captain nodded thoughtfully. "The day we met; do you remember?"

Avery shoved his hands into his pockets and moved to the window. "Arlington. Your friend's funeral. I remember."

"As I recall, you knew something of my history. The broad strokes, at least." Neill's eyes bored into Avery. "But you left out a few things. I've often wondered why."

"Your personal file lacked details," the big man replied. "I expected you to fill in the blanks, but you didn't. That got me curious." He wore a thin smile. "I take it you've never seen the Agency's dossier?"

Neill shook his head, poker face intact.

"Chunks of that one are redacted—*heavily* redacted," Avery emphasized. "I didn't get the full story until recently."

"And what is the full story?"

Avery wandered back to his desk. "I've been authorized to read you in." He retrieved a folder and handed it to Neill. "Those answers you're looking for. I think you'll find them here."

* * * *

"I'VE GOT TO HIT THE GYM." CHRISTINA STIRRED her coffee, a look of frustration forming. "I can't keep doing this."

Viktoriya smiled and took a sip. The two had found a table in the Bristol's café. "The food is rich here. And a properly made cappuccino—" she lifted her cup, "—could double as dessert."

"We've already had one of those today." Christina's brows were furrowed. "Do you work out?"

The question caught Viktoriya off guard. "Clearly not as much as you." She patted the Marine's hand. "Relax, *ma chere*; I don't think you're in any danger."

"Define *danger*." Christina's thoughts returned to the morning, but her eyes went to the menu board near the entrance. "What's an *espresso corretto?*"

"You don't want that; it comes with a splash of liqueur." Viktoriya's grin broadened. She shrugged and amended her comment. "But after today, maybe you do."

"You could be right." Christina laughed softly and began to relax. The café charmed with its art nouveau interior. "Tell me how you met Michael."

The Ukrainian woman looked surprised, but pleasantly so. "You get right to the point, don't you? Are you sure you're not a journalist?"

"Counter-intelligence. I guess you could say the vocations are similar."

"I suppose so. He was a lieutenant at the time." Viktoriya's expression was playful. "But I suspect you'll want to know about the opera."

* * * *

NEILL STUDIED THE FOLDER'S INTERIOR. THERE were several pages inside, along with half a dozen photos. Despite Avery's earlier comments, there was nothing held back, and Michael read the report with great interest.

"IRON HARVEST," Avery intoned. The operational designation appeared numerous times. "Ambitious, creative—"

"—and completely at odds with government policy," the captain concluded.

"There is that," Avery said. "Desperate times, desperate measures—you know the drill. Back in those days, Eastern Europe resembled the wild west."

"Still does, in some ways," Michael murmured evenly. He never looked up, and withdrew one of the images from the dossier's sleeve, a wounded expression on his face. "My parents."

The national security advisor nodded. "David and Jean Neill. American missionaries; not the first to Ukraine, but arguably the most effective." He gave the Marine a chance to let that sink in. "And that's why they were recruited."

"As what? Government agents?"

Avery shook his head this time. "That's just semantics. We supplied a measure of material support. Your father was our point man. We laid out our objectives, steered him toward a few key figures—and let the Gospel do its work." He caught Neill's smile, his first since stepping into the room. "Oh, I know all the lingo, son. Granddad was a Baptist preacher, after all."

"Tell me about those objectives," Michael asked. He wanted a summary that wasn't laced with bureaucratic jargon.

"The idea was to foster democracy; but to get there, Ukraine needed a push in the right direction.

"Consider the situation, Captain. Kiev was a study in chaos. Simply being freed from Soviet domination wasn't enough; the country needed something to fill the void." Avery's tone softened. "The nation's moral fabric was in tatters, and social assistance only went so far."

Neill eyed the report. "And this was your answer?"

"That was all before my time," Avery was quick to reply. "But it was decided that faith-based programs were the key— and as a result, IRON HARVEST was born."

"A government-sponsored religious initiative." The young officer's grin persisted. "A bit unorthodox, to say the least."

"Quite," Avery granted. "Christianity was deemed to be the

most effective change agent. And your parents' goals dove-tailed nicely with the State Department's intent."

Neill focused. A name jumped from one of the pages. "Who was the point man?"

"Allan Hayes. An up-and-coming Army officer at the time; tank commander. Got side-lined in a training accident, so the powers-that-were gave him a new assignment."

"He knew my parents?"

"Not really. Allan only met them once. He acted as a contact, providing logistical support when it was required."

"He did the paperwork," Michael observed. "How did all that square with the First Amendment?"

Avery almost cringed. "It didn't. Well, not exactly. The people in charge found a way to justify it. Since the operation was conducted on foreign soil—" His words trailed off. "Probably wouldn't have stood up in court. The whole thing was kept hush-hush—for that very reason. And for a while, it worked."

Neill closed the folder. "For a while?"

Another pained expression. "A freshman senator caught wind of it—a member of the select committee on foreign affairs. He was a hotshot lawyer from Rhode Island. You know him as—"

"—Mark Breese?" Neill didn't appear to be shocked.

Avery was shaking his head. "He threatened to go public with the whole thing. State had no choice; they pulled the plug."

The captain narrowed his eyes. "What aren't you telling me?"

Avery drew in a breath. "Your father made inroads with some very important people in Eastern Europe. The old guard didn't like that." Neill could see where this was going. "After the program was discontinued, we couldn't protect men like your dad anymore."

The son of David Neill wasn't angry. "We can't lay this at the president's feet."

"I suppose not," the big man admitted. "That was the Chechens—"

"No." It wasn't Neill's style to interrupt. "They're not to blame either. It was a Russian—a man named Ilya Maersk."

"Excuse me?" Avery's face darkened. The name didn't ring a bell, and ran counter to everything he'd come to believe.

Michael exhaled, and for the first time his composure slipped. "Thirty years ago, Maersk was a double-agent; a mole in the British clandestine services."

"MI6," Avery grunted. *Where did the Marine get this intel?* "What else do you know?"

The officer recovered. "Very little," he answered. "We need more information. And we need it fast."

The man's playing the revenge card, Willis decided. Another characteristic that didn't fit. "That's an empty road, Neill. Three decades have passed." He thought of something else. "Besides, this Russian's probably long gone."

"That's where you're wrong." Michael's mouth became a thin line. "He's coming to Warsaw. He's planning to kill Viktoriya Gavrilenko—and possibly worse."

The morning's events had underscored a certain vulnerability. Thankfully, Christina was armed, but Michael didn't want that scenario playing out again. Another layer of protection was needed, and in the back of his mind, an idea had taken root.

Avery felt a chill. "Where did you get all this?"

"From someone who did know my father. The connection's hard to pin down, but I trust the source."

"And the trail back to the Brits?"

"That path's a little murky," Neill allowed. "But I can make a few calls."

Avery contemplated turning the man loose. He'd certainly delivered before.

"If that's the case, then I've got a phone number. I want you to bird-dog this, Captain." Avery was smiling again.

"Make your calls."

* * * *

THE STORY TOOK TIME IN THE TELLING, AND

there were parts that Christina had never heard before. Viktoriya spun the tale with unconcealed relish, and the staff sergeant hung on every word, trying not to look obvious as she soaked up details.

Viktoriya finished and pulled out her cell phone. "Did Michael ever show you these?" She tabbed to the image directory and handed the device across the table.

"No." Christina made it sound like two words, not one. "It must have slipped his mind." She scrolled through several photos, and one eyebrow shot up. "Wow, that's quite a dress. I wish I could wear something like that."

Viktoriya blinked. "Of course you could. We're practically the same size." She inspected Christina from head to toe. "Granted, you are more toned. And—" she giggled, "*bigger*—up here, I mean, but—"

Arrens ignored the observation. "These were taken at the opera house?"

"*Oui*. After the curtain fell."

Christina continued to stare. "You're very photogenic," she permitted. "Both of you." She handed the phone back and looked down at the table. "Did you enjoy the performance?"

Viktoriya almost didn't hear her. "We had a wonderful time. But the best part came later," she had a waggish look, "—after we left the theater."

The narrative had taken a decidedly uncomfortable turn, and very quickly. Christina's face felt warm. Sitting before her was a woman who could have any man she wanted—maybe even Michael—and she feared that her perceptions were about to be shattered.

"I don't think I want to hear this."

She started to push away, but Viktoriya's hand restrained her.

"Sit down." She had a commanding tone, and the Marine was startled by it. "Christina, you need to listen."

Arrens refused to look up. "Why should I? This is about you and him."

"Don't be silly," Viktoriya snapped. Customers nearby had started to take notice and she began to whisper. "He took me back to my apartment—so what? Do you know what happened next?"

Was she taunting her?

"I don't want to know," she replied curtly.

If this was a challenge, she was ready for it. Christina's cheeks were flushed, and a fire suddenly burned in her eyes that frightened the Ukrainian woman.

"You tried to seduce him, didn't you?" Instead of getting louder, her voice dropped. "And how was that performance? Did you enjoy your little conquest?"

It was clear that Viktoriya had made a wrong turn.

"*Yes,*" she blurted. "I mean *no*—it wasn't like that." She took hold of Christina's hands. "*Please*; there's no reason for you to be angry. I did try to seduce him—I admit that. I was angling for a story. But your Michael is a gentleman." She released her grip and caught her breath, hoping to quench the Marine's jealousy. "He didn't want me."

Christina felt chastised. The tense moment had passed, but she wasn't completely convinced.

"He—turned you down?" A single teardrop fell.

Viktoriya's nod of the head was very animated. "He told me good night. All I got for my troubles was a cavalier's kiss—and then he left me standing on my doorstep." She folded her hands and laid them in her lap.

"I'm sorry." Arrens' head dipped again. "It's been a very stressful day. I don't know why I reacted like that."

"I do," Viktoriya chirped. "You're in love with him—aren't you?"

Christina's chin came up. She was trying to halt the flow of tears.

"I told you, we have regulations." It was a weak response. "He's an officer. Sometimes I think he cares," she stopped. "That's not right. I *know* he cares, but—" she didn't finish, her words trailing off.

"Rules can't change your heart, Christina. And regulations don't govern emotions." She reached out again, squeezing her fingertips. "How can you expect him to show his feelings—when you deny your own?" Viktoriya straightened in her chair, thrusting out her other hand. "Now—do we still have a truce?"

Near Dorohusk, Ukraine

THE TRAINS RAN FREQUENTLY BETWEEN Belarus and Poland, but Maersk couldn't use that mode of travel. The weapons he carried prevented it. Instead, he crossed the border as a passenger in Anton's van, skirting the northern edges of Ukraine. Once past Dorohusk, Ilya would take the wheel and cover the distance to Warsaw alone.

As a party to the Schengen Agreement, getting to Poland from Europe was trouble-free, but coming over from Ukraine was a different story. It hadn't always been that way. New restrictions were in place, intended to reduce the black market trade of vodka and cigarettes. Ukrainians waited in line for hours before being allowed access, and many felt the rules cast them as third-class citizens.

For Anton and Ilya, the control point between countries was less of an obstacle than expected. Both men had Russian passports and visas, which eased their entry. The border agent was typically churlish, but waved them on. Anton steered the van through the left lane—they had nothing to declare—and within minutes they were moving west across Poland's eastern frontier.

"You have everything you need," the younger man announced. He retrieved two envelopes from beneath his seat. "For you; Major Pirogov sends his best."

Ilya opened one and then the other. The first held a wad of Polish banknotes. He would need that, given his stand against plastic. The second envelope contained final instructions from his handlers. These new orders would have surprised a less mercenary heart, but Maersk accepted them coldly. He read the message twice and then stuffed it into his coat.

"Stop at the crossroad," REMORA directed. He stared ahead. There was an exit further on, with a fueling point, and traffic was light. It was a suitable location for his purposes. "I need to stretch my legs."

The driver muttered something about relieving himself. Thankful for the opportunity, he eased off the road, just beyond the petrol station. The van rolled to a halt and both men jumped from the cab.

ANTON found an out of the way spot and watched as the steam rose from the ground. With his personal business at an end, he cinched his belt and trudged up the embankment. Maersk had opened the van's side door, his back turned to the Russian hireling.

"My apologies, Ilya Nikolayevich. The cold always—"

Anton stopped in mid-sentence. The old man was facing him now. He held a pistol, its barrel lengthened considerably by the suppressor attached to its end. His hold on the weapon was steady, and the muzzle was pointed directly at Anton's chest.

"And my regrets, *tavarisch*." That was a lie. Maersk was free of remorse. It allowed him to excel at his job. "But our masters must be obeyed."

Anton's eyes were wide with fear and surprise. There wasn't time to voice an objection, and there was nowhere to run. Maersk squeezed the trigger. Two slugs pierced Anton's heart, and the younger man fell lifeless to the snow.

ILYA replaced his sidearm, and then strolled to the ridge and rolled the body down the grade. Gravity did the rest. He watched the corpse until it came to a stop; it was always a source of fascination to him—how the freshly dead could be so limp once life had slipped away.

"Sleep, comrade."

The bitter cold sharpened his words. His utterance was the only benediction Anton would receive. Maersk knew nothing of heaven or hell, and gave no thought to his colleague's soul.

Some men attached philosophical meaning to mortality. They wrapped it in the trappings of religion; but for Ilya, the passage from life to death was purely clinical.

Sleep, he mused. *Those little slices of death...*

The deed was done, and the Russian's empty heart beat no faster than before. He got behind the wheel and turned the key. The engine sputtered to life, and with his face set to the west, Ilya Maersk continued his journey toward Warsaw.

Chapter Twenty-Two * Context

THE PRESS CONFERENCE DID LITTLE TO SET-
tle anyone's nerves. Reporters for the local outlets
were in a kerfuffle; Dobrogost's staff had naturally
asked for discretion, but short of that, they were willing to
negotiate. In a best case scenario, the Polish government
hoped to keep news of the attack under wraps. That request
had not gone over well, but the journalists agreed to soft-
pedal their coverage—in return for some assurances from the
presidential residence.

Avery's briefing broke down three ways. First came the as-
sertion—vehemently expressed—that no member of the delegation was ever at risk. Faction Red was tacitly acknowledged but
their role was quickly minimized. The press corps grumbled,
but they swallowed their objections and recorded the remarks
for public consumption.

Next came a subtle interrogation about the summit. The national security advisor fielded most of those concerns—with an
assist from Tomas Krol—then deftly steered the proceedings
away from the more nonsensical inquiries. Neill and Arrens
were in attendance, and watched with amusement as Avery
side-stepped one question after another. A few dealt with the
conference's chances for success, and the man in the rumpled
suit offered up his answers with a positive spin.

Michael estimated that at least part of the group consisted of spooks or free-lancers posing as correspondents. The Russians had been snubbed, so naturally their interest was piqued. Neill was sure that a handful of the assembly included members of the FSB, possibly even a chief of station or two, but he didn't bother to poll the cortege by nationality.

The last few minutes were devoted to questions related to SMOOTH STONE and RESILIENT EAGLE. Some asked about the escalated tensions at the border with Kaliningrad. Avery had also gauged the audience and used his closing comments to underscore NATO's commitment to Poland.

He finished abruptly and stepped away from the podium with the hope that diplomacy—and a smattering of forceful rhetoric—would somehow reach the Kremlin's ears.

* * * *

NEILL ROSE EARLY THE NEXT MORNING. He shook off sleep and turned to his devotions, choosing a passage from Colossians. The verses there dealt with forgiveness—an appropriate theme, he reasoned, given the news about Ilya Maersk—and those were followed by words that seemed fresh to Michael's eyes.

"Let the peace of Christ rule in your hearts, since as members of one body you were called to peace."

He meditated on that, letting the Scriptures shine a light on his soul. Michael's parents had taught him that real peace flowed from a clean heart—one that refused to harbor hatred. It was a lesson in life that he'd embraced at an early age.

Neill had already come to terms with his father's death. That was in the past. *What was different now?* He considered that as objectively as he could. The names had changed, and so had the circumstances—Captain Ling had said as much. And it was the latter that proved troublesome.

White Dragon's revelation added a new dimension to Neill's understanding of the subject. An old wound had been re-opened, bringing fresh grief and a reasonable dose of concern for Viktoriya. The news also raised a few questions.

Who was Ilya Maersk? And what had made David Neill a target?

His mind broached another topic. In this very room, he and Christina had shared something. At the very least, it was a brief moment of intimacy. Michael had come to realize how she truly felt about him. It had taken some time, but things were becoming clearer, and his own emotions were more transparent as well. Staring into her eyes, he'd wanted nothing more than to express his tenderness, but thankfully, she had put a stop to that.

What did that say about his discipline—and hers? Terryton had told the man to behave himself, and technically, nothing had happened. Still, Neill's actions the day before would not have sat well with the colonel.

His feelings went past physical attraction. His desire was real, but his faith called for depth, and a spiritual dedication that went beyond the flesh. God's leading couldn't be denied. That was something else to meditate on, and Michael's next steps would require a great deal of prayer.

THE captain slipped on his sweats and was met in the hall by Richard Aultman.

"You're up early." Neill was impressed.

"Since five," Aultman crowed. The man was clean-shaven, and wore a coat and tie. He held a folded newspaper in one hand. "You going for food?"

"Caffeine," the Marine replied, a bit of desperation in his voice. "Do you have that phone number?"

Richard pulled out a folded slip of paper. "Your contact's name is Brian Weston; a major in the RAF. Lately seconded to the Secret Intelligence Service." He grinned. "Kind of a clothes horse, too."

Neill studied the number. "Secure line?"

"This goes directly to MI6. He'll be expecting you. This gets you in, but you'll need CONTEXT."

"What kind of context?" Michael was confused. He could really use some java.

Aultman stifled a laugh. "CONTEXT is your pass-key to Weston's office. You'll then be challenged for a priority code. Use the phrase SEMAPHORE, or your call will get backed up in the queue—and probably end up in the major's voice-mail."

"Roger that. When should I call?"

"Ten a.m. Sharp. London's one hour behind us."

"Same time the conference kicks off," Neill mumbled.

"Try to be punctual." Aultman's face twisted into a grin. "The Brits aren't all that hoity-toity; they just let us think they are."

"*Hoity-toity,*" Neill repeated. "I'm not familiar with that phrase."

"Forget it. Mr. Avery and I will leave at eight. Have your people ready to go by nine. Oh—have you seen this?" He shoved the newspaper under the Marine's nose.

Neill read the headline and skimmed the first paragraph. Some journalists had ignored the president's subtle edict; a few of Warsaw's dailies published accounts of the shooting, but those reports were buried deep, and appeared below the fold.

"At least it's not on the front page," Michael offered. He held up the contact information. "And thanks for the number."

"Make sure you use your cell," Aultman advised. "They're still working to encrypt the lines at the Palace." He struck a dignified chord. "And you're quite welcome, Captain."

"My friends call me Mike." He stuck out a hand.

"Richard." The two shook, as if meeting for the first time.

Neill started to go but Aultman stood his ground. "Is there something else?"

Avery's assistant drew a hand across his chin. "One more thing. I know you've got this Bible thing down—" his voice dropped, and he hesitated, "—I just have a couple of questions."

"Fair enough," the Marine grinned. "Let's grab some forty weight and talk it over."

* * * *

Hours later, Neill and Arrens stepped into the lift. Both Marines wore their service alphas. The Bristol's concierge had seen to the captain's uniform and no trace of blood could be found.

"I brought you a gift." Michael produced a small wrapped package. "Don't open it now—it's for Christmas."

She was surprised, and her face brightened. "That's sweet of you." She turned it over in her hand. There was a pause before she spoke up again.

"I wanted to tell you something—but I needed to wait until we were alone."

"That sounds mysterious." It was the only response Neill could come up with.

Without warning, she gripped his arm and pulled him close, pressing her lips against his cheek. Just as quickly, she stepped away, acting as if nothing had happened.

Michael was taken aback, and he lifted a hand to touch his face.

"You talk funny—but I like it," he blushed. Christina's clean scent surrounded him.

"That's for Odessa," she announced.

Neill wasn't sure what that meant, but he suspected it had something to do with Viktoriya. His fingertips rested on his cheekbone.

"For that kind of a reaction, I can go again." He was grinning and decided to press his luck. "Is that the best you've got?" The man was clearly flirting now.

The elevator reached ground level. Christina turned her head, smiling in his direction.

"You're a good man, Captain Neill. But if you want my best, we're going to need to make a few changes."

That dulcet tone again. Her comment was innocent, but her eyes were not, and Michael was left to wonder just what those changes might mean.

* * * *

Pyotr's stare swept Plac Teatralny—Theater Square—as the limo followed Senatorska Street and then banked south.

"This used to be the heart of the city."

"What happened?" Christina asked. The question was an expression of courtesy, and she took in the view, noting yet another *Ulica* that she couldn't pronounce.

"The war, *pani* Christina. Much of *Varshava* was changed after that."

Michael turned in the front seat and gave his friend a glance. Despite his youth, Pyotr now looked much older than his years.

Arrens was searching for a comforting word when her mobile started to buzz. A look at the display brought a smile.

"Do you know this address?" She held it out for Pyotr to see.

Stanislaw read the screen, rebounding instantly. "It's a little out of the way," he granted. "But not too far."

Neill was curious. "Who—"

"A text from Viktoriya," the staff sergeant answered. "She wants to hitch a ride."

"You two are texting now?"

"She's my new best friend," Christina grinned. "We have a lot in common." *You, for one thing,* she didn't say.

Pyotr eyed the available space. "We have plenty of room, Mischa." He seemed enthusiastic, adding, "And I would be willing to sit between the ladies."

"Very noble of you," Neill observed.

The lieutenant took that as agreement, and without another word he relayed the directions to their driver.

The Palace of Culture and Science was huge, its presence up-ending the surrounding architecture. The limo proceeded south, and as they came near, it was more difficult to gauge the full breadth of the structure.

"The Russian Wedding Cake," Pyotr announced, waving a hand. "There are other names, of course, but in polite company—"

Neill had heard a few of those. "Point taken."

Security was tight. After passing muster at the entry control point, the car pulled up to the western entrance. Attendants were quick to snatch open the doors, and the group spilled out and moved toward the columns framing *Salon Kongresowa*.

Neill slowed his steps. The Palace had a familiar air; something about its lines tugged at his memory. He tried to place it but came up short.

"Moscow," Viktoriya prodded. "Is that what you're thinking?"

The captain's thoughts raced to the past. "You're right. This place looks very much like the State University."

The interior was just as impressive. More Policja, carrying Glauberyt machine pistols, were inside. A circular hall wrapped around the sprawling auditorium, with marbled pillars and red carpets stretching out in every direction.

A reception area had been set up in the lobby, known prestigiously as the Hall Coulois. Diplomatic passes were distributed from a long row of tables. Neill pinned his on and then helped Arrens with hers.

"Don't look now," he warned, his voice low, "But it appears that Viktoriya's white knights have arrived."

"At the far end?"

"I told you not to look," Neill chided, grinning.

Christina ignored him, her eyes probing the crowd. "Doesn't look good. Some kind of trouble with their papers."

"Well, we can't exactly vouch for them. Blown cover and what-not—too messy."

"We just can't shake those guys," she remarked.

Michael raised a brow. "Before it's all over, I have a feeling we might be thankful for that."

Christina let him lead the way as they left the foyer. They found themselves directed to Congress Hall where another attendant escorted the group to their seats.

"WHERE are you going?" Christina asked.

Viktoriya squeezed her friend's hand. "Here is where we part ways, *ma chere*. The press stall is on the next level." She lifted her chin and admired the amphitheater. Entry points along the perimeter gave access to anterooms and private booths on two floors.

"Does this remind you of something, Michael?" Her words were Ukrainian, and a knowing smile lit up her face.

Neill had already made the connection. "The opera house— on a much larger scale, of course." He checked his cell. They still had ten minutes before the conference began. "Come on, I'll walk you to your seat."

He scanned the stage as they moved. Ulyanov, Avery and Aultman were seated on the dais, having an animated discussion with Tomas Krol. An interpreter had also joined their huddle. The flags of a dozen countries were arrayed behind them, and there was no small stir when President Dobrogost's party entered the room.

Viktoriya wasn't impressed. "Michael, you know I don't like to butt in—"

"Since when?"

"Don't make fun," she glared, and then cast a glance in Christina's direction. Her voice dropped. "You know she's in love with you."

Neill feigned annoyance, dodging her eyes. "Did she tell you that?"

A classic re-direct. It occurred to her that Michael was good at such tactics. "No—not in so many words," she faltered. "But can't you tell? Everyone else can see it."

His head came around. "Slow down. Who's 'everyone else'?"

The question was enough to produce exasperation. "*Me*," Viktoriya answered. She stared into his face and then broke into a smile—before placing a kiss on his cheek.

The Marine couldn't help but grin back. "What was that for?"

"Odessa." She spun on her heel and entered the press booth.

Odessa again. Neill's ears reddened. There were a few amused expressions on those who mingled nearby. Something he'd done in the port city had brought flattering attention, but Michael couldn't guess what that might be.

He could puzzle over that later. Deciphering either woman's intentions would take more time, and right now the young officer had a phone call to make.

* * * *

TWO HUNDRED KILOMETERS AWAY, CHRIS Prentice pointed the nose of his Raptor east. He was the lead element for RAVEN Flight, and as he angled the fighter away from Gdansk, the colonel looked down and to his left.

His wingman today was a Polish lieutenant, fresh from of the Academy in Deblin. The young pilot jockeyed an F-16. The respective aircraft were flying a 'loose deuce' formation, with vast distances between their wingtips. In reality, the aviators were jetting ahead at different altitudes, which under normal conditions, wouldn't hinder their ability to fly as a team.

For that, Prentice groused, *we'll just rely on the disparity in language.*

The colonel's kvetching was done under his breath. All of the Polish pilots spoke English, or so he'd been told, but the truth was a little more revealing. Joint ops had all the ingredients for miscommunication, at best, and the alternative—well, that wasn't even worth thinking about, now was it?

Prentice gave the Poles an 'E' for effort. The Europeans had certainly bested their U.S. counterparts; many spoke a handful of languages, prompting Christian to consider the percentages for bi-lingual speakers in the American military. Spanish probably topped the list, to be sure, but he wondered—

"RAVEN-2, turn right and form up on my three o'clock position." The colonel spoke slowly; the Pole's responses had so far been sluggish—an indication that his command of English left something to be desired.

"Turning right, RAVEN Lead," the lieutenant repeated, almost immediately. His heavily accented voice crackled in the colonel's headset. "Forming up on your three o'clock position."

Sunlight pierced the canopy and a surprised Prentice smiled under his visored helmet. "That's a good copy, RAVEN-2. Kilo's just ahead."

The so-called Kaliningrad Corridor was the grid square designated for RESILIENT EAGLE. Location names were typically shortened—hence the reliance on acronyms, Christian decided—and *Kilo* was quickly adopted.

The colonel checked his scope. To the east, and headed in the opposite direction, another pairing of American and Polish flyers traced the southern reaches of Kilo's airspace. Their path lay parallel to RAVEN Flight. Two more groups followed from the west, and while their presence was encouraging, what he saw to the north was not.

The tactical air control center at Lask was coordinating with other assets; a Boeing E-3, with a rotating radar dish atop its fuselage. Their combined efforts gave a bird's-eye view of the playing field, and for the first time, coalition forces had a clear picture of the Russians' base of operations.

At this distance, they were far out of sight, but Christian's long-range display showed Ivan's fighters filling the sky. Hardware in the Raptor's nose identified the aircraft as Sukhoi 27s, along with two Su-34s, the brightly colored FULLBACKs he'd seen just days earlier. The birds now aloft had sprung from the base in Chkalovsk.

Their point of origin was telling. Chkalovsk was owned by the Russian Navy, and the Su-34s were operated by their Air Force, the *Voyenno-Vosdushnye Sily Rossii*. That mouthful of Slavic flowed easily enough from the locals' lips, but Prentice became tongue-tied at just the thought of saying it.

The colonel mulled over the collaboration between Russia's forces. Fighters from the Navy *and* Air Force were now working in tandem. The word had been passed that elements of the Rocket Forces were now in place, entrenched along Kaliningrad's southern border with Poland. The Russians were clearly intent on showing some muscle.

According to Prentice's software, eight fighters representing the opposing force were now airborne, with a couple of lumbering support platforms nearby. One was probably a refueler, and the other, with its larger radar return, was undoubtedly a Beriev A-50. This aircraft was far more robust than the E-3, but fulfilled the same role.

He looked on the bright side. None of Russia's assets had behaved provocatively. Christian gave them that. Ivan could be very disciplined. The Sukhois stayed behind their line, playing it safe and observing strict rules of engagement. Coalition pilots did the same, and no one—American, Polish, or Russian—had raised their radars to paint a hypothetical target.

Prentice whispered a prayer that everyone involved would act circumspectly. Stretching out far below were the ground forces of several nations. Getting twitchy now wouldn't help. Wars had begun over lesser things, and with everyone poised on the brink, he couldn't imagine a happenstance better suited to ruin everyone's day.

* * * *

"NOT NOW, CAPTAIN. AND NOT LIKE THIS."

Brian Weston—Major, RAF—was dispatching inconvenient news, doing so in a way that sounded like a favor. His thoroughly British accent was as smooth as honey, and he used it to great effect on those rare occasions when he was obligated to say *no*.

"What *can* you tell me?" Neill was on the receiving end of Weston's delivery. He'd found a small alcove off the main hall.

"Well, I don't mean to be a *dismal Jimmy*, Captain Neill." The MI6 officer was at his desk in London, peering out over the Thames. "Security being what it is, I'd prefer something more discreet."

"SIPRNet?" Neill returned.

"Your internet protocol router," the major agreed. "Our systems *do* talk to one another. And a bit of discretion wouldn't prove amiss."

Hoity-toity. A smile spread across Michael's face. Weston's measured phrasing sounded a bit pretentious, and Neill was beginning to understand what Aultman had meant.

"Do you have a pen, Major? I'll give you my address."

Chapter Twenty-Three * The Spy Game

THE FIRST DAY OF THE SUMMIT ENDED ON A predictable note. Delegates listened to the welcoming speeches and then traded opening remarks. The usual formalities were observed, with customs and courtesies filling most of the morning. To anyone with a discerning ear, this meant that very little was actually accomplished.

The display of protocol wasn't without a few redeeming moments. Neill gave Dobrogost and Avery a lot of credit. The two worked well as a team, laying out their goals in unmistakable terms. Each man emphasized the need for unity; standing up to the Russians would require more than just good intentions, after all. Their admonishments were appreciated, but Neill felt that the process was moving rather slowly.

"You must show some patience, Michael." General Ulyanov was ever the statesman. "Diplomacy takes time; look at the founding of your United States."

"I know," Neill frowned. "But we don't have two hundred years to get this done."

THE American delegation met at the Marconi for dinner. Avery invited a few others, as well; the Ukrainian officers accepted, as did Viktoriya, and Pyotr's presence was practically required. Each member of the group had changed into civilian clothing, and Avery was thankful to be rid of his tie.

Seeing Major Yaroslav lifted Neill's mood and encouraged a smile. "We missed you today, Dmitri. Did you sleep in?"

Yaroslav chuckled. "No such luck. I told you I would make inquiries, and so I have."

"Turn up anything?"

"Your hunch was right, Michael." Dmitri's gaze broadened, and he addressed everyone at the table. "At the Directorate's request, a Berkut unit has been dispatched by my government. A four man team. They have orders to protect Miss Gavrilenko."

Neill translated the major's words, and a look of relief passed over Christina's face. "Then she's in good hands."

"I wouldn't put that Colt away just yet," Michael replied. His tone suggested that he wasn't kidding.

THE national security advisor was interested in the news from Brian Weston—and MI6. After the meal he indulged in a few pleasantries, and then yielded the floor to Captain Neill.

Given the subject, and his own personal involvement, Michael wasn't quite sure where to begin. He decided it was best to start with a name.

"Ilya Nikolayevich Maersk." Neill's expression was sober. "The patronymic is disingenuous, since the name itself is a pseudonym. No one, not even the Brits, know his true identity.

"Some things are beyond dispute." He paused, giving Pyotr a chance to interpret for the other officers. "Her Majesty's Secret Intelligence Service recruited Maersk in the eighties. His cover was ironclad. At the time, he was pegged as a coveted asset—a Russian national, fleeing Soviet oppression and smuggled into London. And without a pound, a penny, or a ruble to his name."

"He was a plant," Ulyanov grumped. "The British couldn't see that?"

Neill shrugged. "Their frame of mind was different during the Cold War. MI6 was looking for resources. They were fishing, throwing out bait—"

"—but it was Maersk who reeled them in," Avery growled.

Aultman whistled softly. "Classic tradecraft."

Michael nodded. "Almost legendary, in fact. In an age before digital capabilities, Maersk practiced his skills as an old school *agent provocateur*." He drew in a breath. "He was embraced for his knowledge of Russian secrets. But after several years it became obvious that what he provided was just clutter." Neill shook his head. "It never yielded anything substantial."

Avery swore under his breath. "And at the same time, Western agents began to die or disappear." This story was beginning to sound familiar.

"That raised a few flags. MI6 was forced to admit they had a mole on their hands." A server appeared and began filling their cups. Neill waited until she had finished. "Parts of the file are blacked out, but this much is certain; the British closed in, and Maersk turned the tables. He killed five agents in one day—and then fled back to Moscow."

"What happened next?" Viktoriya was on the edge of her seat.

"The picture blurs at that point. Field reports indicate he continued his work as an FSB operative. There was also speculation over his involvement with the Hungarian Secret Police, but that was never proven."

"Our people were forced to shorten their reach," the national security advisor added glumly. "But even so, we lost agents."

"Yes, sir," Neill agreed. "Maersk was an assassin without equal. He became known for his ability to shadow his victims without their knowledge." Avery's head came up, and Neill looked his way. "Quite the *nom de guerre*, too. The Brits called him—"

"REMORA." The big man uttered the word with a detached dread. "*That* name I do know."

Dmitri's eyes fell on Viktoriya, and he posed a cautious question. "And now he's coming to Warsaw?"

"Maersk might be here already. I've turned over everything Weston sent to the agent in charge." Michael switched to Ukrainian. "And I'd like to brief your Berkut team. Can you arrange that?"

Yaroslav smiled evenly. "Within the hour, if you wish."

The general was very pensive. "And Mayakovsky—Michael, do you think—?"

"—that it was Maersk who killed him?" Neill nodded his head. "Absolutely."

"What about photos?" Christina asked.

"There aren't any," Neill said. "Before he left London, Maersk scrubbed the records."

"Clever." Avery had a wry look. "Thirty years ago a file was just that. The migration to electronic storage hadn't happened yet."

"You said he's old-school," Aultman threw in. "Does that mean he's off the grid?"

The captain nodded again. "That's exactly what it means. And it gives Maersk a tactical advantage. You can bet he won't be carrying a cell phone—not for this stage of the operation. Telecomm can be monitored, and this guy's too cagey to risk that."

Christina shifted to analysis. "He'll stay away from credit cards for the same reason. Cash-only transactions—so his logistics line will be short."

"Sounds like biometrics are out," Aultman offered glibly.

"So how do we find him?" Pyotr asked.

"We go on the offensive," Avery answered. "Captain Neill?"

"I have some thoughts on that. You and I can discuss it offline, Mr. Avery." Michael sipped from his coffee. "In the meantime, I suggest we proceed on two fronts." He stopped, and Christina whispered a translation to the journalist. "We can't protect Viktoriya and hunt Maersk at the same time. If this is going to be a joint op, we might as well treat it like one."

"The Berkut team?" Aultman asked.

"Exactly my thinking," Neill replied. "The name means

'golden eagle.' Special tactics police, for simplicity's sake. They're here to protect Viktoriya, so let's pool our resources." He faced Dmitri and shifted languages again. "Two of them had trouble getting into the conference this morning. Can you talk to the Directorate, maybe elevate their access?"

Ulyanov took that one. "The Ministry of Internal Affairs can help. I'll make a call after we break."

"At this hour?"

"I'm a *general*, Michael. I'll wake someone up if I have to."

"What else?" Avery broke in. Trying to unravel the variety of languages had his head spinning.

"We finish our coffee." Neill's smile widened. He viewed Avery with a steady eye, trying to gauge his mood. "And after that, sir, I'd like you to phone the Commandant."

The advisor-turned-diplomat raised a brow. "You want more boots on the ground?"

"Just one pair," Neill answered. "It's time we brought in a hunter; someone as stealthy as REMORA. And I know just the man—if we can find him."

* * * *

"You're wound up," Christina remarked.

"Too much caffeine." Michael walked slowly, and the group began drifting away from the table. The ever-watchful agents of the Secret Service stood nearby. They were concerned with keeping an eye on Avery, and their focus had sharpened since the previous day.

"It's getting late. What should we do about Viktoriya?"

Neill bit his lip. "That's right. She rode with us."

"And thanks to a certain Captain, she knows about REMORA." Arrens watched as the journalist lingered near Dmitri. "I think she'd rather stay here."

Neill shook his head. "How do you women communicate without saying a word?"

She shrugged. "It's more like intuition. Any ideas?"

"She can have my room," Michael teased.

"I will punch you," she warned.

"Feisty. I like that."

"Very funny," Christina squinted. "Forget all those nice things I said about you."

He grinned back. "It was just a suggestion."

An alternative sprang to mind. "My suite has two beds. She can bunk with me—at least for tonight."

"Agreed. Tomorrow we'll bring her guardians up to speed on Maersk." He peered through the window, his eyes sweeping the brightly lit streets of the Royal Route. Neill knew they were out there, but he couldn't see the black Mercedes. "I'll pass the word."

"Wait." Christina touched his arm. "I want to tell you something."

"What did I do now?"

She was thoughtful and considered her next statement. "The way you talk about Maersk. Very objectively—no emotion."

"On the surface, maybe. Let's just say I'm dealing with it."

"You're doing a good job," she returned. "There's no anger in your voice. If it were me, I'd go for revenge." The young woman frowned. "I still might."

Neill stepped closer and their eyes met. "The café's open. Would you like to talk about it?"

His tone was warm and inviting. The man could certainly turn on the charm. Christina wanted to accept—

"It's getting late."

"You said that already." Michael was being assertive, not pushy, but his attentions now gave her pause.

"I know." She couldn't stop staring. "Tomorrow will be busy. Let's get Viktoriya settled, and then we should all get some sleep."

* * * *

TO THE EAST, IN NEIGHBORING UKRAINE, THE general's wife used a sharp blade to slice the cucumbers and then scraped the vegetables into a bowl. Chopped dill came next, along with lemon juice. Sour cream, pepper, and salt were added for taste. She was known for this dish, and with all the ingredients mixed together, she covered the concoction and put it into the fridge to chill.

She realized she had made too much. It was a common mistake, she told herself, but at least it would be fresh—even if the stuffed dumplings from the freezer were not. Preparing meals for one, in any country, could be a challenge, and Mrs. Ulyanov could be forgiven her lack of focus.

There was good reason for that. Irina had spent the better part of the day nursing a restless anxiety. Andrei had called the previous evening to share the news from Warsaw. It had taken some time, but she managed to extract all the details—including a few that he would have preferred not to share.

Most alarming was his account of the shooting outside the Bristol. She felt no great loss over the death of one terrorist, and was grateful that her husband had arrived after the event. But when she heard about Michael's injury—

For a woman who had borne no children, her maternal instincts were strong indeed. Irina had known Jean Neill, and despite her reserved and cautious personality, she had come to love and respect the younger American woman. A wary nature was typical for many who lived in Eastern Europe—an unnatural by-product of the old Soviet paranoia. The thought brought a tear to Irina's eye. Many of her countrymen still lived in oppression, long after communism's demise, and even more had no knowledge of the Truth.

But life had long since changed for the Ulyanovs. Shortly after their arrival, the Neills introduced the Ukrainian couple to an extraordinary faith. Irina resisted at first; besides, what good could come from this foreign religion? Its founder had been dead for more than two thousand years, and the Party opposed His teachings as a matter of course.

The State declared that Christianity was a dangerous influence. That was true, but for reasons that neither Moscow nor

Kiev were willing to disclose. Irina could see that now. Her eyes had been opened when Andrei came home with a Bible, gifted to him by David Neill. The following morning, after her husband had left for the air base, she began to read. The old texts captivated her heart and mind for hours, and within the week, the Western missionaries had two more believers to add to their growing list.

It was late when Irina finished her supper. The *salat z ohirkiv* was satisfying, and would taste better tomorrow, but she would not be there to enjoy it. Over the course of her meal Irina had come to a decision, and now there were travel arrangements to be made.

An Austrian Airlines flight, bound for Warsaw, would leave from Kiev on the following afternoon. Irina's skills with the internet were modest, but she managed to purchase a one-way ticket. The departure time was set for seven p.m., and before she locked up the house the next day, Mrs. Ulyanov's famous cucumber salad would relinquish its place in the icebox and be passed to the family that lived next door.

Chapter Twenty-Four * Hunter of Gunmen

"WE'VE BEEN MADE."

Voskov was not in the best of moods. He slid the cell phone across the table and then ambled to the second floor window. The view faced east, and Xander was greeted with glare as the sun rose over Warsaw.

"So I gathered," Yuri replied. The tall Ukrainian had heard Xander's terse conversation, even from the tiny kitchenette. Stepping into the small living space, he poured steaming water into two cups and then dropped teabags into each. "It was only a matter of time, boss." He looked for a spoon—and sugar. The captain preferred his *chai* sweet and Yuri didn't want to frustrate him further.

"It was the hotel," Xander grated, but it was a useless observation.

"Of course it was the hotel," Yuri said with a laugh. "You wrapped those gorilla arms of yours around a red-headed damsel. I jumped on top of a man with an automatic rifle. Did you think they wouldn't notice?" He turned and opened the microfridge. "You don't want cream, do you?"

Xander smiled evenly. "This Marine is clever, *tavarisch*. He wasn't just taking pictures of that sergeant."

"Ahh. My *krasyva zhinka*," Yuri sighed, recalling the young woman—and then snapped back. "Did we get new instructions?"

"Our credentials have received an upgrade—Yegor and Iosef, too." Their comrades had the night shift, allowing Yuri and Xander a chance to sleep.

"When?"

"Today," the officer replied. There was ice in the streets below and more glistened on the exterior pane. "We will be met by a Major Yaroslav when we reach the Palace. He's part of the State Security Directorate." Voskov moved away from the window. The morning light hurt his eyes.

"And there is someone else who would like a word."

Northwestern England

THE SUN WASN'T QUITE UP ON THE SEFTON Coast, a stretch of beach and woodland spanning the miles between Liverpool and Southport. Bounded by the estuaries of Mersey and Ribble, this wide expanse of dunes and marshes was a natural habitat, and the home of a variety of animal life that included wading birds, sand lizards, and a short-legged amphibian known as the Natterjack toad.

Nestled in the heart of this preserve was the staid military base known as the Altcar Training Camp. The site included indoor and outdoor shooting ranges, and was a favorite of Her Majesty's regulars when it came to honing marksmanship. Recently, the camp had attracted American leathernecks, drawn by special invitation to compete in the Royal Marines Skill at Small Arms Meeting. The yearly competition was designed to test shooters on both sides of the Atlantic.

Participants from the U.S. were not full-time competitors. These Marines were generally drawn from infantry units. A healthy percentage came from the Second Division, an arm of the Corps based at Camp Lejeune, in North Carolina. Drilling deeper, First Battalion/Eighth Marines had three representatives, but only one of those could claim an affiliation with One-Eight's scout/sniper platoon.

First Lieutenant Nathan Crockett yawned, stretched, and

then swung his legs over the edge of the bunk, his bare feet landing on the floor of his billet. A hint of dawn teased from the windows of the Nissen hut—a precursor to Quonsets—and in the soft light, Crockett checked his surroundings.

Last night's festivities had left him with a strong case of buyer's remorse . The visiting Marines had won handsomely during this year's meet. Celebrations were naturally in order and the camp's watering hole, the Red Rose, was located just behind officer's country. Crockett and his comrades had made rather merry—well into the early hours—before finding their way back to the huts.

The lieutenant's service alphas lay strewn across the top bunk, right where he'd left them. His sea bag sat upright, stuffed with gear and secured to the rack with a cable. A locker stood in the aisle—a necessary concession to the curved wall of the billet. The rest of his uniforms, a garment bag and civilian clothing hung inside the metal cabinet. And no matter where he found himself, Crockett's waking eyes always searched for the one indispensable tool of his trade.

Iron Mike. The lieutenant smiled. To the common man, he bore the unflattering title of HOG, but that was merely an acronym for *hunter of gunmen*. That was the handle given to those who completed the Corps' prestigious sniper school. As such, his rifle was normally a constant companion, but the M4 carbine was now locked away in the armory. It was a shorter version of the venerable M16, designed for CQB, or close quarters battle. Crockett had used it during the competition, along with the bolt-action M40, the standard issue firearm for Marine snipers.

There was no one else in the room. The front part of the hut was partitioned, affording guests with rank a little privacy. Crockett was thankful for that. Right now he required caffeine and his hosts had thoughtfully equipped the room with a coffeemaker.

The lieutenant pulled on his socks and padded across the cold floor. He emptied half a bottle of water in the back of the brewer, loaded one coffee pack, and then jabbed the switch.

A trip to the head came next—or the *loo*, as his English cousins called it. Fortunately, his accommodations included a bathroom. He'd spent many deployments where that wasn't the case—scurrying down a hall, or worse yet, to a tree line or sand dune when nature called.

As the brewer sputtered through its cycle, the Marine returned to the comfort of his bunk. He had just burrowed beneath a wool blanket when the shuffling sound of footsteps broke the stillness; there was movement outside, and for his sake, Crockett hoped that whoever was passing by would keep going.

"Rise and shine, Lieutenant." There was a light rap as someone tried turning the knob. "Open up."

The response was muffled. "I'm not here."

"Not buyin' it, Crockett." The caller was insistent. "Up and at 'em. You've got new orders."

The sniper groaned and stumbled out of bed. He recognized the voice of his unwelcome visitor. Crockett eased the door open and braced at the icy air blowing in from the coastline.

The man on his porch was well-protected against the cold. Captain Vincenzo de Hoyas wore camouflaged utilities along with a Gore-Tex jacket and fleece liner. His woodland eight-point cover was perched on the crown of his head, the bill shielding intensely dark eyes. He was broad-shouldered, but narrowed dramatically at the waist.

His close friends called him Vinnie, but De Hoyas' short legs and V-shaped frame gave rise to another label. His Marines called him *Spinner*, for his resemblance to a child's top—but also for the way he allowed circumstances to control his actions.

The captain sized up the man before him. "You look awful, Lieutenant."

"It's your fault," he grumbled. "You bought the first round."

"And then I left. Which is what you should have done."

Crockett ignored the retrospective advice. "No orders— I'm on leave." He muttered something about the hour and then retreated to the relative warmth of the hut.

De Hoyas followed him inside, grinning. "Not anymore,

sunshine. Five little words—all leaves are canceled. Belay that; not *all* leaves. Just yours."

Nate frowned, counting on one hand. "That's four words." He found a dirty mug and filled it to the brim. "The coffee's for me," he mumbled. "But there's water if you want it. Now explain yourself."

De Hoyas wasn't a coffee drinker, which Crockett found annoying. "H & S called at three a.m.," the captain began. He was referring to the Headquarters and Service Battalion. "We're talkin' Henderson Hall, not Lejeune. *They* got a call from SECNAV—it goes higher, but I didn't ask."

"Sounds very cloak and dagger," Crockett said. A half-smile formed on his face. He settled into an overstuffed chair and sipped from his mug. "You'd better be nice to me."

"No worries there, Mr. Crockett." De Hoyas planted himself on the end of the bunk. "I'm here to see to all your travel needs."

He gave De Hoyas a sideways look. "So where are these so-called orders?" The captain wasn't carrying paperwork.

"Vocal authorization," Spinner replied. He looked at his phone. "You're on an airplane."

Marines sometimes described future events in the present tense. That practice was widespread at Parris Island, the Corps' recruit depot east of the Mississippi. De Hoyas had spent a tour there as a series commander and the habit had stuck.

"No, no, *no*." Crockett's grin slipped away. Voco orders meant the tasking was a response to an unplanned event. "Come on, Cap'n—we won the match. Why am I being punished?"

De Hoyas removed the cover from his head. "Hey, I'm just the lowly officer in charge. You, on the other hand, have popped up on somebody's radar."

"If you look the other way—"

"Neither one of us can wiggle out of this, Crockett. Now pack your trash. We're on the road." He was doing it again.

Petulance wasn't working, so Nate gave in. "Where am I going?"

"A C-130's been tasked from Mildenhall. We'll meet them

in Manchester. The way I hear it, you're headed to Poland. You know where Lask is?"

"Never heard of it."

De Hoyas pushed ahead. "We have an air base there." He pulled a folded sheet from his breast pocket. "Manchester to Leipzig, and then northeast into Central Europe. Your contact is a guy named Neill. I understand you two have worked together."

Neill? It all made sense now. Crockett stared into his mug and finished the coffee before it cooled. Nine months had passed since OPERATION HEAVY ANVIL—but the lieutenant, a butter-bar at the time, sat that one out. Neill's ties to friends in high places had made sure of that.

Nathan Crockett didn't like to admit it—much less to Neill—but he'd thoroughly enjoyed their little adventure in the South China Sea. They'd had their fun, broken a few rules, and managed to help avert a war. There had been a few bumps along the way; Neill getting shot wasn't part of the plan, and that business aboard the British submarine was the stuff of nightmares. Of course, Crockett could never *tell* anyone about those events, and the rank he now wore was partly a recompense for his troubles.

The brass had certainly pulled some strings; it was more like high-test line, Nate decided. At least it should prove interesting. Central Europe was someplace he'd never been, and Poland was an ally now. He resigned himself to the situation and hoped that this time the operation was planned for dry soil. If that was the case, he wouldn't even have to get his feet wet.

Chapter Twenty-Five * Sharp Elbows

Near Gora Kalwaria,
South of Warsaw

JEAN-PAUL GRIPPED THE RAIL AND WATCHED the divers, pirouetting slowly on the surface as they grew accustomed to the chill. The safety checks came first; the two immersed themselves, gauging the flow of oxygen from the tanks on their backs. Their neoprene wetsuits blended perfectly with the jet-black waters, and in seconds, Toussaint lost sight of the men as they receded into the depths.

His gaze shifted. The boom of the derrick was poised above, but it would be some time before the hoist could be used. The winching station was unmanned, and the span tackle and halyard swung lazily, moved only by the icy gusts that followed the Vistula south.

Henri Minouche stood at the entrepreneur's side, a clipboard clutched in one gloved hand. First he checked the diminishing stack of vinyl conduits. These were being fed below, positioned beneath the keel of the Swedish barge and the mud that held it fast. His next concern was for the electronics monitoring the divers' efforts. The river bottom was murky and the view from the cameras trained on the hulk required a discerning eye.

"We have made considerable progress, fore and aft," Minouche reported.

"Any obstacles?" Jean-Paul asked.

"None that we haven't been able to overcome." The compressor kicked in, forcing the men to raise their voices.

"That is good news." Toussaint seemed to relax. As the excavation progressed, he came to trust Henri's judgment more and more. The biggest question went unasked and Minouche decided to reward his employer with an unsolicited reply.

"A few more days, Jean-Paul—barring mechanical problems and a shift in the weather."

Toussaint said nothing. He hoped Henri was right. Each day on the Vistula was costing him thousands and results were needed to recover his losses. In any case, the expenditures incurred by this enterprise would pay dividends—icon or no icon. Taking on this project was a boon to public relations, and had earned Archaeologique François a form of capital that went beyond money.

The river had drawn lower, receding from its banks. That was a good sign and offered some consolation. Jean-Paul was hardly a devout man, but he whispered a prayer that the same circumstance wouldn't drain his reputation.

* * * *

WILLIS AVERY LIKED NEILL'S STYLE, SO HE PERsuaded him to lead the morning preamble at the Palace. The Marine didn't object. He was well-versed in the system and walked the delegates through a detailed summary of SMOOTH STONE's benefits.

Most attendees spoke or understood a great deal of Ukrainian, and Neill supplemented his discourse with as much Polish as his limited training would allow. This impressed most of the emissaries. His delivery was tailor-made for those who had chafed under Soviet rule, and his avoidance of any pronouncements in the Russian tongue had won many in the crowd.

A few of the representatives were nudged into a conciliatory mood. They peppered the captain with reasonable questions—some in English—responding thoughtfully to his tempered answers. It was a ploy of sorts. NATO was a major sponsor of the missile shield, but the elephant in the room was the United States. Some republics showed reluctance over choosing sides. Most knew it was necessary, yet mistrust was a difficult thing to overcome. Neill's fluency helped, and his reverence for the culture put a friendly face on the West's efforts—which had been Avery's intention all along.

By mid-morning, the captain had spoken at length, emptying a bottle of water as his voice became hoarse. He wrapped up his presentation and yielded the lectern to Tomas Krol, slipping behind the scenes to meet with Dmitri and Pyotr.

* * * *

"THERE ARE A LOT OF SHARP ELBOWS HERE TO-day, Michael," Yaroslav observed. "But I think your words have helped."

"Maybe, but they aren't exactly eating out of my hand," Neill cautioned. "Estonia and Romania worry me."

Dmitri's expression was hard to read. "I believe General Ulyanov is working to leverage their support," he said softly.

The Marine checked his cell; this morning's docket was a bit crowded, and he was concerned they might run late. "Did you catch up with our friends?"

Dmitri nodded. "Captain Aleksander Voskov. His subordinate is Senior Sergeant Yuri Tereshenko. Both are seasoned veterans of the Berkut."

"Are they on board?"

"Captain Voskov seems a little stiff, Mischa," Pyotr volunteered. "But I think they're relieved to have our assistance."

"And vice versa," Michael replied. Plan B was forming in the back of his mind. "I'll brief both of them when I get back—no time now." He caught Richard Aultman's approach from the corner of his eye. "Ready to go?"

The man dangled a set of car keys in one hand. "Whenever you are." He smiled and pointed a thumb toward the dais. "Dad let me borrow the car."

"Time to meet our guest, then," Neill said, and then told Pyotr, "Richard and I are headed to Lask. Tell Christina to keep an eye on Viktoriya."

A wicked grin creased Stanislaw's face. "Did she bring her purse?" he asked.

The Kaliningrad Corridor (Kilo)
Three hours later

CHRIS PRENTICE WAS PAIRED WITH HIS WING-man, RAVEN-2. The pilots angled their aircraft to the west and the Polish lieutenant took point while the colonel followed in a trailing position. Prentice smiled. *Sometimes*, he thought, *you had to let the youngsters take a crack at being lead dog.*

The senior officer dipped his starboard wing and eyed the horizon. Thick bands of nimbostratus pushed south. The clouds were heavy with moisture—more snow, Prentice determined—and hugged the landscape at an altitude of five thousand feet. At 'angels ten'—ten thousand feet—the sun was bright, but the air beyond his canopy was well below freezing.

The colonel's gaze swept north. The expanse was oddly qui-et. Across the border, above Kaliningrad, Ivan hadn't come out to play—or he was just beyond visual range. Prentice squinted. Apart from an Airbus to the east, the skies were clear.

Next, he checked for incoming threats on his HUD, or heads-up display. Eight kilometers due west, two contacts were rocket-ing toward them at nearly eleven hundred KPH—awfully fast. The Raptor's avionics told him they were below the ceiling, but little more.

The colonel was frowning now. Weather could have an adverse effect on forward looking radar—especially in the in-frared range—and the cloud cover beneath RAVEN Flight was giving the system fits.

* * * *

IN HIS SUKHOI-27, CAPTAIN MAXIM KUDRIN kept his targeting electronics off. His wingman did the same.

Neither Russian wanted their gear to signal their positions.

Passive radar was spotty, but between their infrared search and track suite—and the information provided by the eyes and ears of the Beriev—Kudrin knew his adversaries were closing from the east.

The captain looked through the heads-up display, noted his airspeed and began to climb. By the time the nose of his FLANKER entered the veil overhead, the Russians had pushed their engines to full afterburner.

* * * *

PRENTICE WATCHED THE RADAR RETURNS EMA-nating from below. He should have been able to identify them; equipment on friendly aircraft was designed for that, with sensors transmitting coded messages intended to separate the good guys from the bad. But the frequency at the moment was just so much dead air.

One inoperative transponder was possible—but two?

His mind raced; he knew that YANKEE Flight was on a parallel track far to the south. JOLLY ROGER was the lead element for that pairing and Prentice had marked their location just before turning west. There was no way YANKEE could have covered that distance to intercept them—much less appearing on RAVEN's doorstep . . .

Something was amiss. Prentice keyed his mike, preparing to call RAVEN-2 back to a tandem position. The Polish lieutenant was a little too jumpy, and with tensions being what they were—

The colonel cursed out loud. He should have seen this coming. Digits on the HUD spiked; the newcomers' altitudes were rising. Ivan had burst through the clouds and now both aircraft were arcing their way.

* * * *

KUDRIN WAS PRESSING HIS LUCK. INCLEMENT weather called for caution and there were unfriendlies nearby. Putting his fighter on the roof—and at this rate of speed—

risked a mid-air collision.

His first thought after breaking into the open was to survey the battle space ahead. He breathed a sigh of relief; the NATO component was close, but the Russian still had plenty of room to maneuver. Two American-made interceptors were directly ahead. The lead aircraft belonged to Poland; the A-50 from Chkalovsk had already confirmed that. The F-22, on the other hand—that bird was definitely a U.S. asset, as Raptors were not sold to foreign governments.

The captain pitched his nose down. He leveled out quickly, and then flipped the switch on his radar and painted the targets, setting up a shot with one of his R-27 Vympel missiles.

* * * *

THREAT INDICATORS ABOARD THE F-22 BEGAN to buzz in the colonel's ears. Sensors in the F-16 did the same. RAVEN-2's master arm switch was locked and cocked—a state of readiness Prentice had warned against. The Polish lieutenant was high-strung, and seeing Ivan appear before them sent the young officer into a panic.

RAVEN-2's instincts kicked in, but not his discipline. He was far too edgy for his own good. The continuous tone in his headset told him he had a positive lock on the FLANKER; time seemed to compress, but the clock was ticking. The Sukhoi was bearing down on them, and if he waited, the Pole would miss his chance—and most likely get an air-to-air rocket in his teeth.

PRENTICE could almost sense what was happening in his wingman's cockpit. He banked left and brought up his nose, then called over the radio, "Ease off, RAVEN-2. He's goading you. You are weapons hold; I say again—*you are weapons hold*—"

The greenhorn was beyond taking orders. Reacting to the stimulus of his warning systems, RAVEN-2 made a fateful decision. His thumb hovered over the weapon release, and in the heat of the moment, he depressed the red button, triggering the launch of an AIM-9 short range missile.

IT was a snap shot. The Sidewinder slid off the rails and followed a steady course in to the target. The colonel could only watch from above—and pray that the weapon might fail in mid-flight. That request was about to be denied.

A 20-millimeter cannon was embedded in his right wing; Prentice had over four hundred rounds at his disposal, along with four AMRAAM missiles tucked into the weapons bay. Those were for offense. Defensively, the Raptor employed ECM, or electronic counter-measures, as well as chaff and flares to decoy incoming kill shots.

Things might get dicey, and he was queuing up those when his worst fears came to pass.

KUDRIN hadn't expected this. His eyes widened at the sight of the incoming ordnance. He sucked in his breath and started to throw the control column to the right, but that would have put him in the Raptor's path. Banking left wasn't a good choice either. His reflexes failed him, and in the end, the captain simply choked.

The opposing jets' closing speeds enabled the Sidewinder to reach its target quickly. The AIM-9 struck the Sukhoi amidships. Two jarring *whumps* came next. Kinetic energy and the exploding warhead split the fuselage, shearing off the wing and sending the twisting airfoil up and back before it began to plummet to earth. Fire, debris and smoke bloomed briefly, and then the mortally wounded FLANKER heeled over on its left side and tumbled from the sky.

The Russian had intended to frighten his adversary. His ill-conceived actions backfired in the worst possible way, and he was lucky to escape with his life.

Maxim's ejection seat still functioned and jettisoned him from the cockpit—and the burning plane—at a ninety degree angle. Everything had happened so quickly; with his adrenaline flowing, Kudrin was completely unaware that his right arm was shattered.

Dazed by the one-sided dogfight, the second Su-27 rolled hard to the north. Without his wingman and flight lead, the fight had just gone out of him, and his thrust rate didn't diminish for a full minute.

* * * *

FOR HIS PART, COLONEL PRENTICE CHECKED HIS instruments. Relief came as he noted the GPS readout on the HUD. It was clear that RAVEN Flight was well within Kilo's boundaries, and it was also very evident that the Russians had crossed the border—into Polish airspace—to pick a fight.

RAVEN-2 formed up once more on his three o'clock position. There was no way to tell, but Prentice imagined that the man's complexion had blanched. He managed a wry grin. The repercussions of this incident would undoubtedly dog the lieutenant's career for quite a while.

THERE was radio traffic in the colonel's headset. JOLLY ROGER had heard the brief exchange on the common mission channel and was asking if Prentice needed an assist.

The colonel watched as Ivan's parachute reached the cloud cover. "Nick, we're gonna need the search and rescue boys." The red and white canopy drifted evenly and then disappeared. "Ivan punched out and my guess is he sustained a few injuries."

Prentice powered down his defensive systems and wondered if that was a conservative estimate. For all he knew, the Russian might be dead. Only the fact that he bailed gave the colonel a little hope.

He'd have to call it in. Undoubtedly, the Air Operations Center at Lask had monitored all this, utilizing the airborne assets of the E-3 that seemed to be continuously aloft. And they would not be happy. RAVEN-2—*his* wingman—had just shot down a Russian fighter, creating an international incident—and possibly igniting the next world war.

Chapter Twenty-Six * Hostile State

"**N**O TORPEDOES?"

"Nope," Neill shook his head. "None whatsoever."

"What about submarines?" The lieutenant shuddered. "I hate those things."

"There are no submarines in Warsaw," Neill assured him. "The country's basically land-locked on three sides. And there are some aspects of this you'll probably enjoy."

Nate Crockett sank into the back seat of the diplomatic car. "The limo's definitely a nice touch," he conceded. "How's your shoulder, by the way?"

The captain rotated his arm in its socket. "Feels great. No residual effects at all."

Crockett cast a cautious glance at Richard Aultman, who was driving. "Should we be talking about all this . . . you know. In front of—?"

"Richard's the executive assistant to the national security advisor," Michael replied. "I think his clearances are adequate."

"And I'm a pretty good chauffeur," Aultman quipped. "Are you hungry, Lieutenant?"

"The flight crew passed out box nasties in Leipzig." Crockett leaned forward and watched as the countryside rolled by. "Hey, I don't mean to be rude, Mike, but—"

"—you want to know what you're doing here."

A grin. "That thought did cross my mind."

Neill was riding shotgun. He turned to face his friend.

"I remember a conversation we had aboard the *Lexington*," he began. "What you said that day stuck with me."

Nate's grin widened. "I'm a regular Chatty Cathy. Can you be more specific?"

The recollection worked its way to the surface. "Something about visual acuity and crystalized thinking. A sniper's perception of the world—remember that?"

Nate was nodding now. "Those two concepts go hand in hand, as far as I'm concerned. Eyesight's a key factor—and don't discount peripheral vision, either. Crystalized intelligence is the stuff that flows from experience. Plus the knowledge base built up over the course of a lifetime." His tone bore a trace of swagger. "It's all rolled into my philosophy."

"So you fancy yourself a philosopher?" Neill was amused.

"You asked," Crockett shot back.

"Explain how that relates to you."

Nate was spun up. He'd slept on the plane, and his headache was gone. "A sniper uses his eyes. A lot. He gathers intel from what he sees around him."

"I think I see the connection," Neill answered. "You said that both eventually peak; and at some point, they converge—overlapping to give shooters a kind of sixth sense."

"That's a bit simplified," Crockett hedged. "Eyesight starts to wane in our forties, but reasoning tends to heighten. The trick is to make the most of our *sweet spots*—capitalize on that age where both are working at optimum efficiency."

"Have you reached your sweet spot?"

Nate deliberated. "I think so. Vision hasn't degraded, and my thinking's more mature every day. Is that why I'm here?"

"Yeah. I need your super-powered eyeballs and that polished maturity." Neill held back a smile. "More than anything, I could use your ability to see through camouflage and identify what doesn't belong."

"What's the mission?"

"Overwatch. We're protecting someone."

Crockett was all business now. "Snipers don't do that, Mike. We hunt people down and shoot them."

Neill held up a hand. "Hear me out. If you feel the same way two minutes from now, we'll put you on the next flight back to Lejeune."

"Liar." Crockett leaned back again. "All right—make your sales pitch. Is the target a Pole, or one of our guys?"

"She's Ukrainian."

"She?" His brows went up. "A Ukrainian woman?" Nate winced. "Please, tell me she's not one of those potatoes-and-cabbage-every-day types. I've seen pictures, Mike."

It was time for a little fun. "Her diet's none of our concern. And what difference does it make?"

Oh, geez, Crockett wanted to groan. "I think I left a box of get-me-the-heck-out-of-Dodge back on the flight line. *Driver*—"

The Marine in front pulled out his cell phone. "Hang on. I might have her photo." He scrolled through a few images and handed the mobile across the seat. "This is her."

There was a stunned silence. Aultman grinned and watched the lieutenant's expression in the rearview mirror. After a moment, Crockett whistled softly.

"Mercy me." Nate continued to stare. "Neill, you set me up."

"Still need that box?"

"What box?" His eyes never left the screen and he whistled again. "Look at that dress. She could catch cold in something like that."

Michael shrugged. "She seems healthy enough."

"I would not argue with that." He started tabbing through the images. "I might need you to send these to my phone. For identification purposes." It took Crockett a second to focus on anything else. "In this photo she's standing next to *Lieutenant* Neill—so this isn't recent. What's her name?"

"Viktoriya."

"Of course it is," Nate chuckled. "I've said it before and I'll say it again, Mike—you are one sneaky preacher-man."

"What other details can you pick out?"

"Testing my theory?" Nate asked. "Okay, it's on. These were taken in Eastern Europe—probably Ukraine. You two were attending the theater." A pause. "In the company of friends—and it was winter."

Neill nodded his head. "Right on all counts. I'm impressed."

"I'm the one who's impressed," the Marine said, eyeing the picture on the phone. "Why would anyone want to kill *her?*"

Neill took the next few minutes to explain his mission to Odessa. He supplied details about Russia's acts of terrorism—including the stolen warhead—and then spelled out Viktoriya's contributions in bringing down the Murovanka presidency.

"She did all that?" Crockett asked.

"Well, she did have help," Neill granted. He left out Ivan Malyev's name.

The phone buzzed softly, and Crockett checked the screen. "You've got traffic."

Neill retrieved the cell, did more listening than talking, and after a moment he ended the call. His face had a concerned look.

"That was Christina. There's been an incident." He shot a glance back at Crockett. "Nice goin', Nate. You've been here two whole hours and we're practically at war."

Further explanations would have to wait. The vehicle's in-dash Bluetooth winked on. Willis Avery was on the other end and his call would dominate much of their ride back to the capital.

* * * *

WARSAW'S OUTWARD APPEARANCE WAS LARGE-ly an illusion. The façades ran deep; vast chunks of the city had been destroyed in World War II, and then restored to match the look of an older age. Reconstruction had dominated much of the past seventy years, and while some medieval stones still stood, 'rebuilt' was the common term used to describe the castles and cathedrals that dotted the Royal Route.

It was a monumental effort that had paid off. As cities went, *Varshava* was as picturesque as any postcard, and so the old man decided to play tourist. He was alone and on foot—a bit unusual; aside from that, he fit the mold perfectly. Locals were quite accustomed to having visitors, and who would begrudge, much less even notice, the presence of one more excursionist?

Sightseers often chose winter for its seasonal attraction, but the old man wasn't here for that. Professional considerations had brought him to Warsaw. He had a job to do, and to him, these so-called 'holy days'—venerating a dead Jew— were nothing more than a myth and a distraction.

ILYA Maersk was no stranger to Warsaw. He had visited before the fall of the Soviet empire, and several times since. He knew the districts well, with landmarks and thoroughfares etched in his memory. The skyline was little changed since his last trip, and for a man with few friends, the city offered an anonymity that he felt comfortable with.

Maersk stood at the northern corner of the City Center. How he found himself there was a mystery. His eyes were fixed on a memorial, one that was jarringly graphic—a railway car piled high with black crosses, commemorating the hundreds of thousands carried away and murdered in Soviet labor camps.

A cross, of all things. The symbol itself was puzzling. It was an instrument of torture and death, yet it had become a treasured emblem for an impossible faith. Maersk had never understood the attraction; there was no need to complicate the here and now with fantasies of some heavenly being. It was simple, really. Life was finite. Death was final. The former

offered some hope; the latter, none. Couldn't the Priest's fol-
lowers see that? He shook his head. The religious were a su-
perstitious lot, and Ilya's cold intellect could find no rationale
to explain their beliefs.

Maersk turned away and followed the Ulica back to the
van. He had spent the past two days studying the local papers.
One story had gained his interest. It bore the Turandot byline,
and the feature's content gave him two possible clues to the
journalist's whereabouts.

The lengthy narrative described the opening day of the
summit, but it also mentioned the attack on the American
diplomat. This Gavrilenko woman—he was convinced it was
her—had written about both as if she were an eyewitness. If
that was the case, then finding her might be easier than he
imagined. Getting close enough to kill—

That was something else.

* * * *

It was late afternoon when the diplomat-
ic car reached the palace. Neill escorted Crockett inside—there
hadn't been time to generate credentials—while Aultman met
with Avery.

"That's your Christina?" Nate asked under his breath. "She's
a doll."

"She's not *my* Christina." Neill was flustered. "And gorgeous or not, I should probably remind you that she's an NCO."

Crockett was amused. "I didn't say she was gorgeous," he
grinned. "Is there somethin' you wanna tell me?"

"Yeah, there is." The captain became serious. "She's the
other part of the equation. I want you to keep your eyes on her,
too."

Half the delegates had left. The rest conferred where they
could—in the main auditorium, on the dais, or in the anterooms found on both floors. The press box was empty and
the two women greeted the Marines as they entered the hall.
Introductions were made and Christina confirmed what Avery

had already told them.

"You look tired," the captain observed. Arrens' expression made him regret the comment.

"Thanks," she said dryly. "It's been a long day."

"Want to sit?" Neill asked. "What's the latest?"

She sighed heavily. "Initial reports are sketchy. NATO's been very tight-lipped, but not so much with the Kremlin. According to them, a 'state of hostilities' now exists between Poland and the Russian Federation. Suvorov and Moscow have condemned *our* military action as 'highly provocative.'"

Nate's dander was rising. "A *state of hostilities*? What the Sam Hill does that mean?"

"Just typical bluster," Neill dismissed. "If you rant, people start listening. Do it long enough—"

"—and they start to believe it," Arrens smiled. It was one of Neill's axioms and she had heard it before.

"I was afraid of this," Michael frowned. He might need Plan B after all. "Where's Pyotr?"

"With Dmitri. Smoothing feathers—the golden type."

Neill had a knowing look. "Our friends in the Berkut," he said.

"What's next?" Viktoriya asked. Her eyes drifted to Crockett. The lieutenant stared back. This mission had begun to grow on him.

"Time to phone a friend," Neill cracked. "Anybody know what time it is in San Diego?"

Chula Vista, California
0730

SIMON CHAU STIRRED FROM SLEEP. THE GENTLE tone of his cell was incessant and the Navy officer frowned; he was sure he'd killed the alarm before going to bed. He rolled over, fumbling toward the nightstand and discovered that his wife was missing.

A look at the display told him he was right; it wasn't the alarm at all. A call was coming through. The screen ID brought a smile, and conjured images of a rather harrowing night on the island of Huo Shan.

"Morning, Si." Neill's voice was chipper. "You at the shop?"

Chau's feet hit the floor and he returned the greeting. "Leave day. Just got back into town." A hand rubbed away sleep and the aroma of breakfast drifted in from the kitchen.

Six thousand miles away, the Marine's eyes widened. "Honeymoon," he recalled bluntly. "Sorry, Simon—I hope I didn't interrupt—"

"You didn't. What's up?"

＊ ＊ ＊ ＊

"Who called?" Kelsi Pressman-Chau asked. She turned strips of Angus beef in the skillet, and before he could answer, she gave her groom a morning kiss.

"That was Neill." Simon savored her affection. "He needs a favor."

"Michael Neill?" Kelsi's face became a scowl. The meat sizzled on cue. "Stay away from that guy. He's trouble."

"Steak?" Simon leaned over the range and sniffed the food. "What's in the marinade?"

"Cherry juice, olive oil, and smoked paprika." A shrug. "I got inspired."

Chau reached out and stroked his bride's arm. "It's not like last time. He's in Poland." He retrieved the phone and checked his messages. Neill had sent an email, and he read it out loud.

Kelsi grabbed a pair of tongs. "That's a little dramatic, don't you think?"

"He must have his reasons," Simon shrugged. "But I told him I'm not a designer."

She turned off the burner and removed the pan. "You don't have to be. A simple algorithm will get the job done. What's the deadline?"

"Yesterday."

"We'd better get to it then. Want me to give it a shot?"

A shake of the head. "Man want food," he growled. He embraced his new wife, planting a passionate kiss on her neck. "Breakfast first. Or maybe some coffee. Neill's algorithm will just have to wait."

Chapter Twenty-Seven * Son of Ukraine

The Kremlin

ONLY TWO NEWSPAPERS WERE DELIVERED each morning. It was a concession to habit that they were used at all. There was very little in the dailies that could be considered up to date, and they were only accurate in the broadest of strokes. On the other hand, immediacy came from the cable networks, or even better, the internet.

Major Pirogov eyed the broadsheets and made a choice. *Izvestia* and *Pravda* lay in the center of General Karpenko's desk. Both were published in Moscow and the ink on their respective pages had been dry for hours. Each had a history of providing news and propaganda—and where one ended and the other began was a matter of perspective.

Izvestia's circulation figures were larger, but a pittance compared to its heyday. Pirogov lifted it from the desk—the journal weighed much less these days, he noted—and began reading the headlines. One story caught his eye. Eighteen hours had passed since the West's provocation in the skies over Kaliningrad—or more factually put, above Poland.

That detail was glossed over by the Russian media. *Pravda* hadn't even mentioned it, and an editor at *Izvestia* had sanitized the account. According to the official narrative—the one approved of by Moscow—defective instruments had caused both aircraft to wander. *Stray* had such a negative connotation. Weather was also a factor. Faulty equipment and poor visibility had caused this unfortunate incident, and a son of the *Rodina* now lay badly injured. Of course, had NATO respected the peace of the region, none of this would have happened, and—

"Dobrogost's support is crumbling," the major scoffed. "We couldn't have scripted this better."

Karpenko grunted. These circumstances were completely satisfactory. He turned in his chair and retrieved a tablet from the credenza. The Polish summit was trending on several websites, and the general was pleased to see that Turkey had recalled her delegates. Things were moving quickly now, and their *rezident* in Belarus had reported similar details.

"What of the pilot?" He wasn't really concerned, but the question needed to be asked.

Pirogov frowned. "A Polish hospital, near the border. In *custody*, no less," he spat. "Our ambassador is making arrangements for his return."

Karpenko studied the developments online. The Ministry of Defense had been busy and General Suvorov's staff set a frenzied pace; indeed, the lights on Arbatskaya Square had burned late into the night. There would be little rest for the executive body today. Suvorov's directives were being followed to the letter. Additional regiments were ordered into the Russian enclave, and Kaliningrad would soon be teeming with Federation troops.

Warsaw

"WHERE ARE WE NOW?"

Neill settled into a chair next to Christina. Pyotr was seated beside her and muffled conversations filled the hall. The auditorium seemed very still.

"Nobody knows what's going to happen next," she whispered. The venue was softly lit and even the stage looked dim. "Where have you been?"

"Meeting with the Berkut," Neill answered. "Tereshenko's a good egg; both seem very capable. Captain Voskov's a little rough around the edges, but that's his job."

"Good cop, bad cop?"

"Something like that."

"Have you seen Mr. Avery?" Christina asked.

A nod. "He and Krol are hashing things out in the wings." He was weary and it was only ten a.m. "Some of the deputies are ready to bail."

"I was afraid of that." A question came to mind and she asked, "Did you get a read on Ulyanov?"

"The general's been pretty cagey," Michael admitted. "He's up to something, but I don't know what."

"I didn't see him at dinner last night."

Neill stretched and drew in a deep breath. "Irina got in late. He and Dmitri picked her up at the airport. Probably explains why we haven't seen him this morning."

"And where's your roommate?"

Someone must have turned over your question box, Neill mused. He forced a smile. Crockett had spent the night on Neill's couch; the Bristol had no vacancies, but that was about to change.

"He's keeping tabs on Viktoriya." His gaze went to the press box. The journalist caught his attention and waved back.

Two rows behind, Nate was staying under the radar.

THE third day of the conference had begun on a decidedly somber note. Some justification had been ascribed to Poland's actions, but that didn't ease the tension. The papers were full of Moscow's rhetoric, and the results could be felt everywhere—including the Palace.

To the north, there was more tangible evidence of friction. Military checkpoints were hardened; traffic in and out of Kaliningrad came to a halt, and the ground forces of both nations maintained a heightened vigilance.

Neill had seen this type of bluster before, but it was hard

to determine which side would blink—or if either would push the stupid-button.

DOBROGOST led the morning session, extending his greetings, and then broke off his comments to meet with the deputies on an individual basis. It was time to gauge the temperature of the room, and the next few hours would decide the summit's future.

The captain checked his cell. His in-box displayed a new message. "Perfect timing—Chau came through," he announced.

"So why the long face?"

"I forgot my thumb drive," he cringed.

"Boys," Christina taunted. She pulled out her tablet—and a high capacity memory stick. "Forward the file to me. I'll decompress it and copy it over."

"Done," Neill grinned.

* * * *

"HE DOES REALIZE THE SECRET SERVICE IS UP to this, right?"

Avery blinked. "What do you mean?"

"Rhetorical question," Aultman replied. The two were backstage, looking out across the auditorium. "Don't get me wrong. I like Lieutenant Crockett. But his skills are a little redundant."

The national security advisor seemed to understand. "Neill trusts his instincts," he defended.

"And you trust Neill. Is that why you worked so hard to get him to Poland?"

"I think you know the answer to that, Richard," Avery returned. "He's here for several reasons. For one thing, he speaks the language. And he's got a grasp of the culture."

"It has helped," Aultman confessed. "But what about last spring?"

"I'm not following you."

"The South China Sea. We had plenty of SEALs to do that

job. You picked Neill instead." He eyed his boss thoughtfully. "You're grooming him for something, aren't you?"

Avery was guarded but wore a smile. "May I remind you that I asked the captain to gather intelligence." He added wistfully, "Those Chinese troops were simply a complication."

* * * *

THE LUNCH HOUR CAME AND WENT. DELEGATES filtered back into the Palace in the early afternoon, expectantly for the most part, but with a measured dose of reality, and rumors began to ripple across the floor.

The Russians were exerting pressure. It was subtle in some cases, but not so in others. Federation aircraft were ordered to alert status. Four additional missile batteries were re-tasked, and the media was on hand to broadcast their movements—Moscow made sure of that. The coverage had the desired effect, and given this news, there was a palpable sense that Dobrogost's plans were unraveling.

* * * *

"THAT'S IMPRESSIVE." ARRENS' VOICE CAUGHT in her throat. She dabbed a tissue against her eyes. "Was this your idea?"

"Most of it," Neill dodged. The screen dimmed and faded to black. "Simon added a few embellishments."

"He outdid himself."

"Can't deny that," Neill said.

The Marines had slipped into one of the galleries, huddled around Christina's laptop. "The file's pretty big—will that be a problem?"

"We'll find out," she answered. "It works fine on my computer. And the application is common enough." She peeked through the doorway. Tomas Krol was moving toward the podium, and his expression was like a mile of bad road.

"You know what's about to happen, don't you?"

"I have a pretty good idea," Michael surrendered. "There's not much optimism out there. Think you can do this?"

"Can you?" Christina didn't wait for an answer. She powered down the device and removed the thumb drive. Her eyes scanned the room. "Now where's Viktoriya?

"It's time she and I made some new friends."

KROL'S appearance caught everyone's eye. In a hushed voice he asked the delegates to find their seats. Neill followed the aisle toward the front—and was intercepted by the Ulyanovs.

"I wondered when you'd get here," Michael whispered.

Irina squeezed his hand and smiled. The time for fellowship would have to wait.

* * * *

THE LIGHTS FADED AND THE AUDITORIUM BEcame silent. There was movement backstage; the principal dignitaries emerged and the deputies stood as Karl Dobrogost walked to the lectern.

Neill turned and looked over his shoulder. The audio/visual booth was near the back and he could see Christina through the glass. Viktoriya was at her side; her Berkut protectors hovered at a respectful distance, and Nate wasn't far away. A glimpse ahead revealed the presence of Avery and Aultman, standing before the flags on the dais.

"Take your seats, please." The president's tone was subdued. "I have a prepared statement. When I finish, I will answer a few questions."

Dobrogost pulled out a pair of glasses and began to read. He thanked the assembled delegates for their efforts and then alluded to the events of the past twenty-four hours. There was no need to belabor the obvious. Some had harbored doubts from the beginning, and the clash at the border only sharpened their fears.

"Events beyond our control have conspired against us," the

president intoned. "It is the considered opinion of the majority that we suspend our work here—for the time being, at least. I would prefer a different outcome, but perhaps this is best. We will revisit this proposal at a future date."

HE'S backing down, Neill thought. The emotion surprised him, and he felt something bordering on rage.

"That's not good enough," he said forcefully.

General Ulyanov braced. The voice came from the man sitting next to him. He looked to the left and could see Michael rising to his feet.

Heads were turning now. The president's eyes searched the darkened hall. Neill had reached the stage, and climbing the steps, he repeated his words in Ukrainian.

VIKTORIYA'S mouth fell open. She faced Christina, but the staff sergeant was intent on the sound board, coaching the technician working the controls.

One frantic question popped up, and she asked—

* * * *

"WHAT'S HE DOING?" RICHARD AULTMAN tensed.

Avery cautioned the man at his side. "Hang on," he urged. "Maybe we can use this."

Standing on the dais, the Marine had already launched into his presentation.

SHOWTIME, Neill. He faced his host. *Go big or go home.*

"Respectfully, Mr. President, you're not negotiating some *quid pro quo* agreement here. Compromise won't work—Moscow will expect that, so you can't back down. The Russians don't believe you've got the guts—any of you. They're looking for weakness." The delegates before him were hidden by the glare of the stage lights. "Maybe they've found it—maybe they're right."

The president's fatigue gave way to anger. "You break protocol, *Capitan* Neill. Please—"

"Mr. President—if I may?" Avery stood and came forward, smiling to ease the tension. He was applying a little Kentucky windage of his own. "I defer to your judgment, of course, but I suggest we indulge the young captain."

The Polish leader heaved a sigh, staring at Neill. "Very well, then. I yield the floor—to the representative from the United States." He stepped away, and added with a flourish, "By all means, *Capitan.*

"Entertain us."

* * * *

CROCKETT FOUND A SEAT AND SLIPPED ON A pair of headphones. In the booth, Christina did the same, listening to the translation. Neill pressed on.

"What's changed?" He took his place at the podium, adjusting the microphone and addressing the assembly. "You came together to stand up to a bully; now you're all surprised when he acts like one. You have to focus on the common ground you share—the threat facing all the republics. Success or failure is up to you."

In front, the minister from Lithuania scowled. "Petty words from an American," he snorted. "What do the privileged know of oppression?"

Michael had been waiting for that. "You're right, Mr. Ambassador. I am privileged. It was my good fortune to be born in this part of the world—right next door, in Ukraine, as a matter of fact. My family bled and died there." He turned and faced the president. "They knew sacrifice—much like the people of Poland and much like the rest of you.

"Most can remember Soviet rule. Some thought those days were over." He shook his head. "They're not. The Russians will continue to press their agenda; Crimea is lost and a third province has fallen in Georgia. Ten thousand troops are positioned along the border with Ukraine, and as we speak, they're working overtime to field additional Voronezh radars.

"Moscow will settle for nothing less than complete domination. They've been waiting for this, and you of all people—the deputies in this room—should know better than to think they've been tamed by democracy." Neill stepped to the edge of the platform and paused for effect.

"Lights, please."

THE harsh glare receded, and only the footlights remained. At Neill's back, the towering screen began to glow, and eighteen sets of eyes now stared down from above.

"Warriors die in battle. That's to be expected. But far too often, the innocent are also among the casualties."

Tomas Krol stirred. "We're not at war, Mr. Neill."

"Not yet," Michael granted. "But how long can you cherish peace by cowering in the shadows?" He gestured to the faces on display. "These men and women thought as you do, Mr. Krol. Conflict was the last thing on their minds. They hadn't counted on an Iranian missile ending their future—a weapon supported in part by Russian technology." He cast a glance toward the projection booth and the images faded from view. They were replaced by a teenaged girl who looked all of seventeen.

"This is Elzbieta Mistewicz. She was the youngest victim on that tragic day. First responders tell us that she died instantly. Parts of her body were strewn across the crash site, and a positive ID could only be made through dental records." Neill's voice escaped him, and some in the assembly flinched. "Needless to say, her family was not allowed to view her remains."

The young woman's features began to grow. Her eyes soon filled the screen, but there was something odd about them. They had a pixelated look, and as the image expanded, it was replaced with a patchwork of undefined shapes. These soon came into sharper focus, revealing hundreds, if not thousands, of individual photographs that made up the whole. All were black and white portraits, depicting a cross section of age and gender. Many were studio shots, while others were more candid, and each picture appeared to be very old.

"We tend to forget that no generation is safe from atrocity. In World War II, Poland's Jewish population was decimated." Neill looked to the screen. "The men and women you see here faced two evils. The fascists came first and then the communists. Both offered genocide.

"I'd like to ask a question." The Marine strode across the platform, his words a challenge. "Can any of us leave today— our work unfinished—with our humanity intact?" He scanned the darkened hall.

"Oh, and there's one more thing—"

The archival photography receded, coalescing into a new image. Another pair of eyes began to form; these were darker, piercing, and set deep in their sockets. The software continued to pull back until a different figure dominated the assembly's view, and her face was instantly recognizable.

"Everyone here should know this young woman. She was a Dutch Jew, born in Germany. She lived during the rise of the Third Reich, and like those you've just seen, she, too, was a victim of 'ethnic cleansing'. She died in the Nazi prison camp at Bergen-Belsen, but her spirit lives on, in every nation, and her voice will not be silenced.

"I can imagine what she might say to us here today. I believe she would issue a warning, and urge free men to stand in the gap to prevent more atrocities.

"I just wonder if any of you will take the time to listen."

* * * *

THE DIARIST'S IMAGE REMAINED ON THE screen. Theater or not, there was no escaping her powerful stare. Michael descended the steps as a different kind of hush fell over the hall. He walked the center aisle to find his place beside Irina.

Andrei Ulyanov was the first to stand. As Neill took his seat, the general's hands came together; once, twice, and then in sustained applause. Those around him also rose.

Irina's eyes glistened. "*Bravo*, Michael. Well done."

NOT everyone joined in, but the majority of the delegates gave the captain a standing ovation, and after the din faded, Ulyanov remained on his feet.

"Mr. President—a point of order."

Karl Dobrogost's spirit had found new life. "The chair recognizes the deputy from Ukraine." Even Tomas Krol was buoyant.

"I move we put this proposal to a vote." Andrei's tone carried a hint of impatience. "Let it be known that Ukraine stands with Poland." He looked to his left and right, making eye contact with a few of the others. "The rest of you can join us—or continue to live as serfs. The choice is yours, but I say we teach those dogs in Moscow a lesson."

* * * *

Downtown Warsaw

IF HE WERE TO FIND HIS TARGET, MAERSK needed to employ a proven strategy. It was important to view the world through Viktoriya's eyes—to think and react as she would. Practical concerns also played a role, and if he could sort through those logically, he might be able to locate his quarry sooner rather than later.

There were several factors to take into account. Economics would be a major consideration. The woman had probably taken a flat on the west side of town, choosing accommodations that would fit a newspaper's budget. Maersk pulled the map from the glove box. The most affordable apartments were on the city's outskirts, but searching for her there was pointless; it was early afternoon, and the journalist would be out, someplace where she could follow a lead or put her nose into a story.

Let her, the old man thought. REMORA also had leads to follow. So long as she moved about freely, Ilya's chances for success increased. Her protectors would be close, he was sure of that, but there was no reason to believe they'd been tipped off to his presence. They would have eyes for an active assailant, while Maersk's passive methods could be just as deadly.

His own flat was near the park named for Marshal Pilsudski, and the clues in his possession pointed to the Royal Route and the City Center. Maersk stored the map and took the van north, following the Ulica to the Square. There were only two locations to scout, and he'd already spent the morning casing the Bristol. His pursuits there yielded nothing, but he wasn't ready to close the book on the hotel just yet.

His second destination loomed on the skyline. The rest of his day would be spent there. The boulevards merged—Warynskiego ended at Konstytucji Square—and the route ahead would soon deliver him to the eastern face of the Palace of Culture and Science.

Chapter Twenty-Eight * Chemistry

Headquarters Marine Corps

H ALF A WORLD AWAY, OWEN ETHRIDGE squinted. "Sky News?" he asked.

"Reuters." Colonel Terryton appeared pleased. He adjusted the monitor to give the first sergeant a better view. "They're citing Interfax."

The news agency was an off-shoot of Moscow Radio. It was an independent outlet, and that made it more trustworthy. The C.O. smiled, recalling some of Captain Neill's words—*if it's fiction you want, try Pravda.*

Owen's glasses were on his desk next door. He planted himself in a chair and leaned forward. "What's it say?"

"The votes are in," Terryton began simply. "The majority has agreed in substance to the shield. Ukraine and Estonia have signed up to provide radar installations; Romania too. Half a dozen more have okayed relay stations on their soil, including Turkmenistan and the Kyrgyz republic. There are some details to be worked out, but SMOOTH STONE is essentially a done deal."

"Anybody abstain?"

The colonel sighed. "Turkey wasn't happy. They voted *in absentia*—against it—after they'd gone home."

Ethridge voiced an appropriate epithet for those delegates before offering an opinion. "Sounds like the Russian media's on top of things," he grunted.

"Interfax has a bureau in Warsaw," Terryton replied. "And they do mention an 'impassioned speech' by an American military officer. Apparently his words turned the tide."

The senior NCO stared. "Neill?"

"Who else?"

"Son of a gun. So now the kid's a diplomat. What's next on the agenda?"

"Formal signing." Terryton spied his watch. It was getting late, and aside from the duty officers, the rest of the staff had been released for the holidays. "The agreement will be ratified by all parties at noon tomorrow—Warsaw time—at the Royal Castle."

* * * *

IT WAS EVEN LATER IN POLAND.

"You were sandbagging," Neill grinned. "Practically the whole time."

"Sandbagging?" Andrei Ulyanov looked startled. Wearing a blue blazer and a button-down shirt, the general's attire gave him a relaxed appearance. "I'm not familiar with that term, Michael." He hadn't called him *little* Michael since the shooting.

"Kind of like bluffing," Neill explained. He was also casually dressed, nursing a bottle of ginger ale as the two sat in the Bristol's bar. "Holding back; saving your best cards for last, I guess you could say."

The tavern was softly lit, enhancing the mischievous gleam in Ulyanov's eye. "I simply played the hand I was dealt. Our Estonian comrades believed we had doubts. Pledging our support at the end shamed them." He sipped Chardonnay, feeling all the better for it. "To save face, they joined us."

Not far away, the rest of the American and Ukrainian delegates had commandeered a table—and a good portion of the bar's floor space. Irina was seated between Christina and Viktoriya, appropriately matriarchal in the midst of the younger women, and despite the differences in language, the three got along quite well. Across from the ladies, laughter flowed from Nate, Richard and Dmitri, with Pyotr acting as interpreter. Even Willis Avery was in good spirits.

"You've done well, Michael." Ulyanov admired Christina from his barstool. "She's a refined and virtuous woman. Your mother would be pleased."

At the table, the staff sergeant sipped Cabernet. She smiled and gave the officers a nod, with a stare intended for her captain.

Neill returned the look—and blushed. "It's not exactly like that."

"Oh? And what is it like, my young captain?" *Who's bluffing now?* Andrei thought. "I've seen the way she looks at you. Don't tell me you haven't."

Neill paused long enough to deflect the comment. "This isn't over yet. Not by a long shot. Maersk is still out there. And Dobrogost has poked a stick into the hornet's nest—we all have. Anatoly Rurik will bluster, but it's Karpenko I'm worried about."

Andrei agreed. "I share your concerns, Mischa. The Russians will attempt to derail this alliance. Fairly soon, I should think."

"The signing?" Neill asked. "Or the dinner?"

The general weighed that. "Both are symbolic. Endorsing the agreement will be rich with ceremony; everyone will be on their best behavior. There will be lots of sharp eyes. But the *dinner*—" he swirled the wine in his glass and smiled, "—that will be more of a celebration. Our senses will not be so sharp."

"Then we'll have to be ready," Neill breathed.

A chuckle. "*You* must be ready, Michael. This occasion is more than just food and drink." He considered having one more glass, but it was too sweet for his tastes. "Have you ever taken the time to educate yourself on state protocol?"

The Marine drew a blank. "Protocol? What—"

"Michael—" the general was enjoying this, "—the members of Warsaw's Philharmonic will also be in attendance. Not to put too fine a point on this, but have you ever learned to waltz?"

"Waltz?" Neill was alarmed.

"It will be expected," Ulyanov replied. "Your performance this afternoon has caught the attention of the press. Everyone will be watching the American delegation. There is a phrase— very Western, I believe—'optics matter', yes? Taking your place on the dance floor just goes with the territory."

"Ballroom dancing's not in my bag of tricks."

"Perhaps not." Ulyanov motioned for his wife to join them. "But I believe there is a solution."

* * * *

IRINA STOOD AND VIKTORIYA WATCHED HER move toward the bar. As she slipped away, the journalist turned to the windows. The table had an excellent view of the street, and she could see a single black Mercedes parked not far away.

"Are you sure?" Christina wasn't convinced.

"I'm sure." Viktoriya's gaze fell on Yaroslav. "Dmitri?"

The women eased out of their chairs, heading for the exit with the major in tow.

Nate waited till they'd left before falling in behind. His scouting instincts were subtle, but on full alert.

* * * *

PROTECTING A MARK COULD BE MENTALLY TAX-ing, but Voskov kept it fresh. He tested his visual skills, imagining an invisible net around Viktoriya, all the while focusing on her whereabouts. His peripheral vision was like a sixth sense, and in this case alerted him to movement at the tavern's entrance.

"Boss?" Tereshenko's head came around.

"I see them, Yuri," he grumbled.

This was bound to happen sooner or later. Since the SSD boosted their credentials, Voskov and Tereshenko had abandoned the pretense of covert surveillance. Secrecy was no longer needed, and Yuri argued that shadowing their charge at a closer distance could only help. Xander had protested—they risked contact with the woman, after all—but the tall Ukrainian managed to persuade his boss that taking chances was part of their job.

Viktoriya left the lounge and crossed the expansive lobby. The Berkut team sat near the entrance, and the young woman was making a beeline directly toward them. Christina was at her side, clattering heels announcing their approach. Dmitri edged out in front, arriving just as the hesitant soldiers got to their feet.

For their first official meeting, the formal introductions were kept short. The men already knew Major Yaroslav; and since the shooting, Xander's face had been imprinted in Viktoriya's mind. The brooding captain had likewise been studying her.

"Georgios Tereshenko, senior sergeant—my friends call me Yuri." For the women's benefit, the Berkut NCO took charge, presenting his superior last. "Captain Aleksander Voskov, of the Special Purpose Police." The boss was notably taciturn.

"I'm indebted to you, Captain." Viktoriya made eye contact. Xander was taller by inches. "Without your team's intervention, I'm afraid I wouldn't be here."

Voskov wasn't quite prepared for an act of contrition. "We do our job," he managed. His tone was respectful but nothing more.

The officer struck Viktoriya as indifferent; his response was certainly less than effusive. She tried a smile, but her delivery was a little off.

"And you do it well. I just wanted to offer my thanks."

"Keep your thanks." Xander brushed aside the remark with a cold stare. "Your gratitude means nothing to me, *zhinka*."

Yuri cringed. "Boss—"

A spark of emotion flashed in the journalist's eyes. *One more time,* she thought, drawing a shallow breath. Maybe she could pull him out of this contentious frame of mind. "Captain, I'm only trying to repay your kindness—"

Xander wouldn't have it. "Do you think high-sounding phrases will compel me? Try another audience. Your words are hollow," the Berkut leader sneered. "Duty guides my actions; caution should dictate yours."

Caution? Was that the reason for his indignance? Viktoriya was stung. "I have my own duty," she huffed. "And I'm sorry if my vocation has inconvenienced you."

Xander pressed ahead. "So now you take a stab at remorse. It's a little late for that, don't you think?" He lifted his chin. "Regret won't keep you alive, Ms. Gavrilenko. For that you need us."

Christina was lost in the swirl of language, but the Ukrainian's tone was clear. Viktoriya was speechless as Dmitri stepped in to end the escalating squabble.

"Captain Voskov—"

"Reporters," Xander mocked. He ignored his superior's intrusion. "Where is your eloquence now? Cat got your tongue?"

Viktoriya's face was hot, and she gave it right back. "It's just that I hadn't expected an editorial opinion from a *policeman.*" Her sensibilities were offended and her phrasing was meant to wound. "But I'm sure everyone is duly impressed with your genteel civility. If you think so little of me, why bother?"

"Have a care, woman." The captain's tone was condescending. "You take far too many risks with your life."

"And I'll give your advice its due consideration," she promised with a glare. With that she spun on her heel and marched away. She was still fuming when Christina found her in the taproom.

"I didn't catch all that," the Marine offered. "Were you

two—"

"*Fighting?*" Viktoriya turned, peering over the major's shoulder as he joined them. "Not at all." She glowered at Christina. "Why would you say that?"

"But I didn't—"

"I was being *polite*—he was trading in contempt." Arms folded, she stamped a heel into the tiled floor—and did it a second time for emphasis. "The man has no sense of courtesy. I shouldn't be surprised; he's just a simple constable. A *gendarme* with a pretty face." The hint of a smile pulled at the corners of her mouth, and she wore an untamed look.

"So you've noticed," Christina grinned. "I think he's growing on you."

Viktoriya's face twisted into a scowl. "That brutish oaf?" She appeared incredulous, but then added breathlessly, "Do you want to know the truth?"

"Please—don't hold back."

The encounter had excited her emotions and forced an admission. "I can't stop thinking about him."

* * * *

NATE DRIFTED BACK IN AFTER THE FIREWORKS. He offered his friend a shrug but nothing more.

"What was that all about?" Neill asked.

Christina found a place at the bar next to Irina. "Just a little misplaced passion," she smiled. "Nothing to worry over."

Michael raised an eyebrow. "Anything I should know?"

"We'll let those two work it out," Arrens advised.

In the lobby, Viktoriya ignored the elevators and took the stairs. Her exit was anything but subtle.

"Where's she going?" Crockett's curiosity got the better of him.

"I gave her my key. She's staying here tonight."

Neill was thoughtful. "I could speak to Captain Voskov. I'm sure he could arrange a ride back to her apartment."

"Trust me; I don't think that's a good idea." Christina's

eyes cased the lobby, but the Berkut team had returned to their car.

THE Ulyanovs stirred from their barstools. Andrei pushed his glass aside and gave his wife a furtive look. "It's getting late. We'll leave the rest of the evening to these young people."

"Don't go," Christina pleaded. She was charmed by the couple. "Stay for one more."

The general spoke neither French nor English, but understood the young woman's intent. "Not tonight, *moloda zhinka*." He lifted her hand and gave it a gentle kiss, and his gaze returned to Irina. "What do you think, *mati?*"

Mrs. Ulyanov beamed, regarding Christina warmly.

"She isn't Ukrainian, but I approve."

* * * *

"WOULD YOU LIKE TO GO FOR A WALK?" NEILL watched as the Ulyanovs exited the bar. Crockett rejoined Pyotr at the table and the Marines were now alone.

Christina's expression was coy in every way. "Where to, Captain?"

"Old Town," he suggested. "We'll take a taxi to market square. Stroll the plaza. There's a question I'd like to ask you."

Something had warmed her blood. Probably the red wine, she decided. "Pyotr said the square was for lovers—won't we be a little out of place?"

A sly grin formed on Michael's face. "I suppose that depends."

His answer intrigued her. "Let me get my coat."

* * * *

AULTMAN NOTED THE MARINES' DEPARTURE with interest. In spite of the late hour, they were very earnest.

"Where are those two going?"

"It's date night, Richard," Avery teased. "Young people do that." He sipped his drink slowly, none too surprised to find Kentucky bourbon on the wine list.

"Those two can't date," Aultman chuckled. "He's an officer. She's a sergeant. That's fraternization." *And just plain trouble,* but he kept that thought to himself.

"She's a *staff* sergeant," Avery corrected. "And be that as it may, Miss Arrens is going to need an escort for the dinner."

The boss was shrewd; Richard gave him that. "I suppose the selectee for Secretary of Defense can waive those restrictions for the occasion."

"Dang right." Avery was practically in his cups. "There will be lots of young ladies at Dobrogost's soiree. I want Neill focused. Having her on his arm—in uniform, no less—will help keep the other distractions to a minimum."

Aultman had seen the NCO in her blues. In his considered opinion, she just might create the diversion Avery was hoping to avoid.

"What else is bugging you?"

Avery's scowl deepened. "I'm worried about the Poles. They should be on offense." He drew in some air and tried shrugging it off. "I'll tell you about it later."

* * * *

THE OLD MAN HID IN THE SHADOWS, AWAY FROM the watchful eyes of the American Secret Service. He was especially vigilant this evening; a few of the more ambitious agents had wandered beyond the Bristol's perimeter, but Maersk identified those officers early on and managed to keep one step ahead of their attentions.

Ilya had adopted a sauntering gait and a disguise of sorts, complete with a French beret and thick glasses. He chose the appearance of a befuddled tourist, making a show of peering aimlessly into shop windows. Meandering along the boulevard in such an obvious fashion served to blunt the operatives' interest, and the ploy also gave REMORA the obscurity he needed for reconnaissance.

His foray to the hotel was intended as an exercise in surveillance, nothing more. Maersk's stake-out at the Palace had paid off. He'd witnessed Viktoriya leaving in the midst of an entourage of diplomatic vehicles; the convoy of armored SUVs cruised north by northwest, and their passage through the City Center ended at the Bristol. The assassin followed them from a safe distance and then parked the van several blocks away.

THE woman had a suite at the Bristol—or so it appeared. Maersk entertained the other possibilities. She might have joined one of the delegations at the bar, or chose to dine with a colleague in the hotel restaurant. At the very least, she had friends here, acquaintances who allowed her the use of a room. Ilya gave it no more thought. He frequented the shops and cafés along Krakowskie Przedmiescie—just to get out of the cold—and hours passed before any significant movement caught his eye.

First to exit the hotel were the paramilitary types. Ilya had seen them at the Palace and pegged these two as Viktoriya's personal bodyguards. They certainly fit the profile; when she moved, they mirrored her steps. The team leader scrutinized every face in the crowd, and Maersk knew the man could handle himself in any situation. The taller one was surprisingly light on his feet; a trait cultivated by specialty troops the world over. They were always too far away for a clear look, but both had an Eastern European air about them, and there was no doubt in his mind that these men took their direction from the State Security Directorate.

Probably Berkut, Ilya reasoned. Knowing that might prove useful. *Were they on to him?* That wasn't likely. Maersk was a professional when it came to stealth. He watched as they took their first steps into the night air. Each man studied the streets and their fields of vision overlapped. *Situational awareness,* Maersk smiled to himself. It was a tactic common among seasoned officers.

It was getting late, and Maersk's instincts told him she had settled in for the night. He considered doing the same. Viktoriya's protective detail had returned to their vehicle, a powerful Mercedes parked across the street. The woman was nowhere to be seen. Ilya's gloved hand fumbled for the keys and he began to trudge west on Karowa. What happened next shook him to his core, and that had not happened in quite some time.

The young couple emerging from the entrance hailed a cab. Maersk moved closer. They lingered on the flagstone long enough for him to get a good look. The memories came slowly—almost reluctantly, the old man deemed; the woman was a stranger, but her companion's features evoked the past. He was built like his father, with a face to match, and against the warm glow of the hotel's windows, his silhouette was even more recognizable.

* * * *

THE AGENT HAD BEEN IN THE FIELD LESS THAN a year, and his assignment to the Polish detail was a feather in his cap. He had excelled at the Training Center down in Glynco, Georgia, honing his skills in firearms training and— of all things—technical writing and reports.

He was high speed and low drag, but every agent took a turn at overwatch. The youngster was presently working Grid Two, near the Church of the Visitation. From this vantage point, he could clearly see the Europejski Hotel and the boulevards crisscrossing the Royal Route. He found a bench and sat down; standing drew too much attention, and he still had three hours left before his shift came to an end.

Like Maersk, he'd seen the Berkut team leave the Bristol and also watched as the Marines spilled from the entrance to catch a cab. The junior agent had been briefed on the names of all four, but he took an extra moment to focus on Christina. She was quite attractive, after all, and there was no reason why he couldn't do his job and enjoy the scenery at the same time.

He chided himself. His professional bearing had slipped and he redoubled his efforts. Stealing glances at members of the official party could get him into trouble. Just days before, one of his superiors had let that red-headed journalist distract him—and caught a bullet in the vest for his lack of focus.

With his tradecraft now fully engaged, the young agent spied an elderly man on a late night promenade of the city streets. He'd been trained to notice the unusual and the aged figure certainly fit that bill. He had seen him earlier, yet something was different now. His shuffling pace and stooped posture had disappeared, and the tourist was in a hurry.

His presence at this hour was odd, but didn't call for alarm. The agent would mention him at shift change, but the visitor's wanderings would garner little more than a footnote in his report.

* * * *

"ARE YOU WARM ENOUGH?"

Christina was lost in the magic. Nightfall had transformed the square into something wholly different. Christmas lights twinkled in the bistros and coffee houses; strands also hung from awnings, swayed by the breezes that moved through the plaza. The staff sergeant felt vibrancy here, and a few souls appeared willing to brave the falling temperatures—walking hand-in-hand and taking the airs, just as Pyotr had said.

And on top of that, Michael Neill had just expressed concern for her comfort.

"It's like a dream." She spoke softly, for fear of breaking the spell. "I know it's childish, but still."

"It's not childish at all." Michael took in the view. "And it is like a dream. A very special one."

"You're being kind, Captain," she smiled. "But I'm talking about the whole experience." She squeezed his arm. "Christmas in Poland. It's like stepping into a storybook."

His next line came naturally. "That would make you a princess."

A flash of color came to her cheeks. "Aren't you the clever one," she teased.

Christina's heel landed between cobblestones. She was in no danger of falling, but the captain decided to use the missed step to his advantage.

"Easy there, Marine. Here—" He extended an elbow, and without hesitation, she hooked her arm in his. She knew the gesture went beyond chivalry. At the moment she could find no reason to object.

Christina huddled closer. "So what's with the hike?"

He lifted his shoulders. "I thought it would be nice to spend some time together. Enjoy the sights for a change, just the two of us."

"I should tell you something before I forget."

Michael pretended to be shocked. "I knew it. You're married."

She laughed and pressed in again. "No, silly. I'm being serious. You were very noble today." Her face was radiant and Neill found himself staring. "At the conference. Your words inspired me." She gestured around them. "And now all this."

"Better than dinner and a movie?"

"Much better."

They passed a few shops and Neill could see his breath. "It's nice to know I can show a girl a good time."

She would have liked to test that statement, but chose to ignore it instead. "We're probably breaking half a dozen regulations right now." She became sullen.

"Rules are just an excuse not to try. Don't give up yet." He tried a little good-natured ribbing. "Of course, if you keep glowing like that, we're both going to have a lot of explaining to do."

"I can't help it." Her joy started to return. "You make me happy. But we have to be careful."

"Which brings me to my question."

"I'm listening."

"Tomorrow's the signing. The state dinner's the next

night." He stopped and turned to face her. A light snow began to fall, the scattered, irregular flakes lifting in the air around them. Illuminated by the lamps in the shops, they had the appearance of a swirling sea of stars. "Mr. Avery has suspended certain restrictions—just for the evening."

"Are you asking me out—or is this just another assignment?" Her tone was more playful than guarded, and Michael was thankful for that. He preferred a happy Christina.

"I have to take credit for this one. It's been on my mind—since the day we met." Her face registered surprise. "I'd like to be your escort. Would you consider it?"

"I already have," she smiled broadly. "The answer is yes." She was suddenly ebullient at the thought, and didn't mind letting him know it. "Will everyone else be there?"

"It wouldn't be a party without 'em. Nate's looking forward to it." Neill was relieved and he chuckled. "He makes friends wherever he goes."

"And what about Viktoriya? Is she invited too?"

He blinked. "Sure. I doubt she'd miss it. Why?"

Christina thought it over. The journalist's presence meant that her protective detail would also be there.

"She's had someone on her mind lately—a certain Ukrainian captain."

Neill seemed confused. "Dmitri's not a captain."

"Not *Dmitri*," she scolded quietly, braving a pinch of his arm. They were walking again. "That Berkut officer. Aleksander Voskov."

"She's got a thing for *him?*" Neill was surprised. The dimple in his cheek was showing. "I never would have guessed."

She shrugged, and a tuft of hair fell across her forehead. "He did save her life. Possibly more than once."

Neill's eyes narrowed. "You saved *my* life." He paced his words slowly. "If that's the criteria for attraction, maybe I should be the president of your fan club."

"Stop it," Arrens cut him off. "It's more than that. They have chemistry—I can tell." She turned away, as she often did when the truth might be painful. "That's not a problem, is it? The two of them together?"

Michael pulled her to his side, surprising the young woman. *We have chemistry*, he didn't say. He dipped his chin, inhaling Christina's perfume, and then gave a reply that made her heart soar.

"I'm quite happy with present company."

Chapter Twenty-Nine * Standing on Ceremony

THE DELEGATES RATIFIED SMOOTH STONE IN the Senators' Chamber of the Royal Castle. The treaty was signed in the midst of its tapestried hall, the interior spaces trimmed in vivid hues of ivory and gold—opulent, yet oddly simple—and completed by the presence of a restored throne at the far end of the room.

The ceremony began earlier than scheduled. There was no reason to delay it. Karl Dobrogost's enthusiasm was contagious, and none of the dignitaries complained when the president pushed the itinerary forward. Two antique credenzas, draped in scarlet linen—the furniture itself dating to the seventeenth century—dominated the space before the throne. The red fabric fell halfway to the floor, revealing intricately carved table legs, and other appointments complemented the regal setting. The large alcove brimmed with as much history as the rest of the kingly residence. Everything about the observance paid homage to the assembled deputies, and was also a nod to the rich traditions of the Polish court.

Seated far behind the ambassadors and emissaries, Captain Neill was decked out in evening dress bravos. Staff Sergeant Arrens was likewise in uniform; for this occasion she wore a long skirt. Lieutenant Crockett was positioned on their right. His alphas weren't quite as resplendent as Neill's formalwear, but the officer still cut a dashing figure.

"Somebody got in late last night," the lieutenant observed with a grin.

"Don't whisper." Neill was annoyed by the comment and kept his voice low. "Just murmur if you've got something to say," the captain advised.

Nate was getting antsy. "Is that like mumbling?"

"It's like—*muttering*—but with clarity."

Crockett's voice rose to an uncomfortable level. "I think you meant mumbling."

"Hush." Arrens gave them a stern look. "Both of you pipe down." *For crying out loud,* she thought. *You're sitting right next to each other—just send a text.*

"Party pooper," Nate smirked.

IT was a solemn event but held a bridled exuberance. Late morning light filtered through the high windows ringing the second tier. The delegates were brought up one row at a time, patiently waiting their turn to sign their names—and pledge the support of their respective nations.

Willis Avery was first in line, followed by Karl Dobrogost and Tomas Krol. General Ulyanov was next and the rest of the ministers were queued up in succession. A photographer's flash captured the event for posterity. After individual and group pictures were snapped, the delegates were ushered into the Royal Princes' Rooms for champagne.

* * * *

"WHAT'S NEXT?" CROCKETT WAS ON THE JOB now, and chose to abstain from the celebration.

Neill sipped a soft drink and watched as the consuls mingled.

"Back to the Bristol. They found you a room, by the way; recently vacated when the Turks left town."

Nate frowned. "When did all this happen?"

"I was told yesterday," Neill confessed.

"So I didn't have to sleep on your couch last night?" The

sniper feigned disgust. "Some friend you are."

"Knock it off," the Marine said. "After we get you squared away, you and I are headed to the gym."

"All *three* of us are," Christina warned.

Nate was full of protest. "What about lunch?"

"You've had breakfast, pal." Michael patted his stomach. "We could all stand to lose a few inches before tomorrow night."

"Speak for yourself," Christina countered.

Nate shot a glance at his mid-section. "Where's this dinner taking place, anyway?"

"Here at the Castle. In the ballroom—the wing facing the river."

"Sounds like a par-*tay*."

"Aside from the fact that you'll be working," Neill reminded him.

"That's right. I have to keep my eyes glued to your super-model friend." Crockett seemed to pout. "Just my lot in life, I guess. Embrace the suck. I hope you plan on letting me eat before then."

A big smile creased Neill's face. "I'll see what we can do—but no promises." He scanned the hall and the Marines could tell he was looking for someone. "Hang tight. There's something I have to do first."

* * * *

THE PRESS CORPS WAS WELL-REPRESENTED AT the signing, but it was a very select group. Avery ensured that Viktoriya was granted total access; he felt that she'd earned it, and the courtesy of a state invitation was just one more perk.

Michael found the two of them near the main vestibule, a vast corridor running the length of the Castle's northern wing. A proxy of the Polish legate was bending Avery's ear and he looked in need of a rescue.

"You wanted to see me, sir?"

Willis was relieved and excused himself. Michael gave

Viktoriya a wink; she nodded back and watched as the Americans stepped into the chamber next door.

"THIS is just between you and me, Captain." Avery's words carried in the empty room. He lowered his voice. "Our hosts have altered their strategy. It's a predictable reaction, but their thinking has become a little one-dimensional.

"Those Faction Red clowns have put them on edge," Avery grumped. "The Poles are now focused on known terrorist threats—they're not buying the idea of some invisible assassin. At the moment, they're straining at gnats and swallowing camels, or something like that." His brow furrowed. "Can your source prove Maersk is still alive?"

"White Dragon?" Neill hadn't seen the problem from this perspective. He shook his head. "I doubt he'd be regarded as trustworthy. Not by the Poles, anyway. They're still a bit wary of us—they won't give much credence to a Chinese intelligence officer."

"Do you trust him, Captain?"

Neill returned Avery's stare. "He did save my life."

The national security advisor grunted in response. It wasn't exactly the answer Neill was looking for.

* * * *

TWO STORIES WERE PROMINENTLY FEATURED in the morning edition of the *Gazeta Warszawa*. Both dealt with the Royal Castle.

The first was focused on an undeniable force of nature. It was related to the Vistula's receding waterline; the wearing away of the river's banks and the escarpment above and below. Journalists were drawn to such potential calamities, bandying terms that were designed to entice readers, descriptives far more romantic than *erosion* or *long shore drift*.

Scientists were under no such compulsion. They tossed around phrases that included *morphology*, *land degradation* and *hydraulic action*. The erosive effect of a flowing river was a major consideration not only for them, but also for architects and engineers, especially when it came to structures on the Vistula's sloping ridge. History was at stake there, and extra precautions were required to safeguard the national treasures that stretched from the Royal Route to Old Town's waterfront.

Regardless of terminology, it ultimately boiled down to man versus the elements, and without constant vigilance, the natural world would always hold sway. The heart of man tried fighting back; establishing methods to shore up—in the most literal sense of the word—the edifices he'd constructed. There were practices common all over the globe to do just that.

In Warsaw, appraisals of sediments were frequent. The most recent survey of the shoreline uncovered an alarming development. Far below the surface, currents had scoured the watercourse, siphoning deposits of gravel and silt away from its margins. Ancient stream beds beneath the Castle—one was located under the southeastern corner—threatened the citadel's very foundation, creating what could legitimately be called a sinkhole effect.

Warsaw's university geologists were abnormally skittish types, but in this case, they sounded the alarm with discretion. While there was no immediate danger, they announced, appropriate action was needed. They agreed that the most effective remedy was to simply reinforce the bedrock supporting the palace wing.

The second newspaper story was linked to the first and addressed the gathering of delegates to codify the agreement. Ironically, the last day of the structural audit coincided with the signing of the treaty, but the work done at the Castle bore no consequences for the assembled deputies.

A postscript to the article mentioned Dobrogost's banquet, planned for the Great Hall. The list of attendees included the emissaries present for the summit, and a host of others that weren't, in addition to Warsaw's social elite.

* * * *

THE CONSTRUCTION TEAM HAD ARRIVED THREE days earlier. Municipal workers taped off the survey area and began their site readings. Preliminary inspections would be finished within the week. A contractor had been hired, a list of required materials drawn up, and a step-by-step course of action for the repairs was firmly in place.

It was unusual to see an inspector so soon. One had been on hand the first day, which was altogether normal, but now another had shown up. Wearing a hard hat and reflective vest, much like the surveyors, he poked and prodded the soil along the southern wing, taking voluminous notes, as bureaucrats often did. His unremarkable features were obscured by a dappled gray beard.

Pencil pushing functionaries rarely spoke to the common laborer, yet this inspector produced official looking credentials that were, nonetheless, completely bogus. None of the working stiffs thought to question the documents; they preferred keeping their jobs. Earning the ire of a city administrator was the quickest route to unemployment.

And so the survey team resumed their work. In just a few short hours their holiday would begin; significant repairs weren't scheduled until after the New Year. The inspector had vanished, possibly disappearing through an entryway left open for the tradesmen. It wasn't surprising; one moment he hovered nearby, practically invisible, and the next, he was gone. He got close, and then receded from view. That was how REMORA kept his name.

Beijing, China

"HE HAS POLONIUM." THE OPERATIVE FROM Third Department trembled, his face awash in fear.

"Govern your emotions, Lieutenant." Zhu Ling lifted his eyes, regarding his visitor seriously. "Who has polonium?" He'd already guessed the answer to that question.

Third took a breath, measuring his words. "REMORA—

Ilya Maersk. We thought ricin the extent of his methods—he used that in Chernihiv, at the stockade. Now we know more."

Ling pushed back the paperwork before him, staring into Third's face. "How did you learn this?"

The junior officer had never brushed aside one of Ling's requests, but he did so now. "I would prefer to guard the integrity of my source, Captain."

Zhu grunted. He understood the value of an uncompromised asset. It was enough that Third stood by his assessment.

Inwardly, Ling winced. "Can you arrange another call?" The hour was late, and unorthodox exchanges to a supposed enemy were a delicate matter.

Third shook his head. "My contact in the Communications Directorate has left for the night, *tongzhi*. His shift won't begin again for another twenty-four hours."

His cringe was clearly visible now. Someone in the Russian Federation had extended themselves, Zhu Ling knew—someone who could uncover the specifics of REMORA's movements. That individual was willing to help the government of the People's Republic of China. The captain wondered how they might react at aiding the West.

Now that the Cold War was back on, such assistance would be branded as treason.

Chapter Thirty * Predictability

Excavation site,
near Gora Kalwaria

JEAN-PAUL TOUSSAINT BLEW AIR INTO HIS chilled hands; the designer gloves he wore had been left in the trailer, and the mercury had fallen since early morning. More to the point, the outside air was nearly freezing. He was cold, and was forced closer to the platform's portable stove to warm his frozen fingers.

Toussaint looked around him. His director of public affairs hovered nearby, guiding a photographer and his lens to key points aboard the salvage flat. On the stern, near the gangplank, a clutch of university students took direction from Henri Minouche, preparing to transfer boxes of supplies ashore. And just beyond, an additional barge had arrived, pushed south by a tug from Warsaw. The ample deck of this flatboat was empty—and ready to receive whatever prizes the French society could wrest from the Vistula's stubborn grip.

Above his head, the derrick pointed to the sky like a spire. Tackle hung below, and nylon winching straps splayed out equidistantly from their connecting points before disappearing beneath the river's surface. The lines of the halyard had a rated capacity of five thousand pounds apiece, and connected to the cradle, they were more than adequate for the mission at hand.

Everything *appeared* ready—but that was not the case. The winching motor at the base of the derrick had stopped working. A gasket sealing the relay box had deteriorated, allowing rainwater and condensation to build up inside. Terminals within had failed—sparking a small electrical fire—and the entire operation had ground to a halt for want of replacement parts.

"Tomorrow, Jean-Paul. Two days at the most. " Henri wandered stove-side. He wanted to encourage his employer. "The repairs will not take long."

"And the riverbed?" Toussaint could feel his hands again.

"The volume of water flowing beneath us has removed much of the silt. We are only left with mud."

"Will that be a problem?"

Minouche smiled shrewdly. Jean-Paul was always seeking assurances, sometimes subtly, but more often not.

"I won't say *no*." It was an honest admission. "Until we begin hoisting, it's difficult to say. What I can tell you is that we will have answers very soon."

Toussaint considered that. Things had gone smoothly, for the most part. Some variables could not be foreseen. He was guarded—which was prudent, for an archaeologist, but the businessman in him wanted results. Henri's assessment meant they might have the treasured icon in less than forty-eight hours, and that would be a very welcome Christmas gift indeed.

* * * *

NEILL, CROCKETT, AND STANISLAW BOUNDED UP the stairs, each dressed in PT gear. It seemed to be a race; the Marines had made two trips to the Bristol's gym, in as many days, and both were pushing hard as they reached the landing. Pyotr wasn't quite as accustomed to their standards for physical fitness, and placed a close third.

The hotel staff had found space for Crockett on the fourth

floor. His room was down the hall from Neill and Arrens' respective suites. With the signing behind them, and Nate's lodging taken care of, the officers had more time to catch up and get in some cardio. The captain relished the exertion. Stress had built up since the shooting and he needed an opportunity to bleed off the tension.

"Lunch?" Crockett's first thoughts always went to food; he and Neill were very much alike in that respect.

"Count me in," the Pole gasped.

"Something light," Neill allowed, using a t-shirt to wipe his face. "No point stuffing ourselves before dinner."

"You sound like my mother," Nate razzed. "What's on the menu?"

"Traditional Polish cuisine, from what I hear." He smiled. "I'm sure whatever they serve won't offend your palate."

"Glad to hear it. I'm working up an appetite." Nate stared down the hall. "Have you seen Arrens this morning?"

"She's planning a day with Viktoriya. Girly stuff. Shopping, nails, facials; that kinda thing." He noted his friend's concerned look. "Our friends in the Berkut will keep their eyes peeled. And the Agency's never far behind."

Nate decided to try a little fishing. "She's a nice girl, Mike. You two aren't an item, are you?"

Neill let the statement hang in the air, but only briefly. "Officially, no." A frown. Every Marine knew the rules, and the ubiquitous regulations were becoming an annoyance. And why the expectation that they should be ignored? Neill tempered his answer, adding, "But I have to admit—"

"Never admit anything." As far as Nate was concerned, the subject was closed.

Pyotr chuckled. "Mischa was always the cautious one, especially in matters of the heart."

"I guess some things don't change," Nate grinned. "How 'bout I buy you two a beer after chow? There's nothing else on the schedule till 1730."

Pyotr was warming to the idea, but Neill shook his head.

"Can't do it, buddy." He supplied more, but Crockett didn't catch it. The years spent on rifle ranges had degraded his hearing, but the sniper could have sworn he'd heard the words *dancing lessons* as the captain made for his room.

✱ ✱ ✱ ✱

"I TAKE IT YOU'VE BEEN THERE BEFORE?" Christina's eyes were wide, intent on the map provided by the concierge.

"*Vitkac?* Oh, yes," Viktoriya answered. She adjusted her rearview, pushing on a pair of oversized sunglasses. "Window shopping, mostly," she admitted with a smile. "Half the boutiques there are far beyond my budget."

Christina smiled wryly. "Nothing wrong with looking."

"Nothing at all—except when that's not enough." Viktoriya held back a more impish comment. A glance in the mirror offered reassurance; the Berkut boys were two cars back.

"Our escorts appear ready to go," she observed.

The Marine pushed aside her bangs and had a bold thought. "Maybe I'll get a new haircut."

Viktoriya sized her up before easing the car into the morning traffic. "And a new gown—unless you brought something to wear."

"Got that covered," Christina replied. "I'll be in uniform. Evening mess dress."

The journalist applied the brakes and turned with a frown. "No, no, no, *ma chere*; are you serious?"

She blinked. "For a state function? It's expected."

Viktoriya laughed and shook her head. "Do you always act as expected?" She clucked her tongue. "Men don't want predictability, Christy."

"What did you have in mind?" She was ready to defer to the red-headed woman at the wheel.

"A new plan," Viktoriya prattled. She eased off the clutch and gave the Duster a little gas. The prospect of a conspiracy was too much to resist. "Leave everything to me."

Window shopping. Arrens considered that concept from a different angle. She'd done her share over the past few years. Viktoriya's avant-garde thinking had inspired her, and she decided that tonight just might be the appropriate time to change a few things.

Chapter Thirty-One * A Faceless Enemy

THE COLORS OF SUNSET FADED, AND AS DUSK fell, light of a different kind began to gleam in the byways of Warsaw. Christmas decorations abounded along Krakowskie Przedmiescie—or *K Street*, as Nate now called it—with twinkling strands and bright bulbs adding a seasonal glow. A fresh snowfall caught and reflected their radiance, and in places, it appeared as if the stars themselves had descended to grace the city's thoroughfares.

For the first time in years, Willis Avery sported a neatly-trimmed head of hair. His cowlick was gone, and the thatch of gray on top had been recently acquainted with a comb. The contrast was matched by a stiff white shirt, bow tie, and the fashionably-tailored tuxedo that hugged his frame.

Richard Aultman was formally dressed, as were the agents assigned to the protective detail. The attire of some was disingenuous; beneath their greatcoats and jackets, the black and white fabric hid servers' tunics. A select few had been given the role of wait-staff, a shell game of sorts intended to obscure their true assignment.

The sea of formalwear was offset by the varied uniforms of American, Polish and Ukrainian officers, all gathered in Avery's fifth floor suite. Ordinarily spacious, the front room now felt crowded. The national security advisor held court in their midst, his rumbling voice filling the air with last-minute directives.

The dinner was intended to honor the conference delegates, Avery told them. "President Dobrogost has pulled out all the stops; it should be quite festive, but we all have a job to do. I think everyone here has received my presser—" heads nodded around the room, "—so stay sharp. Quite frankly, we don't know if our mark is anywhere near Warsaw, but we aren't taking any chances."

Avery ended his speech with a few more admonitions and warnings before yielding the floor to Captain Neill.

"THERE are no photographs of this man." Michael's brow deepened. "He's a faceless enemy—but don't let that sway you. Ilya Maersk has left bodies all across Europe; most recently, we suspect, in Ukraine—not many days ago—where he assassinated a former military officer.

"Unfortunately, the Polish government hasn't rallied behind this idea, and we can't prove he's going to strike."

"So if he does get into the building, how do we identify him?" Pyotr asked.

Crockett had a roguish expression. "We flush him out, into the open."

Neill looked to his friend. "What's your plan?"

AN economy of words was the mark of an effective briefing. Too much had been said already, so Willis dismissed the troupe. The security detail filed out to prep the motorcade. Neill, Ulyanov and the rest of the company stayed behind and Avery added a few closing thoughts.

"The catering staff has been thoroughly vetted. Along with Dobrogost's people." He peered at Crockett over his glasses. "You all set, Lieutenant?"

"Yes, sir; my gear's in place." He smiled. The Secret Service had been very accommodating, giving Nate carte blanche to stage a few weapons in spots he deemed handy.

"Nice tux," Neill grinned back. "Are you driving the Aston tonight?"

The captain's mood had suddenly shifted, and he struck Willis as a bit more animated. Considering the woman who waited for him downstairs, Avery could hardly find fault. It was time to go, but before he could release them, Neill raised a hand.

"Do you have something to add, Captain?"

"Just a prayer, sir. I think it's fitting that we ask God for protection."

"Always appropriate," Avery grunted. "We can use all the help we can get."

Michael bowed his head. The petition he offered was short and sincere. When he finished, he lifted his chin and gave Avery a nod.

"All right, gentlemen," the NSA brayed. "I suspect there are a few young ladies in need of escorts, so let's turn to.

"I'll see you all downstairs in fifteen minutes."

NEILL took the stairs one flight down to the fourth floor. Leaving the landing, he adjusted his blues, and then stepped off smartly toward Arrens' suite.

He passed Yegor and Iosef on the way, and rounding the corner he saw Viktoriya enter the hall. Dazzling in ivory—with matching heels and wrap—she gave him a smile, closing Christina's door gently behind her.

"You look stunning," the Marine conceded. There was no other way to put it. Viktoriya was at her best and he paused to appreciate the young woman's beauty.

"*Spaseeba, moi capitan.*" Crimson tresses fell around her shoulders, the sienna tint blazing against the haltered straps of her gown. She ran her hand down the sleeve of his uniform, in a touch that lingered, and then moved toward the lifts.

"Hey—wait up." Neill was puzzled. She seemed to be in a hurry. "We can all take the elevator together."

"This might take some time," she answered cryptically. "And I'm meeting Dmitri in the lobby."

Viktoriya threw a glance over her shoulder. Michael appeared taller; it was probably just the uniform. She would have liked to stay, to see the look on his face in the next few moments.

That sight alone would have been worth the price of admission.

THE women were up to something, but Michael was oblivious to their stagecraft. The captain tapped on the door and a voice on the other side told him to come in.

He eased into the room slowly. One lamp was on, leaving the suite softly lit, but Christina was nowhere to be seen—and her uniform hung in the open armoire.

"You're not ready?" Neill checked his cell, raising an eyebrow. This wasn't the occasion to run late—and it didn't fit her character. "Where are you?"

"In the bedroom."

Okay. He chambered an answer and let it fly. "And I'll be in the hall."

"Don't leave, Michael."

That melodious tone again, completely irresistible. Her voice froze him in place and Neill watched as Arrens stepped into the parlor.

Her approach was tentative. She stopped in the center of the room. Neill's senses were fully engaged; his eyes widened, and only one word escaped his lips.

"*Wow.*"

The woman before him *was* Christina—but a version Michael had never seen until now.

From head to toe, she was transformed. Neill was greeted with color—a splash of vibrant red that began at her ankles and continued upward. Everything else about the gown was more daring. It had a V-neck cut, and the fabric hugged every curve. Crossed panels lifted the bodice, with attached cap sleeves that were barely there, flattering her exposed shoulders.

There was no doubt about it. The look was definitely a scene-stealer.

"You aren't saying anything, Captain." Christina started to

worry. She spun slowly; the dress had a square, open back that ended at her waistline. "Is it too much?"

Michael remained quiet. Her beauty had stolen his voice—but the silence was hardly a compliment to Christina's ears.

"I knew this was a mistake," she blanched, turning away. "There's still time to change. Just give me five minutes—"

He rejected that idea. "As you were, Staff Sergeant." Neill's tone was commanding. He stepped forward in unabashed wonder. "You're not changing anything—and that's an order." His eyes were full of something and caused her to blush. "Trust me; there won't be a single objection tonight. Certainly not from me."

She hesitated. "So—do you like it?"

"I love it. You look breathtaking," he blurted.

That was more like it.

"Your hair." Michael took in the rest of the view. "You've changed it."

Her fingers brushed at the loose curls framing the side of her face. A partial updo graced the crown, while the rest fell in waves down the center of her back. "Just trimmed the bangs—they kept falling," she replied.

"I'd fall, too," Michael charmed. He moved closer and lifted her hand, kissing it lightly. He then extended his arm. She accepted it without reservation. "Shall we go?"

Chapter Thirty-Two * Pomp and Circumstance

THE NEW DEPUTIES' CHAMBER WAS LOCATED on the first floor, above ground level, near the Castle's southwestern wing. This hall was positioned far from the ballroom, and in a storage area close to the water closets, Ilya Maersk had found a place to spend the night.

His accommodations for the evening were narrow, a system of damp and mildewed air ducts that laced throughout the confined spaces in the ceiling. REMORA had hidden himself there since completing his 'inspection' on the previous day, and now, hours before the banquet, he lowered himself to the floor and moved toward the Great Hall.

Hunger and weariness tugged at him. For the former, he consumed a few protein bars stashed in his satchel. He satisfied his thirst from the sinks in the lavatory, and the fatigue he felt would fade as he worked his joints and muscles. In any event, Ilya could find plenty of rest once this mission was over.

Success meant blending in. To do that, Maersk would need the appropriate camouflage. The clip-on badge he chose was simple; it identified him as an *inspector*, displayed a false name, and bore the city seal in one corner. It was one of several he'd requested, and had been supplied by his handlers in Moscow.

The ID's features were designed to be bland, enough to produce disinterest in the simple-minded. But he could only wear it briefly. As the evening progressed, security would tighten, and the tag would invite scrutiny. To submerge himself from view—and effectively hide in plain sight—Ilya required more.

The caterers arrived early and began their preparations. Two panel trucks brought foodstuffs, compact fridges and portable warming stoves. A separate van delivered the serving staff's uniforms—starched white tuxedo shirts, with contrasting vests for those in public view; and chefs' jackets, tabards, and stewards' tunics for the cooks. The apparel was wrapped in plastic and the wheeled racks stored in a niche next to the Knights' Hall.

The passage nearby was a busy place. Maersk was just one of many who found his way into the alcove. When he re-emerged, he wore a long-sleeve dress shirt and steward's vest. His badge had disappeared, having served its purpose, and he melted into the background. No one gave him a second glance.

* * * *

"EVERYONE HERE?" NEILL ASKED. THREE LIMousines were required for the American and Ukrainian delegates. The Marines arrived last.

Dmitri nodded. He gave Christina a second look. The trio mingled with other guests in the Castle's Oval Gallery, waiting for their turn to be announced.

"Viktoriya is next door, touring the Marble Room—" he chuckled, "—and all four members of the Berkut are peering over her shoulder. Discreetly, of course."

"That should keep her out of trouble. What about Crockett?"

"Right here, *moi Capitan*." Nate appeared from behind. His eyes were fixed on the fiery red dress. "Mind if I borrow your date for a minute?"

"Just remember where you found her."

"Roger that. Right this way, miss."

Neill watched as they vanished in the crowd. "Have you seen Pyotr?"

"Lieutenant Stanislaw is making a sweep of the north vestibule."

"And the official party?"

Another soft laugh, and Yaroslav lowered his voice. "Take a breath, Michael. Avery has gathered with Dobrogost and Krol, and I believe the Ulyanovs are with them."

Arrens returned after a moment, but Crockett wasn't with her.

"Everything okay?" Neill asked.

"Just dandy." She smoothed the front of her dress, hooking her arm in his.

After his third glance, Dmitri stood tall and voiced a compliment.

Michael turned to the woman at his side. "The major wishes to express his admiration for the sergeant's gown." A grin. "I told you there'd be no objections."

"*Spaseeba*, Dmitri." Christina spied the minister of protocol. "That reminds me." She pulled the captain close, whispering into his ear.

Neill faced the entrance. Chamber music drifted in from the next room. "I think we can manage that."

* * * *

ZHU LING'S PRAYER TIME WAS THREATENED BY A common foe, one faced by all believers. He had good intentions, but his focus gave way to a relaxed state and his mind began to wander. He closed his eyes—ostensibly to meditate—but finally succumbed to fatigue and fell into a deep sleep.

It was a dream that woke him. An old, gray wolf, with a black heart—how he saw that, Zhu couldn't say—stood on the banks of a river, watching swimmers as the current swept them from his snapping jaws. The disheveled beast couldn't reach his prey but he didn't need to. Lapping water from the stream, the broad channel became full of death, and everyone passing by slipped beneath the surface and drowned.

Ling sat upright, his heart racing. He wasn't one to spiritualize visions, but the image of the wild animal was too vivid to ignore.

He picked up his cell and checked the time. He recalled his last conversation with Third. More than twenty-four hours had passed and the lieutenant's contact in the Communications Directorate was undoubtedly on duty by now.

* * * *

GUESTS PASSED THROUGH THE RECEPTION LINE at a moderate pace. Honoring Christina's whispered request, the minister of protocol announced the Marines, introducing Neill as a captain, but dropping the sergeant's rank, addressing her simply as *Miss* Arrens. For this occasion, she preferred to be recognized as an elegant woman and not as a staff NCO of the Corps.

General officers were entitled to special privileges. The Ulyanovs had already been seated, as had Avery and Aultman. Richard got to his feet and waved the couple to their corner of the room, a spot close to an enormous Christmas tree.

The gentlemen stood as Christina came near. "Your chair's right here, Mike." Aultman had memorized the place settings. "Very enchanting, Miss Arrens. My compliments." He bowed slightly, and his admiration was sincere. "You're at the captain's side."

Christina smiled demurely. "As it should be."

* * * *

ILYA MAERSK HAD TWO IMMEDIATE GOALS. HIS first was to identify the security presence and avoid them at all costs. He inspected the interior and after several minutes was able to satisfy that priority. REMORA had no illusions of roaming about freely; the American Secret Service would be looking for out-of-place individuals. But he didn't need to evade them for long, either.

Under the right conditions, his mission could be accomplished in mere minutes. After that, he would make for the nearest staircase and slip away. Until that time, he would blend in, and practice his special brand of obscurity.

The second objective was to locate his targets. Maersk had an interest in only a few of the attendees. He strolled past the statue of Chronos, entering the ballroom from the Knights' Hall. With a glance to his left, the assassin managed to pick out two of his principals.

Dobrogost's table was much larger than the rest—hours had been spent making seating arrangements—and the president and defense minister were now in place. Ilya cut through the center to the rose-colored foyer of the Council Chamber, but Viktoriya could be found in neither of the rooms.

Maersk touched an object in his pocket. To the undiscriminating eye, it looked for all the world like a smoker's butane, but had a far more sinister purpose. It was larger and heavier than other lighters, and the aluminum outer shell enclosed a thick lead case.

The deadly implement had been machined to exacting specifications and required delicate handling. A tiny aperture had been drilled at its base, and a stud on top gave Ilya the means to dispense its contents in small doses—one microgram at a time.

* * * *

VOSKOV WATCHED FROM THE COUNCIL Chamber. "Your sergeant is out of uniform, Yuri."

Tereshenko stood at his side, rocking on his heels.

"I'll complain later," he grinned.

* * * *

THE ORCHESTRA WAS LOCATED ACROSS THE room. Dinner music filled the air as the wait staff brought entrees. Nate showed himself among the army of servers, along with a mix of agents from the Secret Service. He made a point of dropping by Willis Avery's table, fawning over the guests as any attentive *maître d'* would.

Crockett asked the seated patrons if they had any needs. He spoke English, of course, but Neill was surprised by the passable accent he employed.

"We're good so far," Michael answered. He resisted a dig. "How are things on your end?"

The response was typically Nate. He lifted his hands and shrugged.

"You know how it is, *Capitan*. Three days ago I was plinking targets in England; tonight I'm serving green beans in Poland."

* * * *

IN BEIJING, ZHU SIPPED TEA AND WAITED AS PATIENTLY as he could. He was wide awake now, his cell phone pressed to one ear; the voice on the other end came and went. The lieutenant from Third Department was juggling calls, and doing so under the constraints of discretion. The officers' faith formed a loose alliance between them, but their ties to the Comm Directorate were more tenuous.

Third came back after a pause. "He is trying, Captain Ling. But we must tread lightly. Not all Party members are willing to look the other way in these matters."

Ling nodded his assent. "Do what you can."

* * * *

MICHAEL SPOKE TO ONE OF THE SERVERS. SHE smiled, responding in Ukrainian, and gestured to the General.

"Twelve dishes—to honor the president's guests," Neill announced. "In Ukraine, we call this the *Sviata Vecheria*—the Holy Meal." He wondered if this was standard fare at other tables.

Dinner took some time. The food was exquisite and it was customary to sample each course. Fish was served, with borscht, pierogies and varenyky. Kutia—a sweet pudding—was also on the menu.

Ulyanov smacked his lips. The servings were small. He managed to consume each course, and his plate was now empty. "This is normally a meal for Christmas Eve," he explained. "But President Dobrogost wants his guests to experience a taste of Poland a bit early."

"But we haven't prayed, Andrei." Irina was unusually distressed. "What is the Holy Supper without a proper benediction?"

"We can remedy that, *moya druzhnya*," her husband answered. Something about his tone suggested theatrics. He spied a small bottle of honey and turned to Neill. "May we prevail upon you, Michael? I seem to have forgotten the words."

Pyotr translated and Avery perked up. "Is there some role you need to fulfill, Captain?" he smiled.

"It's a traditional blessing, sir." Neill knew where this was going. He returned to Ulyanov. "Despite years of repetition, the prayer has escaped the general's memory. But if you insist—"

Ulyanov rose to his feet. Lifting a water glass, he tapped it lightly with his spoon, attracting the attention of several tables. "Come now, Mischa. Stand up—and your companion, too."

Michael pushed his seat back and stood. He took Christina by the hand, gently pulling her chair aside as she rose. By now half the room was looking their way, focused on the woman and her escort.

Arrens was still, but smiled nonetheless. Neill lifted the honey and removed the cap.

"What are you doing with that?" she whispered nervously.

Neill had mischief in mind. He was starting to enjoy this. "Do you trust me?"

"I always have." Her dark eyes stared. "Don't blow it now."

"On Christmas Eve," Neill began, "the head of the household will anoint those present with a little honey." He made himself understood in both languages, adding a drop to his finger.

Neill moved closer. He rested his fingertip on Christina's forehead; she could feel the warmth of his hand, and as he traced the sign of the cross, she closed her eyes.

The small talk faded and stillness came over the hall as Michael pronounced the blessing. "In the name of the Father, the Son, and the Holy Spirit; may you have sweetness and many good things in life, and in the new year."

She turned her face, gently pressing into his palm and hoping to prolong the caress. Michael must have sensed that, and his hand lingered. When Christina opened her eyes, she saw that nearly everyone had stopped to witness the custom.

* * * *

MAERSK WATCHED THE MARINES FROM THE servers' alcove, but the tender moment couldn't touch his black heart.

Always practical, he scoured the small room for just the right prop. A cooler claimed space near the back wall, and chilled bottles of Cabernet Sauvignon and Chardonnay filled the first three racks. Above that were two bottles of very expensive champagne, undoubtedly reserved for Dobrogost's table.

Maersk reached out a hand and then reconsidered. The timing wasn't right—and timing was everything. Dinner had been served and light conversation now flowed. The musicians would give the guests time to settle their food before launching into the night's entertainment. If the maestro was worth his salt, he'd keep things moving, splitting the evening in two; soft chamber music before the meal, followed by the waltz as the celebration began.

* * * *

"HOW SILLY DO I LOOK—?" CHRISTINA'S FACE glowed. She touched her forehead, drawing a finger across the sticky substance.

Neill's gaze started at her feet and moved upward. "That word doesn't come to mind." He offered her a table napkin. "But if you'd prefer—"

"And wipe away that blessing?" Christina shook her head. "Not a chance, Captain."

An agreeable tune kept Neill from seating her. The opening bars rippled across the hall; trembling violins accompanied by woodwinds in a familiar strain. It was an easily recognized piece of music, and while subdued, the melody was purely joyous.

He had been waiting for this. Michael gave Irina a nod and then winked before offering Christina his hand.

"Would you honor me with this dance, Miss Arrens?"

"The *Blue Danube?*" A smile was only part of her answer. "Most performances can be very long."

"Not long enough," Neill grinned back, and she laid her fingertips in his. "Especially when you've found the right partner."

* * * *

MAERSK COUNTED A DOZEN HEADS AT Dobrogost's table. Estonia and Moldova were there, along with the Lithuanian ambassador and his wife. He looked to his left, but that proved troublesome; Viktoriya was seated with the Americans, and the geography involved only served to complicate his task.

No matter; he had planned for this. Maersk lived for contingencies. A single journalist was of little consequence, while a dozen enemies of the *Rodina* were a prize worth taking . . .

* * * *

ONLY A FEW COUPLES HAD TAKEN TO THE DANCE floor. Michael and Christina revolved slowly at first, and then found their pace, stepping in time to the metered beat.

Viktoriya watched as they began their graceful turns. The scene sparked a twinge of jealousy, but she immediately dismissed that as immature.

"They look perfect together."

"But Michael seems distracted," Yaroslav chuckled.

"The right gown can have that effect." *That's why she chose it,* the journalist didn't add.

* * * *

TWELVE CHAMPAGNE FLUTES WERE ARRANGED on the tray. Maersk's hand hovered over them, and a dozen soft clicks were repeated in rapid succession. It was a casual gesture that no one saw—save one.

All of the glasses were empty, except for the deadly, microscopic pellet now resting at the bottom of each. With that task complete, he dropped the dispenser back into his pocket—and began to search for an accomplice.

* * * *

"SERRE MOI FORT, CAPITAN." CHRISTINA MADE eye contact. It was an invitation Neill couldn't resist. "I won't break, Michael—hold me like you mean it."

He pulled her closer. His palm pressed against the small of her back and she gasped lightly as he tightened his grip.

"Careful," she warned. A smile crossed her lips. "Keep those hands in international waters."

Pairs of men and women streamed onto the floor. Andrei and Irina followed the Marines, and Dmitri and Viktoriya weren't far behind.

"So far, so good—" Neill judged. "I haven't stepped on your feet once. Are you enjoying yourself?"

"Immensely." Christina was jubilant. They twirled closer to the orchestra and she abandoned herself to his embrace. "I can die happy now."

"Please don't," he ordered. "That's not what I had in mind."

She offered a grin. "And what did you have in mind?"

Color came to Neill's cheeks. The young officer was captivated. "Are you flirting with me, Staff Sergeant?"

"Just following your lead," she returned.

They crossed paths with Dmitri and Viktoriya. Christina was impressed by Michael's footwork and had come to anticipate his movements. Their sweeping turns gave him an excellent view of the hall. Stanislaw and Willis Avery had joined the president's table, with Aultman in tow. The four were engaged in dialogue, and the national security advisor seemed to be dominating the discussion.

Neill glanced toward the Council Chamber. Tereshenko was nowhere in sight and Crockett was likewise absent. Only Voskov was visible, stationed near the entrance. He had the chiseled look of a hawk, and his gaze panned the room.

"Has Viktoriya patched things up with her bodyguard?"

Christina sighed heavily. "Not that I know of."

"So what's the attraction?" Neill pressed.

"He's the rugged type," she answered. Her hand left his shoulder, and she traced a finger alongside his face. "Kind of like you—but not as smooth."

"I have a few rough edges," Michael defended. His smile faded. "Still, he is a bit melancholy. Like someone acquainted with tragedy—but resisting God's grace."

* * * *

MAERSK NEEDED A DISTRACTION. HE WOULD bide his time, as professionals were often forced to do, but his wait was almost over.

"Young man." The Russian's tone was brusque. He snapped his fingers and the steward was instantly at his side. "Take this tray and follow me; the president is calling for the toast."

The server looked confused. He'd heard the word *president*, but nothing else rang a bell—until he saw the bottles of champagne in Ilya's hands.

And then Nathan Crockett's eyes brightened.

"*Na zdrovyeh!*"

"*Tak—na zdrovyeh,*" Maersk smiled. A simpleton, he mused. All the better—a pliant *garcon* would ask no questions, and with an acknowledged server, Maersk's chances of success were greatly improved.

* * * *

THE DANUBE RACED TOWARD ITS CONCLUSION; the final bars of the piece were furious, but few on the dance floor were willing to yield to its strenuous demands.

Michael and Christina circled back toward their table. The decorated tree loomed before them, with colored lights burning steadily. The Ulyanovs were spent and neared the corner just as the melody ended with a resounding flourish.

The performance was over, but Neill continued to hold Christina in his arms. She peered around him at the Ukrainian couple. The general was breathless; he lifted his eyes, and Christina did the same.

"Oh, no." She regarded Michael suspiciously. "Did you plan this?"

"Plan what?" Neill felt warm, and a glance overhead gave him the answer.

The hall glimmered with the trappings of the season. Garlands and ornaments graced the columns, and the embellishments also went higher. Ribbons spanned the ballroom, strung from the moldings and intricate coved ceiling, and mistletoe had been placed above the floor at selected points. Somehow the two had ended their waltz directly beneath one of the decorative evergreens.

* * * *

MAERSK PICKED HIS WAY AROUND COUPLES AS they left the floor. The chilled Pinot Noir was cradled in one arm; a waiter's napkin draped the other. Crockett brought up the rear, wheeling a serving cart that held a corkscrew—and a dozen wine flutes bearing the assassin's poison.

* * * *

IT WAS HARD TO TELL WHO BLUSHED MORE. Neill protested, denying subterfuge and proclaiming his innocence. Christina wasn't having any of it and appreciated the chance occurrence for what it was.

"Everyone's watching," Michael pointed out. "Probably bad form to ignore a cultural tradition."

"Always the analyst." Her words came in a breath. "Why don't you just kiss me?"

"Then we can both die happy."

He had no excuses now and was silently thankful for it. Neill wrapped his arm around her waist and held her close. He had never seen anyone so lovely. Christina's eyes were focused on his, and her lips matched the color of her gown. As appealing as she was, Michael felt joy in simply holding her. This was what he'd wanted for some time, and now he could finally—

The spell was broken by the insistent trilling of Neill's mobile. It was buried in the folds of his coat, and a pained expression soured his face.

Christina pulled back. "You should take that."

Michael's frustration was evident. He retrieved the cell and stared. Once again, the caller ID was his own number.

She dropped her eyes. "Saved by the bell, I guess."

"Just delayed," he assured her. He lifted her chin. "This night isn't over yet."

Neill accepted the call, glancing up. A massive painting hung like a canopy overhead. It was a re-creation of a work by Bacciarelli; the fresco depicted King Stanislaw bringing order to the known world. It was entitled the *Disentanglement of Chaos*, but the Marine neither knew nor cared for its name at that particular moment.

Chapter Thirty-Three * Loss

A SERVER KNEW HIS PLACE, AND MAERSK had adopted the persona of career footman. He appeared both abject and courtly, a puzzling combination stuck between extremes. He said nothing and remained aloof, inscrutable in silence. Aultman pegged the old man as a subservient butler or stately chamberlain, but in either case, he wore the experience of years.

Warsaw's philharmonic began to play subdued selections. The music served as a segue to Maersk's approach, and he arrived at the president's table under the pretense of chief wine steward. Opening the Pinot Noir, the Russian handed the corkscrew to Crockett, who applied it to the second bottle, and the two began to pour.

Dobrogost was none the wiser, but Pyotr and Willis Avery had their marching orders. With each glass now full, Nate placed the champagne back on the cart. He eyed the aging steward for further instructions and then gave the national security advisor a subtle nod.

* * * *

"POLONIUM?" NEILL'S CORNER OF THE HALL was a little more frantic. To his way of thinking, any word ending with the letters -ium signaled danger. "Are you sure?"

Captain Ling only added to his anxiety. "Polonium 210, *Mikhail*; very deadly. And Maersk has over 500 micrograms—enough to kill hundreds—if not more." In Beijing, the Chinese officer frowned. "Is there an event where he might use it?"

A chill ran up Neill's spine. His head was on a swivel and he scanned the far corners of the room. "I can think of at least one," he deadpanned. "What's the best way to weaponize this stuff—can it be spread through the air?"

Zhu Ling bit his lip. "That's one form of delivery—but it's more lethal when ingested."

Neill paled. Dinner was over—the damage might have already been done. "What are the effects?"

"Nausea, violent sickness—followed by organ failure. Alpha particles attack from within, destroying tissue." He shook his head. "A horrible way to die, Captain Neill. Once in the bloodstream, there's no way to stop it."

Michael breathed a prayer. He gave Christina a concerned look, and then his eyes were drawn to the president's table.

* * * *

AVERY CALLED FOR QUIET. PYOTR TRANSLATED his words and the orchestra was stilled.

"It's only fitting that we toast our achievements," he announced. "But before we do—" he raised his cell, recalling Crockett's instructions, "—I'd like to ask everyone to silence their phones."

Some had anticipated this moment. The crowd buzzed softly, and across the hall, guests retrieved devices from pockets, coats and purses, briefly thumbing keypads and switches before turning back to the front.

* * * *

NEILL'S BRAIN SPUN INTO HIGH GEAR. SIMPLY poisoning the food would be too mundane for REMORA—or so the captain hoped. Maersk would employ a more symbolic method, a dramatic angle that would fit his legacy.

Gathered around Dobrogost's table were the envoys who stood opposed to Moscow's aggression, and eliminating them all—in one fell swoop—would be a temptation far too difficult to resist.

"The toast," Neill declared.

Christina was alarmed. "What about it?"

Pocketing the phone, he grabbed her hand and started moving forward. "Come on—I think we may have found our assassin."

* * * *

MAERSK HADN'T EXPECTED THIS. THE STIR-ring around him seemed universal; only the old man remained motionless, and his lack of participation made him stand out.

A tactical error, he admonished himself. *Perhaps if no one notices—*

But that was just it. A chilling awareness crept in. This was the Americans' doing, and he should have been thinking two steps ahead. They had been alerted to his presence—and devised a scheme to flush out the traditional, old guard operative.

He'd been tricked, and Maersk wasn't accustomed to that.

"*Pardon*, amigo." Crockett dropped his guise, gripping Ilya rudely by the shoulder. "The man asked you to silence your phone—or did you leave yours back in Moscow?"

The Russian turned, a snarl on his lips. He had drawn everyone's eye, and could see movement; a dark suit edging closer, and moving fast—Polish security, he judged—confirmed by the revolver on the man's hip. Agents of the Secret Service had also taken an interest.

Voskov and Tereshenko noted the drama. They closed in from opposite sides, like moths attracted to flame, but Maersk didn't see them. He gauged his surroundings, searching for exits, and for the first time he looked into the face of Karl Dobrogost.

He'd have one chance before it was over, and it would have to count.

REMORA bowed in feigned resignation—but was coiled like a snake. He waited until the agent was within reach, and then raised his arm, driving an elbow across the bridge of the man's nose and breaking Crockett's grasp.

For a man of his years, Maersk displayed surprising agility. The blow dropped his victim, and as he fell, the Russian spun and reached for the officer's service pistol. It was a double-action .38, just as he suspected, and tailor-made for his present needs.

Nate was fast but not fast enough. Maersk got low and rushed him with the serving cart, building up enough speed to knock him off balance. The Marine staggered and dropped to one knee; wine glasses toppled, and one of the bottles fell, shattering on the tile below.

Maersk wheeled, bringing the weapon up. His bearings were off; the target had shifted, shrinking back, yet still in the open. Pyotr was at his side and instinctively stepped forward as the assassin squeezed the trigger.

The report was loud. The round went high, missing the president and burying itself in Pyotr's shoulder. Yuri Tereshenko came out of nowhere, driving both men to the floor and shielding them with his lanky torso.

Andrei reached for Irina, pulling her close. Richard Aultman pushed Avery back and shoved him to the deck. He wasn't about to witness another attempt on the boss's life. Lying prone, he was kicked in the head as more security personnel arrived, tripping over him in their haste to reach the president.

There were shouts and screams as the hall erupted in panic. Agents began converging from all sides. Completing his mission now was out of the question, and escape was the only option left. Maersk raised the pistol and fired three more rounds; one shattered a mirror, and the second splintered a window pane. The third ricocheted off a column and vanished in the boughs of the tree.

"Stay down," Dmitri hissed. Viktoriya folded into his arms and didn't argue.

The shots had the desired effect. Guests were cowed, with those closest to Maersk crouching even lower. This gave the gunman some leeway, but the chaos wouldn't last. He reached into his pocket and brought out the dispenser—flinging it across the room before fading into the hall.

* * * *

VOSKOV MOVED TOWARD THE EXIT, DODGING diplomats and guests on his way. He scooped something up and was about to push through the doors when Neill caught his arm.

"I've got this, Captain—you stay with Viktoriya." He had to raise his voice; Maersk tripped the fire alarm and the wail of a klaxon sounded, followed by the ringing of bells. This brought fresh hysteria, and some began a rush toward the adjoining gallery.

Voskov tried to shake himself free, but Neill pressed the issue. "REMORA might double back for the kill; don't forget—she was his first target."

He looked ahead. Security spilled into the adjoining hall and turned right, searching for the assassin. The Ulyanovs had found Pyotr. Nate grabbed one of Dobrogost's men but couldn't make himself understood.

"*Mike*—a little help here, please."

Neill grunted a reply, nodding at Yaroslav. "Dmitri, that serving cart's a crime scene—don't let anyone near it." He was marching toward the door and tossed back a sober directive. "No more food or drink—and tell Krol to get his hazmat people in here."

Yaroslav flinched. "What should they be looking for?"

"Polonium," the Marine barked.

"*Wait*—" Viktoriya stood nearby, her words in French, "—tell Michael to be careful, *ma chere*."

"*We* will," Christina answered tersely. She quickened her pace and reached for Neill's hand. "I'm going with you."

"No, you're not. I need you to look after horsefly."

"He'll be fine." Her tone was resolute. "It's you I'm worried about."

Crockett was already bounding to the exit. "Let's go, people. You two can play kissy-face later."

* * * *

NEILL STEPPED THROUGH, SCANNING THE VES-tibule in both directions. To his right, a steady stream of guests was moving to the staircase. The other end of the hall was empty, and the sound of the alarm had grown annoying.

"Geez, Mike, you *wanna* get shot?" Nate growled. "Watch yourself. He fired four rounds, which means he's still got one or two left."

"So which way did he go?"

"What do you think?" the sniper grinned. "Would you follow the flow—or be unpredictable?"

The agents preceding them had reached the staircase. "You're right," Neill nodded. He turned west, away from the crowd, but Crockett's hand restrained him.

"Hang on—we're gonna need a weapon."

"Will this do?"

Barely a heartbeat had passed. Christina now stood between them—holding a sidearm.

"Ruger; 9 millimeter." There was admiration in Michael's voice. "So you brought more than just the Colt."

"Crockett helped," she admitted. "Can you handle this?"

"I've got a pistol badge in my room that says I can," Neill replied.

The trio was startled as Aultman burst through the door. "Where's the party?" he asked, a little breathless.

The captain checked the magazine before chambering a round. "This isn't a parade, Richard. Get back inside."

"Mr. Avery's orders." Aultman was hedging the truth.

Neill frowned. "We don't have time to debate this." He nodded in Crockett's direction. "Go with Nate; take the hall to the west wing and work your way south. Christina and I will head back toward the Old Audience Chamber. Meet us at the staircase." He shot a glance at the sniper. "Can you pick up a weapon along the way?"

"Leave that to me." Crockett was all business but a smile burst through. He had a sideways look for Christina. "I've heard of concealed carry—but where'd you hide that thing?"

"Get Maersk first," she smiled, "—and maybe I'll tell you."

* * * *

THE MARINES TRACED A PATH TO THE CASTLE'S Red Corridor, passing the King's Bedchamber and the Canaletto Room. They reached the end of the wing and were prepared to turn right again when Neill stopped in his tracks.

"Wait."

Christina looked in every direction. "What is it?" she whispered.

Michael was still. He peered into the darkened alcove, where a faint light spilled onto the floor. Far behind them, the din of the fire alarm was merely background noise.

Neill raised a finger to his lips. "This way," he urged.

For the first time, she was apprehensive.

"You all right?"

"I don't like this," she answered. "What's down there?"

"The chapel," Neill answered.

She placed a palm on his shoulder. The captain's training kicked in; he was in ready mode, weapon firmly in hand.

* * * *

A MEMBER OF THE PRESIDENT'S DETAIL PULLED back Pyotr's coat. Andrei and Irina tended to his wound. It was far from superficial, but the Ukrainian couple had staunched the flow of blood.

The Secret Service formed a loose perimeter around the table. Avery pressed in, checking on the Polish lieutenant; Stanislaw was conscious and tried sitting up.

"Easy, son," Willis cautioned. "Just lay back. The medics are here. *Richard*—"

He turned, but Aultman was nowhere to be seen.

* * * *

THE SENATORS' ROOM WAS VACANT. NATE LED the way, skirting around the throne and staying close to the east wall. Coats of arms hung above, bathed in the soft glow of the dimly lit chamber.

"The Guards' Gallery is coming up," Crockett announced.

"You're well informed."

The lieutenant shrugged. "I've got culture—I read the brochure."

"You stashed a gun down here?" Richard tried to mask his anxiety.

"Beyond the Gallery." Nate stopped short of the entrance, his gaze sweeping the open spaces before searching the corners. "We need to catch up with Iron Mike."

"Iron Mike?" Aultman repeated. "Not—"

Crockett shook his head. "A different Mike." He stepped through, guided by a sense of caution and urgency.

"Come on; I'll introduce you."

* * * *

THE CHAPEL WAS A STUDY IN MARBLE AND stone. Jade columns lifted high overhead and held a dazzling cupola of ivory and gold. Aside from their color, these capped, upright pillars matched those in the Great Hall.

At the far end, a Biblical scene hung high, ornately framed, and was set against polished burgundy. The chancel table below was covered by a cere cloth of white linen, accented with candles, and a small prayer rail faced the altar.

Like Nate, Michael's senses were heightened. He stepped forward cautiously, his eyes clearing the room. The alcove was small; its vertical lines intended to focus one's attention upward.

To be sure, there was stillness here, but the peace of the staid little shrine was a façade, and a somber air spoiled the vestry's noble purpose.

"What shall we talk about, Captain Neill?" Maersk's voice was wrapped in ice, his words in Russian. "And which language do you prefer?"

The Marine stayed in place and turned slowly; Christina stood at his side. She was chilled to the bone and she wished for her Colt.

"I've always had a fondness for Ukrainian. I believe my father would have shared that sentiment." His arm went out, forcing Christina behind him.

"As you wish." REMORA's laugh was soft and surprisingly deep. There was a preternatural quality to his presence. He emerged from the shadows much like a ghost. "We come to the subject of your father rather quickly."

"I think of him often," Michael countered.

"As any son would." Ilya held the cold steel of the revolver in his hand. "I must admit, there are times when he haunts my own thinking."

"Maybe that's what's left of your conscience. Taking innocent lives can exact a heavy toll."

"I think not," Maersk asserted glibly. His face was pensive. "Still, I must applaud your family's efforts; David Adamovich has raised an honorable man. Somewhat unbending, perhaps, but he would be proud of you, *Mikhail*. After all, he died to save your life."

"My life?" Neill hadn't expected illumination—especially from an assassin.

The Russian stepped closer. "Yes; a professional courtesy between soldiers—in separate causes, of course." Maersk regarded the Ruger in Neill's palm. "Lower your weapon, *Capitan*. While my pledge to your father is still in effect, I would feel no compunction in killing the *serzhant*."

* * * *

"Take this." Crockett held out a Beretta. His carbine was cradled comfortably in his arm.

Aultman took the pistol and eyed the lieutenant's M4. "Do you have a bullet in the barrel of that thing?"

Nate smiled; he was paired with a novice. "There's a round in the chamber, yes. And the safety's on." He adopted an instructive tone. "Do you know how to use that?"

Richard was sheepish. "It's been a few years since my days in the Army."

"Our army?" Nate grinned. "Here. It's easy. I've already prepped it; just flip this and you're good to go." He demonstrated. "And stay away from that trigger—unless you mean to use it. Got that?"

Aultman licked his lips. "Yeah, I got it."

They were tracking west, along the Four Seasons Gallery. Nate led with the muzzle of his rifle, checking rooms as they moved.

"We'll clear one alcove at a time," the Marine told him. His gaze was fixed on the Prince's Apartment. "Stay in the hall and watch both ends—and give me a head's up if you see that Russian."

* * * *

"No more violence, Maersk." Neill tossed the pistol into a chair. It bounced before clattering to the floor. "There's been enough killing."

"I wonder." Maersk smiled evenly. "Would you turn the other cheek—as your father did?" He studied the officer's face and found himself staring into the past. "Or would you embrace your training and take my life?"

"Put down the gun," Michael directed quietly. "Let's find out."

* * * *

AULTMAN'S HEARING WAS KINDLED. THE ALARM had been stilled and a different clamor reached his ears. It had the sound of metal tumbling across stone and was over in an instant.

The minor tumult had sprung from the southeast corner, beyond the Hall of the Horse Guards and the staircase that led to ground level. It wasn't far, and Aultman reasoned he could be there and back again before Crockett reappeared.

He checked his weapon and drew in a deep breath, then gathered his courage and ventured forward. The elegant flight of steps fell away to his right, and Richard had barely passed the balustrade before recognizing the sound of men's voices.

* * * *

TIME COULD ONLY WORK IN THEIR FAVOR, NEILL decided. The Castle would soon be overrun with security personnel, combing the halls and anterooms for the shooter—which meant the old man couldn't wait much longer.

Michael was determined to draw this out. Keeping Maersk occupied would serve to protect them, and he tried to provoke a conversation.

"We know about your visit to Chernihiv."

Maersk's steps brought him in front of the exit, blocking their path. Christina peered around Michael's shoulder. She was anxious for a change in circumstances, while the captain continued to shield her with his frame.

"You are gifted with subtlety, *Capitan*. But try being more direct." REMORA was impassive. "Mayakovsky's death will not diminish humanity. There are those who warrant a quick end. Vadim's was unnecessarily delayed."

A twitch on Neill's part; his eyes went left, sensing movement. Maersk caught it too, and the light in the room was altered by a shape in the door. Both men were now aware of Aultman's arrival.

"Put the gun down, Maersk," Richard ordered. His hands

were locked around the Beretta and he trained the barrel on the Russian's chest.

Ilya kept his stare fixed on the Marines. He wasn't the least bit concerned with the pistol pointed in his direction.

"Put it down, Maersk," Aultman repeated. Sweat dotted his forehead.

Neill had tried stalling. In time, he knew Crockett would bring his special skills to the moment—but this scenario was unexpected, and filled him with dread.

Where the blazes was Nate?

"Richard," Michael began. His tone remained steady. "I want you to step away and go back into the hall."

A wicked smile creased REMORA's face. He wasn't backing down. There was a sing-song tone in his voice. "You should listen to him, Mr. Aultman."

"You talk too much, Maersk." This wasn't turning out the way Aultman thought it would. "Now put down the gun."

The assassin grinned widely now. He had already determined what Aultman's reaction would be. This was not something the American had been trained for. He would hesitate, giving Ilya the chance he needed.

"I'm afraid our time is at an end, *Capitan.* I've enjoyed our talk—"

"Maersk, wait," Neill raised his voice. "*Richard*—"

"—but for now I bid you *adieu.*"

Maersk shifted his aim to the right and was otherwise motionless. He squeezed off one round, but Aultman wasn't quite as hesitant as Maersk imagined. Richard pulled hard on the trigger. The second discharge followed REMORA's, but the round went low.

The Russian fired again, emptying the cylinder. The first shot had pierced Aultman's heart; the second severed his aorta, ripping through his lung.

The revolver's report was deafening in the columned room. Richard's eyes widened, his body toppling to the floor.

"Richard!" Christina cried out.

Neill pushed toward his friend and for the moment ignored Maersk altogether.

AULTMAN landed awkwardly, still holding the pistol. The Marines rolled him to his back and Michael's hands tore open his shirt.

"Stay with me, Richard," Neill pleaded. "Come on, buddy."

Christina was saying something; Neill didn't catch her words. Blood gushed from two holes, but not in a pumping action. The flow was caused by the shattered artery and the sudden fullness of Aultman's chest cavity.

"We have to stop the bleeding." Christina was frantic but in control, kneeling in a rapidly expanding pool. Like Neill, her hands were drenched. "Give me something to stop this."

He pulled off his cummerbund and tried applying pressure, but a look into glassy eyes told him that there was nothing they could do.

The chapel was empty. Maersk had slunk away. Neill started to reach for the Beretta. He considered going after the Russian before Christina gripped his arm.

"Michael," she fairly shouted. "We have to *stop the bleeding*—" but the words caught in her throat.

It was too late for that and she knew it.

"Christina, he's gone."

"No." Her tone was wretched.

Christina peered into a face that grew paler by the moment. She leaned closer and breathed a goodbye, her fingertips gently closing Richard's eyes. Her lips pressed against his forehead and the tears began to flow.

Neill's hand rested on his friend's still form. With the other he pulled the sobbing woman close. Christina buried her head in his chest and seemed to collapse under a weight too great to bear.

"Why, Michael?" Her voice was muffled. "Why?"

She couldn't take any more and didn't want to. The scene

was just too painful, but for Richard Aultman, the view ahead had become a bright horizon, and arrived much sooner than the morning light.

Chapter Thirty-Four * Aftermath

THE WORDS HAD COME FROM GREECE, BY WAY of an historian whose name Neill could not recall. *Every end does not appear together with its beginning.* It was an axiom of old, and while less than Scriptural, the phrase held boundless wisdom—and no small measure of hope. The principle itself could be seen in everyday life. Winter yielded to spring; heartache to joy; and pain, more often than not, to relief. All were natural processes, providentially ordered; and each took time, invariably leaving their own indelible marks.

Or *scars*, depending on the perspective.

Neill was a man like any other, more so in some ways, and certainly no stranger to pain. Enduring grief was an old saw. In the past, God's grace had always been sufficient to see him through. That was a consequence of his nurtured childhood; his parents hadn't just raised him. David and Jean Neill had brought him up, and the distinctions between the two could only be measured in eternity.

But the loss was different this time. Guilt was a tangible concept, and for want of clarity, self-reproach sought to fill the void. Neill felt the need to assume responsibility for Richard Aultman's death—or assign blame, at the very least. It was not an unexpected reaction, yet the Marine's conscience was clear, and he realized that culpability for the crime rested at Maersk's feet.

* * * *

FEW RESTED AND NO ONE SLEPT. THE NIGHT HAD rushed headlong into turmoil after the shooting. Priority was given to Pyotr's wound; EMTs stabilized him and took him to the nearest hospital. Equally important was the safety of the guests. All were evacuated to the presidential residence next door. Each was interviewed and released, and none seemed any worse for wear—aside from a few who protested the evening's inconveniences.

First responders secured the ballroom and isolated every trace of polonium. Word of this threat was kept quiet. Full disclosure would come later, but the *Policja Kryminalna* wanted to avoid panic; they had a massive crime scene to investigate and didn't need any additional headaches.

Crockett had dashed to the small chapel after hearing gunfire. The Russian had vanished, but Aultman's errant discharge had apparently found a target. Security discovered traces of blood on the ground floor, the trail ending at the southeast corner. A window had been forced there—undoubtedly Maersk's escape route. The assassin himself had long since disappeared.

* * * *

"CAN YOU STAY?"

Neill was numb. He stood outside Christina's room, and for the second time in days, his uniform was stained with blood.

Viktoriya's eyes were cast downward. "I can't leave her now, Michael."

"How is she?"

"In shock; understandably upset." The journalist was exhausted. "I need your help with something—can you come in for a moment?"

The two eased through the door. Christina was on the couch, clad in a robe. Her hair was wrapped in a thick towel, and she looked as she did on their first day in Poland, her eyes now misty and red.

"I'll be back," Viktoriya promised. She gathered a bundle

in her arms. A moment later she vanished into the hall. Neill had seen Yegor and Iosef on his way in and knew she was in good hands.

The curtains had been drawn back; Michael took in the pre-dawn view and found a place on the sofa. He had barely taken Christina's hand when she posed a question.

"Where was God tonight, Michael?" Her voice trembled.

Neill remained silent. He knew she wasn't really looking for answers and only needed to vent.

"Christ's disciples must have had the same question," he said at last. "God's purposes are sometimes hard to see—especially at times like this. Jesus conquered death." He squeezed her hand, and mustered a smile. "Richard's an overcomer now, too." He thought to say more, but then decided it might be best to stop.

Christina released him and walked to the bureau. She pulled open a drawer and then returned—sitting closer, this time—holding the gift Michael had given her on the first day of the summit.

"I'd like to open this now. Do you mind?"

"I can't think of a better time."

She carefully tore through the paper. The package was small, and Neill's wrapping skills had been tested. Beneath the foil was a box. She removed the lid and peered inside.

"It's a heart." A glimmer—it looked like hope—and she held the gold trinket in the palm of her hand.

"A pendant," Michael supplied. "My mother wore a charm bracelet. This was a gift to her, on the day I was born."

"From your dad?"

"Yes."

She tried to protest. "Michael, I can't accept this."

"You have to. When you see the inscription, I think you'll understand."

Christina turned it over and read the engraved words. In a moment's time she felt a peace that warmed her soul.

"For my follower of Christ—love always." She looked up.

"That's the meaning of my name. Your father wrote this?"

"Cross my heart."

She squeezed the charm tightly. "Your mother's faith was very important to him."

Neill smiled. "More than anything."

* * * *

THE BLOODSTAINED GOWN NEEDED CLEANING. A concierge was on duty at all times, but at four a.m., there were few needs to be met. A receipt was signed, the dress was bagged, and the attendant in charge whisked it from sight.

Viktoriya's phone chirped as she returned to the elevator. It was a text from Jean-Paul, promising imminent discovery. It was much like the rest of his messages and asked if she would call at the earliest opportunity.

It's early now, Viktoriya thought. Too much so. She would call him later, at a more respectable hour. She rode the lift in silence, and stepped into the hall to find a familiar face.

* * * *

SHE WAS BACK, WITH CROCKETT IN TOW. "LOOK who I found," the journalist announced. It was an attempt at distraction, but levity was too much of a stretch, and the effort fell flat.

In like manner, Nate was one to use humor as a springboard for conversation. Jokes or disarming comments were part of his forte. That seemed inappropriate now, and he fumbled his way through an awkward moment before Neill came to his rescue.

"Have you seen Avery?"

"Downstairs. He wanted to make sure Richard . . ." his voice drifted off. "The man looks rough."

"We all do," Michael observed tiredly. "What's the situation?"

Crockett drew in some air. "Polish security found Maersk's

weapon. A pistol he smuggled in; not the one he used to—"

Neill cut him off. "Where was it?"

"Storage room. New Deputies' Chamber. Smart move, too—he couldn't have got it past the metal detectors."

Neill was laconic. "He did enough damage without it."

"Agreed." Crockett's gaze was a little too focused. "You going over to check on Pyotr?"

The captain read his friend's eyes. "I'd like that."

"I'll go with."

* * * *

"WHAT'S ON YOUR MIND?" NEILL ASKED. THE Marines stood in the hall, their voices low.

"I told him to stay put, Mike. So why'd he do it?"

"Why do any of us do what we do?" Neill began. "Richard just wanted to help. You can't blame yourself, Nate—that dog won't hunt." He shook his head. "This one falls on my watch."

Crockett had a skeptic's look. "Sauce for the goose is sauce for the gander. As I recall, you told him to go back inside." He glanced at both ends of the corridor, but they were quite alone. "What about his family?"

Michael winced in pain. "A wife, but no kids. I don't envy the phone call Avery had to make."

"Jesus." Crocket spoke the Lord's name, and meant it as a prayer. He hung his head, not knowing what else to say, but it was time to change the subject. "There's something else—one thing they didn't find."

"What's that?"

"I saw Maersk doling out that polonium. He had some kind of device; it was silver, in the palm of his hand. When things got heavy, he tossed it."

"And it hasn't been recovered?"

"Nope. The guests were screened after the shooting. None of them had it—and those Berkut boys haven't been seen since."

Neill mulled that over. "You think they took it?"

A nod. "That would be my guess."

"I'll talk to Dmitri—there has to be an explanation." Neill had questions of his own. "I still can't figure why Maersk hung around."

"What does your gut tell you?" The scout's instincts were talking.

The captain dug deep. "He said something about my dad, and how he saved my life. I think he wanted to tell me more."

"Maybe that's all you needed," Nate offered. "Maybe that's enough. Just don't let Maersk get inside your head, Mike. Those kind of mind games will tear you up."

"I suppose you're right."

Crockett shifted the discussion. "What's next?"

"A dignified return," Neill answered. "Mortuary Affairs is ready with a transfer case. As soon as it's light, I'll give Welles a call." Fatigue was tugging at him. "I just don't think Avery should have to make the arrangements."

Excavation site,
near Gora Kalwaria

HENRI MINOUCHE KNEW THE VALUE OF CON-trolling his employer. He seldom gave Toussaint truly accurate timetables, choosing instead to pad his schedules for situations beyond his control. The principle was as old as salesmanship itself—under-promising and over-delivering was always tactically clever, in a broad spectrum of circumstances. When properly applied, the practice worked especially well for bosses with high expectations.

In this case, the project leader outdid himself. The mechanic found the needed parts and the repairs to the winching motor were quickly made. Lifting the wreck at night was too dangerous, but Minouche persuaded his roughnecks to start work early the next morning. Jean-Paul had arrived long before sunrise. His messages to Viktoriya went unanswered, but in her place, the society's public affairs chief had been roused from sleep to cover the occasion.

The tackle and halyards were ready at six, and by noon, the cheers went up as the scow was ceremoniously lifted from the depths of the Vistula. Toussaint was ecstatic. He was convinced that Henri and his men were miracle workers, but the celebratory mood cooled as the day wore on.

The ancient vessel was placed on the second salvage flat, resting on a makeshift cradle of crossties—railway sleepers, as they were called in Europe. A cursory examination of the hulk revealed two mysteries. The first seemed inconsequential.

The second was far more devastating.

* * * *

"IT ISN'T HERE, JEAN-PAUL." MINOUCHE gripped the railing and watched his crew remove debris from the recovered barge. There was no point in prolonging Toussaint's hopes and the time had come to face reality. He shook his head, a bitter wind stealing moisture from his eyes. "Everything pointed to this location—but our prize eludes us."

"And what of the Swede's letter?"

Minouche shook his head again. "The parchment mentions the sacred vessels, but not the icon. Thinking we might find it here was simply a leap of faith."

"C'est la vie," Toussaint uttered. His tone was glum. Henri was right, and he wondered if the icon had ever been there at all. If it had, there was always the chance that it had been swept away by the river, or stolen by plunderers known only to God. He resigned himself to any number of possibilities, but in the end none of them really mattered.

"Remember our goals, *monsieur*." Henri tried to soften the blow. "Think of what we've already recovered. Much of Poland's treasures can now be returned."

"But not the Treasure of the Heart," Toussaint pointed out. Archaeology was at the same time a field of wonder—and disappointment. "In its place we can offer her people a new mystery."

"*Oui*—what has become of Olm's sacred relic? A worthy question in light of our efforts today." Minouche stared at the front of the Swedish boat. "But I'm curious about something else."

The scow's construction followed a horizontal plane, but her lines were broken at the bow by a thick, stocky shape rising vertically. Bulbous on top, the anomaly had a certain symmetry, and at first brush appeared as a human figure emerging from below. Minouche recognized it immediately. Seeing it beneath the surface, his divers avoided the disturbing form, and had taken to calling it The Boatman. In reality, it was far less dramatic.

"It's a cannon, mounted on the foredeck." He shrugged. "Probably the type used for riverine operations; a bit heavy-handed, but more than adequate to do the job."

Toussaint frowned. "What job?"

"The muzzle points downward, lashed in place. The deck below has been obliterated. And there is evidence of a pitched battle elsewhere on board." Henri gauged the entrepreneur's understanding. "Don't you see, Jean-Paul? We can't blame poor seamanship for her loss, or bad weather. Someone had mayhem in mind."

"Are you saying this vessel was deliberately sunk?"

The project chief watched as the river flowed under their feet. "History is silent on the subject. Perhaps your journalist friend can dig up the truth. Have you been able to reach her?"

Toussaint checked his cell once more; still nothing. This was frustrating, to say the least. He could have used Viktoriya's help right now, to put the proper spin on this outcome—and to help salvage his reputation. He'd managed it in the past, and enlisting a clever wordsmith couldn't hurt.

In his mind, after all, that was what the press was for.

Chapter Thirty-Five * Treasures of the Heart

Morning, Christmas Eve
Hotel Bristol

"ALL SET?" NEILL ASKED.

"All set," came the reply.

Willis Avery stood inside his suite on the fifth floor, eyeing the turmoil around him. Agents of the Secret Service were in and out. His garment bag lay on the couch. A suitcase waited by the door, and the hotel bellmen removed two others from the bedroom. The national security advisor was chagrined by the baggage.

"I tried to pack light," he defended.

Neill gave Arrens a wink. "Some people have trouble with that." From behind, Christina pinched him gently on the arm. Her gesture went unnoticed.

An agent stowed Avery's laptop. A second officer was arranging folders in a satchel. Willis moved to the desk and took over. "What's your schedule look like, Captain?"

"Breakfast." Neill answered. "One more meal together before check-out." He'd almost said one *last* meal, but finality was something he chose to ignore. "We're meeting downstairs at nine. I was hoping you'd join us."

Avery was heartened by the invitation. "Wouldn't miss it. How's our hero?"

"Pyotr?" Michael grinned. "The hospital cut him loose last night. Dmitri's helping him pack as we speak."

"And his shoulder?"

"On the mend," the Marine said. "But he won't make the chin-up team this year."

A thoughtful nod. Two days had passed since the shooting and the frump was making a comeback. Avery's unruly shock of hair had sprung to life, and without a jacket, Neill could see a shirt tail threatening to escape. Each of them had begun down the difficult path toward normalcy, but to the captain's eyes, a part of Avery seemed lost.

"What's the mood among the deputies?"

"Invigorated," Avery harrumphed. "Maersk's actions have galvanized their resolve. What with everything else, Moscow's scheme has backfired." The alternative would have meant days of additional effort, but that hadn't been necessary. Avery chuckled, adding, "The envoys are ticked." The word he used was more caustic.

"Sounds like the treaty should hold, then," Christina volunteered.

"It would make a nice legacy—for Richard's sake. He died trying to protect it." Avery was sullen. "I've spoken to Dobrogost. The agreement has a name now. We're calling it the Aultman Accord."

Christina's eyes grew moist. "He would have liked that."

Avery pressed on. "Karl's people have arranged transportation to Lask. They've got a car for Richard's—" he swallowed, "—for Richard. A Globemaster's flying in from Germany. I'll be going back with him, and Dover will handle things from there."

"When's the memorial?" Neill asked.

"The thirtieth, D.C. Can you make it?"

"We'd be honored," Arrens replied. "What time does your flight leave?"

Avery's melancholy faded. "The new job has some additional perks; departure's pretty much when I say it is." He regarded Neill. "What about you two?"

"Terryton's agreed to some down time. We'll be spending a few days in Olm."

"Stanislaw's family?"

"Yes, sir. Pyotr's sister's driving up," Christina explained. "We've been invited to their Christmas Eve service."

"Mass?" Avery gave the captain a quizzical look. "I thought you were a Baptist."

"That's our little secret," Neill joked.

"I suppose we could all use a little church right now," the big man admitted slowly. "Who's 'we'?"

"Viktoriya's coming. So's Crockett." Neill ran down the list. "The Ulyanovs are flying back later today—Major Yaroslav too."

"I imagine Miss Gavrilenko is disappointed. Her story about that icon didn't play out."

"She's taking it in stride," the captain said. "It remains a mystery, and she can work that angle." The mention of Dmitri stirred Neill's thinking. "Any word from the SSD about that other matter?"

Avery seemed amused. "It's been addressed, Captain." He dismissed the porters, waiting until they'd disappeared, and then continued. "Tomas Krol gave me an education on polonium; very bad stuff." His chin came up. "Do you know who discovered it?"

Christina surprised him with the answer. "The Curies?"

"Bingo. Mrs. Curie was born right here in Warsaw, and the element was named after Poland." Avery wore a sad smile. "Ordinarily, that's a detail Richard would have brought out."

Railway line,
Near Donetsk, Ukraine
Late afternoon

THE TRAIN SURGED FORWARD, ACROSS THE Ukrainian steppes, a shining, silver line racing through the frozen countryside. This was a regional express, built for long distance travel to points east, and included a restaurant car and passenger coach at the rear. Operated by the *Ukrzaliznytsia*—a tongue-twister that translated to the *Ukrainian Railways*—the electric locomotive was modern, surprisingly fast, and without any resemblance to the more common trains that dominated the rest of Eastern Europe.

Ilya Maersk ambled along the through-way corridor, past open berths and the occasional passenger. He was making his way toward the saloon car. His gait was punctuated by a limp; the 9 millimeter slug from Aultman's Beretta had punched through the quadriceps in his right leg. The wound was in and out, the bullet missing an artery and transiting the thickest part of the muscle. It was swollen and painful, but the spy had cleaned and dressed the injury, packing it with gauze to stop the bleeding. After more than forty-eight hours there was still no sign of infection.

Maersk pressed through the door and found a seat at the bar. A thick haze hung in the air at the rear of the carriage; many Eastern Europeans considered smoking an inalienable right, and that privilege was not curtailed within public conveyances. Ilya blinked away the stinging sensation assaulting his eyes and studied the liqueurs that lined the shelves.

"Barkeep," he growled. The steward approached from the far end. "Something strong and cold. Vodka."

The barman gave him a shrewd look. "Gin and tonic would suit you better."

"Too sweet for my palate," Maersk muttered.

"It's all in how you mix it, my friend. Try mine. You'll like it, I promise." He produced a chilled glass and poured the tonic water. Gin came next.

"No wedge of lime?" Maersk smirked.

"Patience," the barman said. "Taste it first—too syrupy?"

Ilya smacked his lips. "A touch bitter, I think."

The bartender's eyes lit up. "Now the lime—and a splash of club soda." He placed the cocktail on a napkin.

Maersk lifted the glass and sipped. He was surprised by the taste and nodded approvingly.

REMORA nursed the drink and considered his next step. Returning to Sverdlovsk was out. By now Karpenko and Pirogov knew of his failure, shocking though it was. Maersk couldn't redeem himself in their eyes, which meant that resuming his life in the Russian Federation was impossible, at least in the short term.

"Another?" The barman was very attentive.

The drink was refreshing and slaked Ilya's thirst. He pushed the glass forward.

The former Soviet empire was vast, and there were options available. Half of the assassin's retainer had already been paid, and Maersk had other resources at his disposal. His first posting was to Dagestan; he still had contacts there, and two former colleagues from his KGB days had retired to provinces near the Caspian Sea. That republic was in the North Caucasus region, ethnically diverse—and far from Moscow.

Crimea was also a good choice, or anywhere in the east, for that matter. He could easily blend in, and then consider relocating after the Kremlin's anger had cooled.

MAERSK finished his drink, holding an unlit cigarette. The compartment was getting crowded. From the rear, a tall patron appeared and sat two stools away. He looked familiar, and Ilya searched his memory to place him.

From behind the bar, Aleksander Voskov dropped his pretenses. "You were quite parched, old friend." He held up the empty glass to the light and retrieved something from his pocket. "Can I get you anything else? A light for your cigarette, perhaps?"

The scales fell from his eyes, but by then it was too late. Maersk froze. His face was pale. He'd seen these two before; leaving the summit, and again at the Bristol. The throbbing in his leg diminished and was replaced by a sickening feeling in the pit of his stomach. Whether it was real or not made little difference.

Ilya also recognized the silver object in the 'barkeep's'

hand—and it was anything but a lighter.

THE old man had slipped, but his deficiencies would be short-lived. Given the dosage Maersk had ingested, the Berkut officer estimated that he had one week—possibly two.

Exposure to polonium was rare. A victim's mortality was hard to determine, while the final outcome was not. It was only a question of when, not if.

The captain had erred in only one detail. The poison was far more lethal than he imagined. Even in very small quantities, the isotopes were deadly, and Voskov's range of seven to fourteen days was extremely optimistic.

Mazovia, The Lublin Region,
Southeast of Warsaw

"MON DIEU, MICHAEL!" VIKTORIYA GRIPPED the wheel, a hint of irritation creeping into her voice. "Why do you drive so slowly?"

In the back seat, Christina leaned forward. On the road ahead, Neill drove Pyotr's van, and she could see the Opel's tail lights in the distance.

"That's pretty standard for Captain Safety," she grinned.

"*Bozhe moi,*" the red-head carped. "He drives like an old woman."

Christina drew back. "That's twice you've called on God—in vain," she teased. "Just remember; we *are* going to church."

Next to Viktoriya, Tula slumbered peacefully. The trip to Warsaw had taken its toll, and after check-out, the young woman handed the keys to Neill. The ride back was segregated; boys in the van, girls in the car, and with each vehicle packed with passengers and baggage, the group started south again.

THE road to Olm was well-traveled and followed the river, but on this Christmas Eve, the route saw little traffic. Few wanted to brave the weather; the winter air had gone from brisk to bitterly cold, and the convoy arrived in Deblin just as the sun began to set.

The cars eased off the highway and started west. Potholes jostled the little Duster, but in time Viktoriya learned to follow Neill's lead and avoid them. The rocking motion seemed to have no effect on Pyotr's sister; and if anything, it lulled her into a deeper sleep.

The journalist studied Tula's face, and then glanced at Christina in the rearview. "Could you live the life she's chosen?"

Arrens blinked. "As a nun?" She considered it and answered slowly. "No—but I'm not called to."

"So—it's a calling, you think?" The concept of being chosen hadn't occurred to her.

"Yes; it's like marriage or being in the military. You don't do it for what you can *get*, but for what you can *give*. It takes a step of faith. Can you imagine doing anything else with your life—being something besides a journalist?"

Viktoriya gave the Marine a knowing smile. "I see your point," she conceded. "I suppose it's like falling in love."

✶ ✶ ✶ ✶

MATI'S HOME OVERFLOWED WITH FOOD AND guests, and after a day of fasting, the family observed the *Vigilia*—the Holy Meal—complete with traditional blessings. It was Pyotr's father who did the honors this time.

In the spirit of hospitality, a place setting was left open. It was intended to honor the Christ child, or kept as a spot for hungry wanderers in need of food. Neill noted the empty chair and raised a glass to Richard Aultman. Everyone at the table joined him in the somber toast.

"NOT a fan of cabbage, I take it," the captain observed. Supper was over and their hosts cleared the dishes.

Crockett winced. "You know me, Mike. I'm more of a meat and potatoes guy. My tastes run in a straight line between peanut butter and jelly."

A smile. "That doesn't leave much room for anything in-between."

The lieutenant was quick with a response. "Spread it on some bread and it *is* the in-between."

Christina cornered the officers. "You two ready?"

"Yep," Michael responded. The meal had left him sleepy. "Let's go witness this miracle horsefly's been telling us about."

Tula began herding everyone, including her parents, toward the front room. Neill found her efforts amusing, and the group pulled on coats and jackets before pushing off into the night.

It was a short walk to St. Mary's. The little company clustered together for warmth, and as they neared the church, bands of the faithful filled the sidewalks. Many carried candles and lit them when they reached the square. In spite of the bone-chilling cold, the old village had a warm glow.

"*Hurry*, Mischa—" Tula linked arms with the Marines and spirited them toward the front of the crowd. "It's time!"

Neill stood tall, peering over the heads of those crowding the abbey's porch. Alone in the open narthex, the priest turned the key. He twisted the knob, released it, and after a moment's pause, the thick, ancient door creaked and slowly opened.

* * * *

THE AMERICANS AND VIKTORIYA FOUND SEATS in the back row. Pyotr escorted his parents and sister closer to the front. The sanctuary filled quickly. The air was cool at first, but soon the chancel was warmed by the fellowship of kindred spirits.

"Nice pendant," Neill whispered.

Christina beamed and touched the charm around her neck. "It was a gift—from someone very special."

"Anyone I know?" Michael tried to memorize the look on her face. It was good to see her smiling again.

"Are you fishing for compliments, Captain?"

"Harpooning's more like it," he grinned. The pew was hard

but he made himself comfortable. "All kidding aside—I'm very glad you made this trip."

"So am I."

"No regrets?"

"None at all." Neill's words gave her the opening she'd been waiting for. "Can I tell you something?"

"Sure."

"It's about the banquet." Christina turned to look him in the eye. "That night was very memorable, for a lot of reasons. You blessed me, and then you protected me—but most of all, you cared for me." She reached out and squeezed his hand. "Whatever else might have happened—and for everything that did—I want you to know that I'll never forget that."

Neill started to speak, but Nate broke in, studying the altar. "What does it mean, Mike?"

The captain looked toward the front. "The Scripture?" He retrieved his phone. "Hang on, I'll check."

"You don't speak Latin?" Christina gibed playfully.

"No more than you," he grinned. Michael thumbed through his devotional app. "You're right, though—it's from the Latin Vulgate. Psalm ninety-one, verse eleven. *For he shall give his angels charge over thee, to keep thee in all thy ways.*"

Christina translated for Viktoriya's benefit. The journalist pulled out her notes. "Sobieski's favorite verse," she supplied. "It's said he carved it himself."

"I remember," Neill answered. "Horsefly said he was good with his hands—maybe he could have fixed that door."

Viktoriya eyed him in shock. "You're the last person I'd accuse of being a skeptic. Are you discounting the legend?"

Neill shook his head. "The spiritual world is very real, don't get me wrong. But in this case, I'm not buying the locals' story." He lowered his voice. "Father Sobieski didn't open that door. It's off-balance; you can tell just by looking at it."

The journalist was in the mood for friendly debate. "But this—act of God—or whatever you call it, didn't begin until after his death. How do you explain that?"

"Shhh," Christina warned. "The service is starting."

THEY sat back as the priest took his place. He began with a short prayer and then called the young people to the front for the ritual blessing. The gathering was small; in another time and place Neill would have been encouraged by it, but something about Viktoriya's question bothered him.

"That's sweet, don't you think?" Christina watched as Pyotr stood and walked Tula forward. "Even with his arm in a sling, the older brother takes care of his sister." She pressed gently against Michael's shoulder, and whispered, "Has she always been his 'treasure of the heart'?"

"For as long as I can recall," Michael returned. The priest waited until everyone had taken their places and then moved down the line. "He's always kept her close."

"I guess that's only natural." Christina's tone was soft. "When something's precious, we want to keep it near."

Neill's eyes fell on the verse, and faced with the Scripture, he became abruptly detached.

"Say that again."

Christina couldn't recall the exact words. "Which part? I just said it's only natural."

"No, that other thing. About being close."

The comment resurfaced, and she paced her remark. "When something's precious, we want to keep it near."

Neill turned in his seat. It couldn't be that simple.

Or could it?

He repeated the verse. *"For he shall give His angels charge over thee . . ."* His gaze locked on the narthex and his brain spun up. "If it were that easy, someone would have noticed by now."

"Noticed what?"

Michael was having a one-sided conversation. "Except for one thing—" a smile formed, "—everyone thought the Swedes had it. They never would have thought—

"Penknife." Neill turned to Crockett. "Do you have a penknife?"

"Will a Gerber do?" Nate cringed. Parishioners two rows ahead gave them angry stares.

"Gerber's fine. Hand it over."

The lieutenant fished the tool from his belt and gave it to Neill. "What are you doing, Mike?" he asked evenly.

He was already on his feet. "It's a *façade*—like so many others we've seen since we've been here."

Neill moved carefully toward the carved figure on the port side of the arch. He shoved the Gerber into a pocket, pressed both palms against the door's surface and then took a step back. His fingertips traced the wooden panels before his eyes settled center-left.

Nate slipped out of the pew. "You're starting to scare me, buddy."

None of this went unnoticed. At the altar, the priest laid his hands on Tula's head, and began to pray as she knelt. But the rising commotion in the back caught his eye.

"Whiskey tango, Mike—" Nate growled. "We're in church, for cryin' out loud. Can't this wait?"

"Not if you want a Christmas miracle." Neill peered into one of the seams, gripping his friend's arm. "Right there—see it?"

Crockett leaned in. "Not really. Your phone have a flashlight?"

He pulled out the mobile. "How's that?"

A frown. "Looks like—fabric. Or canvas," Nate answered. "What's that doing in there?"

Indignant whispers rippled through the crowd, beginning in the last pews and sweeping forward. Pyotr stood, visibly disturbed, and marched down the aisle. A very stern priest followed, and by the time they arrived, the Marines were fully engaged in their scrutiny.

"Mischa—"

"On the right," Neill was saying. An index finger probed the narrow space. "Probably there."

"Got it," Crockett grinned. "Two of 'em; hinges, spring-loaded, on the top and bottom. Deeply recessed. There should be a latch—"

"—on this side." Neill extended the blade on the Gerber. "I see it. Son of a gun; Father Jakob did fix the door."

Nate was skeptical. "We'll see. It's been a long time."

"Mischa," Stanislaw repeated. His voice rose above a whisper, and the priest pressed in. "Explain yourself."

"I will, old friend," Neill answered. His eyes lifted, and he voiced a prayer. *"For there is nothing covered that shall not be revealed.* God, I hope this works."

The Marine slipped the knife between two wooden slats. Using the point of the blade, he depressed the catch, and for the first time in over three hundred years, the release mechanism gave way. Pressure within the portal did the rest. There was a loud cracking sound and the panel that lay flush within the door swung open.

By now everyone was standing, eyes trained on the visitors.

The compartment inside was three feet square. Its contents filled every inch, with no space for overflow. Neill reached out a hand to steady the cache, but it showed no signs of being dislodged from its resting place.

Pyotr was stunned. *"Bozhe moi."*

"It *is* cloth," Crockett observed.

"Looks like hemp." Christina had joined them, and Viktoriya was snapping photos with her cell. "And very old."

"Practically ancient," Neill breathed. "Someone went to a lot of trouble to hide this. Any guesses at what's inside?"

"You're the man holding the knife," Nate reminded him. "What are you waiting for?"

Pyotr started to urge caution, but Michael had already set to work. He began at the top of each corner and brought the blade down. With the left and right sides open, he moved to the top, carefully slicing through the thick material. The fabric resisted at first, but with three edges free, the cloth fell gently away.

MANY dropped to their knees, and most made the sign of the cross. The angered whisperings had given way to bewilderment and surprise. All were swept aside, replaced by gasps of joy—and no shortage of tears—as the Treasure of the Heart made a grand reappearance.

"The icon—it's here?" Pyotr was puzzled.

"It never left," Neill shot back.

Christina gripped Michael's arm. "What about the prophecy?" she whispered, adding with a smile, "I think we need a virtuous maiden for this next part."

"And a nobleman's son." The captain searched the crowd. "Where's Tula?"

"Excuse me, Father." Pyotr stepped into the aisle and returned with his sister. "She's here, Mischa." Her eyes were moist, filled with wonder, blessing—and a hesitant reluctance to believe.

"Horsefly," Michael announced. "You're up, too."

The eldest sibling shook his head. "Not with this arm, Mischa. You do the honors."

Neill took Tula's hand and led her forward. "I'm like you, pal—there's no royal blood in my veins. But if it gets the job done—"

He took hold of the icon's frame; Nate did likewise on the other side, and between the two of them, they removed the centerpiece from its narrow niche and placed it reverently into Tula's hands. The congregation parted before them, and with the Americans' help, the young woman led a processional to return the relic to its rightful place above the altar.

* * * *

"YOUR STORY HAS AN ENDING NOW, VIKTORIYA."
The service had come to a halt and Neill cast a look to-

ward the back of the chancel. The centerpiece completed the triptych. Candlelight gleamed from the gold that framed the painted imagery, and a throng of worshipers crowded the altar's rail, taking in the wonder of the moment. The more devout lay prostrate and the sanctuary hummed with excitement at this unexpected revelation.

The friends huddled in their pew near the back. Viktoriya sat transfixed, furiously adding notes to her tablet. The greatest human interest story of her career had just landed in her lap, but she still had a few questions.

"I don't know where to begin," she blurted. The journalist stared at Michael in amazement. "How did you know?"

"I didn't," Neill admitted. "But you made a good point. The miracle of the door didn't begin until after Sobieski's death. I realized there had to be a connection." The two had been speaking in Ukrainian, and it took a moment to spin their words into English.

"So the priest hid it there?" Crockett asked.

"Who else?" Christina answered. "And he took that secret to his grave."

"Father Jakob knew the Swedes would eventually come," Neill told them. "He fashioned a hiding place—right under their noses." A grin spread across his face. "You have to admit; the good Father was pretty clever."

Nate was still fitting the pieces together. "The inner cavity was off balance—is that why the door swung open all those years?"

Michael nodded. "Probably. The added weight of the icon shifted its center of gravity."

"And so the mystery is solved—one, at least." Viktoriya was thinking of Voskov. She took the time to catch her breath, but the sight of the relic inspired her. She recalled Jean-Paul's press conference. The entrepreneur's rendering of the artifact paled by comparison.

Crockett eyed the centerpiece narrowly. "Shouldn't we—you know, call somebody?"

"No," Neill said sternly. He gestured toward the back. "This belongs to the people of Olm. We need to let them decide how the story gets told." He paused and gave the journalist a warm look.

A mischievous light shone in Viktoriya's eyes. "What did you have in mind, Michael?"

"The icon's in great shape," he continued. "But after three centuries, I'd say it could use a cleaning. Do you think your newspaper would front the expenses?"

Viktoriya considered it. "Under the right circumstances. Do you think the priest would give me exclusive rights to the story?"

"Wouldn't hurt to ask. I think a partnership between you and the village could be mutually beneficial. But you might want to jump on it, before some university decides to underwrite the costs—and take all the credit."

"Then what am I waiting for?" Viktoriya lifted her purse from the bench and found her way into the aisle. The Americans watched as she strode purposefully in the altar's direction.

"Would you excuse us, Nate?"

Crockett blinked. "Sure." He stepped off after Viktoriya, his steps halting.

"Oh, and Nate—" Michael's call was an afterthought.

The lieutenant turned. "Yeah?"

"Merry Christmas."

Both men smiled. "Merry Christmas, Mike."

* * * *

CHRISTINA VIEWED NEILL WITH INCREASED AF-fection. "Another triumph for the captain. There'll be no living with you now, will there?"

Michael pretended shock. "That's awfully bold of you, Staff Sergeant."

She tagged his arm softly. "You know what I mean."

Neill's spirits were riding high and he laughed it off. "I

think so." He took her hand and moved toward the narthex. "Come on. You and I have some unfinished business."

Word had spread, and the Marines skirted around newcomers as they filed in from the cold. Neill reached for the door—it would now be famous for other reasons—and led the young woman into the empty vestibule.

"Where are we going?" Christina's heart had begun to warm.

"Not far," Michael answered. He stopped in the center of the room and gently took hold of her hands. "In fact, this should do nicely." His eyes traveled to the ceiling and then back to hers.

She glanced upward. Hanging over their heads was a traditional holiday decoration.

"Again with the mistletoe?" Christina yielded to his grip and pulled him close. "Did you plan that, too?"

"This was just a happy accident."

She took a more deliberate tone. "And do you need an excuse for something like this?"

"No, Miss Arrens," he said with feigned gravity. "But from now on, I'll always look for one."

"Clever answer." She leaned in, softly whispering into his ear. "You know the rules, Captain."

His blood raced. "I know what they *say* about the rules," he replied. The phrase echoed in his head, and he realized he was starting to sound like his uncle.

Michael smiled. Christina smiled back. The excuses were ignored. His lips met hers, and in the moments that followed, the two forgot about the regulations—and found a reason to try.

Epilogue * Children of the King

January 1st, 1656
Poland

SHE WAS HARDLY SEA-WORTHY, NOR WAS SHE graceful. The Swedish flatboat was less than a barge and more of a mule; a piece of flotsam to carry home the spoils of war. Seeing her did nothing to impress the eye—her lines were awkward, with little consideration for true seamanship, and at best, she was merely a river-going platform.

The cavalryman pushed that fact aside. Form followed function, and beauty wasn't needed; not in this case. The officer required passage for his plundered riches, and the scow sitting low in the water—and far too narrow for a proper load, he judged—would simply have to do.

Johannes Angstrom cursed the priest afresh. The night was late, and he watched his men load their pillaged goods. There was little of value to be taken from the monk's village *(Olm, that was its name, yes?)* and his pursuit of the wagon had been a bootless errand. Still, the blooded soldier had found other trophies worth taking. Castles and monasteries throughout Poland had fallen, and boatloads of treasure were now being sent up the Vistula on their journey to the Baltic Sea and then to Sweden.

There were a few surprises along the way. Some items

were more precious than others, though many were not. The soldiers-turned-looters discovered valuables in unexpected places, yet the most sought after prize was tantalizingly absent.

Captain Angstrom didn't find the icon. He was forced to take comfort in the possessions crowding the deck, but his trove had become a mooring. He was slowed by his burdens and blinded by greed. His men were also overcome with avarice; they dropped their guard, and the cruelly efficient shock troops became a wandering mob of thieves.

And it was then that Krystophor Nilscovic found them.

* * * *

THE ASSAULT BEGAN AT MIDNIGHT, JUST AS THE ciborium and Sanctus bell were being brought on board. The Swedes forgot their spoils, and in the danger of the moment, the treasures of the sacristy were dropped into the murky depths. Infantrymen suddenly remembered their vocations, but their attackers had the element of surprise and soon overwhelmed them.

With twenty trusted Husaria, Nilscovic descended on the marauders. They put their blades to the necks of each, but for Johannes Angstrom, the nobleman had other plans. He bested the Swedish officer with his karabela and spared his life from the edge of the sword. The reprieve was short-lived. Rage consumed his heart and he was driven by a sense of revenge. Krystophor beat the man senseless and then dragged his dazed body to the shore's edge.

THE Vistula carried ice in its veins, and in less than three feet of water, the freezing river filled the Swede's lungs. Nilscovic held him there for several minutes, and then pulled his lifeless form out of the shallows before casting his body adrift.

The Pole's blood ran hot. The scow's deck gun was a short-barreled affair, a *carronade* of less than thirty inches.

Nilscovic pointed the muzzle down and lashed it fast against the pedestal. He ordered his troops to scatter what horses they couldn't take, and in a tumultuous blast, he sent a cannonball through the decks and dispatched the ungainly vessel to the bottom of the river.

* * * *

KRYSTOPHOR FULFILLED HIS VOW TO THE priest. He returned to the holy man's estate and found his stride with Helena. The fire that had burned in his heart was tempered by time—and the affections of the woman who would become his bride. When the pain of losing Jakob grew too hard to bear, the young lovers would comfort one another with the cherished memory of a priest, a brother, and a friend.

But the embers of Olm had grown cold in the couple's hearts. War had changed the landscape and left its mark on the Commonwealth. The devastation was staggering; the blood of those slain drenched the land, and property losses couldn't be told. Jakob was dead; the icon lost, and Krystophor and Helena could no longer find the same zeal for the village. Each became restless, dreaming of places far beyond the horizon; undiscovered vistas where they could put down roots and start their family. Someplace new, a land untouched by conflict. When the Deluge ended, the two made good on their wanderlust and did just that.

Krystophor spent years searching for Olm's prize. Ironically, his quest took him far afield of the centerpiece, and with Helena at his side, he followed the Vistula and traveled northwest, crossing Poland's borders in search of clues. The rage he felt the night he found Angstrom would sometimes haunt his dreams, but God's grace—and Helena—were always there to soothe his conscience.

Between the blended families, it took only a small part of their fortune to stake their dream. The couple traveled west, with many exploits along the way, and finally settled in Germany. Their estate was humble at first, but Krystophor wisely bought up vast tracts of land, enriching their already considerable holdings. Children followed, and in the next hundred years, their descendants would spread to Spain, France and even the Netherlands.

One ancestral line crossed the English Channel and made their way to Ireland. Krystophor's great-grandson—his identity lost to history—shortened the family name. This amendment was difficult to pronounce, so the next generation changed it again. The new surname better suited the surrounding clans and helped the immigrants to blend in. Going forward, there would be no more alterations.

A legacy of honor would be passed down, and while the Neills had descended from nobility, that ancestry was long forgotten. A few would regain it; not the earthly birthright of landowners, nor the inherited eminence of a royal. Their claim to majesty would come from on high; a heavenly reward bestowed by a gracious and loving God—freely given to those who would accept the sacrificial gift of His Son, and become the children of the King.

Look for the next book in
the Michael Neill Adventure Series.
Coming Soon!